Driving Sideways

JESS RILEY

BALLANTINE BOOKS NEW YORK

Driving ↓ Sideways ↗

a novel

A Ballantine Books Trade Paperback Original

Copyright © 2008 by Jess Riley

Published in the United States by Ballantine Books, an imprint of The Random House Publishing Group, a division of Random House, Inc., New York.

BALLANTINE and colophon are registered trademarks of Random House, Inc.

Library of Congress Cataloging-in-Publication Data
Riley, Jess.
Driving sideways : a novel / Jess Riley.
p.   cm.
A Ballantine Books Trade Paperback Original
ISBN 978-0-345-50110-3
1. Self-actualization (Psychology)—Fiction.   2. Donation of organs, tissues, etc.—Fiction.   3. Psychological fiction.   I. Title.
PS3618.I53275D75 2008
813'.6—dc22   2008000479

Printed in the United States of America

www.ballantinebooks.com

1 2 3 4 5 6 7 8 9

Book design by Susan Turner

All photographs in this book are by the author, except for the ones on page 210 (by Jill Schwartzman) and page 322 (by Jed Hicks).

For my grandpa Herb Walker,
who taught me to always root for the underdog

Driving Sideways

CHAPTER ONE

I am alone no longer.

It's strange how much you can change in just one year. Twelve months ago, I'd have laughed in your face if you told me I'd be packing for a road trip this morning. Not rudely, of course, but because traveling anywhere remote was a remote possibility for me at that point. I'd have sooner believed you if you'd said, "One year from now, you will become a Scientologist, learn the pan flute, and join a Bay City Rollers tribute band."

But I've had a change of heart. Well, kidney, really. I'm leaving for Los Angeles this morning, about to do some things long overdue. My Saturn is idling in the driveway, stuffed with suitcases I've never taken anywhere but to hospitals. I feel as if I've just discovered that the cure for cancer is dark chocolate followed by two orgasms. I think I've forgotten to pack my toothbrush, but I don't care. I can buy one on the way. The thought thrills me.

"So you're really doing this," my brother, James, says from behind me, sending me out of my skin.

I jump, making a hair ballish–noise like *aak,* and spin around to face him. He crosses his arms and fixes me with his practiced stare:

one part condescension, two parts disbelief. It's the same look James gives the paperboy when the *Fond du Lac Reporter* misses the welcome mat on the front porch by an inch or more. I lean back into my car, pretending to check my cooler of snacks and bottled water while trying to regain my pretrip composure. As my surrogate parent for the last sixteen years, James has always been able to sneak up on me—catching me in an innocuous act like reading and still making me feel as if I'd been caught stealing from a quadriplegic. "Yes, I'm really going."

"Does Kate know?" he snipes.

"She will," I reply. I shut the cooler and turn to face James.

"Leigh, why do you even care? She's such an asshole. She's a *footnote*."

"I just do, is all." Kate is our mother, who developed the curious conviction when James and I were younger that she would one day become a great actress. The morning she left us for Hollywood, she crouched next to me and whispered absently, "Never settle. Take big risks." Then she stepped into her Ford Pinto and lurched away from the curb, her silver bumper glinting in the sunlight, the scent of Charlie cologne mingling with exhaust in the air. I was five years old. I sat on the curb waiting for her until *Sesame Street* came on, after which I returned to the curb to wait for her return. Twenty-three years later, I'm still waiting.

"You've got to be kidding." James walks around my car and stands directly in front of me. He looks spooky without having had his first cup of coffee, a little like a B-list actor with an emerging heroin addiction. Not that James has ever done heroin. James actually times his alcoholic beverages—one per hour—to ensure he never "loses control." Eighty percent of my friends have had a crush on him at one point or another. Even the guys. They all want to *be* him, until they spend more than an hour in his presence. "When's the last time you even talked to her?" he continues.

I ignore him and pretend to examine my kayak, which I've secured with bungee cords to the roof of my car. Exhaust forms a foggy pool around my ankles. I don't think it's a good idea to tell him Kate has no idea I'm dropping by. Or that the last time I talked to her was about seven years ago.

"And how well did that conversation go?"

I ignore him some more. If I ignore him long enough, James usually gives up.

"Leigh, be reasonable. You're in no shape for some . . . *road trip* . . . that will just disappoint you."

His tone makes my stomach contract into a fist. "I'm in fine shape. Dr. Jensen said so last week." I adjust my kayak one last time. Why couldn't I have just gotten up ten minutes earlier? I suddenly hate the snooze bar. I wish I could think of something clever to say, but the best I can do is, "Besides. I've been reasonable my whole life. That's the problem." James rolls his eyes: *Give me a break.* Even now, he knows exactly how to make me feel like a twelve-year-old who still can't read a clock.

"People wait for years on kidney transplant lists. . . . You're lucky enough to get one, and all of a sudden you're Peter Fonda in *Easy Rider*?" He shakes his head, almost knocking me down with a sonic boom of disappointment. I think he's more upset by the fact that I'm growing as a person—his little sister is changing from unassuming, vanilla *Leigh*, with a spine like a warm Twizzler stick, to independent, empowered LEIGH, with a firm handshake and excellent posture. I once was lost, but now am found, thanks to a kind stranger named Larry Resnick.

But more on him later.

"James," I say, "Peter Fonda had a motorcycle filled with drugs and money. I've got a Saturn with a kayak on the roof." I also think of asking James if he would prefer I join a convent and sew my lips shut, but instead I say, "I'm tired of living vicariously through everyone else. I want my own life." And really, that's the meat of the matter. *I want a life.* I try to sound rational and convincing as I explain this to James, but I know if this conversation goes on much longer, my voice will grow higher and tighter until it sounds like I'm sucking helium. As the person who used to sign my report cards and once met with my ninth-grade principal to discuss the lewd cartoons I'd drawn in my math book to amuse friends, James has always had that power over me.

"What if you get sick again," he says, challenging me. "Then what?"

"Then I find a hospital." Simple logic, right? I think James is just afraid of change. Either that or being left behind with his wife, Marissa, who makes hot tuna casserole every Tuesday and leases a new beige Volvo every year. As if on cue, Marissa opens the back door. In a gauzy lilac robe, her hair in purple rollers, she looks like she'd be much more comfortable had she been named Mimi or Lady Bird.

"Everything alright?" she asks timidly.

James crosses his arms and glares at me. "Leigh still thinks she's going to California."

Marissa appears confused. "Oh?"

"I'm just taking a trip. People take them every day," I say, trying to sound calm. Would James ever just let me *breathe*? I feel chest-deep in a vat of pudding and sinking fast.

"Leigh, you are not going alone."

"I'll be fine. I'm only going for two weeks," I insist, but I don't sound too convincing. I'm growing claustrophobic and sweaty, so I decide to just take action before I change my mind completely. "James," I say with as much finality as I can muster, "I'll call you from Sioux Falls." With that, I slide into the driver's seat, shift from park, and begin my journey. It's one of those hyper, surreal moments where you might escape after all, where you think for a minute that you've actually convinced the Jehovah's Witnesses peering through your front window that you're not home, even though they clearly saw you streaking through the living room and diving behind the couch wearing nothing but a towel.

I leave James looking hurt and perplexed in the driveway, and suddenly I feel guilty. But not guilty enough to stay, and not guilty enough to quash my excitement.

I'm really doing it. Two left turns, a series of intersections, and one long graveyard on my right (which I drive past holding my breath, to add a day to my life), and I'm leaving Fond du Lac, Wisconsin.

Good-bye, Tucker's Hamburgers, Gilles Frozen Custard, Lakeside Park, and the Miracle Mile, where a dozen people bought winning lottery tickets and thousands more bought losing ones. I wish I had a convertible, so I could wear Jackie O sunglasses and a scarf over my hair and carelessly toss something fluttery and symbolic into the wind—maybe a love letter from an old beau, or ancient to-do lists, or just bundles of money, because if I had a convertible and Jackie O sunglasses, it stands to reason that I'd have a much more exciting life involving a surplus of inherited or ill-gained money.

I turn my stereo up and Jefferson Starship assaults me: "We built this city . . . !" I rush to find something that won't trigger my gag reflex. (Ah, yes: "London Calling," by the Clash. For some, not just a band, but a way of life.) I suppress a delirious giggle. *I'm really doing this.* I begin to sing along and ease onto Highway 23. My MedicAlert bracelet glints in the sun, looking much more like a sterling silver Return to Tiffany™ heart tag bracelet than the old-school stainless steel plate the kid with diabetes wore around his wrist in fifth grade. Humming down the highway with the rising sun at my back, I snake a hand down my side to touch my scar. I can almost feel my new kidney jouncing around in me. It feels less like an alien jelly bean and more like an old pal. I decide to name it Larry. After its namesake. I am alone no longer.

I was diagnosed with polycystic kidney disease when I was twenty-two, but hadn't felt quite right since high school, really. I spent my late teens like an extra from the set of *Flowers in the Attic:* pale, fragile, dark half-moons under my eyes. I napped often. You'd have thought I grew up on melba toast dusted with arsenic. It wasn't until my brief stint in college that anyone had a clue what was going on inside of me. The overworked staff at the university clinic put me on benazepril for high blood pressure and Tylenol for a low, grumbling back pain that wouldn't go away. Minor, right? It was nothing gripping and urgent like meningitis or syphilis. I had more bladder infections than anyone else I knew, but I figured I was just prone to them, the way my friends were prone to cold sores and bad taste in men. And my fat ankles? Well, they were just another of the many physical traits that would never make me a qualifier for *America's Next Top Model*. Nothing to write home about.

One day while filling out a doggy report card at Fuzzy Navels for Kermit, a high-strung pug, I collapsed with a blooming, amazing pain in my lower abdomen. (Fuzzy Navels is the doggy day care I work at. I was beta "paw"ssociate.) They wheeled me out of work on a pop-up gurney, and everything happened so fast after that: the ultrasound that diagnosed my disease, a million blood and urine tests, a parade—no, a *hailstorm*—of needles, new words like *creatinine* and *erythropoietin*. . . . My kidneys were infected with cysts that were multiplying, bleeding, taking over, blossoming like mini mushroom clouds. People with polycystic kidney disease (or PKD) aren't supposed to get sick until their midlife crisis, until they've had time to save for retirement and build equity in a home. It's supposed to progress slowly, plodding along at a nice, glacial pace. But I guess my particular PKD skipped class the day they handed out the syllabus. Over the next few months, the painful cyst-bleeds ramped up in frequency and intensity, as did the resultant hospital stays. And then one day, my cysts just wouldn't stop bleeding. The pain was radioactive. My abdomen swelled up like the bloated belly of a refugee. I became a revolving door for dozens of blood transfusions.

My kidneys, then working as successfully as Todd Bridges after *Diff'rent Strokes*, were excised from my body during a bilateral nephrectomy from which I now have a fifteen-inch scar. And I became the second-youngest patient on kidney dialysis at St. Luke's.

I remember I wasn't quite sure what to make of it all. I felt as if I were hurtling toward earth without a parachute. I stepped outside my body, avoiding eye contact with everyone: the boy who bagged my groceries, the teller at the bank, even my closest friends. In an orgy of self-pity, I let tears collect in my ears at night while I mentally catalogued everything I'd probably die before doing or seeing or touching or tasting. I eventually stopped returning my friends' calls. I became a nonperson pulling into my brother's driveway in a noncar. I hadn't quite received a death sentence, but I knew my odds. About 55,000 people are on waiting lists for a kidney transplant at any given time, and 12 people die each day before they get one. That's 4,380 people dead every year, just off the transplant list. I tried to stay optimistic. If 12,000 people receive a kidney transplant in a given year, I had a 37 percent chance of making it to thirty. Even the Miracle Mile couldn't help me.

Talk about putting things in perspective.

PKD is genetic (although I can't recall anyone in my extended family being formally diagnosed); so thus programmed from birth, my getting sick was inevitable. And maybe I lit the fuse with a few too many college visits to Bullwinkle's for dollar Captain and Cokes on Thursdays, but what could I do now? By the time I decided that *anyone* in their twenties could be hit by a truck before they made it to thirty, my doctors had me on a list for a kidney transplant. James wanted to give me a kidney, but he wasn't a good match. We seldom are. I love James, and I owe him more than the average person owes an older sibling. But there's something in James that's like lemonade on a canker sore.

But that's a story for the ride.

So anyway, six years, hundreds of hemodialysis sessions, and a million bad poems later, I'm the proud parent of an adopted kidney donated by a good-hearted stranger named Larry Resnick. Sadly, he wasn't a living donor. I have no idea how he died, but I'm sure it wasn't of old age.

God, I sound flippant. I don't mean to sound so crass. I guess there's no telling what kind of reaction you'll have when told you may or may not make it to thirty due to an organic rebellion occurring inside your body. And how you'll swallow the prescription for that ailment is something else entirely. My doctors told me the new kidney was not a cure-all. That I should think of it as just one more piece of my total ongoing treatment plan, the key word being *ongoing*.

I know I'm not cured, but when I woke up after surgery, I wondered if I was in the wrong room. Or the wrong body. I felt as if I'd been living in the dream where you're trying to run away from a lurching horde of zombies, but your feet are tied together, so all you can do is shuffle, and I'd finally woken up. Once my anesthetic wore off, I wanted to devour a deep-dish cheese pizza, then take a sun-dappled bike ride through Paris. Well, I was probably incapable of riding in the pace car of a parade, given my hospital gown and stitches, but damn I felt great!

My transplant team said that sometimes people wake up after surgery feeling quite well, and I shouldn't push myself, and a million other dos and don'ts. And as long as my kidney functioned, I'd have to take medication every day that suppressed my immune system so my body wouldn't reject it. Of course I listened. I've been listening all my life. And I'll do everything I'm supposed to, but . . . something's different. I can't help feel I've been given a free ticket to the destination of my choice. My mind keeps playing that song from *The Wizard of Oz* when Dorothy and the gang wake up from their sleep in the poppy field and dance right on into the Emerald City—"Optimistic Voices," I believe it's called. (You can almost imagine the conversation that led to that title. "But we need to name the song!" . . . "I don't know. It's a pretty hopeful tune. And those gals' voices—so cheerful, so positive, so . . . optimistic. Jeez, I don't know. This is a tough one!")

After the operation I returned to my brother's place and gradually resumed my life. The first perk was that I didn't have to return to work at Fuzzy Navels for about five months. And when I did, I didn't have to pick up poop anymore. Too germy. Too much risk of infection.

But then things got a little strange. Before my transplant, I lived in the rigid little bubble that many chronically ill people call home. Every morning for breakfast, I had a bowl of shredded wheat and soy milk. I measured all of my portions. Every day for lunch I ordered a veggie sandwich on a sesame bagel from the Bagelmeister Café. For dinner each night I had a salad of mixed greens and iced tea with whatever low-sodium, low-phosphorous, low-potassium casserole Marissa had taken a well-meaning stab at that evening (mmmm, right?). After dinner, I watched *Animal Precinct* and ate an entire bowl of salt- and taste-free popcorn. You get the picture.

But after my surgery, I began having strange cravings for food

I'd never tasted before. Gazpacho. Falafel with cold cucumber salad. Candied ginger. Once I found myself standing in the Copps checkout line at two A.M. dropping five bags of frozen edamame on the conveyer belt. Five bags! I'm sure the checker thought I was completely stoned.

In addition to my new food cravings, I also completely lost interest in the music that had propelled me through three years of college. Dido? Barftastic! Third Eye Blind? Shittacular! At first I chalked it up to a simple change in tastes. This happened to everyone, didn't it? I mean, we all used to have mall hair and jelly pumps, but then we developed common sense, right? One night, I found myself on line at the Exclusive Company holding CDs by Elbow, Nick Drake, and Wilco. I'd never heard of these people—or heard any of their songs—but I *knew* I'd love them. And I did. A new soundtrack for a new me.

James knew something was up when he came home one afternoon to find me on my knees digging up his front lawn. "What are you doing?" he asked, in a tone that suggested he was making a mental note to price straitjackets online later.

"I'm metal detecting," I answered. Wasn't it obvious?

He frowned. "I didn't know you owned a metal detector."

"I just bought it," I said, removing my gloves and grinning. "You won't believe the stuff I'm finding!"

After I showed him the collection of rusty nails and old coins I'd dug up, he left, looking slightly ill. Later he began referring to my new hobby as "mental defecting."

I discovered metal detecting by accident at the park one afternoon with my new favorite reading material, graphic novels. I saw a man who bore a strong resemblance to Ernest Borgnine skimming the ground with a machine like the starship *Enterprise* on the end of a long stick. It occasionally emitted a muted *bwoop*, at which point he crouched down, dug around in the dirt, and unearthed a mud-caked artifact that he carefully examined. I forgot my pretransplant shyness and asked him what he was digging up, and he showed me. Dirt-crusted coins, worn dog tags, and even a rusty contraption that looked like an old polio brace. I bought my own metal detector the next day. I checked with Dr. Jensen, since I knew I wasn't supposed to be digging around in the dirt, and he said it was okay because my surgery had been more than six months ago. As long as I wore gloves and washed my hands. Which I would have done anyway, given the fact that I despise dirty hands.

I know, this sounds like a hobby for retired accountants who wear black socks with sandals. But since I have such a short attention span, I figured it'd be a great way to meditate on the go and make some pocket change in the process. And like the man who scours used book stores convinced he'll discover an inscribed first edition of *Anna Karenina* for five bucks, I am positive I'll one day unearth a pocket watch that belonged to Ralph Waldo Emerson or maybe a flask used by Janis Joplin. I'm going to have to keep this one a secret from my friends, though. They just wouldn't understand.

Weirdly, I also had a strong urge to go kayaking. Before my surgery, I thought of kayaks as the Canoes of Death. The very idea terrified me. Lacking any semblance of upper-body strength, I knew I'd just roll over and trap myself underwater the second I sat in one. And I only knew how to doggy-paddle—my version being much closer to the flailings of a stroke victim than that of a flat-coated retriever gliding through the water with a duck in his jaws. I also thought only people with really expensive sunglasses and huge backpacks kayaked. But guess what? With my new kidney, I bought my own smallish recreational kayak and joined a kayaking club. I talked my friend Wes into buying a kayak and joining the club, too. Wes turned out to be pretty good.

While I was reexamining my life, I decided to take this road trip. I call it my Unfinished Business Tour. So here are the major pit stops during the tour: First, stop in for a chat with Seth Bradley, whose last words to me were, "We can still be friends, right? [*Long pause.*] So are you gonna eat that?" Second, pick up my road trip partner for the next leg of the journey—my best friend, Jillian, who moved to Colorado shortly after we graduated from high school. Oh, and while I have her attention, talk her out of marrying her eye crust of a boyfriend, Geoffrey (yes, with a *G*—even my neighbor's

cat had the good sense to be named Jeff with a J). Third, personally
thank Larry Resnick's family for his gift of life to me and learn if I'm
really channeling him. Last but not least, I want to confront my
mother about how she could abandon James and me. I know that
at this point I shouldn't care, but I do. I'm finally ready to ask the
questions that have dogged me my whole life.

You may be thinking that this is an errand for the chronically
and optimistically deluded, or maybe a person who's eaten some
bad bologna. You may also be thinking, *Channeling the kidney
donor? Is she high?* I know. It does sound like I'm smoking lawn fertilizer. So let's throw this narrative in reverse. The Seth thing, well,
that's just basic curiosity about the old college boyfriend who broke
my heart. Okay, *broke* is too kind a word; more like he sliced my
heart from my chest, sautéed it in butter and garlic, and ate it during a date with Kara Rivers, his next girlfriend. On a whim, I
e-mailed his old Hotmail account, not really expecting a reply. But
he wrote back, and he sounded genuinely happy to hear from me.
Really happy, like I was the Megabucks lottery commissioner with
a big check for him or something. Turned out he landed a job after
college in Sioux Falls, South Dakota. We made plans to meet for
lunch. Since I was headed west anyway, I figured, *What the hell?* I
was *so* over him, and maybe he's gotten bald and fat, which would
be kind of fun. But he was my first major deal, and the last real one,
so you know how that goes.

The Jillian and Geoffrey thing is a bit more complicated. They
started dating six months ago, and now they're engaged. While I realize this isn't terribly absurd, here's the problem: I've never met
Geoffrey, and neither has Jillian's family. And Jillian is *close* to her
family. And to me. We've always had veto power over the men she's
dated, and there have been a lot. Sure, she and Geoffrey live in
Colorado, but you'd think they could've squeezed in at least one
trip back to Wisconsin somewhere during their whirlwind
courtship. I wasn't really paying attention while this developed, because I was deeply absorbed in discovering and mentally catalogu-
ing more ways I was channeling Larry. And *that* whole idea is
Jillian's fault anyway. But through conversations with Meg, another

friend who moved to Aspen with Jillian a few years back, I learned some disconcerting things about Geoffrey with a G.

He seems to be your average self-deluded weirdo—not nutty enough to be a lunatic, but not endearing enough to be eccentric. He runs a health club called Crunchtime in downtown Aspen, and one of his more memorable print ad campaigns compared a photo of his buff thonged ass to a photo of a friend's saggier ass in a thong ("Become ass-tounding again! Join Crunchtime!"). When *The Passion of the Christ* was released, Geoffrey printed an ad featuring a crucified weight lifter and the tag "Resurrect Your Body!" That wasn't even the worst part. He'd superimposed a photo of his own smiling face over the face of the crucified weight lifter. Can you believe that?

He gets terribly possessive of Jillian, once driving ninety miles to extract her from a night out with girlfriends because she'd sounded "weird" when she called to check in with him at midnight as he'd instructed. Maybe because she was having *fun*? And he is completely obsessed with fitness. Before Geoffrey, Jillian was like me: laid back, slightly pudgy (and *fine* with it—my kidneys couldn't handle low-carb if you paid them), and easily talked into spending an entire day in pajamas watching Brat Pack movies on DVD while eating Cheez-It crackers, caramel corn, and gummi bears in a nice little snack rotation. You know, *normal!* After Geoffrey, Jillian became decidedly not like me: chiseled, dedicated to "food as fuel," and awake at four A.M. daily to train with Geoffrey for their next triathlon.

Oh, and did I mention he has two ex-wives and a son with each of them?

So I have to rescue her. I haven't told her this, though. It's kind of a surprise. It's also a wonder he's letting her leave for a few days, but I suppose those are the freedoms granted when traveling with a well-medicated, frequently hospitalized friend. (The assumption being that I am less likely to introduce Jillian to hillbilly heroin and swarthy men intent on seducing her, since I've had a kidney transplant and all.)

My third and fourth reasons for taking this trip are self-explanatory. And right now is the perfect time for a road trip. Fuzzy Navels is closed for the month of July, since my boss, Mindy Vandenheuven, the alpha pawssociate, is trolling Europe for young backpackers to bed. I'm not dating anyone because, well, do I want to have a miserable time out with some guy who's comparing my legs to his last girlfriend's, or would I rather eat an ice cream sundae and take in a sunset? And I need time away from James to figure out where to go from here. I think I'll just take this summer to be alive. I can worry about the rest later.

The farther west you drive in Wisconsin, the more interesting the scenery gets. Once you cross I-39, the expansive cornfields and potato fields give way to the occasional cranberry bog and lush rolling hills flecked with mature oak trees and family farms complete with old red barns, twin silos, and the requisite herds of impassive black-and-white Holsteins. The views from the interstate are postcard-worthy, but I'm only a few hours from home and already I'm sick of the billboards for cheese shops, casinos, U-pick apple orchards, flea markets, and Amish furniture.

You never see signs for Catholic furniture. But I do think we Catholics have cornered the market on yard art, with the Saint Francis of Assisi bird feeders and the Virgin Mary in a mini amphitheater/half bathtub. I've counted eight such Mary in a Bathtub statues in front yards in the last two hours. My great-aunt Pansy had one in her yard, too; my cousins and I would arrange our Barbies in a semicircle before Mary for a concert from the Giant Virgin Soloist. Sometimes all of the Barbies would make a pilgrimage to Mary in the Bathtub to confess their sins, which usually revolved around a deviant, sex-addled Ken and, once, a large armless G.I. Joe action figure with post-traumatic stress disorder and blackouts when he drank too much.

Closer to the Mississippi, the hills segue into rocky gorges and steep sandstone bluffs. Tenacious pines and birches cling to the rocky outcroppings. All of the local geology has something to do with the last ice age, but I may have been passing notes during that particular lesson. Maybe the next rest area will have some brochures.

Four hours after leaving James and Marissa in Fond du Lac, I become the last person in a long line for an empty stall in the women's bathroom of a rest stop on the Minnesota border. The girl in front of me turns around and fixes me with a bright smile. I jump, because she looks exactly like me. Well, not exactly, but close: blond, shoulder-length ponytail, billboard of a forehead, a spray of freckles across the nose. Her lips are plumper than mine. We're both wearing denim shorts and white T-shirts, but she's wearing baby blue sneakers without socks and I'm wearing sandals. It's like gazing into a dirty mirror at a younger, cuter me. Mini-Me.

She says, "I'm totally convinced there are more stalls on the guys' side." She smiles again, and I smile back, disarmed. Her teeth are crooked, but not distractingly so.

"There's this disposable paper gadget called the Magic Cone that girls can use to pee standing up," I blurt. Where was I going with this?

I'm glad when she laughs. "That would save time. We could switch lines."

I glance at the line ahead of us. Everyone looks exhausted and uncomfortable, shifting from foot to foot like dazed cattle.

"Where are you headed?" she shouts over the din of constantly cycling hand dryers.

"California."

"Oh, me too!"

"No kidding," I say. "Where in California?" The line inches forward a bit into the industrial warehouse of a bathroom.

Her eyes flick over my shoulder. "Long Beach, to visit my aunt."

"Cool. Ever been?" I ask.

"Once when I was younger," she says dreamily. "All I remember are palm trees and strip malls."

We inch forward again. Wads of paper towels have spilled from the trash cans and are now blowing across the floor like tumbleweeds. Mini-Me and I continue to make small talk, bonding over the annoyances of public bathrooms. After about two days, we're at the front of the line. A stall bangs open and releases a white-haired woman in a Disney sweatshirt who is yapping into a cell phone and wiping her free hand on a thigh.

At this point Mini-Me smiles at me and says, "It was great meeting you. Nature calls!" And she's off to the newly vacated stall before someone else jumps the line. *What a nice girl,* I almost muse aloud, entering my own empty stall seconds later. I hardly even mind that she used the phrase "Nature calls!" which is one of my least-favorite colloquialisms in the English language. Only "silly goose" and "heavens to Betsy" rank lower.

Sweet, sweet relief. Larry's working beautifully. I stand and wipe, checking the bowl for signs of blood or strange coloration. Nothing but yellow, baby. Afterward I fight the herd to the sinks, wash up, and am pushed by the mob to the hand dryers. Somehow, the bathroom chaos has its own order. I set my purse on the tile floor between my feet and punch the silver button on the dryer. To my right, a woman has turned the nozzle up and is attempting to dry her hair. I wonder where she washed it. In one of the sinks? That's a bit off-putting.

As a blast of hot air hits my dripping hands, a swarm of girls in soccer uniforms stream into the bathroom, giggling and shouting the call and response lyrics to a song that's been playing on Top 40 radio lately. They break through the endless line, victors in a restroom game of Red Rover. I overhear one of them say, "And I'm, like, 'Didn't you get my messages?' And he's all, 'What messages?' Like his phone is broken or something." At this, her audience protests. *Men,* I think. I try to dry my hands faster, rubbing them vigorously together as the machine instructs me. Just then the strap of one of the shouting girls' purses breaks, sending coins pinging and rolling across the tile floor. The mob in front of the sinks parts, as if the coins are little bombs, while the girls bend down to pick up the change.

As I glance at the woman still drying her hair, a blond girl picking up pennies bumps me. Hard. "Sorry!" she shouts, while I stumble to keep my balance. Because she apologized, I give her a lame smile. I really start smiling when I notice she's wearing an armful of the same kind of jelly bracelets that were popular when I was a kid. Who knew they were making a comeback? My hands are finally dry, so I bend to pick up my purse.

I find nothing but air.

My purse is gone. I irrationally wonder if I left it in the stall, but I know I put it between my feet. *My purse is gone,* I think as my pulse goes from a walk to a trot. I'm sure it's around here somewhere. I scan the gray tile floor, finding nothing but crumpled balls of damp paper toweling. I fluff through them a bit, making a show of the fact that I've lost something so people won't think I'm a bag lady. More people drift in and out of the bathroom like drones. I find nothing under the wads of paper. My pulse shifts from a trot to a gallop. I latch onto a sane-looking mother with a mopsy toddler in tow. "Excuse me. I can't seem to find my purse. Have you seen a big black purse anywhere?"

We gaze together at the big black purse on the shoulder of every woman in line. *Dear God.* She gives me a pitiful look while her toddler hides behind her knees, clearly sensing my imminent mental collapse. "Sorry. Try lost and found," she offers. I drop to my knees and peer under the stalls. Nothing but feet marching away to the back wall. Feet that get smaller and smaller, a study in perspective. Feet with places to go, purses to see. I study the counter, finding only puddles of pink liquid soap and water.

I dash out of the restroom area into the lobby. I force myself to imagine that I've locked my purse in my car and that I'll have a good chuckle at myself when I discover it sitting on the passenger seat like a well-behaved pet. Of course, I know this won't happen. At this point, locking my purse and keys in the car seems almost whimsical, like a play I once enjoyed.

I feel faint. I scan the travelers plugging quarters into the vending machines and browsing the wall display of local brochures. No big black purse.

I shove the glass doors open and jog into the parking lot, jostling a man in a blinding yellow polo shirt. He stumbles backward. "Hey!"

"Sorry," I squeak. I scan the parking lot, blinded by the sun's reflection bouncing off dozens of cars. Around me, families are stretching or lugging coolers to the shaded picnic area. I imagine for a moment that I am one of them, with nothing on my mind but stretching my legs and the chilled peanut butter and jelly sandwich I'd packed earlier that morning.

I dash up and down the sidewalk, frantic, seeing my purse everywhere and nowhere. A parade of cars flows through the parking lot. Brake lights flare. A yawning father sits in the passenger seat of his minivan, pouring flat soda onto the asphalt. It splatters and runs past my feet. And over it all a façade of normalcy that almost makes time travel seem possible—yes, I *could* go back ten minutes and find my purse in the bathroom! Of course! I could go back ten hours and get up earlier! I could even go back ten years and never get sick at all!

I sink onto the curb in front of a black Acura and watch a girl in bright pink flip-flops walk a sheltie to the dog-friendly area. I can hear her saying, "Make a doodie, Shotzi. Make a doodie." The sky hangs above me like an inverted lake. I think of making the slog back to my locked, purseless car, but I can't yet summon the energy.

My purse is gone.

My keys are gone.

My money is gone.

And sweet, sweet, *sweet* Jesus, my antirejection medicine is also gone. Did I mention that I need to take these pills every day? In a specific order? Or my body could reject Larry?

Someone has stolen my purse. The thief (presumably a woman) and my purse and my money and my medication are probably doing seventy down I-90 on their way to Las Vegas, where the thief will max out my credit cards on blackjack, sleazy hotel rooms, and fur coats. Later the thief will discover my meds and down them with champagne and probably have sex with a male hooker named

Mario who was purchased with my MasterCard. Afterward, they will make fun of the family photos she finds in my purse. Then I imagine her using my Visa to purchase tickets for Céline Dion's show, and I absolutely lose it.

I can already hear my brother's "I told you so" ringing in my ears.

CHAPTER TWO

Why didn't you just *ask* me for a ride?

It might sound surprising, but I didn't wake up from surgery with a zealous urge to discover whose kidney I now carry. It happened gradually, once I felt well enough to ponder such things. Oh, and developing new tastes in food and music helped.

Organ procurement centers (how's *that* for a euphemism?) keep the identities of cadaveric donor families and transplant recipients anonymous and confidential. I could, however, write to the donor family via my transplant coordinator, who would forward my note to the center, which would in turn send it on to the family. So I composed a brief thank-you letter and dispatched it, telling myself not to expect anything in return. I couldn't even say my full name or where I was from. If I waited for a year and the kidney was still in working order, the transplant program would arrange for me to meet with the donor family. But that made me uncomfortable, because it reminded me of court-ordered supervised visits arranged between dazed children and their incompetent parents in a public park.

I couldn't believe it when I received an even briefer note in re-

turn. It read, simply, "You're welcome. I'm glad Larry can live on."
It was obvious by the persnickety cursive that an elderly woman
had written it. Cryptic. And even more interesting, there was a return address label—the kind you get for free in the mail from the
American Cancer Society to guilt you into donating a few bucks.
Clearly, someone at the organ rodeo had been daydreaming
about what to make for dinner as our correspondence crossed her
desk. The author of this little ditty was Betty Resnick, resident of
608 Maple Lane in Cedar City, Utah. I had no way of knowing
whether or not Larry lived in Utah, although it wasn't likely; most
transplants are regional, as there's a forty-eight-hour window between death and operation. So the mystery was only half-solved.

But my curiosity had been kicked into overdrive. Especially
after a conversation I had with Jillian six months ago at the Blue
Moon Café one week before she returned to Aspen and met
Geoffrey with a G. I'd been describing some of the weird urges
I'd developed since the transplant, like my new penchants for
edamame and Wilco, and she pounded the table with enough force
to send a drop of water from my glass onto my right hand.

"Oh my God." She finished chewing and gasped. "I was just
reading about this!"

"About my transplant?"

"No, goofball. About recipients taking on the personality of the
dead donor!"

I rolled my eyes. This was fairly typical of Jillian. Whenever I
bemoaned the downward spiral of humanity in general, she shook
her head and said, "But children are being born *every day* with *gifts*
that will save the human *race!*" Jillian also believed in the power of
crystals and was once nearly trampled by a throng of people while
visiting a woman simply known as the Hugging Saint.

"I'm serious! There was this woman in Rhode Island—"

"Is this going to be like that story about the guy whose hand was
replaced with the hand of an evil serial killer and the hand makes
the guy start hacking people to death?"

Jillian shook her head. "This is real. It's called cellular memory.
I heard about a woman in Newport, Rhode Island, who had a liver

transplant, and she started to acquire the characteristics of the dead woman who donated the organ. Like, she used to hate Indian food, and all she wanted after the surgery was curry . . . and then she began dreaming in *Bengali*! She took a trip to India, became a Hindu, and runs an ashram in Bombay now."

I laughed. "That's an urban legend."

"Believe what you want," Jillian said, shrugging. "I'm only saying that when you open your mind to new experiences, change is possible."

"You said that about ear candling. I still have a scar from that burn."

Jillian tore off another chunk of bread with her teeth and said, "But you *liked* the energy work, remember? You fell asleep, you were so relaxed."

"That's because I'd just left dialysis. I was exhausted."

Still chewing, Jillian opened her mouth, leered at me, and asked, "Do I have anything in my teeth?" Wet bread was lodged in every crevice of her mouth.

I rolled my eyes while she snorted at her own bad joke. "Now, would your Native American spirit guide do that?"

"Sure!" she answered. "He'd do anything for a laugh."

Just then my other best friend, Wes, arrived. Wes, a former college rugby player, is so heterosexually male he could make Clint Eastwood look flamboyant. Jillian does not care for Wes at all. In fact, she finds him terribly offensive, a feeling that I think began eight years ago when we were all playing a drunken game of Truth or Dare in Wes's dorm room. Jillian, who had a major crush on Wes at the time, had slur-whispered into my ear, "Dare him to mash his face into my boobs."

Which of course I did, and which of course Wes did, in an awkward, anticlimactic move that all of us pretend to have forgotten. Afterward Jillian was so mortified by the whole affair that she could do nothing but bray about how she made me eat one of my own pubes during the game just to distract us from recalling her request for the boob-faceplant.

After Wes joined us at our booth at the café, he only reinforced

Jillian's crazy notion about the possibility of channeling organ donor traits.

"I'm serious," he said. "I heard about some guy who left his family, quit his job as, like, the CEO of some big-ass corporation, and sold everything he owned to become a missionary in Guatemala after his kidney transplant because he felt *compelled* to do it." As if to underscore this, he added, "I saw it on the Discovery Channel!"

"Wes, isn't that the network that routinely airs sensational programs about *face-eating tumors* and twins conjoined at the skull?" I asked.

"That's terrible," Jillian added, although I couldn't tell what was terrible—the fact that these physical deformities occur or the fact that I was using them to make a point.

"No, wiseass. That's The *Learning* Channel."

"Same diff," I said, snickering. "The modern freak show, no tent required."

"And you watched it, you heartless rube." He continued undaunted. "Laugh if you will, but there are more mysteries in the known universe than we will ever come to grasp." I thought I caught a glimmer of adulation in Jillian's eyes at his comment, but that was quickly squelched when the conversation deteriorated into a detailed description of the effect two tablets of Levitra had on his latest date.

Later I began to ponder what Jillian had said. Sure, I'd developed some new hobbies and strange food cravings. Sure, I'd begun buying unfamiliar items on impulse, with no real understanding of my urge to do so. Sure, I'd been having some weird dreams, like the one where I was a guy with a ponytail and a crazy girlfriend named Hopi and I lived in Utah and drove a late-model black Volkswagen to my job as an environmental researcher at a well-respected nonprofit.

I think it finally hit me when I received Betty Resnick's note postmarked in Utah. Because I received that letter *after* I'd been dreaming about being the ponytailed guy who lived in Utah. Yeah. But before I hit the gas and barreled headfirst into la-la land, I thought I'd try something else that might help me get a better handle on the evaporating reality of my life. Jillian, having all the right New Age connections, hooked me up with a woman named Helen who billed herself as something of a psychic. Well, she actually called herself a healer. Healer Helen had the biggest breasts I'd ever seen. They filled the room like out-of-control air mattresses. So of course I couldn't take my eyes off them. I became immediately paranoid that she could read my mind and forced myself to think about the time I donated twenty-five dollars to the Small Farmer Relief Fund.

I knew I was in trouble when she wanted to open our session with a prayer. Now, I'm a person who gets the giggles in church. I don't know why, but something about organized religion just tickles my funny bone. Last Christmas I went to midnight Mass with Wes and I had to leave after the priest sprinkled holy water on us, because Wes started hissing, "It burns! It burns!"

Anyway, Healer Helen opened with a prayer to the god of fake psychics or whatever, and I was glad her eyes were shut because I was trying so hard not to laugh that I'm sure I looked deranged. I focused instead on the incense smoke wafting around our heads and the gauzy purple panels draped centimeters above the burning candles placed strategically throughout the room. I leaned back into a pillow, getting comfortable, when Healer Helen finished the prayer and gave me a sweet Zen-like smile.

"Are you ready to begin?"

She began by examining my palms. "You're very sensitive. And you are a very nature-oriented person, no? When is your birthday?"

I told her. I'd thought about lying to see if she'd catch it, but I can't lie and keep a straight face. Especially not with a mind reader like Healer Helen.

She scrutinized me some more. "You have had many lives. Eighty, perhaps ninety."

I disguised my laugh as a cough.

"In fact," she continued, "you were one of the first humans!"

I actually felt honored. How cool is that? Neanderthal me!

Her brow darkened. "Now, you're not pregnant, are you? Be-

cause I keep getting this vibe that two are walking in your footsteps."

I sat up straighter. "I don't believe that would be physically possible."

"I'm getting this amazing *vibe*," she repeated. And then I felt a
bit skeeved out.

"I just had a kidney transplant," I volunteered, instantly regret-
ting it.

She closed her eyes and nodded. "Alright. Your kidney. I'm sensing some amazing energy around it."

A healing wound? I almost asked.

"What an incredible gift," she sighed, oblivious to my skepti-
cism. Then she did a little Stevie Wonder–like thing with her head
and said, "Something with the letter *L*."

Larry! I almost shouted. Then, *Lemon!* And finally, *Leon!* Because that was my father's name. Believe it or not. My father's
name was Leon. Short for Leonard. I just shrugged and pretended
to be confused. But I had goose bumps.

Then Healer Helen had to ruin it by saying my guardian angel
was named Denise.

Denise? No wonder I'd turned out this way. With a guardian
angel named fucking Denise. I knew a girl in college named
Denise, and she'd slept with almost every frat boy in our dorm.
They called her Dirty D and told us much more than we wanted to
know about her sexual idiosyncrasies. How she went *"Hoo! Hoo!
Hoo!"* when she came, like an owl. "Give a hoot. Don't pollute."

Some guardian angel.

But the seeds, already planted, had now been watered. It was
only a matter of time.

Later I tried to convince James that I was channeling Larry
through my new kidney. We were eating dinner—Shake 'n Bake
chicken and veggies with four dipping sauces Marissa had made
from scratch: barbeque, ranch, teriyaki, and a sweet-and-sour
sauce comprised of ketchup, sugar, and vinegar. This was her idea
of Japanese food.

He said, "Leigh, have you fallen and hit your head?"

I had to tread lightly. James's temper was legendary. When I told him about Jillian and Healer Helen, he said, "Those people are just out for your money." He ripped into a chicken strip. "And Jillian, well, she's flakier than a croissant."

"But don't you think it's at least a possibility? Like UFOs?"

He snorted. "Leigh, it's called reality. Pull up a chair."

"More teriyaki?" Marissa asked.

I wonder what my mother would have said. I honestly don't know, as I can hardly remember her. She's always been like a photograph gone wrong to me—so blurry and overexposed that it's hard to tell what the original image was. When I was little, I'd sometimes mold my image of her into whatever mother I'd liked most on the TV movie of the week. One week, she'd be a power-suit-wearing attorney fighting to keep Baby W with her kind, sweater-clad adoptive parents. The next week she'd be a cookie-baking, minivan-driving mom who would stop at nothing until I was head of a Texas high school cheerleading squad. I became a speed-reader at an early age in an effort to catch a glimpse of her name in the credits of every television show or movie I watched. Of course, I never saw "Kate Fielding" slide past before the key grips and best boys. My grandmother (I called her Gram) never said much about her, simply pressing her lips into a tight line and changing the subject whenever her name came up.

James hated her. After awhile, his hate seemed as much a part of his personality as his tendency to quote Elvis when faced with a quandary and to pronounce curtains "coitans" when he was in a good mood. He blamed her for his boring job, for my getting sick, for his fear of confined spaces, and of course he blamed her for what happened to Dad.

For awhile after she left she sent us checks. They dried up when I was fifteen, and then, mysteriously, the checks started arriving again one year later as if she'd returned from a long vacation. Never with a note. Just a check for one hundred dollars, sometimes as much as five hundred. James discouraged me from writing to her, and I only did twice during that time. Her silence was response enough. Once, when I was ten and James was twenty, he ripped up one of her checks right in front of me in the kitchen. "We don't need her fucking money," he raged, stomping over the shreds of paper on his way out the door, pausing only to punch a hole in the kitchen wall. Later that night I came downstairs to go to the bathroom and found James sitting at the kitchen table quietly taping the check back together, his shoulders slumped. I tiptoed back upstairs and reread *Then Again, Maybe I Won't* and began *Lady Chatterley's Lover*, a book I'd found on Gram's bookshelf. I didn't come back down again until morning.

My mother has no idea I got sick and had a kidney transplant. Sometimes, when I see commercials featuring mothers chatting on the phone with their daughters or shopping for wedding dresses together, the weight of her absence pushes me into the nearest chair and I can't breathe for a minute. What kind of strange, detached creature gave birth to James and me? Was she unable to produce oxytocin? Did mercury pump through her veins? Sometimes I imagine myself as a newborn, sobbing myself hoarse in a bassinet while my mother paints her toenails. But I can't think like that too often, because it's hard to get out of bed when I do.

The worst part is, I'm not even 100 percent sure where she is. The last few letters I sent disappeared into a black hole. None have been returned to me marked "Undeliverable," and I suppose that's something. I do have a phone number, but the last few times I called, I got one of those mechanical messages: "The owner of this voice mail box is unavailable. Please leave your name and number at the tone." It's the kind of recording you get when the intended recipient of your call can't figure out how to personalize the voice mail system, is too lazy to personalize the system, or wants to remain anonymous. So I left a message. It felt like I was making a recording for a time capsule that would be unearthed two hundred years from now.

I have a phone number that may or may not be hers. An address that may or may not be hers. I checked public records, and the address is *listed* as hers. Or was. When do they update that stuff? I should have hired a private investigator, but to do so would have required me to actually acknowledge the fact that my mother may not want to be found. Or could be mentally ill. Or dead. And those are painful facts to acknowledge. Denial and postulation are so much more comforting. So I'm taking the chance that I'll find her when I get to Los Angeles, or, at the very least, that I'll figure out *how* to find her when I get there. I'm shaking the dice, letting Larry blow on them for luck, and tossing them across the table.

I suppose when you live without something long enough, it's easy to forget you ever had it to begin with, unless someone rubs it in your face. Sometimes, during meetings at work or particularly long pit class lectures, the question would bubble up and pop in my head: *What happened to my parents?* And I'd feel off balance and unprepared for something, like my mind just stepped off a really fast escalator without looking. This still happens now and then, but much less now that I've quit drinking. It's just another part of who I am, along with being left-handed and never failing to stain my pants or shirt while eating out. I've got James, I've got aunts and un- cles that never forget my birthday, I've got friends that aren't afraid to make me eat one of my own pubic hairs on a dare, and I've got Larry. What more do I need?

Besides my big black purse?

So here I am, fighting tears in the parking lot of a dirty rest stop that straddles the Wisconsin-Minnesota border. A girl in my field of vision is imploring her dog, Shotzi, to make a doodie. My purse and car keys are missing. I can see my be-kayaked car parked down the line, now as useful to me as a condom to a lesbian. A trucker with four chins and a T-shirt reading I BRING NOTHING TO THE TABLE is ogling me, and judging by the flock of seagulls fighting and scream- ing over me, I'm not long for a warm splatter of bird shit on my head.

Not to mention that my body will probably kick Larry to the curb—perhaps the same curb upon which I currently sit—now that my prednisone and Imuran have been hijacked, and then I'll be back in line for the fun little ride called dialysis.

I've hit a new low, even for me. I bet the psychic didn't see this one coming.

•   •   •

I can't believe it. Mini-Me is sitting on the curb next to my car. With my purse in her lap and a scuffed green backpack on the pavement near her legs. She must have seen me pull in, pegging me for a sucker instantly.

Without instruction from my brain, my legs begin to run toward her. I am acutely aware of Larry's kidney. "Hey," I hear myself shout. "Hey, you. Give me back my purse!"

Mini-Me stands, cowering against the passenger door. "Don't be mad. I need a ride to California. Please. I won't hurt you; I'm not a weirdo or anything. I'm just . . . I'm all alone and I need a ride."

For a moment, I can't say anything. I consider screaming "Thief," but I've never been in this kind of situation before. Was I the kind of person who would just stand there and yell "Thief!" after a mugger took off with her purse, helplessly watching her sixteen credit cards and envelope of coupons fade into a point on the horizon? Or did I chase the creep down myself, grab her by the ponytail, and punch her in the face? God, this is one of those times I wish I'd watched less TV and gotten out of the house more. We stare at each other and I can almost feel the earth turning on its axis. I don't want her to take off running with my purse. And medication. So I finally say, "Just give me back my purse. You want money? I'll give you some." I stick my hand out, hoping I looked serious. "Come on. The purse."

She shakes her head. "Nuh-uh. If I give it back to you, you'll just take off without me. This is my collateral."

For a second I almost glance around to see if she's talking to someone behind me, because this is the most insane thing that has ever happened to me. Is there a boom mike behind us? I'd burst out laughing if I wasn't afraid for my life.

"Listen. I need a ride to California. Please. A safe ride. I won't hurt you," she repeats. "I just . . . You just seem safe and normal and I just want a ride."

"Why do you need a ride? How'd you get here?"

"It's a long story."

A semi churns past, whipping up hot dust and ancient candy wrappers. "I can't believe this," I mutter. She seemed so *normal* in the bathroom!

"All's I want is a ride. I don't have much money, and . . . you just seem really normal."

"I'm not that normal," I reply. This is quite amazing. A kajillion people make pit stops here daily, and I'm the one wearing the target. Her forehead knits together expectantly and I notice her hands quivering. What if she's a junkie? I scan her forearms for tracks. I see only chipped red polish on her fingernails, smudges on her knees, tiny beads of sweat on her forehead. "You're not on drugs, are you?"

"No!" She gives me an indignant, pleading look and blinks heavily. I have a sudden image of her sleeping under a picnic table, tucking her knees up into a hooded sweatshirt, retreating into herself like Gram's dog Lucky did after he'd been shot by the neighbor for chasing chickens. Riddled with bullets, he slunk under the porch and died while Gram and I wept.

"Please." She clutches my purse closer to her chest and looks at me with these big, watery, woeful eyes. "I'm not going to rob you or anything. I promise." I stand there gawking at her. *Any second now, I'll wake up,* I think. I blink hard. I chew the inside of my cheek.

I decide to ask my new inner muse: *Larry, what do you think?* I listen hard. I feel weird at first, listening to my kidney, but what the hell—it beats tarot cards.

I could get hurt. Or become an emotional hostage to a crazy little liar.

And that would be worse than my high school boyfriend, Kevin Murphy, *how?*

I could get killed.

Hadn't I told Wes I was taking this trip if it killed me? What supreme irony that would be. But with kidney disease already handicapping my life expectancy, what was the point of hiding out and playing it so safe I became a sheltered shadow of a person—

a person half-alive, never straying beyond the comfortable corner she'd painted herself into? I don't want to be like my great-uncle Harry, who never ventures outside except to pick up his mail, who's in his robe by six each night, watching reruns of *Gunsmoke* and eating Banquet pot pies. Countless television shows and online articles tell me I have one hundred things to do before I die, and I haven't done one of them. Besides, my mother's parting words to me were "Take big risks." Maybe it is finally time to take her advice.

And ultimately, I feel that Larry would have wanted me to give this girl a ride. People did it all the time in the sixties and seventies. And it isn't like she's a member of Hells Angels or a middle-aged trucker with a beer gut and a foot fetish. She's a teenage girl abandoned at a roadside rest stop. A bona fide magnet for the kind of bad things you see on the news at night.

The sudden image of Gram solemnly shaking her head and saying, " 'There but for the grace of God go I,' " seals the deal. I sigh. "Okay, fine. I'll take you part of the way." What choice do I have? She has my prednisone. I hope I won't come to regret this.

Mini-Me shifts her weight and blinks. "All the way? And I keep the purse for insurance."

"I won't leave you, I promise." I sound like a bad boyfriend.

"That's what my first foster mom said. And the second. And the third."

I can't tell if she's being sarcastic or simply factual. "Listen. There's medication I need in there. I had an organ transplant, and I have to take daily medication so my body doesn't reject it." I give her my best *Let's be reasonable* look.

She opens my purse and fishes out a bottle of pills. "Is this it?"

I think I nod.

"How many do you need every day?"

I close my eyes, feeling like a socially retarded third grader bargaining for her stolen underwear at camp. "Come on."

"How many do you take each day?"

I open my eyes again, irritated. "Of those particular pills, two."

She produces two pills and hands them to me like a rail ticket. "Thanks. Just take me to California."

Now, I've never really done too many crazy things before. I usually left that up to my friends, listening like an enthralled five-year-old as they relayed their latest exploits: "And *then* what happened? And *then* what?" I was the designated driver. The reference. The bailer from jail. So this was my big chance to drop some jaws. And what better way to start than to be blackmailed into giving a ride to a teenage runaway abandoned at a rest area? I mean, really. What could go wrong?

As we pull back onto the highway, she kneels on the passenger seat to watch the rest stop disappear behind us, then turns around and begins chatting aimlessly. About the universal strangeness of truckers, about bumper stickers, about things found in canned vegetables. Her monologue is making my brain check its watch, so I decide to interrupt her. "You know, it's really dangerous for a young girl to hitchhike alone."

"I wasn't alone. At least, I wasn't when I left Minneapolis with my boyfriend. We had a fight at the rest stop and he took off without me. I thought he was kidding."

I glance at her. She's still holding my purse, and my anxiety could clear a tall building in a single bound. "What about your family?"

"I don't have one."

"No family at all? Everyone comes from somewhere," I say, sounding far too much like Lady Aberlin from *Mister Rogers' Neighborhood*.

Mini-Me sighs and rolls her eyes. "Three foster homes and counting, when I left. My parents died in a car accident when I was six." It's such an offhand, jaded remark. It's the same tone she'd use to describe poor service at a restaurant. "Beat that one."

I'm not ready to beat that one. Not yet. "Are you serious?"

She nods.

"How old are you?" I ask.

"Seventeen."

"So do you really have an aunt in California?"

"Yeah." She pulls a pack of Marlboro Lights from her backpack and starts smacking them against the heel of her left palm. "Can I smoke in here?"

"I'd rather you didn't."

She stuffs them back in her bag. "So why are *you* all alone? That's not very safe either."

"Wait a minute. Let's back up here. Why didn't you just steal my car?"

"I'm not a thief," she insists. "I just needed a ride, and not with some creepy guy who'd probably rape me and dump my body in a ditch."

"Why didn't you just *ask* me for a ride?"

"Because you probably would have said no. Everyone else has."

I glance at her, bewildered. "How many people have you asked for a ride?"

She shrugs and stares out the window. "I don't know. A few."

"How long had you been there?"

She seems to consider this for a minute. "Just three days," she says finally. "As of today."

"Oh, is that all?" As our grammatically challenged president might say, I am being "sarcastical," but it sails right over her head.

"Yeah. I didn't have enough money for a bus ticket to California. So I panhandled for awhile, but, you know, the cops and all. There was this one state trooper that kept coming around, and I got nervous. So I've been, like, keeping a low profile."

I have never seen anyone so completely untethered and needy. Then again, I haven't been out much. She reminds me of a girl I knew in grade school. Gina O'Connor had broken glasses and unwashed, uncombed hair—a crazy brunette ball of cotton candy— and kids tossed dozens of tiny spitballs in her frizzy hair during silent reading. They taunted her for wearing hand-me-down jeans and bringing her lunch in a paper bag instead of a plastic Care Bears lunch box. Of course, I wanted to rescue her, even at eight years old. And of course, I want to rescue the girl in my passenger seat now. Of course! Ludicrous, I know. She's not a blind puppy in need of paper training, or Eliza Doolittle, or the world's largest unfinished latch-hook rug. I'm still not sure what the best course of action is exactly, but I guess I'll figure it out along the way.

"Look," I say, "we're taking a scenic route. There are a few places I need to stop first."

"Dude! A road trip! I'm, like, so on board with that." She grins. "So where we going?"

"Wait. What's your name?" *Which purse-snatcher do I have the pleasure of addressing?* I think but don't add.

She smiles warmly. "Denise. What's yours?"

It figures.

CHAPTER THREE

South Dakota: Great Faces. Great Places.

So when are you going to give me my purse?"

Denise (I still can't get over that name) nods and says, "Eventually. I promise. Look, I'm sorry to do this, but I have to protect myself." She sounds earnest, like a teacher on her first day in the classroom. I know I should be furious about the whole situation, but I'm strangely exhilarated. I know I could drive her directly to the nearest police station and hand her over to professionals. I know I could refill my prescriptions at the nearest Walgreens, even though I'd be out over a thousand bucks. I know I could ask James to transfer some money into my checking account. Or just go home with my tail tucked between my legs.

No I can't. None of the above. I am on a ride I don't quite want to get off. It's ratcheting up a steep incline and I have no idea what's on the other side, and the suspense is not even close to killing me. In fact, my five senses and I are throwing a party that's only just begun.

We're cutting through desperately flat and dull southern Minnesota on our way to Sioux Falls, South Dakota, where I will see

Seth Bradley for the first time in seven years. Denise has taken quite an interest in our story, convinced that he's the love of my life and that we will again fall madly in love. She tells me the story of the boy who abandoned her at the rest area. Rick. Slick Rick. Rick the Dick. He sounds as compassionate as a tapeworm, and uglier still. His favorite band is Nickelback, which tells me all I need to know. "I can't believe he would just leave you like that," I say to Denise, to which she replies, "You don't know Rick." She also drills me about PKD and my transplant, but for some reason I'm reluctant to share too much with a person holding my purse hostage. So I keep it concise and superficial. Just the facts, ma'am.

Every so often I sneak a furtive glance in her direction. She's tucked both feet under herself on the seat, and I notice a constellation of mosquito bites on her left calf. She's tiny, really. Probably just a size two. And something about her reminds me of a toddler—it's not baby fat, because she doesn't have much. Maybe it's her pouty lips or her round, guileless gray eyes. Or maybe it's her habit of fidgeting: with the zipper and cuffs of her sweatshirt, with her shredded shoelaces, with the lock on my car door.

We pass a billboard for the Spam Museum and Denise turns to me. "Hey, let's go!"

I scowl. "Not a chance." Then I have a thought. "Unless you give me my purse."

She seems not to hear this. "Aw. You're no fun." Denise pouts and resumes staring out the window. "Look how wholesome this shit is. All these fields, all perfect and shit. What are they, fucking Mormons?"

"Lutherans," I say, keeping my eyes on the road. I furtively glance in her direction again, but she's still looking out the window. God, I'd be so much more relaxed if I were alone. I cruise past a solo driver in a beige Buick bearing a sensible AAA window decal. A sun-faded brown box of Kleenex rests in the window above the backseat. I imagine a world where I could teleport myself from my car to his and speed away. *In case of rapture, can I ride with you in the reliable, non-hitchhiker-carrying sedan?*

We pass another billboard for the Spam Museum and Denise says, "Hey. Think of a word that rhymes with Spam."

"Cram," I say, wanting to add *it*.

"Shazaam!"

"Bam." I'm mildly embarrassed to be participating in this game, but more so that this is the best I can do.

There's a long pause, and then Denise adds, "Tram!"

I can't think of any more words that rhyme with Spam, so I feign annoyance. "Okay, enough of the rhyming word game."

Denise shrugs and pulls out a battered copy of *The Catcher in the Rye*. "Mind if I read?" she asks. I'm too surprised to do anything but nod. I'd expected her to lug out a Danielle Steel novel, or maybe *Thievery Digest*. I'm a little unnerved by her choice in reading material. Doesn't a red flag pop up in an FBI computer somewhere whenever anyone checks *Catcher* out of a library? Because didn't Mark David Chapman and Lee Harvey Oswald enjoy the novel? I tell myself I won't worry until Denise starts referring to herself with three names.

Then, all at once, I think of *jam, ram, dam,* and *yam.* Story of my life, man.

We decide to stop for dinner outside Fairmont, Minnesota, at a restaurant called Annie Oakley's Roundup, because Denise enjoyed their billboard two miles earlier. I coast down the off ramp, slicing through the buzzing cicadas. When we get out of the car and stretch our legs, I'm struck by the sweet smell of growing things: corn, ditch weeds, and cut hay waiting to be baled. Even the air, blanketing us in evening haze, seems green and clean and alive.

"This town smells weird," Denise announces, wrinkling her nose.

"It's the smell of plants breathing," I say, immediately wishing I hadn't. I sound pretentious. I once read an article about violence decreasing in the inner city after the planting of trees and bushes. Something about feeling connected to a larger natural universe. I wonder if we should get off the freeway and maybe take a more scenic route to capitalize on this calming phenomenon, but it's probably not a good idea, seeing as how I know more about Fuzzy Navel's FedEx guy than I do about this girl.

Annie Oakley's Roundup turns out to be a crazy cross between a fifties diner and an Old West saloon. All the waitstaff wear cowboy hats and boots, and I can hear a short-order cook crooning along with Patsy Cline in the kitchen. We're seated by a waitress in scuffed boots who looks as if she hasn't slept in months. I order black beans and rice, coleslaw, and an iced tea, and Denise orders their bloomin' onion and a Coke. I wonder if I'm buying.

"So do you have any money?" I ask, genuinely concerned for her. Okay, and for my bank account. I wonder how long she would have stayed at the rest stop had she not latched onto me. The entire situation still seems surreal to me, like I'm watching it happen to someone else in a Lifetime movie.

"Some," she replies, staring at an elderly couple in a nearby booth silently stuffing fries into their mouths. Suddenly she sighs cinematically. "Do you think they're in love or just going through the motions?"

"Maybe they're brother and sister."

"I bet you and Seth wouldn't go through the motions," she opines wistfully, which startles me. She has no idea what Seth and I had been like. How could she be such a romantic? Especially after being ditched at a public rest stop off I-90 by someone who first told her he loved her on the Tilt-a-Whirl at a county fair?

"Denise," I say, taking a deep breath, "I'm worried about you. I mean, you're seventeen. . . . Are you still in school?"

"Listen, it's not as bad as it sounds. I'm going to live with my aunt. I'm finishing my senior year in Long Beach." She won't look me in the eye and I suspect it's actually worse than it sounds.

"And you really don't have any parents? There's no one we can call? What about your foster parents? I'm sure they miss you."

"As if. We had a fight and I took off. I called them from the road before Rick left. I am not going back there, and they know it." Her cheeks color and she begins to stammer. "Stupid, I know. But look. My aunt knows I'm on the way, okay? I just didn't tell her about

Rick ditching me. I was, like, too embarrassed, I guess. But she's
my family."

"So why haven't you lived with her before?"

Denise sucks in a breath and toys with the saltshaker. "Well,
she had some problems with, like, drugs. In and out of rehab, you
know? But she's clean now. She's been clean for over a year. She
said I could live with her." She unravels a bit of sweatshirt cuff.
"And besides, I'm seventeen. I can be legally emancipated."

Our waitress clomps by in her cowboy boots and taps our table
with a lacquered fingernail. "Your food'll be right up, gals." Someone plugs money into the jukebox in the corner of the restaurant
and Bon Jovi begins to insist that everyone listening gives love a bad
name.

At this point I decide to change the subject. Maybe it's because
Denise's family makes mine sound like the Cleavers. Or maybe it's
because I'm beginning to feel like an interrogator badgering a victim of domestic violence. Besides, there's plenty of time to get the
whole scoop between here and California. So when our food arrives
I tell her all about my suspicion that I've inherited more than just a
kidney from Larry Resnick. It does start some great conversations,
you know? Her gray eyes grow large and bright, and despite myself
I bask in the attention. "I've heard of that kind of thing happening!"

Apparently everyone has.

"So what does it feel like?" she asks, excited.

"Most of the time I don't notice it. But sometimes—sometimes
it really feels *alive*. Healthy and alive. I don't know, like it just has
its own energy." I feel a bit odd telling a stranger this, but there you
have it.

"Can I touch it?" Her eyes are still wide, like dinner plates.

I giggle. "Um, okay."

I stand up and she reaches over the booth. I guide her hand
over the scar, feeling like a human Blarney Stone. "Wow," she says
reverently, sliding back into her seat. "That is so cool! His name's
Larry?"

"Yep," I say, still grinning. I lift a forkful of fragrant beans and
rice to my mouth.

"What do you think he was like?"

I think that he was the kind of man to feel very passionate over injustice. I also feel strongly that he didn't hunt, but he loved to go camping and kayaking. And maybe even metal detecting. I think he was a vegetarian and never forgot a family birthday. His nieces and nephews adored him, and he played horsey and monster with them for hours without complaining. I think he was handsome in that thoughtful, intelligent way that artists can be . . . sort of like Chris Cornell, maybe. I think he broke his arm once, when he was nine, and he lost his virginity when he was nineteen in his parents' basement, listening to Jeff Buckley.

Of course, I don't tell her this. Instead I say, "I think he was a kind man. And I think he knew things."

"What kind of things?" she persists.

I shrug and push rice around my plate. "I don't know. It's not like he was a *Jeopardy!* champion or anything. I just think he was wise."

We chew our meals in silence for awhile. Suddenly Denise says, "My first foster mother worked for a psychic hotline. She wasn't psychic, of course. But she was really nice to me, you know? Then she and her husband got divorced and she went all crazy. She couldn't deal with me anymore. So back I went."

What do you say to that? I shake my head, hoping to knock some inspiration loose. I come up with, "A child isn't a pair of jeans. You just can't . . . *return* someone if they don't fit."

She snorts and tears off a deep-fried onion petal. "Oh yes you can. You'd be amazed what can happen. Can I try some of your coleslaw?"

Sluglike, I slide my coleslaw across the table and watch her finish it. Who on earth is this girl? In a parallel galaxy, she'd be my troubled younger sister. In this one, who knows? Maybe she's Aileen Wuornos reincarnated. She looks up at me and gives me a goofy, thankful grin. "This is pretty good. Thanks for stopping here."

Okay, so she isn't Aileen Wuornos. "You want some dessert?" I ask, smiling.

"Ooooh! See if they have turtle cheesecake," she chirps.

When the bill comes Denise surprises me by sheepishly sliding my purse across the table. "I hope you don't think I'm a jerk." So I am buying. But then Denise fishes around in her backpack and produces a crumpled ten-dollar bill. "Is this enough?"

"I can't take your money," I say, suddenly ashamed of myself. But I'm thrilled to have my purse back.

"It's not my money. It's Rick's. So yes, you can take it." Her face lights up in a wide smile and she presses the money into my palm.

We decide to drive another hour and a half toward the setting sun before finding a motel for the night. We listen to a local oldies station, which feels perfect for a road trip, while Denise reads my road atlas in the fading light. To keep my checkbook in the black, I pull into a Motel 6 off the interstate just as the guitar intro for CCR's "Who'll Stop the Rain?" begins. I like this song, and I hesitate for a moment before killing the engine. We step out of the car, travel weary, and stretch. I feel mildly disoriented, as if I've just exited a carousel. Insects fly in loops around the bright white parking-lot lights and a cool night breeze lifts the hair at the nape of my neck. "I'm getting two rooms," I tell Denise. "One for each of us." I may be crazy enough to give a ride to a stranger, but I'm not nutty enough to let her share a motel room with me the night I meet her. Even though I'd done pretty much just that with a few guys in college. But never mind.

Denise seems disappointed. "Oh." Then she perks up. "Can we just hang out together in your room for awhile?"

I shrug. "Sure, why not?"

The night manager is slumped like a jumbo sack of dog food in a Plexiglas booth. I request two single rooms and he slides the keys through a slot in his partition, staring at Denise's chest the entire time. "Rooms 118 and 119. On your left under the staircase."

My room makes me pine for a Holiday Inn or Best Western. Even Super 8 would be a step up. One boxy bed juts like a buck-tooth into the room, which smells of bleach and ancient tobacco. A mysterious black stain in the shape of a hot air balloon splays be-

fore the bathroom door. Denise turns on the dusty television set
bolted to the cheap veneer dresser, and a local nightly news anchor
flickers to life. "What do you usually watch?" she asks me.

"Oh, I don't know." Well, I usually watch Animal Planet or the
Food Network, but I doubt Motel 6 subscribes to gourmet cable.
Plus it's embarrassing to even acknowledge my tastes in television
because, let's face it. I'm not yet thirty, but I'd be right at home in
any senior center in America. I stack a few pillows behind my back
and settle against the headboard that's been nailed to the wall. My
legs twitch from a full day of driving. When I was on dialysis, they
would sometimes cramp. I'll take the twitching any day. Maybe I
could go for a hike tomorrow afternoon. Then I remember I've got
Denise.

"I love old Ginger Rogers movies," Denise says. She sprawls
across the bed, flipping through channels until she finds a black-
and-white movie. "Oh, *Mildred Pierce*! Even better. Joan Crawford
is, like, completely fabulous."

I grin. "Ever see *Mommie Dearest*?"

" 'NO . . . WIRE . . . HANGERS!' " she replies. I guess this
means yes.

We watch Mildred's unfolding drama for awhile. "God, could
you imagine having a mother like her? Someone who would do absolutely anything for you?" she asks, propping herself up on an
elbow to look at me. "What's your mom like?"

"I have no idea."

"What do you mean?"

I'm too tired to really think about it. Which is weird, because
usually I go out of my way to tell people the gory details of how my
mother abandoned me. It's who I am. If you want to know me, it's
as essential as knowing I have kidney disease and an inexplicable
crush on David Cross. Instead I simply say, "She left when I was
five." In the movie, Mildred Pierce slaps her daughter for being insolent.

"Serious?"

I nod. "She wanted to be an actress. She's the reason I'm going
to California."

"When's the last time you saw her?"

"Twenty-three years ago."

"Wow." Denise shakes her head slowly. "That's a long time."

I can tell she's being sincere and it touches me. I'm sure she's lived through worse than an absent mother.

"What about your dad?"

My heart trips over her question. "Oh, it's a long story. Let's save it for another night." I try to sound nonchalant. All of a sudden I'm hit by a sledgehammer of exhaustion.

"Okay," Denise says amiably. She turns back to the television. "Hey, you hungry?"

She leaves the room to buy us a snack from the vending machine outside. When she returns she tosses me a small bag of Funyuns. "How's this for an after-dinner treat?"

"You are trying to kill me," I say in mock horror.

She launches herself onto the bed and says, "You're lucky. I almost got you a box of raisins."

As I dig into my Funyuns, I notice Denise playing piano on the bedspread with her fingers. "What are you playing?" I ask.

"Huh?"

"Your fingers. What are they playing?"

She laughs and blushes. "Oh. A Hall and Oates song. I do this sometimes." She bursts into the refrain from "Private Eyes."

This cracks me up, despite the fact that I'll now have this tepid song in my head for days. "You know Hall and Oates? How do you know about Hall and Oates?"

She rolls her eyes. "I don't live under a rock. The eighties are the new seventies."

It's going to take me awhile to get used to her. But truthfully, Denise is starting to grow on me—although like a boil or a beautiful head of hair, I haven't yet decided. I guess I didn't realize how lonely I was.

When the movie credits roll we say good night. Denise thanks me again for giving her a ride and I'm pretty sure she means it. She doesn't even glance at my purse on the dresser. "Be ready to leave at eight-thirty," I tell her like a big sister.

"Right-o," she says, heading out the door. "Tomorrow's the big day!"

For a minute I don't know what she's talking about. But then I remember. My date with Seth. "Hey," she says, turning back to me. "You're not going to get up early and take off without me, are you?"

"Not if you're ready by eight-thirty," I say. I lock the door behind her and flip open my phone. I have one new voice message. From Seth. Seeing his name on my phone makes me feel both surprised and flustered. How many years had I gone without receiving a message from him, voice or otherwise? Was reconnecting as easy as zapping an e-mail into his in-box? As Gram and a million other wise relatives have advised over the years, if something sounds too good to be true, it probably is. TiVo aside. Maybe I should call him back and cancel the whole thing. Here are how my feelings for him have evolved over the years: First, we had the "Maybe I'm Amazed" period, where everything was like discovering a gorgeous uncharted island near Tahiti. Then we moved into "Making Love out of Nothing at All," which was like finding the cannibalistic natives on our uncharted tropical isle, which slowly slid into "The Way We Were" despair as he pulled away—my heart eaten by the cannibals—and beyond into bitter "You're So Vain"/"I Will Survive" territory (a new island entirely) after he dumped me. Then my emotions hibernated for some time, until finally, years after our fling had ended, I was left with a "Peaceful, Easy Feeling." The healthiest and sanest state of mind, if also the most beige. (The only danger being selective amnesia, wherein I forget the times I waited by the phone for him to call, overlooked his tardiness and/or predate inebriation, et cetera ad nauseam.) The thought of rekindling any kind of interest in him exhausts me a little. Especially after the last few days.

But in the end, curiosity beats apprehension by a yard. I punch in his number and clear my throat. He answers after three rings and sounds both familiar and strange. He doesn't say hello, but instead greets me by name. "Leigh!"

I hate when people do that.

"I'm so glad you called me back."

"Hi." For a moment I'm unsure what to say, and follow up with the obvious. "I saw that you called, so here I am. Returning your call." My cheeks grow hot at my inept conversation skills. Where did I learn to interact with people, the "Draw Winky" School of Human Relations?

"I just wanted to make sure we were still on for tomorrow." It sounds like he's smiling.

"Of course. I'm looking forward to seeing you." It's a fine line between excessive enthusiasm and friendly interest, but I think my response walks it well. I almost tossed in a "really" before the verb, but I managed to stop myself in time.

"Me, too. Where have you stopped for the night?"

"I'm near Worthington, about an hour from Sioux Falls. I'm staying in a motel off I-90." I don't reveal that I'm staying at a Motel 6. Nor do I reveal that I'm not alone.

He sounds disappointed. "You should have called earlier. I could have given you some recommendations on places to stay."

We make more surreal-feeling small talk for a few minutes and I again get the slightly uncomfortable sense that this is all happening too easily. I'm also getting the feeling that I've forgotten something important and potentially embarrassing, like I've suddenly realized four hours into my day that my pants are on inside out. Am I reading more into this meeting than I should be? I tell myself that we're just old friends reconnecting. Nothing more. Well, okay, he was once much more than just a friend. I mean, "just a friend" doesn't try poking his index finger into your anus while you're making out in his parents' basement while said parents are upstairs watching 20/20.

After I hang up I try to get comfortable, but the crispy booger wiped on the bedspread by a former guest isn't exactly comforting. I turn the clanking air conditioner off and throw the bedspread onto the floor, which leaves me with the scratchy overwashed blanket and institutional white sheets. I fluff my pillow and reflect on my strange day. A million questions swirl through my head, bouncing off one another and forming new ones. What do I tell Jillian about my new traveling companion? Wes? *James?* Oh God, I can just imagine what James would say. Then I think of how I met Seth

in college. (We'd both volunteered to be hypnotized by perfor-
mance hypnotist Mark Maverick at a back-to-school show—how's
that for symbolism?) Just as quickly, my brain shifts gears and reminds me that I've got a new responsibility one wall away, sleeping
in another bucktooth Motel 6 bed. Or not sleeping. My mind
buzzes like I've crammed for a final exam. I don't think I'll ever fall
asleep, especially after hearing what could very well be a drunk and
mentally unstable professional cage fighter shouting obscenities
and banging on a door down the hall, but the next thing I know my
travel alarm is beeping in my ear.

When I knock on the door of Room 118, I am answered by only the
sounds of semis blazing past on the freeway. At first I assume she
simply overslept, but then I wonder if she skipped out on me. A
feeling of lightness, fluttery and buoyant, begins swelling in my
body. But then she opens the door, still wearing the ratty T-shirt
and gym shorts she slept in. She yawns and squints at me through
a pair of glasses. She wears contacts? "Morning," Denise says,
stretching. "Just give me a sec to get ready."

I force a smile, suddenly fatigued even before setting foot in my
car. "Rise and shine," I say, and sit on the bed to watch cartoons and
fret about my so-called date while I wait. I glance out the window
and observe a black Acura with tinted windows slowly tooling
around the parking lot. Something about the car seems familiar,
but I forget about it when Denise bounces out of the bathroom.
"Okay, all set!"

So here we are, Tweedledee and Tweedledum, on our way to
sunny Sioux Falls, South Dakota, home of Seth Bradley and the
Sioux Falls Cardinals. "So, like, are you nervous?" Denise asks ex-
citedly, blowing through the hole on the cover of her vanilla cap-
puccino. (We bought coffee and muffins first thing after leaving the
motel parking lot—I can't function with low blood sugar.)

I smile and shrug to conceal the fact that I'm so nervous about
seeing Seth again that I may soon have a seizure, right there in the
car, and we'd have a terrific accident and I'd really die (for real!)

and then in the afterlife they would put me on the lame track, because I'd been just like spineless Albert Brooks in *Defending Your Life,* and I'd have to prove myself fearless in some kind of interstellar stunt. So maybe seeing an old boyfriend is really nothing to get myself worked up about. It's not like I'm trying to defuse a ticking bomb at a day care, is it?

Ah, Seth. When we were together, the very thought of seeing him just about gave me convulsions. I was a journalism major, likely to end up in some shitty little burg covering high school football every Friday night. How could I possibly interest a guy who was going to someday save gorillas in Africa? And how could I maintain the interest of someone who wrote me near-daily amusing notes referencing everything and everyone from Debby Boone to John Waters? Someone who made things look effortless, someone people knew and liked, someone just enough beyond my orbit that, like a flower following the sun, I began to reach for him no matter where he moved?

Seth and I parted ways a year before I got sick. Maybe he could sense my illness, the way they say dogs can smell tumors. Maybe we just hit the three-month wall and never recovered. Regardless, I soon had bigger worries than bumping into Seth on my way to a pit lecture. And then I left school entirely. I told myself I'd go back when I felt better, and after I'd adjusted to my new reality and dialysis routine, I thought about reenrolling. I really did. But I just kept putting it off. And I never really felt better. Anyway, that's another story entirely.

Seth, however, has somehow reappeared on my calendar for today. I wonder if he'll look the same: slightly cherubic cheeks . . . tousled dark hair . . . that innocent, goofy grin that made his blue eyes crinkle and my resolve wrinkle. In college, Seth was really into hemp necklaces and tie-dyed T-shirts. I was a sucker for that kind of thing back then. His only physical flaw (if I forced myself to pick one) was a cute little bald stripe through one eyebrow—the result of a childhood run-in with a garden tool. Seth has affected my worldview more than he knows. When we were making a beer run one long-ago night, I asked if his friends had chipped in. Seth simply replied, sagelike, "No, man." (He called everyone "man," even me.) "It always comes out in the end. I don't worry about keeping tabs." And smiled his sweet, knee-buckling smile. I remember thinking, *How refreshing!* Of course, I'd just come off this thing with a guy who'd once refused me an upgrade from regular fries to crispy curls because they were fifty cents more expensive.

I probably don't need to tell you that James didn't like Seth. He referred to him as "that dirty hippie." Now, Seth was neither dirty (he showered purposefully) nor a hippie (he got regular haircuts and ate fast food), but at that point, little else could have made Seth more attractive to me than my brother's disapproval. James didn't like something? Sign me up!

The sixty miles to Sioux Falls pass quickly, and we spot our first billboard for Wall Drug, which Denise points out, before returning to one of the South Dakota travel guides I've packed. "So are we going to the Corn Palace?" she asks, an index finger tracing the write-up in the book. "How about the Badlands? I mean, it's not every day you drive through here, right? So why not see the sights?" She then sings a few bars of Michael Jackson's "Bad," complete with falsetto *"Wooos!"* at the appropriate intervals.

I don't really have much of an itinerary before reaching Jillian's place in Colorado. Nor am I under a Draconian schedule. We could pretty much stop wherever we wanted, money (or lack thereof) being the only impediment to our travels. I shrug, but even lifting my shoulders has become an effort. I'm too anxious to move, except for my stomach, which feels as if it's doing the fox trot at a dance-off in my midsection. At this point, all I really want to do is travel back in time so I could stay in my driveway yesterday morning. Fuck the Corn Palace.

My phone rings again, which reminds me that I need to change my ringtone, because the only thing that annoys me more than my ringtone is a professional boxer that gives God a major shout-out after a victory. I always yell at the television, "Sorry, but God's hanging out in a children's cancer ward or the Ho-Chunk Casino, you self-absorbed boob!" And why am I watching boxing to begin with? Yes, that's right. Rhymes with "Games," but he's much less fun.

In fact, my gut tells me it's James calling me right now, but wouldn't you know? It's Seth again. The sight of his number almost sends me into the ditch, swerving a little, and Denise reflexively extends her right hand straight ahead. "Watch the road, dude."

I fumble and answer; he greets me with "Hi, cutie. We said Brew Ha-Ha, right? At ten-thirty?"

Hi, cutie! What the hell is this? His overly familiar greeting knocks my nervousness back to make room for a new emotion: mild suspicion. I try to shove it in the corner. I'm supposed to be excited, not wishing we could simply keep driving. I manage to stammer, "Uh, that's right. Ten-thirty." I have to remind myself to smile so my voice sounds friendly and easygoing, like a helpful customer service representative. Brew Ha-Ha is a hip little coffee shop (I looked it up online) in the recently gentrified downtown area of Sioux Falls, and it seemed like a neutral, pleasant place to reunite.

"Can't wait to see you, Leigh."

Hearing him address me by name again does nothing to allay my growing suspicion. Maybe because he once addressed me with laid-back "mans" and "dudes." As in "Hey, dude, you should see how hungover [insert name of roommate du jour] is this morning!" when we met each other between classes. His new greeting feels like a favorite sweater that's shrunk in the wash and now cuts into my armpits. Plus, is he repeating my name so he remembers which woman he's talking to at the moment?

He continues. "God, how long has it been? I hope we recognize one another!"

I search my memory archives for a funny anecdote from our relationship, but I come up empty-handed (brain-celled?). The best I can do is, "Well, at least my hairstyle has improved somewhat since then." I suddenly remember him chiding me for wearing a belt all the time. It was a woven leather belt. My favorite. I thought it completed my outfit, and there my waist was, every dip or turn reminding him that I was definitely not the kind of woman he'd want to share coffee and a newspaper with every morning for the rest of his life.

"Oh man, what did I have . . . that fucking bowl cut?" He

laughs, and I'm relieved that it sounds both real and familiar. At least that hasn't changed.

"Ah, those were the days," I add lamely. I flick my eyes at Denise. She's staring out the window at the endless fields stretching to the horizon, and I can almost feel her eavesdropping.

"No worries, Leigh. I'd recognize your eyes anywhere."

Pass the Limburger and plug your nose, I think. Nevertheless, something flutters deep in my seventh chakra, as Jillian would say. I remind myself to tell her I actually thought this. Well, he didn't describe the color of my eyes. They're brown. I'm sure he's forgotten, unless he's hung on to some old photos of me. I imagine three photos of us together, dusty at the bottom of a box in his closet, edges curled, water spots on my face. Perhaps the one of us taken at his friend Jack's wedding. Perhaps the one of us taken while camping, where I'm sitting on his lap on the picnic table. We're both drunk. I hate that picture, though; I look like I have Down's syndrome.

But anyway, blah-blah. The more important thing is that all of his saccharine flirting is practically dripping from my phone. My ear feels covered in frosting. I force a brittle laugh and decide to confront this behavior. "Ha-ha. When did you become such a flatterer?"

"When I stopped smoking pot, I guess."

I wonder briefly if he's also given up breathing. "Wow. I guess we have a lot of catching up to do."

"So what am I supposed to do while you're on your big date?" Denise asks as we cruise into the city.

"I don't know. You could go for a walk, or window-shop," I say. "Just don't snatch any more purses."

She ignores this, scanning our new surroundings for her options. "I think I'll read my book in a park." *Good,* I think. Hearing her say that she'll be spending the next hour or two engaged in a safe, productive pastime definitely enhances my opinion of her.

I drive around and around a block loaded with touristy bistros and boutiques, searching for a parking space. Huge pots of native prairie flowers and ornamental grasses line the sidewalk, and I watch a woman in flip-flops stub her toe on one. I find Brew Ha-Ha in the nick of time thanks to MapQuest, and then I score a parking spot two blocks away, right near a cute little park with a gazebo and lots of benches. After I stop the car I'm afraid to get out. I become a bigger chicken than the San Diego Padres mascot.

"What's wrong?" Denise asks.

"Nothing," I say. It feels eight thousand degrees, and I'm too scared to even lift my arms for fear of discovering how deeply my antiperspirant has failed me. I force myself to think of the time I had to sing Bryan Adams's "Heaven" solo in front of the entire eighth-grade chorus class, and getting out of the car to have coffee with an old boyfriend in a strange city while my teenage runaway sidekick reads a book becomes much more manageable. "Meet me back here at noon. Do you have a watch?"

"No, but I can ask someone what time it is." She rolls her eyes.

Brew Ha-Ha is filled with young professional types in crisp button-down shirts and a few kids with blue hair and lots of black eyeliner. Everyone's drinking coffee, eating baked goods, and reading newspapers. The blue-haired kids look like they'd be planning a coup if they had more energy. I find an empty overstuffed purple chair near a small table and stake my claim, scoping the room for Seth. I become horribly certain I won't recognize him or he won't recognize me, and we'll both think we've been stood up. I can't believe how nervous I am. It's ridiculous, really. I mean, he's not Christian Bale or something. He's just a dreamy, kinda kooky guy who once gave me an ill-fitting *Partridge Family* T-shirt as a gift.

As I glance up at the blackboard to review the specials of the day, I hear, "Leigh? Leigh Fielding?"

I freeze and turn carefully toward the voice. I'm about to lay eyes once again on the man who once confessed he used to watch me from across a crowded room. My stomach breakdances across my midsection. And there he is—Seth Bradley, with eyes that could still melt a Popsicle, a smile that could calm a crying baby, the same cute bald stripe in one eyebrow . . . and hair that's seen fuller days and the same outfit (light blue oxford shirt over Banana Republican pants) that my insurance rep had on just last week.

Huh?

He leans down to hug me, because I'm too befuddled to stand. His tie arrives first, whacking me on the nose. He smells like aftershave that cost more than my brother's house. "Leigh, it's so great to see you!"

I hug him back in self-defense. "Hi, Seth!" I squeak. I clear my throat. "Wow, you look great," I say. I feel incredibly grubby all of a sudden, like I was the one sleeping under a park bench and giving myself French showers for three days. I wish I'd given more consideration to the simple denim skirt and gray halter top I'd thrown on this morning.

He orders us lattes and baklava and pulls up a chair next to mine. I'm touched because he remembers that baklava is only my favorite dessert ever. Even Larry loves baklava.

So we catch up. He almost falls out of his chair when I tell him I had a kidney transplant.

"You what?" he says. He seems impressed, which both pleases and annoys me.

"And get this," I add. "I know who donated it." We talk a bit more about me and my new kidney, and I feel like a hero featured in *Reader's Digest*. I decide not to tell him the whole "channeling the donor" yada-yada yet. First I want to hear why he looks like an insurance salesman. We never discussed our careers (or in my case, job) in the few e-mails we exchanged before today. When I'd asked about his, he replied, "I'll tell you all about it when you get here." Naturally, this led me to believe he was on the cusp of some groundbreaking scientific discovery, perhaps a wonder pharmaceutical that had nothing to do with easing social anxiety or giving a pensioner a four-day erection, but rather cured one of the thousands of debilitating diseases still striking down millions annually. That, or he'd just been released from prison.

"So whatever happened to studying apes in Africa?" I ask.

He shrugs. "I got a better offer."

"A better offer than being the next Dian Fossey?" This better be good. I wait for him to tell me he's a lawyer for the Rainforest Action Network. Please, let it be so.

"I'm a mortgage broker," he says, and I can tell he's really proud of himself.

Is he kidding? *A mortgage broker?* This isn't the Seth Bradley I knew in college. I wonder if he's taken up yachting as well. "I can't believe it," I admit. A small part of me wishes he was still smoking pot.

"Well, it's true. I dabbled in day-trading for awhile, but then I settled into something a little more . . . regular. I mean, despite fluctuating interest rates. But this city has seen some great growth in the past few years. It's no Minneapolis, but it's got that small-town yet cosmopolitan feel that is a real draw for young families. I'm working with a developer now on a series of upscale townhouses just a block from here."

Who is this guy? He could buy and sell people like me.

"But I don't want to talk about me," he says, clearly lying. "What have you been up to, besides having a kidney transplant, my God!"

"Um, I work at a day care for dogs," I hear myself mumble.

"Oh, how sweet! That's perfect for you."

I chuckle weakly. "Actually, I own it." It's one of those lies that your ego throws out in self-defense, without permission from your brain. I regret it immediately.

His eyebrows shoot up on his forehead. "Wow! Hey, you should think about opening a branch here in Sioux Falls." He takes a bite of baklava and adds, "You know, there's a real market for that kind of thing these days. I could help you get started if you ever wanted to branch out. Make it a multistate venture. I know a guy who's a whiz with marketing."

I decide to change the subject. "So are you dating anyone?"

He shifts and takes a sip of coffee. "Well, yes, actually."

I act completely riveted. "Oh, really? That's wonderful. What's she like?" I form a mental image of his girlfriend: tan and lean, with a face like Charisma Carpenter and a closet full of clothing I'd go bankrupt just thinking about buying.

He looks at his knees. "Well, I'm kinda married."

I laugh. It was too perfect, really. "Kinda married? Maybe sorta? Haven't decided yet? Seth," I say, "you're either married or you're not."

"Okay, I am," he admits, visibly uncomfortable. "But I'm not . . . um, things haven't been the best lately." At that, his face turns into something jaded. Making him look like a complete stranger.

I brace myself. This is exactly how my friend Jody's life went down the flusher. A married man, a lonely girl, confessions of unhappiness, and—boom!—you've got an illegitimate son and you have to teach fourth grade in a different city.

He turns bright red. "It's nothing like what we had. You and I. I mean, we weren't together long, but it was something special. Something . . . unpolluted, maybe. Wholesome."

"Wholesome is for school lunches," I blurt, suppressing a laugh.

Okay, this whole episode has gone way beyond simple catching up and mending fences. He is clearly hitting on me. The knowledge thrills and sickens me. On one hand, I'm receiving very flattering attention from a handsome but veritable stranger, but on the other, I already know many of this stranger's funny anecdotes, such as the fact that one of his college roommates once stuck a carrot up his own ass while masturbating. Also, hello! The handsome stranger is not available! So that's a huge black checkmark by his name. If this were elementary school, he'd have to stay in from recess with his head on his desk for months.

"I know, I know. It's silly." He brushes a hand through his hair and sighs. "Maybe I'm going through a phase of some kind. I mean, all marriages have their rough spots." He suddenly laughs, a little too loudly, startling me. "God, I can't even believe I'm saying this!" His eyes grow wide and crazy, like, *Aren't untimely confessions of marital instability fucking* hilarious?! *Aren't they just* insane?! *Wheeeee!!!!*

"Seth," I say, smiling in a way that hurts my cheeks, "we were a college fling. We had part-time jobs, no worries about things like health insurance or . . . mortgage payments. But we broke up for a reason"—I take a breath, try to keep it breezy, platonic—"the reason being you, uh, dumped me." *See?* my tone implies. *We're just old friends poking gentle fun at the naïve kids we once were.*

He clears his throat and sets his baklava on a napkin. "Leigh, I'm really sorry for the way things ended with us. I was young. Stupid. A real jerk."

My hand suddenly develops a mind of its own and waves dismissively. "Oh, don't worry about it. That was a long time ago." Apparently, my mouth has developed a mind of its own, too. *Don't worry about it?* Jeez. Like my heart wasn't shredded for months afterward. I decide to change the subject. "Do you have any kids?" I ask. I feel slightly schizophrenic, and I blame the way he's staring at me.

He shakes his head like, *Kids? What are kids?* He leans back in his chair and studies me, looking amazed in a way that feels as authentic as polyester. "I can't believe you're really here."

"Me either," I say truthfully. I chew some baklava and avoid his gaze. The Goth kids leave, maybe to start their coup.

"How long are you staying? Will you be here tonight?"

I shrug and say, "I'm not sure," even though I know I'm leaving as soon as I collect Mini-Me and get back in the car. I check the melty Salvador Dali–esque clock on the wall near the blackboard of specials: eleven-thirty. I have to meet Denise in half an hour.

The part of my inner self that drinks whiskey and wouldn't hesitate to heckle a bad comedian entertains the notion of staying overnight and having one last fling with Seth in some seedy hotel room. No, a well-appointed, antique-filled bed-and-breakfast! With a fireplace, clawfoot tub, and four-poster bed. It would smell of lavender. I imagine handcuffing him to the bed, screwing him so completely he would never again be able to achieve an erection, and leaving him there, weeping. I have a very active sex life, in my mind.

"I hope you don't think I'm a jerk if I tell you I still think about you sometimes."

Maybe he has the same fantasy. *Finish your coffee and shut up,* I want to say. *Go play polo or something.* Instead, I say, "Thank you."

Good grief. *Thank you?* Four hundred and fifty miles and seven years of pining and this is the best I can come up with?

"Can I call you?" he asks.

"Probably not," I say.

He shrugs. "Well, I better get back to work. It was great seeing you again." He leans forward, right into my personal space, and says, "We can still be friends, right?" His breath smells like mountain-grown coffee. For a minute I think he's going to kiss me, but instead, he spies the uneaten half of my baklava and says, "Are you gonna eat that?"

And all the wondering, daydreaming, and pining are over. Just like that. It was like snapping your fingers.

After I get back to the car, after my long walk of shame to the car, I fight the urge to sit next to it and bang my head against the driver's side door, repeatedly. It wouldn't hurt. I have dent-resistant side panels.

CHAPTER FOUR

This way to Wall Drug!

Have you ever noticed that the longer you look forward to something—a trip, perhaps, a party, a wedding, a reunion—the longer you anticipate it, build it up in your mind, the bigger a disappointment it always turns out to be? This is what I call the Johnson effect, so named for a highly anticipated yet infamously disastrous wedding Jillian and I attended in college. Drunken declarations of affection were made to objects of longtime lust and it wasn't pretty. Anyway, I've always had the most fun spontaneously, when plans were cobbled together at the last minute. So why am I surprised that a reunion I'd been looking forward to for weeks turned out to be a major letdown? I should have remembered the Johnson effect.

To cheer me up, Denise insists that we go to the Corn Palace. I tell her it will likely spark my final spiral down into the bowels of depression, culminating in a state of permanent catatonia, but she just says, "What's catatonia? That's such a pretty word!" First, while we're in a town remotely resembling civilization, we need to stock up on hygienic accoutrements, mostly for Denise. (Although I would like to buy some new eyeliner, as mine rolled under the dresser at the motel.) She points out a Target near the interstate. I can hear the bills in my purse lining up to sing "So Long, Farewell" from *The Sound of Music*. It's kind of cute when they do, but somewhat distressing when they've exited stage left and all I have is a cartful of impulse buys to console me.

Target is a dangerous place if you're on a budget.

When I find the makeup aisle, Denise says to me, "I'll be right back," and disappears.

I select a waterproof brownish-black eyeliner pencil with a built-in sharpener in the cap. To try and jump-start a festive mood, I also toss some fruity pink lip gloss into my basket. And a new toothbrush, as mine tasted slightly mildewy this morning. And a new pair of sunglasses, because my old ones have an annoying scratch on the left lens. And also this bag of SunChips. And this book, because it's been "Bookmarked as a Breakout." It's about the lovesick matriarch of a jumbled, dysfunctional family. I love books about dysfunctional families. It's nice to feel like part of a club.

I meet Denise near the checkout lanes. She's carrying two Ping-Pong paddles, a big black marker, a stapler, and some white construction paper. "What's that for?"

She winks and says, "You'll see."

Soon we're back on the road, passing the world's largest bull's-head statue on our way to the Corn Palace, Mount Rushmore, the Badlands, the Black Hills, and Wall Drug, not necessarily in that order. Quite an itinerary, I know, but hey, like I said, I don't get out much.

We're barely back on I-90 when I find out what Denise's Ping-Pong paddles are for. As we reach cruising speed of eighty miles per hour while Jim Croce's "I Got a Name" seeps from the car speakers, she snaps the cap from her fat, fragrant black marker and begins to write messages on the construction paper. Messages like "Nice turn signal, ass monkey!" and "Your blinker's still on!" and my personal favorite, "Slow down, Zippy! It's not a race."

"I think driving should be an interactive experience," she says matter-of-factly while she staples her messages into paper pillowcases. She slides the first one over a Ping-Pong paddle and flashes it at me like she's Wile E. Coyote falling off a cliff: "Learn how to drive!" She flips it over and I read, "Thank you! Drive safely!"

I engage my cruise control just as Jim gets to the part about rollin' down the highway. "So you think pissing other drivers off while traveling at speeds in excess of seventy-five miles per hour will get us from A to B intact?"

"You worry too much," Denise says. "Let's just try it for awhile. If anyone tries running us off the road, I'll stop." I must look skeptical because she smiles and adds, "C'mon, it'll be fun."

You might be thinking that not only have I had a kidney transplant, I've also had a good-sense transplant. But I've always envied crazy, spontaneous people like this. People free to say and do the things the rest of us are thinking and censoring for the sake of social conventions. Denise is the kind of person who could talk you into doing things that might land you in a Mexican prison at five A.M., and you'd feel like a star in a John Woo film the whole time.

We get an excellent chance to share our impressions of other people's driving skills almost immediately, right as we cruise up behind a lumbering Winnebago with the right blinker flashing. I begin to pass on the left, and just as we're even with the driver of the Winnie, Denise flashes her "You forgot to turn off your blinker!" sign. The driver, a wrinkled brown man of about 127, squints to read the note. When he finally realizes what it says, he appears surprised, like, *Who, moi?* He checks his blinker to confirm her charge, gives an exaggerated nod, and salutes Denise. She waves back frantically, beaming. The blinker goes dark.

"Well, whaddaya know," she says. "It works!"

A few minutes later, we spot another sign for Wall Drug. Denise writes, "This way to Wall Drug!" and slips it on a paddle.

An hour or so later we're finally in Mitchell, home of the Corn Palace and the Enchanted World Doll Museum, the latter of which I wouldn't visit unless you paid me in men who looked like Jonathan Rhys Meyers. And even then I'd have stipulations.

So let's see. First impressions of the Corn Palace? The building itself looks like St. Basil's Cathedral in Moscow's Red Square, with its sour-cream-dollop roof spires. And yes, there is a giant mural made from corncobs on the front. The theme changes annually. This year, it is "Year of the Rodeo." Across the street you'll find an ice cream shop with plenty of benches upon which to enjoy your frozen novelty on a stick, Uncle Zeke's Black Hills gold jewelry shop, the Enchanted World Doll Museum, and a plethora of creepy mannequins sitting on benches everywhere. One of the mannequins is a politically incorrect Indian squaw. Down the street you'll find the yard statue emporium and more opportunities to spend your hard-earned dollars on souvenirs from your trip to Mitchell, South Dakota. Souvenirs like a stuffed, ready-for-wall-mounting "jackalope," which was invented by some clever entrepreneur decades ago. (You make a jackalope by gluing tiny pronghorn antlers onto the head of a dead jackrabbit. Neat, huh?) And if you're into thin, leaf-shaped pink-and-gold-toned jewelry and Riudoso Old West–style font, this is your vacation destination. Kenny Rogers's "You Gotta Know When to Hold 'Em" streams through tinny speakers on the Corn Palace, assaulting all ears on the street. My cousin saw Kenny Rogers perform live last year and said he was a crotchety old bastard. Kenny yelled at the crowd for not singing along enthusiastically enough and said he was too old to hobble back out for an encore, so everyone better just shut up and enjoy the last song.

Inside the Corn Palace, well, what can I say? If you enjoy the combined scents of popcorn and urine, you've found your personal nirvana. An amphitheater overlooks more corn murals and a pit of—surprise!—more souvenir kiosks full of South Dakota–themed kitsch: magnets, thimbles, bells, spoons for your collection (and what twentysomething doesn't have a collection of miniature spoons?), overpriced felt-bottomed plastic statuettes of Mount Rushmore, T-shirts, hats, calendars, Ass Kickin' salsa mixes, the "World's Largest Gummi Rattlesnake," and enough plastic toys of Asian origin to fill Yankee Stadium. Busloads of senior citizens swarm in for the guided tour. Instantly (and I hate to even say this, I sound completely heartless) I suspect the origin of the urine odor.

This is a place for people in fanny packs, people who purchase souvenir T-shirts and immediately change into them in a public restroom. I'd bet my car that half of the tourists rummaging through the South Dakota thimbles have bought collectible plates or maybe a replica of the *"Titanic* diamond" from the Bradford Exchange—perhaps even clipping the coupon from the ad in their Sunday newspaper insert, carefully filling out their personal information, checking the appropriate boxes with a smudgy pen, and mailing it in. I briefly pity the person who has the job of deciphering the handwriting on those coupons. I briefly pity the people filling out the coupons. Then I remember: Who the hell am I to pity anyone? We all wear pity targets of varying size.

Denise buys two Auto Bingo tiles for the ride, and she somehow talks me into having my picture taken with my face poking through one of four holes cut from a wooden panel propped in the corner. It's been painted to look like ears of corn, with your face peeking out beneath the tassels. The caption reads, "Getting corny at the Corn Palace!" I'm sure my lone face looks ridiculous in the photo, as there are three empty holes around my head. It's a moment designed for a family, and soon enough we're asked to take a picture for a family of four posing in the cutouts. While backing up to frame them all in the photo, I bump into an Amish girl in sneakers. We smile at each other. "Sorry," I say, my hand instinctively reaching for my purse. Not because the Amish are renowned thieves, but hey, you have your purse stolen by one innocent-looking girl during a trip, and you get a bit skittish.

I refocus and snap a perfectly touristy family picture, just the thing for posting on a refrigerator with an official Corn Palace magnet.

The ride after Mitchell is an endless droning trip back in time, a trip to the Land That Time Forgot, where everyone watched *The Dukes of Hazzard* on Friday nights, before Jessica Simpson was even born. Back to a time when little boys played cowboys and indians, not *Grand Theft Auto*. I try to imagine a five-year-old boy on his family vacation in a minivan begging his parents to stop at the 1880 town so he can get his free sheriff's badge, as several ancient billboards advertise along the interstate. But the only image I get is a little 1950s boy in full cowboy regalia, sitting cross-legged and mesmerized in front of a black-and-white television showing the latest *Howdy Doody* episode. Today's five-year-old boy is probably watching a SpongeBob video on his personal DVD player and could give a rat's ass about getting a free sheriff's badge from some college kid in a costume.

The fields along the highway are filled with hand-painted and often misspelled signs touting campgrounds, diners, auto "toe" service, motels, Frosty King "drive-inn" ice cream shops, Western wear and "saddlery," gas station/diner combinations (EAT HERE! THEN GET GAS), casinos, tourist attractions and gift shops, homemade pie, pancakes, antiques, five-cent coffee, ten-cent pop, free ice water at Wall Drug, cowboy boots, Sinclair Dino gasoline, trading post plazas, and CHOOSE LIFE! MY MOM DID. Beyond the signs, giant pills of hay and herds of Black Angus cattle dot endless fields carpeted in dry brown grasses. The land changes after we cross the Missouri River in the middle of South Dakota, shifting from relatively flat grasslands to parched undulating hills pocked with abandoned barns and stands of poplars and willows clinging to old creek beds. The sky is a clear, eye-stabbing blue; heat waves shimmer from the road ahead of us. Denise reads almost all of the travel brochures I've brought along, pointing out places we should be sure to see on our way to California. I realize she's gradually morphing from stranger to traveling companion. I'm beginning to feel more relaxed around her, but I'd still be slightly more at ease hanging out with someone who has Tourette's syndrome. I guess when you spend this much time in a car with someone, it might be better if you don't know that person as well as, say, a sibling or spouse. You're suppressing your cranky auto outbursts, and you can fill the time learning all about each other. Although I'm not learning too much more about Denise. Whenever I fish, she seems happier talking about our itinerary or pulling some goofy-ass stunt. For example: She took pictures of herself posing against our road map with her own camera, just to amuse herself. And then there are her Ping-Pong paddle signs.

We hit our first major stretches of construction, and the interstate narrows to a one-lane highway decorated with bright orange signs: SLOW DOWN—GIVE 'EM A BRAKE! and FINES DOUBLE IN WORK ZONES. The monotony of driving, of the bland, dry scenery, has lulled us into semi-trances, broken only for brief license plate ID or song lyric word games, most of which are initiated by Denise. Somewhere after Chamberlain, I say, "My ass is completely dead. I think I hear them playing taps for my right ass cheek." This makes Denise laugh, which of course makes me happy. When we stop near Murdo to pee, stretch our legs, empty our small bag of trash, eat a light dinner from the cooler I packed yesterday (or was it the day before?), and get gas (in the automotive sense of the word), we run into the same Amish family we saw at the Corn Palace. Playing travel leapfrog, Denise says. A hot wind whips my hair across my Chap Stick–covered lips as I try to eat cut-up papaya, a hard-boiled egg, and veggie sticks with hummus. "You know," I say, "you could pretty much sum up any road trip like this: Drive, stop, pee, eat. Drive, stop, pee, eat." I crunch into a pea pod.

Denise echoes me. "Drive, stop, pee, eat. Don't forget 'Stretch your legs.'"

I sigh. "You know you're getting old when you have to remind yourself to prevent deep-vein thrombosis."

"Yeah, you're sooo old. What are you, like, seventy?" Denise says. We watch the Amish family pile back into their van. "If we see them again at Wall Drug, I'll crap a solid gold brick," I say.

"If you do, can I have it?" Denise asks, her mouth full of half-chewed carrot. Emily-Posts-in-training we're not.

In the cinder-block rest stop bathroom, a woman complains that her teenagers are staying in the camper at all of the scenic overlooks. "And they're watching *Dances with Wolves* in there! Would you believe it?" I chuckle and try to look sympathetic, but I suspect the overhead fluorescent lighting and my general state of wear and tear make me look more like a methadone clinic reject. When her kids pile out of the camper, I'm not surprised to see they're wearing black outfits and sullen expressions. Back at the car, a sweaty man in a tie-dyed Sitting Bull T-shirt points at my license plate and asks if I have any cheese. One of his front teeth has vacated his mouth. He's wearing clip-on sunglasses.

"Huh?"

"Your license plate. You're from Wisconsin, right?"

"Oh, right." I roll my eyes and force a smile. After the Giant of Wit strolls past, I mutter to Denise, "If one more person asks me if I have any cheese, I'm going to slap them. No! I'm going to suffocate them with some Swiss spread."

Denise arches her back and points to her ass. "I got your Swiss spread right here, baby."

The best part is that I actually do have cheese in the cooler. Individually wrapped string cheese and teeny wheels of Gouda.

Come on. I'm from Wisconsin. It's like a law or something.

Minutes after we're back on the highway and seconds after Denise says, "Man, we're going, like, eighty. Those poor bastards from the old days, coming out here in their covered wagons and shit. They probably did five miles in an hour," my kayak blows off the roof.

We'd hit a rough and curvy patch of asphalt near construction, and the bumpy road coupled with the harsh South Dakota wind caused just enough jiggling to undo my (apparently not so) careful securing of the kayak to the roof of my car. "Holy shit!" Denise shouts. "Your kayak!"

I just scream, watching the bungee cord tethered below my front bumper snap free. My bright yellow kayak, paid for with two full weeks of toil at Fuzzy Navels, lifts from the car in a single WHOOSH. I instinctively transfer my foot to the brake, my eyes to the rearview mirror. "Oh my God!"

Luckily, there are no cars immediately behind us. My kayak blows back, back, smaller and smaller, until it lodges on a sandbagged construction barrel a hundred yards or so in the distance. I cross a rumble strip onto the shoulder and park. My heartbeat is almost loud enough to drown out Denise's question: "Now what? Are you going back for it?"

I undo my seat belt and crane my neck around, casing the situation. "It cost too much to just leave it there!" I turn on my hazards and knock a half-empty coffee cup onto the floor, splashing the remains of my Mexican mocha onto our road atlas. "Shit."

Just then, a semitruck rumbles over the slight rise we just crested. The kayak, already trembling under the unrelenting wind against the orange-and-white-striped construction barrel, picks this moment to lift up again, then surf down an air current, soaring directly beneath the tires of the oncoming truck. My paddle, tucked inside the belly of the kayak, is ejected and spins 180 degrees in midair. It flutters into the ditch. There's a slight hiss of air brakes, a tiny crunch, and my kayak disappears beneath the semi, which spits it out seconds later, crumpled and deformed. A slight cry escapes my lips.

"Well, that solves that," Denise says. The semi roars past, rocking my car on its springs and kicking a cloud of hot dust at us. The driver scowls.

"My kayak!" I moan. Five hundred bucks, shredded beneath a truck's tires. With luck like mine, I could get a job as a casino cooler, no problem.

As I stare at the yellow chunks I'd once glided through clear waters in, my cell phone rings. When I check to see who's calling, I'm not quite surprised to see that it's Seth. I wait a beat for the butterflies in my stomach to begin fluttering. But apparently, they've become victims of a heavy pesticide application. I sigh deeply and answer.

He greets me with, "Leigh, I'm so sorry. I should have been honest with you right away."

Two seconds into the conversation and I'm already tired of it. "Seth, it is what it is." I want to add something else, something light and funny, or maybe meaningful and deep, but I'm too exhausted to make up my mind. I feel like one of Fuzzy Navels' regular clients: a colorful woman from Texas who couldn't commit to an opinion, always appending statements like "Oh, last summer in Austin was so hot! The hottest on record" with "Well, actually, maybe it wasn't." I'm drained, like a wetland near a new shopping center. "Don't worry about it," I hear myself add. To be honest, I'm surprised he's calling with an apology. It seems out of character for a guy. Why even bother? I mean, I was only passing through, our reunion went less than spectacularly, and now we know. What a jerk he's turned into, that is. Puzzle solved. Let's head back to the Mystery Machine and all.

Then I realize that he's drunk. "No, no," he insists. "I really mean it."

"Where are you?"

It's funny. I'd always imagined we'd someday live together in a tin shack in the jungle saving gorillas and distributing malaria treatments to the local people. I don't know how a guy with a major college crush on Che Guevara ends up refinancing people's homes. I fantasize for a minute that it was a Halloween costume: the mediocre career guy with a roving eye.

"At a corporate barbecue." His choice in words only reinforces the gap between us. In Wisconsin, you attend a "brat [bratwurst] fry" or you simply "grill out." You barbecue down south, or anywhere else, actually.

"Are you drunk?" I ask. "You sound like you've been drinking."

There's a slight pause, then, "A little."

I glance in my rearview mirror at the remains of my kayak, and a pang zips through my heart. "Seth, please don't worry about it. I've got bigger fish to fry. [Barbecue?] My kayak just blew off the car." I immediately despise myself a little for telling him, as this means I'll now be required to give an explanation, keeping me on the phone longer.

He laughs, too loudly. "Your what? Your what blew off the car?" I pull the phone away from my ear and grimace. Seth's got one lucky wife.

"Kayak. I had a kayak tied to my—oh, never mind." I flip off my hazards, pull away from the shoulder, and get back on the highway, my calf muscle straining from pushing the gas pedal to the floor. I watch my mangled kayak disappear behind me. It's almost metaphoric.

"We're leaving it there on the side of the road?" Denise stage-whispers.

I shrug, semi-despondent. It's been ripped to pieces! I feel guilty littering like this, but I'm not going to strap garbled chunks of plastic onto the roof of my car. I wouldn't know how to keep them there, for one thing. They would probably blow off again, this time into a funeral procession, causing a twenty-car pileup that would necessitate thirty more funeral processions. Or maybe they'd hit a bus full of scientists racing to share their newfound cure for the bird flu with the rest of the world. No! A bus full of *children* who will one day grow up to cure bird flu. That'd be more my style.

Seth rambles on a bit longer about his marital woes and tries to engage me in some nostalgic "Hey, remember whens" from our college days. I refuse to bite. "Where are you headed now?" he asks.

He's asked me this already, in person. I can barely conceal my annoyance when I say, "Rapid City. The Badlands, Wall Drug, Mount Rushmore, you know. All the tourist staples." We pass a truck with Indiana plates and Denise blows a kiss at the driver.

"Oh, you have to go to Wind Cave! Are you going to Wind Cave?" I'm trying to pay attention to the road. His questions irritate me, remind me of a clingy boy I went on two dates with after Seth and I broke up. The clingy boy was named Chad. He had a whiny voice and would call me at strange hours to ask, "What happened to us?" like our two dates equaled a long, passionate relationship.

"I don't know."

He goes on to recommend a restaurant in Rapid City, and I decide that I will now purposely avoid it, as well as Wind Cave. Later, after we hang up with empty promises to stay in touch, I think how sad it is that Seth isn't happy in the life he's chosen. Maybe I'm the last brass ring going past on the carousel, and a familiar one, at that. One once so desperately smitten that it would be easy to assume those feelings would never change. But things are so different now, I don't want him to reach for me. It's a liberating thought. I look over at Denise. She's playing Auto Bingo by herself, with one of the tiles she'd bought at the Corn Palace. It makes me smile.

Things are definitely different now.

• • •

Five hours after leaving Mitchell, after losing my kayak and after flashing signs at six more drivers, one of whom, I swear, is going to hunt us down and murder us in our beds, we enter the famed Wall Drug tourist mecca. Few things in life beyond Eisenhower-era textbooks and seventies porn offer such opportunity for rueful hilarity. Denise insists on having our picture taken near the famous water pump, and a woman in plaid shorts and a leather fanny pack happily obliges. Wild West–style music is blaring from speakers everywhere. Then we have to pose with our heads stuck in some crazy pioneer cutouts while a German family snaps our photo, and then Denise wants us to put on Holly Hobbie bonnets and dresses and pose in a covered wagon. She arranges me in front of the eighty-foot brontosaurus and takes my picture. Afterward she poses me near the jittering animatronic cowboy orchestra, coming soon to a nightmare near you. Denise seems to have reawakened a long-slumbering love for the sucktacular. When we spot our familiar Amish family ordering ice cream cones, Denise punches my shoulder and asks good-naturedly, "Where's my gold brick, bitch?"

I probably don't even need to tell you she wanted to slap a WHERE THE HECK IS WALL DRUG? bumper sticker on my car. And you can probably imagine that I'd sooner plaster signs like I ♥ MY BIG FAKE BOOBS! or HOOKER FOR HIRE; JUST HONK, I'M CHEAP! all over my back window than an advertisement hinting at a fondness for Wall Drug.

After a sanity-challenging half hour roaming the 75,000-square-foot Emporium of Western Kitsch, we hop in the car and head to Badlands National Park. When I was ten, Gram piled a surly James and an obnoxious, Rainbow Brite–obsessed me in her decrepit motor home for a "family bonding" excursion to Yellowstone and other assorted western destinations. Other than James getting severe altitude sickness and almost dying on Pikes Peak (or so he says), me forgetting my backpack (filled with critical items like roll-on lip gloss and grape Bubble Yum) in a Colorado Springs gas station, and all of us being robbed in Albuquerque, it was a great trip. Gram seemed to instinctively know that James and I needed to establish some sort of a bond as siblings. I'd been living with her at the time. James was just getting over his wild stage, a year away from finishing college. Gram sat me down on her fluffy red sofa one day and said, "What would you think about moving in with James in a year or two?"

I just stared at her, hugging a pillow to my chest. It wasn't even in the same solar system with my future plans. "Why can't I stay with you?" I asked, uneasy.

Gram clasped my sweaty little hands with her firm, cool ones. "I'm not going to be around forever, and then you'll only have James. You need to get to know one another."

"But I already know James," I said, pouting. I didn't want to live with my angry older brother and his stupid AC/DC albums and cupboards stocked with Campbell's Chunky soup. I found out later that Gram had ovarian cancer and was only trying to prepare me for the inevitable.

But our trip out west was certainly fun and became the yard-stick by which I would have measured all of my future trips, had I taken any. Gram had the three of us singing "I Am the Walrus" and playing I Spy (with James spying mostly R-rated things), and by the end of the trip, I spied a side of James I'd never seen before. *He's actually human!* I remember thinking.

So here we are in the beautiful Badlands of South Dakota, and Denise is already pestering a tourist to take our picture. The Bad-lands themselves are much better than Wall Drug . . . like a minia-ture Grand Canyon, striped with layer after layer of impossibly well-coordinated earth tones. I buy a National Parks Pass, which will pay for itself if we head to just a few more national parks. Hell, the West is *loaded* with them, so it seems like a good financial de-cision.

We hike away from all the RVs and minivans loaded with kids and luggage, through some parched grass toward the fossil-heavy hills. Everything smells just how I imagine the set of *Little House on the Prairie* would smell: like butterfly wings, sunbaked earth, and a hint of pollen, but also slightly horsey. Strange purple flowers bob in the hot breeze. We take pictures of a prairie-dog town and a herd of buffalo, me with my fossilized Canon (so old it almost needs an oxygen canister) and Denise with her whiz-bang digital wonder, which I suspect may be stolen. But you never know.

We stop to share a tepid bottle of water and I check my watch. It's after four. I wish I had time to do some metal detecting, but that's not going to happen. I say to Denise, "Okay. We have time to see Mount Rushmore or the Crazy Horse Memorial, but just one. What'll it be?"

She looks incredibly torn. I had no idea a seventeen-year-old could be so into large granite sculpture. I guess she doesn't get out much, either. "Let's ask Larry," she finally says. So, Magic 8 Ball–style, she hovers her hands over my hip. I laugh. She's off a bit, but I'd rather not have her any closer to my groin. "I'm feeling a Mount Rushmore vibe," she announces.

So we go. But it's sort of anticlimactic, because I'm more impressed by the hordes of tourists all trying to get a glimpse of some guy's fourteen-year hobby. We laugh at the fact that "Where's Lincoln's mole?" merits inclusion among the frequently asked questions listed in the brochure. We laugh harder at two successive middle-aged couples in matching outfits: first, red Heinz ketchup T-shirts with denim shorts, sun visors, and nylon fanny packs; next, bright green T-shirts embossed with a country music station logo, plus khaki shorts, leather fanny packs, and—bonus—matching cowboy hats. The Black Hills surround us like massive pine-studded gumdrops. The shadows grow long and cool. *No wonder the Sioux didn't want to leave,* I think. Fucking Custer. Goddamn gold rush.

"Let's stay to watch the evening lighting ceremony," Denise says, furtively snapping a picture of a Swedish couple eating hot dogs.

"I'd rather not. That's a few hours away."

She shrugs and continues snapping random photos as we stroll the grounds: of the monument, of adolescents on cell phones desperately trying to maintain a distance between themselves and their families, of the cavernous gift shop and cafeteria, of the shadows creeping across the ragged hills.

"Oh crap, my memory card's full," Denise announces, climbing from the railing near a shady viewpoint. "Can we go back to the car to get a new one?" I try not to roll my eyes, because patience is a lesson I need to learn, and we make our way through the crowded parking ramp back to my car. There's a black Acura with California plates parked next to it. What, does everyone own a black Acura this summer? "Hey, look, what a surprise! It's another Acura," I announce. "What's the sales pitch? *Acura: It's the new Toyota,*" I joke. "Free Acura with every test drive!"

Denise glances around the lot nervously. "You know what? Forget the memory card. Let's go find someplace to eat," she says. "Or maybe we could go to Custer State Park?"

"But I thought you wanted to take some more pictures."

"Well, I changed my mind. Let's go eat instead. I'm starving."

"Whatever," I say. I'm not always patient, but I'm usually flexible.

We make our way through the sprawl of kitschy tourist shops outside the official Mount Rushmore National Memorial area. The valley, clogged with people and campers and minivans stuffed with kids, is home to a strip mall of brightly lit gold-rush-themed "saloons" and T-shirt shops and, yes, many more opportunities to add to your souvenir magnet, spoon, or thimble collection. It's worse than Wall Drug, because when you look up, behind the neon Wild West–storefront façades are the rocky, forested hills the Sioux still consider sacred. I doubt you'd ever see mini-golf on Gethsemane.

We cruise past Wind Cave National Park and decide to have a late dinner at an outdoor bistro in Hot Springs, South Dakota. A young guy at the counter asks us if we're in town for the Miss South Dakota pageant. When I say no, he replies, "Aw, I figured for sure you two would be in it!" Denise and I roll our eyes and laugh. Over grilled panini sandwiches we discuss ghosts, reincarnation, and the most vivid dreams we've ever had. She tells me a story about a set of twins that spoke to each other in their own language, confirmed by linguists to be an ancient, long-defunct Asian language. I tell her that a Ouija board once told me I'd marry a man with a first name beginning in *E* and that I'd later make a killing in the stock market. Since just the thought of investment options makes me go cross-eyed and drooly (and I can barely rub two nickels together between paychecks from Fuzzy Navels—not much in the way of investment capital), this is not likely to happen. After the server lays our bill on the red-and-white-checked tablecloth, Denise pulls out two twenties. "I got it," she says.

"Where'd you get all this money?" I ask, dumbfounded.

"Don't worry about it. Dinner's on Rick." She winks and takes a sip of water. I wonder if she snatched some other woman's purse while I was being humiliated at Brew Ha-Ha by Seth. I begin to wonder a lot about Denise. Like, what if she's not really who she says she is? What if she's mentally ill? What if she's part of an in-terstate identity-theft ring, and I'm the unwitting beard? The fall guy? I decide I'm just being paranoid. I have to call Jillian tonight, and I can just imagine what she'll say when I unload this little morsel on her. I'm also going to call James, but I probably don't have to tell you I'm not even going to drop a hint about my new sidekick.

After dinner, we discover a plaque near our parked car: The hot springs of Hot Springs, South Dakota, really exist, and here we are parked next to the aptly named Kidney Springs. Denise reads the sign: " 'Useful in the treatment of chronic diseases of the gastroin-testinal tract, diseases of the liver and biliary passages, disorders of the genitourinary tract and in sluggish condition of the alimentary tract.' " A knowing expression blooms on her face as she turns to face me. "See? This is all just . . . what's the word . . . ?"

I sigh. "Serendipitous?"

"Maybe. But you know, it's just . . . too weird! I mean, you should totally, like, wash your hands in the springs or something."

"I'm not washing my hands in a public fountain."

"Leigh, it could be like that healing water in Europe. Just a pinky?"

"Not even a pinky. There will be no public hand-washing!"

It's getting late, so I decide to find a place to sleep for the night.

Like last night's accommodations, this one won't be winning any Hotel of the Year awards. It has an outdoor staircase covered in green AstroTurf. A brown, boxy car sits on two flat tires under the stuttering neon VACANCY sign. I think this motel actually might have negative stars. But it's got that retro, Sid and Marty Krofft feel to it, with plastic potted plants, original swag lighting, and a thin wafer of wrapped deodorant soap in the bathroom. This is where people who live in houses that still have lead paint stay on their vacations to Wall Drug. This is where life—the whole seedy, grubby, sweaty, beautiful mess of it—happens. Denise signs the hotel logbook "Amy Jasper."

I decide to take my chances and just get one room. But I also decide to hide my car keys and money under my mattress, just in case. I'm hedging my bets. After investigating the bedding (clean, but slightly musty) and taking my nightly meds, while Denise refills the cooler with ice from the machine near the office, I flip open my cell to call Jillian. When I tell her about Denise she says, "You have got to be kidding me. What do you know about this girl? She could be a crazy drug addict! She could be a serial killer!"

I walk to the window and pull back the stiff drapes to peer at Denise draining water from a bag of apples. "I doubt it," I say. I want so badly to add something like, *At least she doesn't advertise a health club with a crucifixion.* Instead I say slowly, "Well, what do you know about me?"

"That you're missing a chromosome?"

"No," I say, frowning. I'm not in the mood for Jillian's humor, so I try a different approach. "Remember what you said about Larry?"

"Yeah?" she says eagerly.

"I just feel he'd want me to do the right thing. And the right thing was not leaving her there alone."

I hear her sigh. "Well, I would have called the police."

"But you're not me," I say. We hang up and I dial James because I promised to call him and I'm a glutton for punishment. Marissa answers, mouselike.

James comes to the phone out of breath. "Where are you?" he demands.

"HotSpringsSouthDakota," I answer, like it's all one word.

"I thought you were going to call me in Sioux Falls!"

Hot Springs, Sioux Falls, you say potato, I say . . . Okay, I feel a bit guilty for not phoning him when I said I would. But as I was somewhat steamrollered by the events of the day, I doubt I'd have been a stellar conversationalist. "I'm sorry I didn't call earlier," I venture. "But I've just been having a great time, meeting new people, and—"

"Meeting new people?" James sounds terrified, as if the prospect of bubble-girl me meeting germ-covered strangers is just too much to bear.

"James, stop worrying so much about me! I'm a big girl." Across the parking lot, a dog erupts in a volley of barks.

"What's that? Where are you?"

"Somebody's dog," I say. "And I told you, I'm in Hot Springs. I'll be at Jillian's tomorrow." I start to feel like someone's smothering me with a huge, itchy wool pillow. Are all big brothers so protective? My brain is running around, giggling, barely restraining the part of me that wants to blurt, *I've got a secret! I picked up a hitchhiker, shhhh!*

"I don't like you traveling alone," James says for the six hundredth time.

I'm not alone, I think, madly. Instead I say, "I'm fine. You've got to trust me. I wouldn't do anything stupid." Which was, of course, probably the same thing Katie Holmes said to her manager before her first date with Tom Cruise.

James changes the subject. "Leigh, please don't try to find Kate. She doesn't want to be found."

"I have to," I say. But it's pointless to argue this with James yet again. He simply can't understand my compulsion to get some kind of closure from the woman who brought us into the world and then left us, the woman he's erased from his life without a single glance back.

"Leigh, she doesn't want to see you or me. You're just going to get hurt."

"So let me be hurt," I argue dramatically. "Let me be something." Of course, he and I have been hurting each other in little ways for years, but we don't acknowledge this. Our conversation ends in a stalemate, with nothing resolved or anything truly interesting shared.

After I close my phone I hear a terrible thudding, like someone dropping a motorcycle down the stairs. I throw open the door to see Denise sitting on the pavement at the bottom of the AstroTurf stairs, blood dribbling from a knee and a ladderlike scrape along one leg. She looks up at me, lip quivering, dazed, the cooler and its contents scattered behind her. Ice cubes spray the blacktop like a fan. "I fell," she whimpers.

Later, after tossing the food back in the cooler and shepherding her up the stairs, I open my travel first-aid kit and pour hydrogen peroxide on her wounds. She hisses in pain.

"I told you it would hurt. Now, don't look. I'm going to pick out a piece of gravel."

"Ouch!"

I swab her knee with iodine and apply a large bandage.

"You're so prepared," Denise observes, rubbing her ankle.

"I have to be. One of the perks of kidney disease," I say brightly.

"So, like, tell me more about your family," Denise demands while I pack up the first-aid kit. She sounds like a cross between a therapist and a three-year-old demanding another bedtime story. She presses her new bandage and looks at me expectantly.

What a strange question! Maybe she's starting a dossier on me. I sit on the edge of my bed, smiling, flattered yet slightly put off. "Well, I have an older brother, James. He's a very angry person, but he can be really sweet." I pause for a moment, lost in thought. My family. What do you tell a stranger about your family? I wish I had enough siblings to form a baseball team? Hell, I just wish I had parents. Finally I say, "I had a terrific grandma. She died when I was twelve. She was so neat. She knew Joni Mitchell and raised pygmy goats." A sudden memory springs to my mind, from shortly before Gram died. She was undergoing chemo, pale and weak, but still game for late-night movie binges and whatever bizarro questions or challenges I presented her. I'd just read a magazine article about how to determine your face shape (so you could subsequently choose the best hairstyle for your face), and one of the suggestions was to trace an outline of your face in the mirror with a stub of soap. Gram hunched behind me in the bathroom, tracing my face carefully on the mirror while I tried not to giggle. Would I have a heart-shaped face? Oh, how I prayed for a heart-shaped face, just like Valerie Bertinelli's. (I was very into syndicated *One Day at a Time* reruns back then.) The brown, almond-scented soap wobbled. "Hold still, hon," Gram said. I could barely contain myself. Would it be a round face? Or an oval face? I could work with that. Oh, just let it not be square, I pleaded to the patron saint of vanity. After the shape had been traced, Gram and I stepped back to ponder the squiggly blob on the mirror. "Hmm," Gram said. "I think what we have here is a walnut-shaped face."

"She had goats?" Denise asks, breaking my reverie. "Did you drink goat milk?"

"When I was little, yes." I was, in fact, a very colicky baby, allergic to cow's milk. I wonder if Denise is trying to live vicariously through me, like my life is some kind of safe family sitcom full of kooky misunderstandings and kids trying to raise money for their parents' anniversary gift. My real life is much closer to an episode of *ER*.

Later, after I refill the cooler with ice and lock it in my car, I ask how her ankle is. "Stiff," she says. "Thanks for taking care of me." Denise turns on the television and begins flipping through channels. "So what are we doing tomorrow?"

"We're meeting up with my friend Jillian," I say, setting my travel alarm clock for seven A.M.

"Jillian, huh? Do you call her Jill for short?" she yawns, turning off the TV and settling into her double bed.

"No." In grade school, the kids, dull wits all, had called her Jill the Pill and mocked her with the "Jack and Jill" nursery rhyme incessantly. She's gone by Jillian ever since.

"Night, Leigh. Night, Larry."

I smile. "Night, Denise."

"Don't let the bedbugs bite," she says.

I pause before adding, "If they do—"

"Hit 'em with a shoe—"

"Till they're black and blue," I finish. We giggle, and I think, *So this is what having a younger sister might be like. If you picked her up at a roadside rest area.*

Right before I fall asleep to the relaxing sound of what could very well be buffalo stampeding above our ceiling, I think that maybe I should cut James some slack. He's just doing what he thinks he should. Especially with both parents out of the picture. I remember how several of his college girlfriends tried to befriend me—bemother motherless me, if you will. They'd want to take me shopping, invite me over for holiday gatherings with their families. One even picked me up from school when I got food poisoning because I couldn't get ahold of James. Unfortunately, any attempt at bonding was usually met with suspicion on my part. And James tended to feel lukewarm about the ones I actually warmed to. There was one he seemed completely mad for—Tricia McMurphy. She never asked to take me to the mall. She had straight, glassy red hair and cruel opinions about everyone. More specifically, everyone's appearance. Including mine. I remember her laughing coldly at a terrible, poodlelike haircut I'd gotten in junior high; it was one of those cruelly honest reactions that a more tactful and decent person would have self-censored without blinking. "Oh my God! What happened to your head?" she'd said in the smug, mean-spirited tone popular with privileged and insecure bullies. James caught my eye before I slunk away, wounded. "Don't be mean, Trish," I overheard him saying after I left. He sounded almost as dejected as I felt. A few days later, Tricia didn't come around anymore.

Of course, this was long before he assumed a starring role as Angry Man in *Vengeful People I Have Known.* (Okay, so that's a list I once made when I was bored at Fuzzy Navels. It could also be a good TV show.)

I lay my hands over my transplant scar and close my eyes. I can feel tiny, invisible galaxies turning and expanding. I can feel stars being born.

CHAPTER FIVE

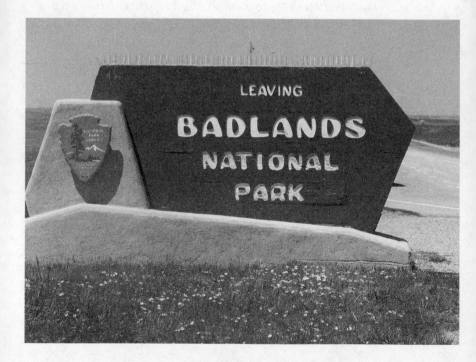

I know my gun safety.

We're just outside Cheyenne, Wyoming, passing endless trains stuffed with coal and herds of cattle clustered around ancient windmills, when we almost get killed again. We're cruising along doing about sixty-five, harmonizing to one of my favorite Wilco tunes ("Impossible Germany"), pointing out pronghorn antelope, when I feel a heavy thud in front of the car, like driving over a log. The car immediately begins to shake violently. I lay off the gas, wobbling toward the shoulder. I have to throw my entire body into control of the steering wheel. Panic lurches into my throat. My wrists tremble as I guide my crippled car onto the gravel away from passing traffic. "What the hell?" I hear Denise say. "What's happening?"

I shift into park and we turn to each other, surprised and shaken. "You okay?" I ask.

"Yeah," Denise says, jumping out to investigate the damage.

"What is it?" I shout, unbuckling my seat belt. "A flat tire?"

"You're not going to believe this."

I leap out and race around to join her on the gravel next to the car. My right front wheel—*the entire fucking wheel*—has caved in, making a courteous forty-five-degree-angle bow to the road. "Oh my God."

"Oh my God," Denise echoes. "We could have totally died!"

This is true. I vaguely knew a girl in college who died after her tire blew out on the freeway; she lost control of her Ford Explorer and it rolled seven times.

I crouch down to examine the wheel. Weirdly, the tire is intact. It's the actual wheel itself that has simply given up and sagged inward, as if to say, *That's about enough driving for the day.* "What the fuck?" I ask the sky. First my kayak, and now this. Is it a plot? I begin to wonder.

We stand there for a moment, watching cars and trucks zip past on operative, smug wheels. A hot breeze is blowing, making the ditch weeds rustle and dance. I press my face into my hands. I can hardly wait to see how much this is going to cost. I will never be able to retire. Ever. I'll probably have to whore myself out as a greeter at some big-box chain store when I'm ninety. I'll die in their break room, and the fifteen-year-old stock boy who finds me will eulogize my passing with "Holy shit, she did a total faceplant in her Noodles and Company. That sucks." After I imagine this I realize, wow! I haven't allowed myself a fantasy where I die of old age in a long time. I must be getting optimistic.

I kick the collapsed wheel. My hubcap slips onto the shoulder with an uninspired clang. I suddenly want to go home to Wisconsin. I want to overhear a nasal "Oh, yah?" or "Dis one time, I seen Harv put a sixer in 'im before he even touched his perch!" at a tavern-league softball game. I want to smell Johnsonville bratwurst sizzling on a smoky charcoal grill. I want to know there will be a cheese, smut, and fireworks store at the nearest highway exit and I even want my brother to tell me, "I told you so."

Denise senses my gloom and gives me a pep talk. "Come on, Leigh. What would Larry do? Larry wouldn't give up and kick his tires."

"I know," I say, reluctant and sulky.

"What would Larry do?" she asks again, brightly.

I sigh and play along. "Larry would go get his phone and call a tow truck."

"Hell, yeah! That Larry, always doing the sensible thing."

This makes me laugh, and I start to feel lucky to be here, broken down on the side of a highway in Wyoming. A year ago, I wouldn't have believed this could even be possible. A year ago, I carried a pager around at all times, in case a functional kidney came on the market. It's amazing how much of an entitlement complex you can get just walking around feeling healthy.

Denise falls back into the passenger seat and takes a long drink of water. I return to the driver's seat and find my purse. As I rummage through it a police squad car pulls up and parks about ten yards behind us. It's not a state trooper, because the driver isn't wearing one of those wide-brimmed funny hats, but he is wearing Erik Estrada sunglasses. My mind barely has time to process this, when Denise sighs and gives me a look I've seen on people before they confess a horrible, urgent secret.

"Okay. Before the cop gets here, there's something you should know, just in case anything happens." Denise unzips her backpack and pulls out a gun.

My heart hits the roof of my mouth, and I gag a little. "You have a gun? When did you get a gun? Where did you get a—*You have a gun?*"

"I found it in the bathroom at the rest stop. Pretty cool, huh?" She holds it at another low angle and admires it. Adrenaline surges through my gut.

"Is it loaded?" I could throw up.

"Yeah," she says, "But don't worry. I've got the safety on."

"Jesus *Christ!*"

"Oh, settle down. I know my gun safety."

I can't believe this. I stick with her long enough, I'll wind up dead or wanted in three states. "Jesus Christ, hide that thing!" I gape at the gun. "Do you know what can happen if that trooper knows you're *armed?*" But part of me, the Walter Mitty–TV Land part (bigger than I want to admit), is pretty damn thrilled to have uttered the words, "Do you know what can happen if that trooper knows you're *armed*?" We're Charlie's Angels minus one. And minus their sex appeal and kickboxing skills.

"I'll hide it under the seat, in my pack. Who would suspect a thing? Unless you keep acting all wild."

"Do you want to get us killed?" I hiss, still wild. Why on earth would she pick this moment to make such a confession? Great timing, Denise.

She sighs. "Nobody's getting killed."

I look in my rearview mirror. The trooper is still sitting in his car. Probably calling for backup, since I'm sure he'll do a search of the car and we'll be arrested and have to spend the night in jail, with a rock for a pillow, massaging the feet of a bull dyke named Blanche. "So what kind of gun is that?" I ask, my eyes glued to the rearview mirror. What is he *doing* back there?

"It's a Glock something or other."

"Put it away. Under the seat. Now. But don't look obvious, like you're bending way over to hide something under there, like drugs. Or a fucking gun." I can't swallow. I suddenly realize she could have robbed me back to the Stone Age and left me for dead in a motel room that's probably already seen its fair share of dead bodies. But she hasn't. Oh my God, but who cares, we're going to be arrested. I refocus and do a mini breathing exercise. *In for three—hold for four—out for seven.* Okay, Leigh, focus. I watch Denise carefully slip her pack under the seat. "Don't bend so low!" I shout. "Okay, now sit up. Look natural."

Denise smiles at me, more natural and wholesome-looking than a teen model for organic butter. "Who's the unnatural-looking one? Chill out, dude. You're going to give us away."

It occurs to me that I'm not quite past my sensible Midwestern middle-class upbringing, despite Larry's entry into my life. Who knows? If I'd been born wealthy, I may have had the means with which to really rebel. I may have wanted to live darkly, through the looking glass, delving into the kind of life Denise was born into— poverty, drugs, violence, danger—if only to feel how thinly we're all skating on life's surface. To get high on the precariousness of it all. But that kind of attitude is pretty rare back in middle Wisconsin. People rebel in Wisconsin by going vegan, by actively despising the Packers, by not baptizing their children into the neighborhood Catholic or Lutheran church. So when your new traveling companion whips out a gun at an inopportune moment, your first reaction is less "Now things will *really* get interesting!" and more "Oh Christ do I wish I were home watching the History Channel!"

Also, I may have mentioned it, but I've already experienced the precariousness of life, and it wasn't thrilling at all. It scared the shit out of me, frankly.

Denise sits up, flipping empty palms up. "Happy now?" I glance in the rearview mirror. The trooper is striding slowly toward our car. Once again, I listen for Larry's thoughts on the matter.

Don't worry, I hear. *Think positive and you'll create a positive destiny.*

Larry seems to have developed a bit of an echoey Obi-Wan Kenobi voice, but maybe that's just me.

I face forward and arrange a natural expression on my face as he approaches the car. "You gals break down?" He pulls off his sunglasses and squints at us. Or smiles. It could be both. I think of Denise's gun again, and beads of sweat assemble on my forehead.

"Her wheel almost fell off!" Denise exclaims, eyes bright. I can tell she finds his dimpled chin, shiny black hair, and eyes the color of glacial ice very, ah, aesthetically agreeable. He's also quite young—probably younger than me. I can barely look at him, he's so gorgeous. I'm afraid the penalty for looking at someone so attractive is having your eyes pecked out by crows.

"How'd you manage this?" he asks, whistling at my wheel's misfortune.

It was wheely hawd, I want to say, but instead I shrug.

"Have you called a tow truck?"

A tow twuck? We shake our heads and I say, "I was about to."

"Let me. I know a guy in town who's not a big rip-off artist. We take our cruisers to his shop."

My car *used* to have free roadside assistance, back when it was newer. Ish. And I didn't join AAA, because I don't do all that much driving, really. "That's very nice of you," I say. "Thanks."

Before he returns to his car to call the tow truck, Officer Hottie examines my license plate. "Wisconsin, huh? You a Packers fan?"

"Oh, no," I say. "Please, no cheesehead jokes." I make a funny noise like *aaaaggh!* and cross my index fingers at him in an anti-cheesehead talisman. Oh, why am I so socially delayed? I often make ridiculous noises during a conversation, and I'm helpless to stop myself. I'll think, *Don't do it. . . . Don't do it. . . . Don't do it*, and then a second later my sound effect is floating around my head, the verbal equivalent of the holiday sweater and matching snowman earrings.

He laughs. "Okay, I promise. What are you guys doing out here in the middle of nowhere?"

"Sort of a vacation, I guess. And what's a vacation to the middle of nowhere without the car breaking down at least once?" With a gun-toting hitchhiker? Ha-ha!

He grins. "Where are you headed next?"

"Well," I say, "we were hoping to be in Glenwood Springs, Colorado, later this evening, but I don't think that's going to happen." Denise's fingers start playing piano on her knees.

"Do you need a place to stay tonight?" For a minute I think he's going to offer us the futon in his living room, but then he says, "Because it's Frontier Days. I think most of the motels are booked, except for the Days Inn on Lincoln Way. You want me to call and see if they could squeeze you in? I know the manager on duty right now."

I glance at Denise. "I guess we'll need a place to stay if my car's in the shop." And given the severity of my car's mishap, I can't see this being a simple two-hour fix. Looks like we're stuck here tonight.

"Okay. What's your name?" He twirls his sunglasses around in one hand. "So I can tell Jim at Days Inn who to book the room for. I'm Eric, by the way."

Estrada? I think. *Oh, please let him be Erik Estrada!*

"Eric Gardner," he finishes. He smiles at me and it's like step-ping into a spotlight.

"Leigh Fielding." We shake hands. "This is my sister, Denise," I lie. Denise gives a little wave, a funny smile plastered to her lips.

"It's nice to meet you," she stammers. Cars cruise by, their pas-sengers rubbernecking to see why we're chatting with a police offi-cer. We watch him retreat to his squad car and make the calls. Denise grabs my wrist and hisses, "He is soooo hot!"

"Eh. That whole Colin Farrell thing just doesn't work for me."

She makes a face like I just told her I drink my own urine. "Okay, he is *way* hotter than Colin Farrell."

Officer Hottie returns and says, "You're all set up at the Days Inn. And Frank should be here any minute with the tow, and they'll get your car in the shop and have you back on the road in no time."

Embarrassed by his kindness, I'm pretty sure my face is the color of a tomato. "Thank you so much. You really didn't have to go to all that trouble."

"It was nothing. Say, if you get a chance, you guys should check out Frontier Days. Since you're stuck in town and all. Ever go to a real rodeo?"

I shudder involuntarily, hoping he doesn't notice. "No, but I've been to a bar with a mechanical bull."

"They have that there, too," he says, squinting and grinning crookedly. He has dimples, of course. And probably three dates for Frontier Days, just for tonight.

At that very moment, the tow truck appears on the horizon. "Well, I should get back to work," Officer Eric Gardner says. He slides his sunglasses back on. "Nice meeting you both. Good luck with the car!"

While Frank examines my wheel and hooks the car to the truck, Denise grins slyly at me. "You called me your sister."

I can only blush and shrug.

After we tow my wounded car to the repair shop and get an es-timate for my busted ball joint and tie rod ($600, enough to feed a family in Bangladesh for a year), the shop's courtesy car drops us off at the motel and we check in. The Days Inn is probably the cleanest place we've stayed thus far, although I wouldn't want to hold a black light over the bedspread. Denise and I claim our respective beds and organize our luggage.

We call a local Chinese restaurant that delivers and order veggie lo mein (me) and garlic chicken (Denise). Exhausted, we lie on our motel beds watching *Beyond the Valley of the Dolls* while we wait for our food to be delivered in white waxy boxes. I have to say, Denise is a much better movie-watching partner than Jillian, who always seems to take a call during the film's opening scenes, then plops back down next to me and starts in with the litany of questions: "What did I miss?" "Are they divorced?" "Where are they going?" "Is he going to kill that guy?" "Why did she hit him?" "Who's that?" and my favorite, "So how did this war start?" Jillian doesn't watch films so much as she needs them translated for her with sign language, cue cards, props, and interpretive dance. Watching movies with Jillian could someday carry a warning label: *May cause bouts of psychotic rage, cerebral bleeding, uncontrollable crying, and premature death from brain implosion.*

Something about the moment feels familial, if a tad dysfunctional. Maybe that's what makes it comfortable to me. Denise asks me suddenly, "Do you ever think about dying?"

"I hope this isn't a trick question," I say. I glance over at her, but she's lost in thought. So I say, "All the time. When I got sick, I didn't expect to make it to thirty. I still don't, some days." I try to submerge myself in the movie, because while I can admit this, I can't accept it, deep down. Wes tells me not to say that I probably won't make it to thirty, because then I probably won't, but I can't help it. I wonder what I will feel when I exhale my last breath. Would I know it was my last breath? I hope I'm asleep.

An all-too-familiar panicky feeling swells inside me like a toxic balloon. I don't want to die yet. I have far too much to do.

Denise lies still, barely breathing. "I tried to kill myself, once. When I was fourteen." She lifts her left forearm to show me a soft scar across her wrist.

"Jesus, Denise."

"I had a knife in my hand, pressed against my left wrist. I didn't really want to do it. I was just so . . . You know that feeling you get when you're treading deep water and you can't touch the bottom and you're ready to give up because you're just so tired? I felt like that, but really sad, too."

She pauses for a moment, and I look over at her. She's staring at the ceiling, flushed. Her voice is soft when she begins speaking again. "I prayed for a sign. Something to tell me what to do. Nothing happened. So I pressed the knife down, and then, all of a sudden, the phone rang once. There was a long silence, and then it rang again, just once. I ran into the kitchen to answer it, but nobody was there."

"Did you tell anyone? Your foster parents?"

"Ha! They're, like, the main reason I wanted to kill myself."

For a minute I'm speechless. Then I say, "Suicide is a permanent solution to a temporary problem." It was something I'd heard James say a few times, like a mantra.

"I know," Denise says. "Anyway, that was a long time ago."

Yeah, thirty-six whole months.

I lean back, only slightly relieved. But I've learned something about myself. I'm way too socially awkward to ever man phones at a suicide hotline. Just as we refocus on the movie, the phone rings, startling us both. Denise and I stare at each other for a moment like spooked children playing with a lively Ouija board. "It's probably the delivery guy," she says with false confidence. I answer the phone, expecting God herself.

I hear a man ask, haltingly, "Hi, uh, is this Leigh?"

"Yeah." I swallow hard. Who could be calling us here? Maybe it's the auto shop calling to tell me they don't have the right parts in stock after all and I'll be in Wyoming until Christmas. Oh, and is that a gun I have under one of the front seats? "Who's this?"

"Um, this is Eric. Eric Gardner. Officer Gardner."

"Oh, hi," I hear myself say. I frown. What could he want? I become instantly paranoid that Denise's backpack is full of crystal meth. Did he see her gun? Was a bloody arm hanging from my trunk? Oh Jesus. Denise mouths, *Who is it?* I wave my hand dismissively: *I'll tell you later.*

"I hope this doesn't seem weird, but I was wondering if I could take you guys down to Frontier Days."

"Uh—"

"I just got off work, and I figured you were probably going to be stuck at the Days Inn all night, so I thought I'd see if you wanted to check out Cheyenne while you're here."

I pause to pick my jaw up from the floor. Okay, yes, this is weird. I form a mental image of him pulling over behind dozens of stranded female motorists . . . the Casanova Cop . . . offering a lift, a night of frivolity at Frontier Days, a cocktail on his futon, a fertilized ovum . . .

"You still there?"

"Huh! Oh yeah. I'm here."

Denise can hardly stand it. She's giving me an insane, wild-eyed look. Her eyebrows have surged to the top of her head.

"So what do you say?"

I consider my options: stay in the motel room with Denise and discuss death, or watch some bronco buckin' with Officer Hottie. I hate to sound heartless, but it's no contest. "Um, sure. What time?"

"Pick you guys up at seven?"

I hang up and tell Denise what I've just signed us up for.

"Wait a minute. That was the cute cop?"

I nod.

"And he wants to take both of us to Frontier Days?"

I nod again.

"Hmmm," she deliberates. "Ummm, I think I'll stay here."

My pulse picks up, and I suddenly realize I'm very thirsty. "Why?"

"*A*, I don't do well as the third wheel. *B*, he's way more into you. *C*, what if he's a freak?"

I roll my eyes. "*A*, this isn't a date. *B*, he's not into anyone. This is a charity date. *C*, he probably is a freak, so aren't you curious to learn what kind?"

She sighs. "I really don't feel like going to a rodeo."

"What's wrong?" I ask.

"I just don't want to go out, okay?" She stares past me at the wall.

"Are you sure you're alright?"

She flips through a few channels, tuning me out. "I'm stellar. I'm just gonna hang out and watch TV."

Okay, she is clearly pissed about something. "Larry wants you to go," I try, giving her a jovial, encouraging face. I even do a little jig.

"But I don't want to go," she repeats curtly, and I finally decide to drop it. I know better than to argue with a gun-toting runaway. Our food arrives, and we eat in silence, save for the occasional slurp of a spicy noodle.

I tiptoe while I get ready so as not to disturb Denise. Her ornery mood fills the room like a cloud of carbon monoxide. Maybe she's just worn out from the day. My emotions are certainly capable of changing their mind at a moment's notice, given my hormones, blood sugar level, environment, and the amount of REM sleep I've had the night before. (Although it pains me to admit this. I like to think of myself as a very calm, levelheaded person not prone to pitching fits.)

So what do people wear to Frontier Days? Besides assless leather chaps, boots, fringy shirts and vests, roach-clip feathers, bandannas, ten-gallon hats, and belt buckles you could eat spaghetti from. I'd forgotten to pack any of those particular items, mostly because they make my eyes scream when I look at them. I guess I'll settle for a khaki skirt, navy V-necked top, and some sandals I found on sale at DSW. No fashionista me, because when you're going to Frontier Days with Officer Hottie, you want to be as comfortable as possible.

Denise comes into the bathroom and leans against the doorframe while I curl pieces of my hair. Or try to. Annoyed with the dry environment and Cheyenne's brand of treated water, it's simply not cooperating. "Maybe I will go, after all," she says quietly.

I glance at her, slightly amused. "Okay, great! But you've got only ten minutes to get ready." I wrap a chunk of hair around the iron.

She tears around the room, throwing on a short skirt and preen-
ing, applying more makeup than necessary. "What do you think?"
she asks.

I study her while she twirls. *Too much makeup,* I think, but I
say, "Gaw-jus. Simply *gaw*-jus, dahling." I make a purring-trilling
kind of noise. (See, what did I tell you?)

She seems pleased with this. The phone rings just as I run some
gloss over my lips. It's Officer Hottie. "We'll be right down," I say in
my best attempt at nonchalance.

I examine myself in the full-length mirror. If I suck in my gut
and stand really tall, I could pass for someone who almost makes it
into a Sears ad. Not too shabby.

The off-duty Eric Gardner is waiting for us in the lobby. In a
ten-gallon hat, cowboy boots, tight jeans, and, yes, a belt buckle
as big as a TV tray. Denise snickers, and I feel my lips curl into a
snarky grin. "I've never gone out with one of the Village People," I
say.

He laughs, still blindingly gorgeous. My Rip VanGina wakes up
and rubs her eyes. Hello! "So are you guys ready for Frontier Days?"
he says through perfect lips.

Hoo-wee, am I!

Turns out everyone at Frontier Days is wearing boots and a cowboy
hat except Denise and me. And after about five minutes, Denise
buys a straw cowboy hat and I'm the only one sans hat. Which is
fine by me.

I'm not all that enthused about going to the rodeo part, since
I'm not really into calf roping and horses that desperately don't
want to be ridden. So we just stick to the midway, which proves to
be entertaining in a kiddie-end-of-the-gene-pool kind of way. After
we buy cotton candy and nachos, I spot a red-haired guy in a cowboy hat the size of a lawn tractor and a BODYBUILDERS FOR CHRIST
T-shirt. I'm not kidding. I wonder if he knows Geoffrey with a *G*.
We see lots of be-hatted people throwing darts at balloons to win
mirrored panels embossed with the names of country singers and

arena rock bands. We see a toddler singing, "You'se a fine mutha-fucka, won't you back that ass up," over and over while plucking plastic floating ducks from their water sluice, and we see one whopper of a lovers' spat between two drunk people wearing, yep, you guessed it, cowboy hats—with feather roach clips. Denise wins a stuffed pink dragon by hitting a target near the bull's-eye with an air gun. We walk past a dunk tank, which turns out to be a mistake because the clown perched above the water starts heckling us im-mediately. "Hey, Ken! Hoo-hoo, Ken with Barbie and Skipper! Betcha can't hit me." Eric chuckles and buys three throws for five bucks. He misses every time. "Nice shot, loser!" the clown shouts. "C'mon, pretty boy, let's see you throw like a girl one more time!"

Eric tries to laugh it off, but I can tell he's pissed. His manhood has been ridiculed.

But boy-howdy, did we get a compliment! "Barbie and Skipper," I say, trying it out. "I like it!"

Denise says, "Ha-ha," like a chickadee. (Or like Nelson from *The Simpsons,* if you're more a pop culture kind of person.) We get in line for a ride that will probably inspire my veggie lo mein to make an encore appearance. I take a deep breath. The air smells like funnel cakes, corn dogs, and an industrial hog farm. Eric turns to me and says, "Having fun?"

"Sure! When do we get to see the mechanical bull?"

"Oh, we'll get there. So tell me about Wisconsin," Eric says, like I live in a mythical land somewhere between a rainbow and Uranus.

Denise and I glance at each other. "Well, if you like beer, bratwurst, cheese, and the Packers, you'll do fine," I say. Then I blurt, "Eric, can I ask how old you are? I'm just curious."

Eric blushes. "Twenty-three. Do I look that young?"

Denise makes this really interested face. "I'm eighteen," she pipes up.

Eric nods without looking at her and asks me, "How old are you?"

"Twenty-eight," I say. Closer to thirty than twenty-five. When I turned twenty-five, my aunt Sally made a huge deal about it, bray-ing "Quarter of a century! You're a quarter of a century!" every time I glanced her way during dinner. I'd been diagnosed with PKD three years earlier, and everyone was trying to maintain a brave, optimistic front while my health rolled steadily downhill. Two years later, I had my transplant, and the sky cleared itself of clouds. I could see thirty on the horizon, and forty, and maybe even fifty. Half a century.

We make some more small talk that you might have on a one-time date with a cute guy who still has dinner four times a week with his mother. Denise starts to get a little sulky, because we're both getting the vibe that Eric is more interested in me than in her. On the ride, all of the change falls from my pockets and I keep sliding up against him, sometimes with enough centrifugal force that my leg actually sticks to his. This makes me impossibly flustered, because I'm pretty sure if there's much more of this, I might have an orgasm that could warp time and bend light, but he doesn't seem to mind.

Later we go on the Ferris wheel. Denise decides to smoke and get a snow cone so she can flirt with the tattooed guy behind the counter. As we ride up and around in our little Ferris wheel seat, I ponder whether or not to tell Eric about my kidney. I guess if it's not relevant to anything we're talking about, why bring it up? I probably won't see him after tonight, and it's not like you can just blurt, "Hey, guess what? I had an organ transplant!" on your first and only date with a hot guy in a huge belt buckle. Instead we talk about dating disasters. "I once dated a girl who ate dog biscuits like a snack."

"I once dated a guy who thought tigers were female lions."

"I once dated a girl who knocked my best friend out with one punch."

"I once dated a guy who lifted weights with his neck."

I opt not to tell him about the guy who went down on me after eating a bucket of five-alarm chicken wings. Who knew you could get hives down there?

My stomach goes into a free fall as we float down again. Eric is staring at me in a way that suggests he sees something in me I clearly do not. Does he not see my puffy moon face? The wispy hair I've developed on my cheeks and upper lip as a result of my medication?

Other than the Seth debacle and a few minor mishaps here and there, it's been years since I've had anything even remotely resembling a date. In fact, for the last three years, the only dates I ever saw or discussed were the edible ones, which put me right below C-SPAN on the fun-o-meter. After I got sick I joined an online support group for people with kidney disease. I started this e-mail–phone thing with a guy in the U.K. who also had kidney disease. He was such a trouper, training for some big bike race (not the Tour de France) in between dialysis sessions. He wanted to be the next Lance Armstrong, minus the testicular cancer. My mood at the time was a black squiggly line and his was a cool blue room. Sometimes I couldn't stand talking to him, because the following words simply didn't exist in his magical language: *hate, can't, never,* and *doomed.* His mother gave him one of her kidneys, and his body rejected it. Isn't that awful? I'm sure there's something Freudian or Oedipal in there somewhere. In the end, I simply couldn't handle his optimism, his unflagging belief that things were always just about to get better, because it completely broke my heart. We still e-mail now and then, only now we don't talk about how horny we are.

I smile at Eric and feel my face flush. Could I allow myself to fall in love again? I mean, not necessarily with Eric (although the Ouija board did say my future husband's first name would begin with an E). But with anyone? With the right person? *What would that be like?* I wonder. Shopping for groceries together, assembling a computer desk, getting annoyed at a raised toilet seat. Little luxuries, all. Gifts I thought I could never afford.

Right at the top of the Ferris wheel, Eric leans over to kiss me. It's straight out of a cheesy eighties teen movie (I think that's what he's going for), but with more spit. In fact, he's a bit of a slobbery kisser, doing this weird lickety-lick thing on my lips with his tongue like he's a mother cat trying to clean Fancy Feast stuck on her kitten's mouth. But his tongue feels like velvet and I haven't had sex since the Pleistocene Epoch, so you can guess what associations my dirty little mind made next. My vagina starts hurling herself at the fence.

Unfortunately, the mood is broken when I happen to glance down and see Denise lift a wallet out of someone's backpack. At least, that's what it looks like from up here. Denise is picking pockets? I don't say anything to Eric, but my stomach shrinks into a hard stone.

I almost take a nasty tumble as we step off the ride, reminding myself why I don't do ski lifts, and we meet up with Denise. She's in a fantastic mood, jabbering on about the tattooed guy in the snow cone stand who said her lips reminded him of rose petals.

I temporarily forget about her kleptomania (if that's actually what I saw—we were pretty high up). "Ew! He actually said that?"

She nods and laughs. What is it with guys in Cheyenne and lips?

"Did she tell you about her kidney?" Denise asks Eric. *Dammit, Denise,* I think.

He shakes his head, confused. "Your kidney? What's this?"

I resist saying anything about urine production. Instead I mumble, "I had a kidney transplant a year ago."

Denise adds, "And now she's channeling the spirit of the organ donor!"

Thanks, Denise. Eric looks at me like I'm not the well-adjusted girl he licked on the Ferris wheel. "Sounds kinda New Agey to me," he says.

"It's nothing," I say, rolling my eyes.

"Oh, yes it is," Denise blathers on. "Her taste in food changed, and music, and it's like she can feel his energy!"

Eric gives me a long, considering gaze, and I actually feel myself shrinking. I become Lilliputian. "I never met anyone who had an organ transplant. That must have been something."

"It was something, alright." I wait for him to say a sentence with the phrase "I reckon" in it, but he says nothing more. We walk to the Buckin' A Saloon, a bar at the end of the midway. The bouncer knows Eric and lets us in without checking our IDs. I begin to sus-

Driving Sideways   101

pect that Eric is a local celebrity. He orders a beer for himself and asks what we want. I request a Coke, and Denise orders a Bud Light. Cowboys lope around everywhere. After a minute Eric hands us two Cokes. Denise pouts but soon begins flirting with a guy wearing two silver belt buckles: one on his belt and one on his hat, like a miner's light. The dual-buckled cowboy calls her Missy. Eric rides the mechanical bull, a disturbing sight indeed. If after your first kiss, your date starts humping an animate object that isn't you, the night's probably over.

For the rest of the evening he keeps looking at me like I've shaved my head, wear an orange robe, and hand out flowers in an airport. But I don't even mind. Hey, he humped a fake bull, not me. And even though I won't be marrying Eric and probably won't ever see him again, he has renewed my faith in the human drive to couple. Because if Officer Eric "Hottie" Gardner could ask me on a date to Frontier Days, other just as unlikely dates might be right around the corner. Plus, he made me feel purty.

After he drops us off (without asking for my number—no surprise there), I confront Denise about what I saw from the top of the Ferris wheel.

"What? Are you kidding me?" she answers, indignant.

"But it sure looked like you did," I say. "You can tell me the truth, Denise. I won't be mad. I just want to know if you did it or not."

"Leigh, I am telling you the truth. There's no way I would, like, steal some guy's wallet, even if I *am* fucking broke. Besides, I was too busy talking to John."

"John who?"

"The snow cone guy." She can tell I'm still skeptical, so she adds softly, "Leigh, come on. I didn't steal anything." She writes, "For real!" on a sign and flashes it at me, making a sad, pouty face. Dammit, Denise.

I let it drop, but something still seems off-kilter. As we lay on our beds watching Conan O'Brien, I feel my earlier confidence seeping away. That Eric asked me out was a total fluke, I tell myself dismally. I imagine myself dying alone, in poverty, the crazy dog lady on Sixth Street, never having my face licked like it was Fancy Feast ever again. So I decide to call Wes for a pep talk. I call him from the parking lot for a little privacy. His first reaction when I tell him about picking up Denise is fairly predictable. "Oh my God, are you kidding me, what if she's crazy," and all that jazz. Then he says, even more predictably, "So you two get all lesbo yet?"

"Nice," I say. Once we get past this formality, I tell him about my date with Eric.

"So who's this guy?" Wes asks like a weight lifter on the verge of a 'roid rage, somehow more concerned with Officer Hottie entering the picture than with Denise.

"Oh, he was a good guy. Young. Very cute."

"I'm sure."

Is Wes jealous?

"He kissed like a cat," I announce. Wes doesn't say anything, so I continue. "He got kinda weird after he found out I had a kidney transplant. I think he pitied me, like I was in a wheelchair, but he feared me as well. Me and my mighty kidney, Frankenwoman of the spare parts." I do a mad scientist kind of laugh.

"Listen, you have to be careful, Leigh. There are a lot of nuts out there. Believe me, I know, I'm a guy."

I rankle at this. "Don't patronize me." Apparently, all of my friends and family think I'm a mentally incapacitated ward of the state. A sudden wave of despair washes over me. "I'll never meet anyone."

Wes sighs. "Yes you will. He's out there somewhere, probably on a bad date with someone else. When you meet you'll tell each other the story of the bad dates you had tonight."

I think of discussing bad dates on the Ferris wheel with Eric and almost say, *Aaaargh!* I get even more depressed and then I say, predictably, "It won't matter anyway, because I'll probably be dead by thirty."

Wes is the one who says, *"Aaaargh!"* Then he says, "Stop feeling sorry for yourself. There's no reason why you can't live to be a hun-

dred. You're going to have to find a good job and settle down one of
these days. Besides, everyone who walks the planet has a terminal
illness. It's called life."

I sigh. Wes is right. I've pegged my entire future on dying by
thirty, but I guess I can't put responsibility off any longer. I'd have
to get my own apartment, which is probably long overdue. I'll
have to find a career that doesn't involve picking up poop (although
I've heard most of them do, figuratively speaking). I'm going to have
to start saving for retirement. And maybe, if the planets align and
Tyson's entire North Carolina hog fleet launches itself into the sky,
fall in love and open a joint checking account.

It's time to put Gram's favorite saying to work. I need to shit or
get off the pot.

CHAPTER SIX

Colorado: Fresh Air and Fond Memories Served Daily

My car is ready to roll the next day around noon. I reluctantly slap my Visa on the counter at the repair shop, and I get another image of my ninety-year-old self dead in her pesto cavatappi at the big-box store. It's like I open my purse and dollar bills fly out, with wings of their own. But I'm thrilled to have my car back, because it means I'm that much closer to seeing Jillian, thanking Larry's family, and—if I'm lucky—being the main course in another face-licking incident that will simultaneously arouse and disgust me.

I call Jillian to tell her we're on our way, but I lose the signal before we can talk for long. It's a day designed for a drive—the sky envelops us, cobalt blue, laced with a few wispy clouds. To our right, grassy foothills march back to the Rockies. The mountains—stubborn hangovers from the planet's adolescence—loom along the horizon. The closer we get to Denver, the more adrenaline courses through my veins. I want to move to the mountains. I want to live in a little cabin next to a towering, tenacious mountain fourteen thousand feet above sea level and eat a bowl of raisin bran every morning in its shadow.

I don't pay too much attention to Denver, because I'm stressing about the right exits and such. The traffic is amazing. I guess everyone has my living-in-the-shadow-of-a-towering-mountain idea. I glance in my rearview mirror and something catches my eye. "Does that black car look familiar to you? I could swear I've seen that car before. A *few* times, in fact."

Denise cranes around in her seat. "Maybe we should try to lose it. What if it's some creepy guy who saw us at our motel and decided to follow us? What if we're being followed?"

We share a delicious, dangerous look, which I finally break with, "Stop it, you're creeping me out." I shudder and press the gas pedal, weaving in and out of traffic to escape our overactive imaginations. And the black car, just in case.

Denise flaps our map of Colorado all over the front seat and futzes with the radio, trying to find a decent station. She settles on a station that bills itself as "rocking the Rockies." In two hours, we'll be in Glenwood Springs with Jillian. And Geoffrey with a *G*. It probably goes without saying (since this is my first trip in four years beyond a radius of fifty miles), but I've never seen Jillian's Colorado digs. To help pay for their various athletic endeavors, Jillian and Geoffrey have two roommates: a nineteen-year-old ski bum who's really into 900 numbers and some thirty-seven-year-old who builds and repairs stringed instruments. I'm told he did John Denver's last guitar.

I haven't seen Jillian since Christmas, over six months ago. Our conversations of late have mostly involved me, perplexed, saying things like "But what's his family like?" and "I thought you just finished a triathlon," and Jillian, Stepfordesque, saying things like "Geoffrey's signing us up for a couple's rock-climbing challenge. Isn't that gray-it?" and "You simply have to try this recipe for energy bars that I found." (*Long pause*.) "Oh, wait—you can't really eat food so high in protein, can you?"

I do admit I felt somewhat bereft, maybe even mildly abandoned, when Jillian moved out west right around the time I got sick. I know, I know, we're both grown-ups and she can live any damn place she wants, get a life and all. But come on, your best

friend—who wept at your grandmother's funeral, finishes your
sentences, and warns you when you've got spinach stuck between
your teeth; your confessor, therapist, partner in crime, and sounding board all rolled into one amazing person—announces she's moving four states away as you're blindsided by a medical tsunami, and
you don't feel even a smidgen of loss, self-pity, or envy? (If you
don't, let's bottle and patent whatever you're on, because we'd make
a fortune.)

So there's that. And I'm toting a metal detector, a teenage runaway kleptomaniac, Larry's kidney, and a pretty large chip on my
shoulder about her fiancé. Even I wouldn't want to make up a guest
room for me right now. But I can't wait to see her, even if I have to
take Geoffrey in the bargain.

The white lines blip by below our car in a highway countdown.
We're twelve thousand feet above sea level, and I decide to queue
up some John Denver on the iPod: "Rocky Mountain High," "Sunshine on My Shoulders," "Annie's Song." I can almost touch the
low-flying clouds. Mountains hem us in on all sides, and the road
weaves between them at crazy angles. We pass through the endless
and somewhat creepy Eisenhower Memorial Tunnel. Vail flies past,
expensive and overdeveloped, followed by towns named Avon,
Eagle, and Gypsum. The ski lifts carved into the mountains are
quiet. Trailers litter the valleys, home to what the vacation-home
crowd euphemistically calls The Help. My car chugs listlessly up
the steep mountain passes; I rub the dashboard and say, "Come on,
baby! You can do it!" We spy a cluster of bored-looking bighorn
sheep on one of the mountains. Our ears pop and we stretch our
jaws to relieve the pressure.

Every fifteen minutes Denise flashes me a sign: "Are we there
yet?" I almost need to send a medic, she's laughing so hard.

Her sign language is really pissing me off. I threaten to throw
her Ping-Pong paddles out the window. "Who are you, Helen
Keller?" I ask.

"No," she writes, and makes like she's going to paddle me on
the head.

"I think this is it," I say, consulting yet another of my MapQuest maps. "715 Mesa Drive, Apartment Number 4, Glenwood Springs." I park our little traveling circus in a driveway next to an elderly Honda sporting bumper stickers that read VISUALIZE WHIRLED PEAS and FREE TIBET. "Now, don't steal anything," I say to Denise.

She just rolls her eyes and finishes my next sentence for me. "And leave the gun in the car." Jillian must have seen us park, because she bounces out in black yoga pants and a coral wrap shirt to greet us in the driveway. Her auburn hair is pulled back into the kind of messy knot that takes more effort to put together than one might think.

"You finally made it!" she says. I step out and hug her. She smells like patchouli, vanilla, and lavender. Her future children are going to grow up with fantastic scent-memories and friends that say, "Dude, your mom is so hot!"

"And this must be . . . Denise?" They shake hands like rivals in a karate match.

"And this must be . . . Jill!" Denise mimics, but not cruelly.

Jillian's smile freezes. "Well, this will be an interesting trip, won't it?"

A minute later we're carrying bags inside. Jillian's four-bedroom apartment is fairly plush, compared to most of my friends' first postcollege pads. The ground floor is home to two bedrooms, an office that appears to double as a mountain bike and snowboard storage room, a crimson and navy bathroom, and a spacious open-concept kitchen that spills into a living room lined with cushiony brown seating. Tribal masks and batik prints of fertility goddesses and priests decorate the walls. A metal staircase spirals up to the loft bedroom that Jillian shares with Geoffrey. A cone of incense wafts smoke from the center of a goofy, brightly painted candle-holder on the coffee table. It looks like someone glued clumps of neon Play-Doh together with their elbows in orbit at zero gravity. I snicker and pick the piece up. "Did you commission a toddler to sculpt this with his feet?"

Jillian gives me a level look, a faint smile playing at the corners of her lips. "Actually, that candleholder was painted by an adult with disabilities."

Denise snorts and I carefully replace it on the table. "Oh." I decide to keep the rest of my comments to myself as I continue to show myself around, noting a Buddhist altar in a corner next to a peace lily.

It's the sort of place I'd want for myself, if I'd received a kidney from a Malaysian medicine woman. "So where's Geoffrey?" I ask, finally. Not that I'm in a mad dash to meet him.

Jillian hauls an air mattress from a closet and says, "Buying some groceries with Todd."

"Who's Todd?" I ask.

"You know, Todd. I told you about him." I just stare helplessly. Jillian looks at me as if I'd just asked her who the president was. "Our roommate Todd? Repaired-John-Denver's-last-guitar Todd? Todd who is practically *dripping* with musical talent?"

"Oh, sure," I say, trying not to look confused. There were too many new people with too many new talents in her life to keep track of.

While Jillian inflates the air mattress between the extreme sports equipment in the office, Denise and I check out the pictures on the fridge. Lots of shots of Jillian and Geoffrey in the mountains, Jillian and Geoffrey climbing rocks or running, Geoffrey's two kids. Jillian tells me she's only met one of Geoffrey's children. Once. Sounds like a recipe for a healthy marriage, doesn't it?

Here are a few other things I know about Geoffrey, via Meg. He won't let his kids watch popular "family" movies that he deems infantile or corrupting, like *Happy Feet* or *Shrek*—one, two, *or* three. And he's rude to waitstaff—avoiding eye contact, barking orders, leaving tips that wouldn't buy a pack of gum at Walgreens—even when his meal meets his standards. And he has standards that would give a Sherpa altitude sickness. Even the last guy Jillian dated would have been better than Geoffrey with a G. Who cares if that guy gave her a gently used stuffed animal on her birthday? At least he also did amusing things like passing out slices of pie at three in the morning to strangers at Perkins. I bet Geoffrey breaks out in hives when he laughs, and the only things that tickle his funny bone are injured kittens or oil spills.

At that moment, Geoffrey with a *G* comes in the front door with Repaired-John-Denver's-last-guitar Todd. Todd's not bad. In fact, for a guy pushing forty, he's mighty edible-looking, with lusher lashes than I'll ever see in the mirror and a physique that tells me he might be part of the Crunchtime cult. Never mind the battered green Converse sneakers, purple cargo shorts, or Rastafarian dreds. As long as he's not wearing a belt buckle, he's fine with me. Geoffrey, on the other hand, has these crazy Gary Shandling liver lips and I can't imagine Jillian kissing them or having to watch him pass forkfuls of food between them. (And forget sex! The thought of Jillian copulating with Geoffrey makes me want to take a sitz bath in bleach.) "Welcome to our humble home!" he announces grandly. This is another of my least-favorite phrases. It's sort of like saying, "Please, foray into a perfection you'll never achieve!" Jillian introduces us and he shakes my hand much too tightly. He's a handshake Nazi! You hear about these people from time to time. When he releases his grip, finally, my hand throbs. I try not to show it on my face. I'm getting pretty good at hiding pain, although I'm not sure if this is a plus or a minus.

We catch up in the living room, over sushi made by Todd himself. I only eat the veggie rolls, because—guess what?—I'm the invalid on a special diet. Apparently, Todd is not only a whiz with the stringed instruments. He's also mighty apt with the raw fish.

"I can't believe you saw Seth again," Jillian says, whirling some wasabi into a tiny square dish of soy sauce. "Is he still following Phish?"

"Jillian, he's a mortgage broker. Alan Greenspan is his personal hero. Also? He's married and he hit on me."

"No way!" Jillian ponders this, amazed. "Didn't he once tell you that monogamy isn't a natural state for *Homo sapiens*?"

"And how, apparently." I remember that Jillian's engaged and quickly add, "At least for him, anyway."

Denise pops a California roll into her mouth. "This sushi rocks. Are you, like, a chef?"

Todd brings five long-stemmed glasses and a bottle of four-year-old Shiraz into the living room. "Just trying to make myself useful," he says, effortlessly popping the cork. I watch the red aromatic liquid glug into my glass with something close to reverence. I haven't tasted a drop of alcohol in nearly seven years. And I'd be a dirty, stinking liar if I said I didn't miss it—the fuzzy warmth of the first drink, the jubilation and easy conversation of the second, the coy, nonsensical flirtations of the third. (I'll stop there, before the inappropriate and obnoxious comments of the fourth, nudity of the fifth, and vomiting of the sixth.)

I pick up my glass and smell the wine grandly—heady notes of blackberries, vanilla, and oak with subtle mossy undertones. My eyes almost roll back in my head. *Just a sip,* I hear a voice say. *You can handle just one sip, right?* I swirl the Shiraz around and around the inside of my glass, mesmerized by the syrupy hang time. Jillian clears her throat like a schoolmarm, breaking the spell. I sigh and reluctantly push my delicious old lover away. "Got any tea?"

So I tell Jillian about the car breaking down, our date with the cowboy cop, about my kayak blowing from the roof of my car. She laughs, drinks wine, and I can feel the old Jillian shaking off the dust and stepping into the room. After she finishes her last sushi roll, Denise turns to Geoffrey. "So what do you do?"

Geoffrey launches into a long, tedious speech about how he started Crunchtime, how fitness wasn't a priority for him until his mother developed type 2 diabetes and heart disease, about the Aspen spa competition, his brilliant marketing strategies, fitness as a lifestyle, nutrition for various training circuits, and so on. It's about as interesting as a lecture on sawdust, as far as I'm concerned. And frankly, I'm shocked to learn he has a mother. I thought he may have hatched from an egg in someone's basement. He talks for so long that I can begin to hear his lips and mouthparts sticking together in an extremely unappealing manner. *Smack-smack-smack.* I check to see if he has white crud in the corners of his lips. At that point he finishes his dissertation and slugs the rest of his wine. Sucking the air from a room and monopolizing conversation is thirsty work! Todd tips another dash of wine into Geoffrey's glass, and I salivate.

Everyone is getting drunk but me. Just then, the fourth roomie barges into the living room, returned from wherever the ski bums smoke pot all night. He's also drunk. "Hey," he shouts. "Let's do tarot readings."

"Oh, absolutely!" Jillian claps her hands. Her cheeks are flushed.

Stoner Ski Bum runs to his room, puts on a Frank Zappa CD, and rejoins the sushi party in the living room. "Sorry. I can't function without music." Denise sits up straighter and smiles at him. He's cute, if you like ski bums with a bit of acne. I think he might be shorter than me, but I can't tell, because I've been sucked into a couch cushion and we'll need a team of mules to pull me out.

We sit cross-legged on our couch cushions and I watch Jillian do tarot readings for everyone in the circle while I wait my turn. Our only light glows from candles scattered throughout the room (including the one in the holder made by the disabled adult). She takes it pretty seriously, so it's hard not to get caught up in things. It's like when you were a kid at slumber parties with your friends, freaking yourselves out by repeating "Bloody Mary" in the bathroom mirror with all the lights out, and you never could say it thirteen times because after the twelfth time you believed you might die of fright (or worse) if you did.

I have to shuffle the cards and divide them while thinking of a question. I cut right to the chase: *Am I on the right path?* Followed by *What should I do next?* Followed by *Will I ever be happy?* And *What about love and a career?* So, it's kind of a glut of questions. I'm leaving it up to the spirits to sort it out.

Jillian deals four cards in a diamond pattern: the Fool, the Wheel of Fortune, the Six of Swords, and the Hanged Man. Great. She tells me that my romantic life is about to experience a new beginning—and that I must be spontaneous and embrace folly. Embrace folly, huh? I'm pretty sure last night's date put me on the right path.

"The next card refers to your finances," Jillian says, consulting her little tarot instruction book. "It's the Wheel of Fortune, so your finances are at a turning point. Maybe moving in a new direction."

"Yeah, out of my purse," I interject.

Jillian frowns. "You're going to gain greater perspective and find opportunity in an accident." She moves on to the next card. "Six of Swords. This deals with health and happiness." She holds the little booklet up, straining to read it in the candlelight. "Wow. This card reveals the blues, recovery, and travel." She looks up at me, awed. "That is totally you!"

Okay, I have to hand it to her. That's pretty good.

"Last card. The Hanged Man. This card refers to your career."

"Or lack thereof," I whisper. Apparently, my career is not in the shitter, as previously thought. It's on the gallows with a noose around its neck.

"You will overturn old priorities and see the world from a new angle. You must live in the moment and wait for the best opportunity. It also means 'sacrifice.' "

"We could have just asked Larry," Denise says. Her reading had a lot to do with falsehood and burdens, so she's irritated.

Stoner Ski Bum, already bored, suggests we go for a walk. "I'm supposed to meet Ben at the Hotel Colorado."

"Oh, you'll love the Hotel Colorado," Jillian says to me. Todd grabs two more bottles of wine for the road.

As long as it's not the Hotel California. Because if I check out, I definitely want to leave.

There's supposedly a ghost—or a few ghosts—haunting the 114-year-old Hotel Colorado, which was modeled after some six-teenth-century Italian castle. We tiptoe down the empty halls, and I'm really starting to get the willies. People have died here, in this very hotel. People have made love, and argued, and complained about vacations gone awry. Doc Holliday and Teddy Roosevelt once stayed here. Families from Delaware, too. I absolutely love it.

After being adequately spooked by the grand, sweeping staircases, flickering chandeliers, potted palms, and ghostly sounds of business travelers getting drunk on martinis in the lounge, Stoner Ski Bum (Mark, I learn) suggests we traipse over to the "hot pots," as his friend Ben is a no-show.

"Hot pots?" I ask, suppressing my urge to do a James Brown hot tub impression.

"They're hot springs right in the river," Jillian says. "You'll love it."

"But we don't have our suits."

"We don't need them!" Jillian gushes. I guess she's on her fifth drink.

On our way, we pass a small outdoor music festival in downtown Glenwood. Bluegrass songs drift over the herd of hippies stomping around by the stage smoking clove cigarettes (and likely more). "Oh, let's dance!" Jillian says, beginning to shimmy her body to the music while she makes her way toward the band. "I love outdoor music!" Jillian's got a great sense of rhythm. Her moves make me look like a windup monkey with cymbals, which is why I keep my distance from her at weddings.

"Jillian," I say, steering her back toward the sidewalk, "hot pots. Remember?"

She pouts for just a few seconds.

The hot pots turn out to be a pocket of boiling water tucked into the Colorado River and hidden by massive, slippery rocks and weeds. The river itself rushes past, cold and moonlit—rapids more experienced kayakers might salivate over. Steam billows from the springs, and everyone's getting naked but me.

"Come on, Leigh," they chide. So I get naked, too, in record time. The guys become suddenly fascinated by the moon and their feet. We hoist ourselves into the scalding water and turn pink. Sharp rocks dig at the soles of my feet.

"Isn't this gray-it?" Jillian asks, sweating against a wet rock. She's wearing a mustache of perspiration.

"Wonderful. Just don't pass out." I feel vaguely guilty for some reason. Maybe it's being naked with strangers. I feel hairy, out of shape, and undersexed. Plus, I've got a bad aftertaste from the Catholic childhood I mentioned earlier.

Todd shuffles to a corner, and the water around him erupts in hot, malodorous bubbles. "Sorry," he says. We all groan and laugh. As another bottle of wine makes the rounds, Jillian slides over to me. "How are you feeling?" she asks, wiping a few strands of damp hair from her forehead. For a minute she's the old, pre-Geoffrey Jillian: maternal, observant, relaxed. Then I glance at her washboard abs and remember where I am.

"Fine," I say. But I wonder about the effect this kind of heat might have on Larry's kidney. I notice Mark staring at my chest and I cross my arms.

"Would you like a foot massage?" he asks.

"No, thanks," I say. Never let a stoned, horny ski bum nine years your junior massage your feet when you're all naked in a hot pool. Unless you're into that.

Denise begins flirting with Geoffrey and his liver lips while Jillian discusses astrology with Todd. I'm trying not to pass out. Mark sidles up next to me, his pubic hair waving in the current around his baby carrot penis. "So where are you from?" His backne glistens in the moonlight.

Check, please.

Mark asks another eighty questions or so (which I politely answer or skillfully evade) while Geoffrey honks laughter at everything Denise is saying. Jillian shoots them a frigid look, which neither notices. Todd is just hanging out, a mellow hippie who repairs instruments. When he abruptly announces, "Hey, I heard homeless people come here to wash their hair," we decide to get the hell out of the hot springs.

Jillian and Geoffrey argue on the way home. I have a feeling it's about him flirting with Denise, and I feel a little guilty for bringing her. But a tiny flicker of hope flares in me. Maybe I won't have to do anything to convince her how weird, manipulative, and controlling Geoffrey is. Although, truthfully, I haven't really seen his weird side yet. And I was kind of looking forward to that. Denise skips ahead, buoyant and young, linking arms with me and encouraging me to skip, too. I can hear Mark and his baby carrot breathing behind me, so I do.

The fight must be picking up speed, because when we get to the apartment, Jillian and Geoffrey stay in the driveway talking in strained, dangerous voices. Jillian sounds as if she might start crying any second. "Are you okay?" I ask, pulling her aside while Geoffrey stalks around, rubbing his face. Todd, Denise, and Mark tiptoe into the building.

"Fine. I'll be right in."

"Are you sure?"

"Yes," she snaps, eager to return to the argument. I know how she feels. Sometimes you just can't let it drop until you win. It's almost viral, an infection that simply has to run its course.

Inside, Todd and Mark pass around a joint (which I only take a teensy hit of) before we crash. I tell Denise she can have the air mattress in the office. I take the couch, because I want to be here if Jillian needs me. Todd turns out the lights and everyone goes to their rooms. I organize a pillow and sleeping bag on the cushions and try to get comfortable, but there's a creepy wooden mask condemning my soul from its vantage point on the wall. I can't hear any arguing in the driveway, and when I peek through the front window, I see only cars. They must have gone for a walk. *Some visit,* I think. Even when I'm in the same room with Jillian, Geoffrey knows how to take her away.

Several hours later, they're still gone. I lay facing the sofa back so I don't have to stare at all the shadows cast by the fertility goddess and high priest of voodoo statues. I might have dozed off, but it's the kind of light, frustrating sleep that makes you dizzy and crabby. The apartment is dark and still. I have no idea what time it is. I can hear Todd snoring lightly, and . . . something like a footstep. I hold my breath, straining to hear . . . and there's another footstep on the living room carpet.

And another. Then stillness. I'm holding my breath so long I'm starting to see spots. The silence roars in my ears.

One more step. Someone's sneaking up on me. At least that's what it sounds like. Because the footsteps are so quiet, so deliberate, and so evenly timed. A second later, I hear another. I lie there, frozen, staring at the sofa, my heartbeat banging in my ears. I decide to turn over to confront whoever it is after two more steps. Oh God, what if it's Denise with a knife, deciding to murder me and dump my body in a ditch after all?

Okay, just do it. Take a breath and do it. After another step I spin violently around and discover my mystery visitor.

Stoner Ski Bum. He freezes. He's a foot away from me, hovering.

I can't believe this. "What the fuck are you doing?" I ask.

He backs off, startled. "Um—"

"Were you sneaking up on me?"

He stutters a bit. "I was just—"

"You were sneaking up on me! Admit it."

He collapses on the love seat next to me and cups his face in his hands. "Oh God. I just can't deal with temptation."

"What?" It's just light enough for me to see that one of his freshly picked zits is bleeding. Ugh.

"The hot springs. It was just too much."

I scowl. "What were you planning on doing to me? Molest me in my sleep?"

He just stares at his lap. A chill oozes over my skin. What if I'd been asleep? *What if?* Suddenly, I'm incredibly grateful that I'm prone to insomnia and have a decent sense of hearing. I'm wildly thankful that I've stopped drinking. I think of the time my friend Meg woke up on a strange couch after a strange night out to find a strange guy on top of her, trying to be real quiet about raping her.

I grill Stoner Ski Bum. I say, "Do you know how much time you'd have gotten in prison for doing anything to me?" (Even though I don't know.) And "Do you know how much the other inmates would love to sneak up on *you* while you sleep?" I say a bunch of other menacing things. He tells me some long, sordid story about his family, and how he's fucked up his whole life, how he was drunk and stoned, and he's addicted to sex and has poor impulse control, and how his dad left him when he was seven, blibbidy-blabbedy-bloo.

"You better learn some impulse control," I say. "It's a tough world without it." I become this dart-throwing, cannibal-sandwich-eating, no-mercy-for-bullies bitch—a new look for me. I lecture him for what feels like two hours in the early-morning dark. Finally—*finally*—he apologizes for the hundredth time and mopes off to bed to call some 900 numbers and jerk off. I hope the bastard beats off so much he gets a zinc deficiency.

The whole ordeal leaves me feeling clammy and dirty. I consider taking a quick shower, but at that very moment Jillian barges through the front door. "Leigh? Is that you?" Her voice is nasal and hoarse.

"Yeah," I whisper from the couch. "What happened?"

"He's such an asshole," she sobs. She finds her way over to me and sits down. "Can we leave in the morning?" she asks, hugging a pillow to her chest. "I've got to get out of here. I can't stand him." Jillian's voice has a crazy note to it. The same crazy note her voice had when she accidentally cut her bangs to a nosebleed-inducing height the week before her senior picture was to be taken.

I sit up, concerned but (I'd be lying if I didn't admit this) kind of euphoric. "What happened?" I repeat.

"I don't want to talk about it right now." Her voice catches.

"What time is it?" I ask. I am, apparently, unable to speak in anything other than questions.

She flips on a table lamp. Four in the morning. Wow. I rub my eyes. "Yes, of course we can leave in the morning. Where's Geoffrey?"

"He's not coming home." She begins to weep again.

Incredulously, I hear myself say, "Hon, I'm sure you two can patch things up. You're going to get married!"

"Not in this lifetime. *Especially* not in this lifetime!"

The plot thickens. "What do you mean?"

She gives me a hostile stare through her tears. "He cheated on me. With a trainer at his gym."

It was the easiest breakup I never had to do.

We lie on adjacent couches, whispering for another hour. I opt not to tell her about Mark's uninvited middle-of-the-night overtures. And I learn, in bits and pieces, that all was not 100 percent kosher between Jillian and Geoffrey for the past month and a half. Jillian cries some more, and I try to comfort her without actually telling her what a creep I thought Geoffrey really was. Or sounded like, since I exchanged maybe ten sentences with him since arriving. The cardinal rule of comforting a heartbroken friend is never to admit your deep-dark-so-honest-they-sting feelings about her slug of an ex-boyfriend. Because (A) she still has feelings for the guy despite his dirtbaggish behavior, and (B) then you've insulted her judgment. I've known friendships that ended after such well-intended admissions. Besides, what if they get back together? Then you have big stinky egg on your face every time she looks at you. And not sunny side up.

As I say things like "He totally doesn't deserve you" and "Okay. Geoffrey? Is so going to regret this," I feel this weird blend of sympathy and relief, and then guilt for being relieved about the demise of their relationship. But that's what happens when your best friend dates and finally ditches a nutso named Geoffrey with a G who has two ex-wives and an ad campaign involving a crucifixion. We sleep for a few hours. When we wake up, Jillian greets me with "Fuck Geoff and his triathlons. You want some pancakes?"

It makes me want to organize a parade.

I met Jillian at a big 4-H Child Development meeting in sixth grade. (Child Development was a project you could sign up for, and all it really entailed was taking a babysitter certification course and making a "rainy day" activity kit full of markers, yarn, Legos, googly eyes, magnets, and other small choking hazards.) A whole gang of us adolescent girls sat cross-legged in a circle, learning hand gestures for the "Little Bunny Foo Foo" song. I noticed the girl across from me making gestures like Little Bunny Foo Foo was really beating the crap out of the field mouse, which tickled my funny bone. I started making Little Bunny Foo Foo hump the field mouse, which turned out to be a hit with her.

Her name was Jillian Wallace, and she had not only a pool and a spiral perm but six rowdy brothers and sisters, one of whom owned a Ford Mustang and a bootleg Nirvana tape before we even knew who Kurt Cobain was. Another had an expensive, aromatic suede jacket and was on the high school dance squad. They threw crowded, destructive parties when Jillian's parents were out of town, with cassette-tape streamers on the ceiling fans and mattresses thrown from upstairs windows. Just like on TV! They were like gods to me.

I doubt I would have made it through junior high without Jillian. I'm not exaggerating. Puberty is a cruel mistress, and humiliation is her favorite sport. Zits, your first period, growth spurts that leave you resembling an orangutan with rickets, vicious cliques and their random attacks, an emotional vortex of hormones that make you as personally appealing as a moldy fish stick. You could show up to school one day in the wrong shoes and be branded an untouchable for the rest of the year. I still don't know how Jillian and I muddled through it. In high school, we were inseparable. I mean, you know how it goes, right? It's fairly typical best-friend stuff. Making asses of ourselves over guys who would one day be prematurely bald and sell insurance, cruising around in rusty cars with temperamental horns and bumper stickers reading FOXY GRANDMA, passing enough notes back and forth to fill six garbage bags, all-night phone marathons, drinking wine coolers and throwing up together in Bill Hanson's backyard, near the Mary in a Bathtub statue. But somehow it was different because I did it all with Jillian.

When I went to college, she enrolled in massage therapy school. Sure, we visited each other on weekends, and the phone marathons simply grew more expensive, but while I was busy lining up paper in my printer for yet another essay on the transcendentalists, Jillian was busy lining up bodies to log some hands-on massage hours for her license. I always knew she wanted to do something that would set her apart, and eventually to leave Wisconsin entirely, but part of me denied the day would ever come. She was my adopted family. The sister I never had. Dubbed "partners in crime" and "attached at the hip" by more than one junior- and senior-high teacher—how would I function without her? This is not a rhetorical question. After Jillian met Meg Phillips in a LaStone therapy class, they decided to move together to Aspen, Colorado, for a financial "happy ending." Before they left we formed a motley trio and adhered to a regular schedule of inclusive activities like hiking and shopping, but I couldn't help but feel that I'd just lost a national election in a tight race.

Meg's great, if you like living in the shadow of the karmically blessed and metabolically gifted. With her airy yet defined curls, childlike, obsidian eyes, and all-around fragile aura, it's a wonder I was never trampled by the mobs of men rushing to buy her drinks or throw themselves over mud puddles in her path. Meg looks like the kind of person that wouldn't make a trip to the mailbox without full makeup and designer yoga duds (if the servants didn't bring her local advertising circulars and credit card offers inside for her). But that would be a wrong assumption. She's always had an effortless style and beauty, and her easy kindness eventually hobbles and assimilates even the cattiest of girls. But I know her weak spots, which together keep her human. For example, dairy gives her incredible gas. I love her for this. Plus she laughs at my jokes, especially if they juxtapose drug paraphernalia with religion. I suppose in some circles, mostly James's, this would also be a weak spot. Also, Meg talked her husband into naming their golden retriever puppy Helen Roper, mostly because it cracked me up. You just can't be bitter with someone who names their dog after an extravagant, sex-crazed secondary character in a modestly popular seventies sitcom.

After unwittingly ruining about twenty-four men for all other women (including Wes), she eventually married the scion of a shipping dynasty. Yes, that's right. A scion. Heir would be too working-class. I guess you can meet them right on the ski slopes, because that's where she met hers. Meg and her scion had a son just eight weeks ago, but she's cleared her calendar to see me while I'm in town. So not only do I have to contend with the fact that I look like Andy Dick's strung-out kid sister in her presence—she's also gracious and thoughtful as hell.

After a quiet breakfast of blueberry pancakes, real maple syrup, and fresh apricots, Jillian begins to pack a bag the size of a mobile home. Denise approaches me, worried. "I thought we were staying another night!" I shrug and tell her there's been a change in schedule. She watches Jillian pack and whispers to me, "Are we going to have room for all of this stuff?" We try to cram Jillian's bag into my trunk, but there's simply not enough room. She drags out my metal detector.

"What's this?"

"It's a metal detector," I say. I brace myself for the impending blizzard of ridicule. But she's too distraught by Geoffrey's philandering to make fun of me.

"Can we leave it here? My bag won't fit." I force myself to do a breathing exercise. *In for three—hold for four—out for seven.*

"Do you have any smaller bags?" I ask as gently as possible.

"I don't have any smaller bags," Jillian snips, tired and tearweary. "This is it."

There's no getting around it, so we stow my metal detector in with the extreme sports equipment. I believe the proper adjective for my mood is *crestfallen.* That it starts to drizzle moments later is only fitting. Road trip from hell, two; my new recreational activity equipment, zero.

After we get in the car, Jillian hangs a traveler's medicine wheel on my rearview mirror and places a clear pyramid statue on the dash. I'm disappointed that I can't make fun of her for doing so, given the circumstances. But Denise pipes up. "What's that stuff for?"

Jillian clears her throat and smooths the chunk of horsehair hanging from the medicine wheel. "Safety, clarity, and guidance on our travels." I shoot Denise an intense look in the mirror, hoping she understands that she is not to laugh at this, no matter how difficult the suppression. Luckily, she catches my eye and seems to understand.

No one talks during the ride to Aspen except to say, "Do you have enough room back there?" (me) and "Yes" (Denise). Denise curls up in the backseat and leaves her signs on the floor, instead immersing herself in a waterproof book dubiously titled *Aqua Erotica*. Jillian sits in the front seat, eyes closed, pretending to sleep. The horsehair from her medicine wheel brushes my forearm twice during the ride, and I discreetly blow it away from me. She wakes up long enough to mumble directions. We're meeting Meg at Explore Booksellers and Bistro, but we're early. We park and decide to investigate the shops first.

Chanel, Gucci, Fendi, and Louis Vuitton are way out of our league, so we go to Mhendi and check out the circa 1976 bell-bottoms and leisure suits. I truly wish we had a disco party to which we could wear some of these duds. Nobody has seventies theme parties anymore. Not since VH1's *I Love the 90s*. Denise does the running man in an Afro wig to Diana Ross's "Upside Down," which would have totally cracked me up if not for the depressive pall of Jillian's mood. I keep a close eye on Denise in case her kleptomania again rears its ugly, pimple-studded head.

Jillian, not surprisingly, steers us into a New Age bookstore. "I need to buy a new pendant," she explains. "I lost my last one." Denise wanders around examining books about aliens and Indian gurus. I point out an array of crystal pendants hanging from a display in the corner. Jillian selects one and holds it above the entire rack. I can hear her whisper, "Am I clear? Should I buy a new pendant today?" The pendant begins to swing back and forth. Rather, her right hand swings the pendant back and forth.

Lordy, lordy, lordy. I scan the shop for Denise, and thankfully she's obsessively sniffing every votive candle on a wall shelf. I'm used to Jillian's pendants and crystals, so I can only smile and shake my head. Once during a phone conversation about whether or not I should quit Fuzzy Navels, I could hear her doing the pendant thing in the background to determine my decision. That day, the pendant indicated I should stay put.

Today, Jillian looks up at me and sighs. "I'm not supposed to buy a new pendant today."

You just have to love her for that.

Damp from a rain-spattered jog, we're early at the Explore Bistro, which is tucked cozily above a first-floor bookstore. Jillian jiggles her knee like she's on speed, vibrating her menu and shaking the table. Occasionally she shoots a look at Denise that could kill a sparrow in flight. I can hardly contain myself at thoughts of the pleasant trip that lies ahead. To distract myself, I furtively stare at a fit, attractive young couple seated behind Denise. They're wearing complementary outfits: fitted T-shirts, sandals, expensive-looking khaki bottoms (shorts for him, a skirt for her). You can tell they're in the early stages of their relationship, because they keep caressing each other's hands and giggling. (Or am I just cynical?) How lucky they are! A fog of loneliness rolls over me while I watch their giddy whispers. I want to throw the saltshaker at their heads and shout, *Quit being so happy! Can't you see there are heartbroken people over here?*

Just as the tension threatens to suffocate all of us and I'm growing increasingly despondent over the happy couple, Meg breezes in, dispersing the storm clouds. It's true. It actually stops raining. I stand for one of Meg's amazing-smelling hugs. "You look wonderful," I say wistfully. Clad in a pink cashmere sleeveless top, silk capris, ballerina flats, and freshwater pearl earrings, she shows no visible signs of having given birth (and shiting on the delivery table) just two months ago. She smells like lavender, not spit-up or dirty diapers. "Where's Ian?"

"Oh, I'm sorry," she coos. "He's with my in-laws for a few days. I wanted to spend as much time as possible with you guys. Plus, his grandma and grandpa want to spoil him rotten while the nanny's on holiday." *Nanny? On holiday?* I feel the chasm between Meg and myself widen. I will never marry a scion or employ a holiday-taking nanny to potty-train and give crustless sandwiches to my children. Because I will not have children, unless I adopt. I have a 50 percent chance of passing PKD on to my children, and I just can't take that risk.

I don't conceal my disappointment. "Aw, Meg, I wanted to meet him!"

She sighs. "I know, but he's just such a handful. And honestly, I just needed some girl time away!" I try not to frown. I hate when people say they need "girl time." It sounds minimizing to me. I hear Denise clear her throat next to me. "Oh! Meg, this is Denise. Denise, my friend Meg."

Only Meg's raised eyebrows betray her surprise at my traveling companion. "It's wonderful to meet you, Denise," she says. Denise simply gives her a weird grin that I can't interpret. Jillian gets up to hug Meg and starts to cry again.

Over edamame, bowls of steaming wild mushroom bisque, and hummus with pita wedges, Jillian brings Meg up to speed on Geoffrey with a G's errant ways. Meg is sympathetic, but I sense a hint of relief in her sympathy. "I know just what will cheer you up," she says. "We're going to a day spa, and then to a party. And you can't say no, because it's on me." We protest (some more enthusiastically than others), but Meg says, "I won't take no for an answer." I love it when my richest and most generous friends say things like that. Though there's something slightly off about Meg. Brittle, almost, and she seems to be flinching more than necessary at loud noises. But then I'm distracted by a postlunch Goldie Hawn sighting, and we shift to wasting time (time we will likely want back at the end of our lives) constructing a filmography for Goldie. All we can come up with is *First Wives Club* and *Private Benjamin*.

Several hours later, after being pummeled, kneaded, and pampered into a blissful stupor, we're in one of Meg's five palatial bathrooms dabbing blush and gloss on our faces. It makes me think of another of Gram's cherished catchphrases: "Like sprinkling sugar on a turd!" Which is harsh and untrue, I suppose, but fun to say nonetheless. I smile and bare my teeth in the mirror to check for lipstick smudges. Skylights in the ceiling give us natural light to work with, and we're surrounded by oxygen-expiring plants and a flattering rose hue on the walls. If my hair doesn't turn out in this environment, I may as well toss my "product" and shave my head.

We preen ourselves to within an inch of our lives and pile into her Land Rover. "I heard Kate Hudson might be at the party," she says, like a mother announcing a guest appearance at children's story hour by Harry Potter himself. I'm still a bit disappointed to miss meeting her son, Ian, and if not for the Pooh-themed nursery (replete with random baskets full of antique rabbits and teddy bears that have movable joints and stitched noses) and cans of Similac formula stacked near the Sub-Zero built-in refrigerator, I'd wonder if he existed only in Meg's imagination. It's the same story with Meg's husband, Brandon. Out of town on business, she said. If not for the framed photos on the walls . . .

"So whose party is this?" I ask, smoothing my slacks. Somewhere between Meg's tar paper shack and her beater of a car, I have managed to develop a brown stain on my pants in the shape of a school bus. Jillian and I climb into the backseat and Denise hops in the front next to Meg.

"One of Brandon's business partners. He's from Kuwait. He's pretty dull, but he knows all the right people," Meg says, smiling at me in the rearview mirror. I feel the gulf between us stretch. Jillian stares listlessly out the window at the mountains. She's called Geoffrey about six times since we left, hanging up on his voice mail every time. I squeeze her hand and make my fingers do the Little Bunny Foo Foo dance. Jillian gives me a pitiful smile that could break Martha Stewart's heart. I glance at Denise, who looks as if she's about to either make a sign or steal something. "So tell me. How did you two meet?" Meg asks, meaning me and Denise, even though I know Jillian already told her the whole sordid story. This irritates me.

"At an hors d'oeuvres table at a bar mitzvah," I say cheerfully. "We both went for the last spring roll and ended up almost brawling. It was the funniest thing." Denise snorts and leans out the window to take a picture of a snowcapped mountain. Jillian rolls her eyes.

I know we're in for it when we're greeted by two uniformed attendants at the gates of a winding hidden driveway. They consult a list, check Meg's name, and wave us on. "Dude, it's, like, a fucking *castle*," Denise whispers to me, jaw agape. I lean over her shoulder to see what she's gawking at, and there it is—Brandon's dull business partner's home game of the Hotel Colorado. For another point of reference, think: desolate, hauntingly elegant hotel in *The Shining*, minus the ax murdering and seventies décor. Backlit fountains throw sprays of what can only be pure springwater into the air. Tan thin people glide across the landscaped grounds and mill around stone balconies wearing white, red, and black couture and enough bling to back a terrorist group for life. "Let's go find Jeeves and get a drink," Denise says.

I'm clearly in the wrong tax bracket to be attending this little soirée. The guests at this party make even the relatively well-heeled Fuzzy Navels clientele look like ragpickers in a Dickens novel. But hey, Larry wanted to see how the other half lives. Inside, Meg wanders off to air-kiss people who presumably also employ nannies and gardeners while we pluck flutes of champagne from a roving tray and try not to guess how much everything in the house costs. Don't worry, I'm not going to drink mine. It's just for show, something to wave around while I talk, because that's what you do at parties thrown by lackluster business partners who know all the right people. Denise, drawn to the insolent smirk of one of the bartenders, leans over the portable bar to flirt with him while he mixes drinks. I spot a bored-looking thirtyish man standing alone near a wall of leather-bound books and size him up. Clean, attractive, probably doesn't live with his mother. No wedding ring on his left hand. Good signs, all. I drag Jillian with me. "Anything worth reading on those shelves?" I ask.

He spins around on a heel to see who dared interrupt his private thoughts. "It's hard to tell. But I doubt any of those books have ever been read." No snaggleteeth, foul breath, or obvious speech impediment. More good signs. I confirm, in rapid succession, that he is childless, unmarried, and gainfully employed. Jillian shifts her weight and darts her eyes around the room, already searching for an escape route. *How to keep her here? Think, Leigh. Think.*

I suddenly blurt, "Ever been to an ashram?"

He looks at me like I've asked him to describe his latest bowel movement in excruciating detail. "Um, no." But he turns to Jillian, amused. "Have you?"

And we're off. Thank you, ladies and gentlemen, don't forget to tip your waitress. I back away carefully, pleased with my meddling. How does the saying go? "The best way to get over one guy is to get under another"? Well, actually, I don't necessarily want Jillian to dive right into another emotional disaster, or even have sex with this guy, but I figure she could use a little flattery and engaging conversation with a cute man. Hey, it beats moping in a corner the whole evening. And staying home with a box of tissues, a bag of Terra Chips, and a DVD of *The Way We Were* is out of the question, under the circumstances.

I load a plate with delicious cheeses and crackers that crossed the Atlantic to reach me. I find a comfortable vintage chair and settle in for a nice session of people-watching. Denise is flirting with a bartender, Jillian is flirting with a scion, Meg is flirting with the Aspen Country Day School parent group, and I am flirting with the finest fromage blanc I've ever seen. All is right with the world.

The next thing I know, Jillian is towering over me, her shadow eclipsing my Gouda and Gruyère. I look up. She glowers down. I gulp. "Thanks a lot for introducing me to Mr. Charisma over there. He asked me to suck his dick in the bathroom."

Yikes. That's exactly what I thought—*yikes*. "Oh my God. I'm so sorry. He really said that?"

"Well, it was implied." She rolls her eyes. "Leigh, I wanted to talk with *you*, not some stockbroker on vacation."

"I'm sorry?" It comes out like a question because I'm too startled to commit to a statement. My face heats up like a rash.

"I would never do that to you! Just ditch you with some strange guy and skip off. How many times do we get to see one another all year?"

I notice a vein throbbing in her forehead. Her fury is stunning and, I suspect, somewhat residual from her fight with Geoffrey. I haven't felt this kind of wrath since I backed over an office laptop with the Fuzzy Navels doggy taxi. "I'm really sorry. I didn't mean—"

"God, what's *with* you lately? It's like I don't even know you any-more."

"I could say the same thing," I mumble under my breath.

"What?" she demands.

"Nothing."

"You're so high on life, you wouldn't notice a speeding truck headed right at you. This isn't a movie, Leigh. It's real life, with re-sponsibilities! And consequences!" She leans in and adds, "And I can't *believe* you picked up that *girl*." I hang my head, my delicious cheeses souring into a lamentable aftertaste. I guess I was too drunk on the possibilities of the evening, too giddy from my prox-imity to Louis Vuitton, to think of anything but having fun. I didn't even pause to consider the true feelings of my freshly heartbroken best friend. I feel like a jerk.

Then I get pissed. Really pissed. Miss Crystal Tarot Card here is a fine one to lecture me on real life. Miss Hypochondriac, calling me once a month for reassurance that she doesn't have cervical cancer or Bell's palsy or scurvy. She has no idea what it means to be sick. No idea! "Well, why can't I be high on life?" I ask, letting the rage build. "While you were off prancing around the Aspen Com-edy Festival and dating ski instructors, I was hooked up to a dialy-sis machine. Week. After week. *After week.* So I didn't *die*! I can't get high on anything of substance, so why not let me be high on life and make bad choices and screw up a few times? Everyone else does it!" I think about adding, in a last dig, that thank God I did pick up Denise, because I'm closer to her these days than I am to Jillian, but thankfully I don't.

Finally it hits me. I wasn't angry about Jillian and Geoffrey. That wasn't it at all. I was angry with Jillian for leaving me six years ago. Right after I got sick. I think I'm also angry about James always chasing after my little light with the candlesnuffer. And suddenly, I'm furious and sad that I've never been to Europe or been truly loved by *anyone*, not even someone my friends hated, someone who tried to turn me into something I wasn't.

I thought I was over this.

Jillian's eyes shine bright with tears and she says, "I can't deal with this right now." She stumbles off through the glowing crowd, leaving me to feel like a jerk. An honest jerk, but still . . . a jerk. I slink off to the nearest bathroom and run smack into Meg. She still smells fantastic. She links arms with me and asks, "Where are you headed?"

"The bathroom. I tried setting Jillian up with some creepy guy, and we got in an argument, and she just took off," I confess. I'm surprised by the sudden constriction in my throat. Am I going to cry? I try to take a deep breath, but my lungs feel like boulders.

Meg leads me to a bathroom through a pink-and-gold outer sitting room lined with mirrors. Women leer into them, searching for flaws and retouching makeup. Once inside the private bathroom, Meg locks the door behind us, leans against the marble countertop, and gives me a tiny, hopeful smile. "You two will patch things up. You always do."

I sigh heavily, my throat still tight with emotion. "I don't know what's wrong with me. Jillian's right. I don't feel like myself anymore. I don't know who I am. I never imagined my life being like this." I bury my face in my hands. "I feel like—I feel like—oh, I don't know what I even feel like." *Do not even* think *about dying. Do not.*

"Sweetie, we all go through the same thing," Meg says in a soothing voice. She hands me a tissue and I blot my eyes, which have indeed grown misty against my will.

I sniff. "Oh, right. I forgot you're also a socially maladjusted orphan with kidney disease."

She shakes her head, smiling gently. "Come on." She washes her hands and dries them on a monogrammed towel. She turns to face me and says, "I haven't told anyone this. Anyone but my family. And Brandon knows, of course. But right after I had Ian I got really depressed. I didn't even want to see him. I was afraid to be alone with him, because I seriously saw . . . I seriously saw images of myself holding a pillow over his face." Her voice drops and she gazes at the floor. "Or worse."

Just as I form a mental image of what "or worse" could mean, she looks up. "Anyway, my doctor was a real help. He told me to just lock up all the knives." She laughs bitterly. "Can you believe that? Some bedside manner. 'Sorry to hear about your suicidal and homicidal tendencies, ma'am. Just hide the steak knives and this whole thing should blow right over.' " She tilts her head to the side, staring off into space. I am rooted to the floor. I don't breathe. "Brandon took me to another doctor the day after our gardener found me passed out in the car in the garage. I'd left the engine running."

"Oh my God, Meg," I say. My beautiful friend. My perfect friend. The gardener found her? I think of Ian's Pooh-themed room and my throat swells shut.

"I'm on some pretty strong antidepressants now. And I've got a good therapist."

I step across the great divide and embrace her. Meg has just confessed a recent urge to erase herself from the planet. I've already seen the brink and involuntarily stared over its edge, with no desire whatsoever to return. But to go there voluntarily? Jesus, Meg. I can't understand it, but I try. I stare at a monogrammed towel, hanging askew on the rack behind Meg's back, and think of how badly Meg always wanted to be a mother. It's been her primary topic of conversation for as long as I've known her. And when she finally becomes a mother, her hormones pull the rug out from under her. We hug and listen to the quiet sound of friendship within the room. Outside, two women laugh like big cartwheels across a lawn, and a tiny idea flares to life within me. Maybe my mother had postpartum depression. Maybe it was the world's longest episode, and the only way she couldn't hurt me was to leave.

Sure. And maybe I'd metal-detect my way right into Cillian Murphy's heart.

CHAPTER SEVEN

Utah! Travel and Adventure

Every family has tragedies, and I know my mother leaving us hardly registers on the misery index when compared to what other people have gone through. I knew a woman whose first boyfriend was murdered while he slept in his own bed. Later that same year, her father died of colon cancer and her brother was diagnosed with lymphoma. I had a friend in high school whose mother and fifteen-year-old sister drove head-on into a garbage truck. Her mother survived the accident. Her sister didn't. A year later the mother jumped from the roof of our town's parking ramp. When you really think of all the opportunities for things to go awry, for despair to vault unannounced into our lives, what choice do we have but to self-medicate with booze, drugs, sex, food, gossip, shopping, gambling, psychic hotlines, religion, spa treatments, collectible plates, grudges, karaoke, and bad sitcoms? It's mind-boggling, really.

My real family tragedy is that almost a year to the date after Mom left, my father shot himself during a solitary camping trip. He left no note. At first they told me it was a hunting accident, but I figured it out a few weeks later. Kids are pretty smart.

Because I was only six when he died, my memories of him are like a watercolor painting left out in the rain. I remember his scratchy mustache and slow, sad brown eyes. He bought bottles of Löwenbräu by the case and always drank one on the ride home from the liquor store while I sat next to him and poured Lemon-heads right from the box into my mouth. He didn't get up and go to work like the fathers on TV did, coffee in one hand, briefcase and newspaper in the other. My dad didn't seem to have much of a job at all. He told us he was a writer, but from what I could see, he just sat in his book-cluttered office drinking wine and listening to *The Last Waltz* over and over with his eyes closed.

He taught me to ride a bike when I was five, running alongside me with his hands steering the handlebars next to mine, saying, "Just keep pedaling. . . . Keep your eyes focused straight ahead!" Like this was also some kind of mawkish advice for the way I should live my life after he let go of the handlebars. Gram told me that he used to have lots of girlfriends in high school. And he had to pick my mom, Ms. Aspiring Actress.

He took me to see *The Karate Kid, Part II* at the Retlaw Theater the week he died. We shared a box of Junior Mints I picked out at the Caramel Crisp Shop down the street. On the way home we sang "Yellow Submarine" and he retold me the story of my birth. How there had been a raging ice storm that knocked out power lines all over Fond du Lac County, and he and Mom almost didn't make it to the hospital. The trees were glazed with ice for three days afterward. Gram took lots of pictures of me sleeping in my pink baby cap and the gleaming, crackling trees on the same roll. My story wasn't funny like James's story, how he came out peeing and the doctor said, "It's the fountain of youth!" But hearing it still made me feel cozy and loved. I remember this night so vividly be-cause it was the first time Dad had been out of bed in clean cloth-ing in months.

So naturally, I figured things were getting better.

The only belonging of his that I still have is a tiny silver tie tack shaped like a four-leaf clover, which I found on the top shelf

of my parents' closet the morning our old house was sold. Seeing that tiny tie tack, looking like a forgotten birthday at the back
of his empty, dusty closet, did something to my heart that made
it hard to take a deep breath for weeks. At the luncheon after
his funeral, Lucky barked endlessly and people parked on Gram's
lawn, leaving ruts. They clomped through her petunias in sad
outfits and hustled Gram into another room when she started
wailing. I watched everyone carrying casseroles into the house
from an upstairs window and read 365 *Bedtime Stories* cover to
cover. My mother, not surprisingly, stayed in California. I found
out a few years later that she signed us over to Gram shortly thereafter.

I remember having headaches for weeks afterward. I couldn't
sleep with the lights off. I became obsessed with time travel, attempting to build a time machine from Gram's card table, some
blankets, and her blender so I could go back to save him. Was Dad
mad at me? I kept asking James and Gram. No, they said, he was
just very sad. Did I make him sad? No, they told me. I became terrified of feeling sad, and of sad people, thinking they were just moments away from death.

Dad's mother, our Gram, took us in after he died. I thank her
daily for being one of the reasons I didn't end up in a juvenile de-
tention center or wrapped around a pole at Beansnappers. Before
she died of ovarian cancer sixteen years ago, she raised pygmy goats
and grew organic heirloom vegetables (and marijuana, though I
wasn't supposed to know that), eventually becoming the sole veg-
etable supplier for three local restaurants. She'd met Jane Goodall
and Annie Proulx. She had a boyfriend who owned a vacation home
in Alaska and his own herd of elk. She left me enough money to be
diagnosed with kidney disease and not hit my own casket shortly
thereafter.

Gram's sort of the reason I met Wes. She and Wes's mom belonged to the same book club, and the two of them would get together once a month to drink Bloody Marys and gossip about
everyone else in the book club, tossing Wes and me into a room and

hoping we wouldn't set any fires or bite each other hard enough to break the skin. We usually ended up making prank calls and paging through the porno magazines Wes had brought in his backpack. On hot summer nights we'd spend hours spitting into the bug zapper while we were supposed to be roasting marshmallows. Once I tried making him kiss me, and I ended up almost losing a tooth. He didn't punch me, just bashed his lips into my own so hard tears sprang to my eyes. "How was that?" he asked, grinning.

"Great," I said as the room grew blurry. My front tooth wobbled in its socket. So you can see why Wes and I never became romantically linked as adults.

This is how we build a family. When I met Jillian, I adopted her boisterous family. And thankfully, they adopted me—although out of true affection, pity, or morbid fascination, I'll never know. I dove into books, finishing almost one hundred in a single summer. I raised a litter of kittens orphaned in Gram's barn, bottle-feeding them and wiping their tiny backsides with damp tissues to help them defecate. They followed me around like I was their mother, eventually crawling behind the refrigerator or under the stove to die of distemper.

As I got older, I stumbled a bit. I was absent from school so much I had to resort to drinking ipecac syrup for real physical evidence of illness after Gram began to doubt my excuses. I just found it so hard to concentrate. What was the point of learning cursive or how mummies were embalmed? My parents were gone. One was dead, and the other was in California and might as well have been dead. For the rest of my life, I would only buy the Father's Day and Mother's Day cards for extended relatives. Each time they sent me home from school with an invitation for my parents to join the PTO, I took it as a personal insult. Once, when a telemarketer asked me if my mother was home, I told her no, she'd left us three years ago and then my father killed himself, so he couldn't come to the phone, either. We talked for forty-five minutes and she sent me a Christmas card that year. I made up fabulous stories in my head of how Yoko Ono wanted to adopt me and raise me with Sean, and

he and I would incestuously make out in his bedroom while watching *The Cosby Show*.

But after awhile, the fact that James and I were basically or-
phans faded into nondescript Muzak humming in the background
while life bustled on. After awhile, you don't even notice it's there.
I fell in love with the wild horses of Chincoteague Island and accepted a small cactus from Tommy Bartell as a token of his affection. My epileptic friend Amanda and I composed love letters to
Michael Jackson, Jon Bon Jovi, and that goofy-ass kid Mackenzie
Astin, who showed up on *The Facts of Life* in season six. I learned
to roller-skate backward in the dark and never missed an episode of
Mr. Belvedere. I realized that I wasn't the only kid in my class with
estranged, divorced, or deceased parents. And if those kids could
learn cursive and how to tie their shoes in a double knot, I guess I
could, too. Just keep pedaling. Keep your eyes focused straight
ahead.

"So where are we going?"

I shrug. My right calf aches from flooring the accelerator to
make it up steep incline after steep incline. "Want to go to Moab?"

Denise lights up. "Hell yeah!" She consults our map. "Should
we visit Canyonlands or Arches National Park?"

Jillian rips a hangnail from her index finger and says, "Why
don't we ask Larry?"

The land here is dusty and rocky beyond the irrigated green
fruit oases near Palisade. (Come for the peaches, stay for the . . .
peaches!) The interstate follows the meandering path of the Colorado River—wide and brown and lined with thirsty vegetation.
The sight of it makes me mourn the loss of my kayak. I can check
the snowcapped Rocky Mountains off the list of potential hazards
to my little four-cylinder car, but the dry western plateaus, past
Glenwood Canyon and the growing city of Rifle, are no Twinkies
for my engine, either. I kissed my good gas mileage good-bye the
minute the elevation started to rise.

Reddish-brown mesas and rugged cliffs sprawl in all directions, prickly with sage and drought-stunted, gnarled pine shrubs. Mesquite, maybe? I count the prairie dog towns as we drive past, their dirt mounds the size of anthills from the car. There was a wildfire burning on a ridge back near Parachute, and the interior of my car still smells of smoke. Mesquite smoke. I smell like a barbecued rack of ribs. This kind of makes me hungry.

"What do people do out here? For, like, fun, I mean." Denise is annoyed by the apparent lack of entertainment in the landscape.

The air dries my eyes out and I remind myself to treat them with Visine later. "They drink lots of water and put drops in their eyes," I answer. We pass a tube of sunscreen around, rubbing the lotion into our arms and on the backs of our necks. I'm developing some nice color on my left arm, despite the closed window. Who says you can't tan through glass? "I'm getting a trucker's tan," I announce brightly. Nobody comments on my mismatched forearms.

Jillian and I have made a tenuous peace, although another argument could flare at any moment. Denise's mood buoys us along. She plays the drums on her lap to a Wilco song and tries to engage us in a game of Auto Bingo. "I noticed you're a big Wilco fan," she says.

"You picked up on that, huh?" I say, smiling as I catch her eye in the rearview mirror.

"Lots of people your age tend to like them," she says philosophically.

"Don't stereotype," I warn. "You're seventeen, yet you like Hall and Oates."

"Yeah, but you're almost thirty and you like Wilco. So, you prove my point."

"I like lots of other bands."

"Like who?"

I am suddenly unable to think of a single band I like, other than Wilco. "Radiohead!" I blurt.

"I thought so. I bet you like Coldplay, too."

"What's wrong with those bands?"

Denise simply lifts one eyebrow in response.

"Well, I guess I'm just not as cool as you." I fish some lip balm from my pocket and apply it to my chapped lips.

"Not many people are," Denise sighs. I catch Jillian cracking a tiny smile.

We do the rhyming word game again, to juvenile words like *gas* and *stink*. We pass through Grand Junction and play interstate leapfrog with a middle-aged cowboy in a pickup truck, who mistakes Jillian's hand—raised to shield her eyes from the sun—for a wave. He drives past, grinning and waving vigorously. "Oh my God, he thinks I'm waving at him," she shrieks. We shriek along. Denise is right: Interactive driving *is* more fun!

I floor the accelerator to pass him, but he speeds up, waving again. We shriek laughter some more. After one more round of passing, he presses three tickets against the glass.

Jillian squeals. "They say 'Jam' something. Oh my God, he's inviting us to Country Jam!"

"*This* is what people do out here, Denise," I say with authority. "They invite strangers to country music festivals."

We laugh when, minutes later, we pass an exit marked for that very country music festival. Our pickup driver turns off with a final wave. At this point, I catch something in the rearview mirror that makes my stomach cold. "The black car's back," I deadpan. A few vehicles back, and I can't be sure, but my gut tells me it's the same black Acura with the tinted windows that I've been seeing everywhere.

Denise jerks around. "Shit."

Jillian just looks at me, alarmed. "What? What black car?"

"There's a black car that's been following us," I say casually, hoping to shock her with my indifference in the face of potential danger. "We've seen it about . . . four times now? Five? But I'm sure it's nothing." There are thousands of black cars on the road, and thousands of black Acuras. I really don't believe we're being followed, do I?

Denise squints and says, "It's probably not the same car. Like, what are the odds, anyway?"

"Shut up," Jillian says, but her voice is eager for the juicy details. She cranes her neck and spots the car. "I can't really see who's driving."

"Maybe it's the ghost of Ted Bundy. Jillian, you're the only one with long dark hair. We're off the hook, Denise."

I expect Denise to laugh, but all I get is a wan smile. Then I remember that the Acura in the Mount Rushmore parking lot had California plates. And the car slowly crunching over gravel in the parking lot at the Motel 6 . . . I don't have the world's best memory, but I'd bet my medication it was the same car. "What kind of plates does it have?"

Jillian shades her eyes and peers back. "I can't tell."

"Does the driver look like Kurt Russell?"

Denise scowls. "What does Kurt Russell have to do with anything?"

I raise my eyebrows to mock her. "What, you weren't cool enough to see *Death Proof*?" It's an arcane Tarantino reference, and I can tell by her reaction that she didn't get it. I love being juvenile sometimes.

"I was too cool to see it."

I squint in the rearview mirror. "Uh-oh, I think I saw the driver wave at us."

"You guys, cut it out," Jillian shouts. By now we've got the willies like fourth graders watching *The Exorcist* at a slumber party, so I zip in front of a semi, skirt a few slower cars towing U-Haul trailers, and zoom off the interstate at the next exit. We crane our necks and watch the black Acura cruise past; the driver doesn't seem to notice our exit, and our anxiety begins to subside when we stop at a gas station to use the restroom, refuel, and stretch. We chuckle at our spooked-out selves, but part of me still feels jumpy and rabbitlike.

Back on the endless freeway, there are no black cars in sight, and relief becomes a welcome passenger in the car. I take the opportunity to tease Jillian to lighten the mood. She's eating almonds from a canister. I reach in for a handful and give her an evil grin. "I barely washed my hands in the last bathroom. And I've been touching the nuts." The former is a lie, but the latter is true.

"Whose nuts?" Denise asks from the backseat.

"Knock it off!" Jillian laughs despite herself.

I kick back and smirk. "Just think. You're eating microscopic bits of something I've already eaten."

Jillian groans, but she's still laughing. "I'm throwing these away now!"

I pop three almonds into my mouth and chew. "Mmmm. Delicious, nutty fecal bacteria."

"That," Denise begins, "is so incredibly gross."

Near the Utah border, traffic almost disappears. We seem to be sharing the vast interstate system with only semitrucks, all of us desperately chugging up the arid, rocky inclines and coasting down the other sides. "My God, this is a long drive," Denise mumbles.

"And we still have two states to go!" I answer cheerfully.

We take the more scenic Highway 128 to Arches National Park. And it's really beautiful, with striated sunset-colored cliffs shading the looping highway, which has been carved from the gorges below. Not an animatronic cowboy orchestra in sight! Larry picked a winner. At the park's entrance we flash our pass and pick up another road map of the local highlights. But first, we pull over to stretch our legs and take in the red and rocky Martian landscape surrounding us. Later, Denise takes pictures of us posing in front of the Delicate Arch, Balance Rock, the Double O Arch, Skyline Arch, and the Windows red rock formations. I'm sweating profusely, and so are the six thousand fanny-packing tourists around me also posing for pictures. "Who are you, Ansel Adams?" I shout.

"Take your sunglasses off and do a funny pose!" Denise replies. Everywhere we look, people are hiking in expensive boots or taking thirst-quenching swigs from plastic water bottles. Jillian doesn't say much. I can tell she's reminiscing about hiking, rock climbing, and biking with Geoffrey. Or maybe she has sunstroke. After yet another posed photo, we watch Denise compare cameras with a

group of Japanese tourists. "She's weird," hisses Jillian. Easy for her
to say. Her dad locked himself in the car to escape his shrieking
brood when they got too crazy to bear. My dad's idea of getting away
from it all involved a loaded shotgun. I was one Gram and one
James away from *being* Denise. It was that close.

We decide to camp in a cheesy rat-hole RV park just outside of
Arches because it's cheap and has shower facilities. Jillian reads a
paperback titled *Autobiography of a Yogi* after we pitch our pocket-
sized tent. We drive into Moab for dinner as a hot wind begins to
blow dust through the decrepit trees clinging desperately to life
amid the RV parking pads.

Moab is the kind of town white-water-rafting guides call home,
defined by red cliffs and souvenir shops with log cabin beams and
CD players oozing Native American flute instrumentals. Cute guys
tool around with mountain bikes attached to the roofs of their
Jeeps. I fight the urge to join the parade and drive up and down the
main drag with a borrowed kayak on my car. *My poor kayak.*

The three of us order various pastas at an Italian restaurant
called Pasta Jay's. I try the gnocchi with red sauce and a lemonade.
Jillian orders ravioli and a glass of pinot noir. Denise picks mani-
cotti and water. There are too many uncomfortable silences.
Denise sucks through her straw at the ice cubes in her empty water
glass, making grating slurpy sounds.

Jillian glares at her. "Must you do that?"

"Excuse me," Denise says archly. I wistfully flip through the
wine list, the way you would a photo album of old, dear friends that
all perished in a plane crash. Jillian and Denise stare at the traffic
crawling down Main Street. So many Jeeps, so little time. So much
tension it's making me rhyme.

Suddenly Jillian drawls, "Denise. Tell me again. How does a
seventeen-year-old girl end up alone at a rest area?"

I listen as Denise repeats her Slick Rick story verbatim.

"Wow, that's quite an ordeal. You're lucky nothing terrible happened to you." Jillian's using her bitchy sarcastic voice.

"Yes, I am," Denise says, in the same tone.

"I just don't get it. Why didn't you call anyone? I'm sure there was someone you could call."

"In your perfect little suburban world, yes, there would have been someone to call. In mine, there wasn't."

"Who wants another bread stick?" I ask in my jovial, Ralph Bunche peacekeeping voice. I get a terrible image in my mind of them throttling each other over a plate of ravioli, spilling drinks, knocking over a candle and setting Pasta Jay's on fire. I imagine Denise sneaking up on Jillian in the night to smother her with a pillow. I imagine Jillian putting drops of Amazon tree frog venom in Denise's water. I can see them in orange jumpsuits, hands and feet shackled, riding a bus to the women's prison and straining to spit at each other over the seats.

A small boy in tight Spider-Man pajamas runs to our table and aims a blue plastic gun at me. "Pew-pew-pew, you're dead."

"Aaaargh! You got me!" I slump over in my chair while he proceeds to shoot up our whole table. After he skips off I steer the conversation to Geoffrey, because my two traveling partners have something in common when it comes to being recently dumped by creeps.

"Have you talked with Geoffrey today?" I ask. *Gentle, gentle.*

Jillian shakes her head and folds her napkin into squares. "I don't want to talk to him for awhile now." She flaps her napkin open and stares at it. "God, it still doesn't seem real."

"I totally know what you mean," Denise says. "I had no idea Rick would ditch me like that. And I'll probably never see him again. But, like, it's weird. I don't even give a shit."

"How long were you and Rick together?" I ask, modeling the appropriate questions for Jillian.

"Six months, take it or leave it."

"It's 'give or take,' " Jillian corrects.

"I know, but in our relationship Rick was always taking and I was always giving."

Jillian gives me a small smile. It requires a deft touch, but by the time our check arrives, we've all bonded. Sort of. I feel like I've just brokered a truce between the Bloods and the Crips. For an encore, I tell them about Stoner Ski Bum sneaking up on me in the night. Ta-dah!

Jillian blanches. "Oh my God. I'm so sorry."

Who's sorry now, baby? I treat everyone to dinner and leave a big tip to keep the mellow good times rolling.

Back at the campground Denise digs her book and this weird flashlight-type gadget out of her backpack. It looks like something a coal miner might wear. "What is that?" I ask.

"It's a reading light. Check it out." She pulls the thick stretchy band over her hair, centering the tiny lamp above her eyebrows. She turns it on, and a blinding white light erupts from her forehead. You could read a book under the covers or do a little spelunking, should the urge strike. Or maybe give your friends optic nerve damage.

Jillian turns away, blinking. "Do you have to wear that?"

Right away I get this feeling that Denise stole it from Brandon's rich business partner's house, but I don't say anything. Maybe I'm just being paranoid. I grab the backpack I got for free when I joined the Sierra Club and head for the showers. Jillian follows me. We claim adjacent shower stalls and arrange our travel-sized shampoos and soaps. I stand under the warm spray of water, amazed at the amount of red sand spiraling down the drain.

Jillian's saying something. I poke my head past the curtain. "What?"

"I said she still makes me nervous."

"Jillian, conventionally grown produce makes you nervous. So do people who overtheme their homes. Somebody wants to collect Monopoly memorabilia, and all of a sudden they've got a neurological disorder." I'm speaking of the woman for whom Jillian did a few home-visit massages: Crazy Monopoly Lady. Every nonfunctional inch of her home was overrun with various Monopoly collectibles or limited-edition board games. Even a few functional pieces had been appropriated, like the knobs of every cupboard or drawer (tiny metal shoes, irons, dogs, and cars). Her kitchen was wallpapered in Chance cards and property deeds. It wasn't *that* disturbing— I mean, she just needed to get a life, and Jillian's in the car hyperven-

tilating before the session. Now, had she requested a full-body rub-
down on a bed of Monopoly money while Jillian wore a top hat,
perhaps a private freak-out would be justified.

"I don't know," Jillian continues. "Maybe you've got Stockholm
syndrome. Earth to Leigh. Come in, Leigh."

"Jillian, you're going Monopoly Lady on me."

"Okay, okay. But you don't know anything about this girl. She
could be dangerous."

I think of Denise's gun and the way she clutched my purse to
her chest. "I know enough. Besides. Anyone could be dangerous,
given the right situation." I'm guessing Jillian would be moderately
dangerous if she ran into Geoffrey's fuck buddy on the street. My
razor clatters to the floor and I pick it up, wincing. Can you get ath-
lete's foot in an armpit?

"Leigh, I know you! You can't pick up every lost puppy you find.
Some of them might bite."

"When did you get so fatalistic?" I shout over the pounding water.
"You're the one who had me listening to the universe and 'trusting the
positive flow of qi,' whatever that means. Anyway, like you would
have just left her there. You let total strangers be your roommates."

Jillian says nothing. I confess I never told Jillian about Denise's
unique method of convincing me to give her a ride. It is sort of
damning.

"I'm not a child," I add. "You've got to trust me on this. Do you
really think I'm that bad a judge of character?" I bite my tongue before I say anything about Geoffrey or Stoner Ski Bum, the Wonder
Roomies. "She needed a ride, I had a ride. Jeez. Both her parents
are dead. Give her a break, will you?"

Also, I don't tell Jillian about Denise's emergent kleptomania.

I drive it on home. "And really. When you think of some of the
so-called friends and boyfriends we've had in the past, it didn't really matter where we met them. Creeps are just as likely to show up
in the Laundromat or church. Just ask a hundred former altar
boys." Crude, yes, but it conveys the point, no? Jillian groans and
tells me I'm bad, but I know she's smiling.

Outside, the wind has picked up. It propels us in our shower shoes back to the tent. Inside, we organize our sleeping bags and blankets. There's barely enough room for two people, let alone three people with plenty of literal and figurative baggage. Despite our bodies as anchors, the tent tries to leap into the sky. The wind has become a gale. I climb out of the tent to search for storm clouds, but I only see stars. Millions of them, gleaming like angry gems in the clear black night. Wrappers, leaves, dust, and tiny stones pelt my legs and lodge in my clean wet hair, which is flying behind me, almost parallel to the ground. I squint my eyes at the debris to prevent accidental blindness. I glance at the tent and see it billowing and flapping, struggling to remain rooted to the earth. Denise and Jillian are silhouetted inside, wrestling with the corner pegs. This is probably a good time to climb into a storm cellar.

The family camping three inches from us suddenly runs past, chasing their tent and swearing in German. Their brown tent is gracelessly tumbling away, top over bottom (ass over teakettle, as Gram used to say), a boxy runaway kite. It plugs itself into a tree and crumples.

We are trapped in a windstorm.

We could be struck by flying debris like D-cell batteries and telephone poles. I poke my head back in the tent. Jillian and Denise glance up at me, alarmed, struggling to keep the tent from collapsing. Or lifting and spinning off the planet. "What's happening? Is there a storm coming?" Jillian asks me.

"No," I say, "it's just the Four Horsemen of the Apocalypse. Go back to your reading."

"Who put the tent pegs in?" Jillian demands, looking for someone to blame. And then the tent collapses. I pull my head out just in time. Denise and Jillian scream, reeling around under the nylon material, which has plastered itself against their bodies. I find the tent opening and peel it from them. "Come on," I shout into the wind and flying dust. "We're sleeping in the car."

In the car everyone's crabby. The wind rocks the car on its springs while we punch pillows, adjust seats, and grumble. "I hate not being able to stretch my legs out when I sleep!" Jillian shouts in a sudden, furious outburst.

Later, when Jillian and Denise are asleep and the wind has died down to a dull roar, I get up and go to the bathroom. Something's wrong. I ache, and my eyes feel like hot marbles. I may have a slight fever. I stare for a long time into the toilet bowl after I urinate. My pee looks fine. Clear, yellow, properly filtered. I flush the toilet and press my palms against my lower back like a pregnant woman. I touch my toes. My back feels fine. But still I ache and my joints grind against one another. I take a Tylenol and a few vitamins. I count and organize my medications under the anemic glare of the bathroom lights. I caress my scars and hemorrhage hope. "Please, no," I whisper. *I'm not ready to be sick again.*

My mind ticks off the other symptoms I exhibited during my first bout with renal failure: itching? I clasp my forearms, test the skin. I touch my face. My neck. No, not yet. Muscle cramps? Again, nothing, thank God. Mental fatigue and irritability? Well . . .

A brunette woman in a flannel shirt and denim cutoffs enters the bathroom. She looks achy, too. Her eyes are puffy. We nod at each other before she locks herself into a stall.

I return to the car and curl into a ball on the reclined driver's seat. I'll call the doctor if I feel sick in the morning, I promise myself. I recite one Our Father and three Hail Marys, every penance ever assigned me in confession. I do my breathing exercises. I fall asleep thinking of my mother's high school yearbook and how she'd been voted "Best Smile." Her long straight blond hair, parted in the middle. I remember the day she cut it into a bob, when I was four. "Mommy, Mommy, who are you?" I said, gaping up at her new strangeness, colliding with her knees in the entryway. Or maybe I remember her later version of it. I imagine my now-self sitting on her Hollywood stoop, gazing up at her and saying, "Mommy, Mommy, who are you?"

In the morning I feel cool and supple, ready for another full day of Denise's photography and Jillian's misguided pining for Geoffrey. I drink orange juice and tell no one of my feverish trip to the bathroom.

After a late brunch in Moab, we top off the gas tank, restock the cooler with bottled water and ice, and chart our course to

Cedar City, Utah. The drive through the San Rafael Desert is un-nerving, as road signs warn that there will be no services—no gas, no bathrooms, no vending machines with bottled water, no rest for the weary at all—for another hundred miles. Nothing but arid iso-lation, and maybe a few vultures circling over human skeletons. As we approach the final warning sign near Green River, Jillian asks, "Will we have enough gas to make it?"

Denise snorts. "Well, you both had veggie deluxe omelets this morning. What do you think?"

Jillian just rolls her eyes. I'm sick of driving (and nervous about my impending visit with Larry's family), so I pull into the last gas station for miles to let Jillian take the steering wheel. I discover I truly enjoy riding in the passenger seat of my own car. Which is sur-prising to me, given my control-freakery. I'm free to watch the scenery, and it does make my soul sit up and rub her eyes: vast, empty plains stretching for miles back to rugged cliffs and brick-colored buttes, sagebrush and grasses eking out a thirsty existence in the ditches, gregarious sky overwhelming in its blue clarity. The road unspools before us, endless white lines running together into an albino snake. Denise leans out the window to take pictures. I feel as if we've driven into a patriotic country-music video, or maybe a commercial for trendy jeans.

The air is still hazy with smoke from wildfires over the painted mesas on the horizon. It stings our nostrils. I'm still a bit shaken from my midnight flirtation with illness, so I take it easy. We listen to the Shins' latest album and I close my eyes, lulled by the tires humming on the highway. "Jillian," I say, getting sleepy and philo-sophical, "what did you like about Geoffrey when you first met him?"

She sighs through her nose. "He was ambitious. He had goals, and plans. He'd been everywhere—Nepal, Japan, Kenya, Costa Rica, India." I feel a sad sort of knowing. Jillian adores travel. Peo-ple who travel, and the stories they tell, are like heroin to her.

"Let's go to Uganda next year," I suggest, closing my eyes. "Go see the last gorillas."

"Nan did a gorilla safari last year."

"Nanzipan?" I ask. Nan was a girl we went to high school with. Jillian kept in touch with her, but I didn't. I never really liked Nan, mostly because conversations with her were always one-sided. Hers, that is. I tried an experiment the last few times we spoke; I let her talk about herself during our entire conversation, waiting for her to ask about me. Anything at all about me. But she never did.

"It was really expensive," Jillian says. "And she claims she was almost held hostage by some guerrillas. Not the hairy ones."

This is Jillian trying to be funny, and I acknowledge it with a cartoon sound effect: "Wah-*wah*."

I think about Larry as I listen to the tires hum beneath me. I hope to meet his family tomorrow. They don't know I'm arriving. I've been too nervous to make the call. For one thing, what if they declined to see me? I'd much rather case the situation as I got closer. Ask a few locals if they knew him, that sort of thing. See if I still have the guts to show up on Betty Resnick's porch, like, "Ta-dah! Guess who I am?" I promise to let you know as soon as I figure out what's wrong with me. Other than kidney disease.

I must have dozed off because I wake to an alarm clock. No, not an alarm clock: the warning "ding" my car makes when I've left my blinker on for too long. "Turn off the blinker," I mumble, annoyed.

Jillian responds with a soft "Uh-oh."

I open my eyes and glance over, still groggy. "What is it?"

"I think we're running out of gas."

I sit up, wide awake. "What do you mean you think we're running out of gas?"

Denise pops her head up from the backseat. "What's going on?"

We listen to my car sputter and chug. I lean over to examine the gas gauge. The needle has dipped far below "Empty," past "Driving on Fumes," to "One Last Gasp—Hope You're Not Lost in Detroit." The low-fuel light shines from the dashboard like a beacon. The dinging drones on. Apparently, my car not only makes this noise when you forget to turn off a blinker; it also tells you when you're about to experience impaired mobility in an unsavory location. "Didn't you see the little glowing gas pump?" I ask, incredulous.

Jillian grows more agitated. "No, I guess I didn't notice. I was just trying not to get lost."

"It's a straight shot on I-70! How could we get lost?" I gaze around at our quiet, non-interstate surroundings. "Jillian, where are we?" I ask slowly.

We coast onto the shoulder, where my car gives one final wheeze and conks out. Jillian gives me a pleading look. "I was so bored with the interstate. I thought I would explore some of the back roads . . . you know, take the scenic route." She flinches at my expression and adds in a whisper, "I wanted to find Goblin Valley State Park and surprise you."

"Well, surprise, we're out of gas!" I shout, doing jazz hands.

Her face shrinks, small and sad.

"We're out of gas in the middle of the fucking desert!" I announce, for anyone who's missed it. I stare through the windshield, fuming. Outside, a tumbleweed bounces—get this—right past a bleached Georgia O'Keeffe–style cow skull.

I flip open my phone. No signal. "Jillian, try your phone."

She can't pull a signal either. Fantastic.

We're all going to die out here in the red Utah desert like cartoon people crawling toward water fountains that don't work.

Even Larry would be pissed about this.

CHAPTER EIGHT

Helluva place to run outta petrol.

Sometimes I make lists of funny or perplexing observations and events in my life so that I won't forget them. Here's a sample:

1. Last night I dreamed my mother was making cookies, only she was using my prednisone and Imuran instead of chocolate chips. A metaphor? But for what?

2. I signed up on my driver's license to be an organ donor.

3. Wes packed me a lunch for dialysis today. Contents: one to-furkey sandwich with a bite taken out of it, a baggie of unblessed hosts, and an apple.

4. Conversation I overheard between two women at Culver's last week: Woman A—"I'm thinking of getting a cat." Woman B—"Why, tired of playing with your own pussy?"

5. My push-up bra insert worked its way out of my bra, down my stomach, and out of my T-shirt while I was talking with Dave Walker, who has the loudest dog at Fuzzy Navels. It plopped on the floor between us. We both ignored it and kept talking. I will never wear a push-up bra again.

6. Another surreal moment at work: Last month, in the middle

of an important meeting with some bigwigs in city management, Mindy asked all of us, "Mind if I put my head down for a short nap?" and then proceeded to do so while I looked on, silently sweating, having temporarily lost the ability to speak. Sure, she has narcolepsy, but what kind of an excuse is that?

7. Gram whistled everywhere she went: "Pennies from Heaven," "Gift of Finest Wheat," "Ain't She Sweet," anything. She could do a vibrato whistle and knew thirty-four birdsongs by heart. She was indistinguishable from cardinals and black-capped chickadees.

8. For two years before she left, my mother hunched over her Singer sewing machine and made me puppets: finger, hand, and sock. And marionettes. And a perfect wooden puppet theater with velvet curtains so I could enact "The Little Match Seller" and "The Frog Prince" for all the preschoolers in the neighborhood. She decorated my post–baby room with masks—the festive, nightmarish kind popular at Mardi Gras. I remember staring at them in terror before falling asleep. My mother also spoke to me in long chunks of dialogue from movies filmed before I'd been conceived.

"Mommy, can I have some juice?"

Her reply, eyes gazing vacantly into space: " 'You're the last great apostle of rugged individualism.' " (Leslie Howard to Humphrey Bogart in *The Petrified Forest*.)

"Mommy, what does *circumcision* mean?"

Her answer, face screwed up in a wiseguy grimace, my nose clamped between her index and middle fingers: " 'You're a very nosy fellow, kitty cat. Huh? You know what happens to nosy fellows? Huh? No? Wanna guess? Huh? No? Okay. They lose their noses.' " (Roman Polanski to Jack Nicholson in *Chinatown*.)

You know that line from Shakespeare: "All the world's a stage, and all the men and women merely players"? Well, my mother took that quite literally. In my house, the acting bug crawled under our beds and in our shoes and latched onto my mother with long, sharp teeth. It looked at me through the eyes of every puppet, every horrific mask. Some days, she spoke only in mime. And you should have seen the day my parents brought home their first VCR: Beta, then VHS a year later. I swear to God, my mother was so insane with glee, I saw seams bursting on her clothing. As I got older, I would ask myself questions like, why couldn't she have simply been an obsessive stage mother, funneling her dashed dreams into my dysfunctional stint as a child star? And why couldn't she have been content to participate in community productions of *Seven Brides for Seven Brothers* or *Fiddler on the Roof*? Well, I might as well have asked why I wasn't born one of the Olsen twins. There's just no point in asking such impossible questions.

I must have been immune, because the acting bug left me alone. All the videos and motivational speakers at school were constantly chiding us to "just be ourselves," like this was the panacea for the bully who called you Dracula Teeth, and other sundry juvenile inadequacies. So the whole acting-like-someone-else thing made no sense to me. In high school, there was the usual invitation (usually from a well-meaning bald English teacher with coffee stains on his khaki pants) to audition for the role of Laura Wingfield in the school production of *The Glass Menagerie*. But it all seemed forced and unoriginal. The stage makeup, the hot lighting, the costumes that stank of mothballs, the single, velvet roses handed out to cast members on opening night. Not to mention the idea of memorizing lines and then reciting them in front of hundreds of critical strangers, which was about as appealing to me as contracting herpes. Whatever the case, I preferred to hunker down with a book and let the scenes on the page play themselves out in my head.

I can almost recall my father badgering my mother to drop the crazy acting fantasies and focus instead on her nursing job before she accidentally killed some geezer in the ICU, but I might have dreamed it. I sometimes like to imagine them having grand arguments about her irrational ambitions as an actress (given our distant proximity to Hollywood and New York and her dubious talent), but I have a feeling my father would have been defeated before even starting a fight like that, given his own doomed ambitions as a writer. I also sometimes imagine my mother staging plays for the patients at the hospital she worked at. (The image of retirees line-kicking in hospital johnnies has always tickled me.)

But she could have won an Academy Award for her role as our mother. Rather, her nonrole. I'm sorry, I sound bitter. Maybe I am. Don't worry, I'm not going to jump off the "Woe is me, all alone in my raggedy clothing" orphan plank here. I mean, it could have been worse. Look at Piper Laurie's shining example of maternal love in *Carrie*.

Damn. I just had to compare her to an actor, didn't I?

I stumble out of the car with my cell phone, leaving the car door ajar, for which it scolds me: *ding . . . ding . . . ding . . . ding*.

Heat waves shimmy up from the blacktop. I can't believe Jillian. How many times have I told her to find a gas station the minute the fuel gauge sinks to one-quarter full? God, I sound perilously close to James. I examine my cell phone again. No signal, not even one fickle bar if I stand on my toes and hold the phone above my head.

"Did you get a signal?" Jillian asks from the driver's seat, fanning herself.

"No." I open the glove compartment and rummage for a map. "Let's try to figure out where we are." With our collective powers of deduction, we conclude we're somewhere near the town of Hanksville. Well, maybe *near* is too misleading a word, especially when it applies to walking in sandals through the desert. My best guess would be six miles one way, and that's conservative.

Shit. I force myself to do one of my breathing exercises. Someone will be along. I scan the clear, hot sky. Okay, someone other than a circling vulture. I slump back into my seat. "Jillian, what about your phone?"

She steps out of the car and flips her phone open. "Nothing. Maybe I should try it up on the hill? You never know."

"Be my guest," I say, fishing in the cooler behind the seat for a sad little ice cube to slide over my forehead. "Christ, it must be a hundred and twenty degrees." Not to mention I'm craving something sweet so badly, I'm ready to eat my cherry Chap Stick. I wonder if this means I'm about to hallucinate or have a seizure. Jillian starts heading down the road while I open all of the car doors to catch the raggedy breeze gasping past.

"How are you doing?" I ask Denise, watching a drop of sweat snake down her forehead.

"Fine. But I have to go to the bathroom soon."

I gesture to the vast, baking desert. "Nature's commode."

"I have to take a shit."

I hand her a napkin. "So, are you sorry you made me give you a ride?" I almost said *"asked" me for a ride,* but that technically didn't take place. Denise misses it entirely.

"No way! I don't know what I'd have done if you didn't come along."

Carjack someone? I want to tease, but instead I say, "You're a smart girl. You'd have figured something out."

She grins. "Maybe. Hey, I'll give you a million dollars if you guess what song I have in my head."

I laugh and scowl. "I don't know." I hate when someone asks me a question like that. It evokes the same disdainful response in me as "Hey, guess the name of this rash!" or "Hey, guess how many lightbulbs it would take to circle the earth!" Completely pointless.

"Come on, try to focus in on what I'm thinking. Here, I'll send you the vibes." She puts her palm on my forehead and hums.

I start laughing again. "Cut that out."

"Do you know? Come on, guess."

"Um, 'Maneater' by Hall and Oates?"

She makes a jarring buzzer noise: *Eeeeenhh.* "It was 'You're a Mean One, Mr. Grinch.' "

I roll my eyes, smiling in spite of myself. "You are so odd. What put that song in your head?"

"I don't know. Did Dr. Seuss write any stories that took place in a desert?"

I study her while she reties her shoelaces. "You know, I still feel like I hardly know you," I say. "I mean, I know what kind of books and music you like, and that you like taking pictures, but . . . I don't

know. Never mind." I don't know why I feel compelled to get
to know her better. I'm just the driver of the bus. Do I really
need to know the family and medical history of every passenger?
It's not like we'll be pen pals once we part company in California.
Will we? I suppose the responsible thing would be to find out more
about her. But how well do we really know anyone—even our families? How much do they really want us to know them, when you
get down to it?

Denise straightens and looks me right in the eye. "What? What
do you want to ask me?"

"Okay, well, tell me more about being a foster child. Like, did
you have foster brothers or sisters that you really miss?"

She fidgets a bit before answering, "Um, the short answer is no.
I mean, sometimes kids just, like, bounced through the system
from home to home, you know?" She pauses and lights a cigarette.
"There was one little boy, Jarrod. He was a real sweetie. Just five
years old. I really hope someone figures out what a great kid he is
and adopts him. The problem is, everybody who can't have their
own kid wants a baby. To adopt, I mean."

I get this insane urge to pluck the cigarette from her fingers and
take a drag. But I don't. "Do you want kids someday? What *do* you
see yourself doing someday?"

"Yeah, I want to have a few kids. And I'm not sure what I want
to do."

"What do you like to do?"

"Jeez, this isn't a job interview," she huffs. She takes a drag from
her cigarette and follows up with, "I like art. I like acting." She tips
her head and stares into space behind me, pondering her next
statement. "I was thinking of becoming an actress," she adds with
certainty.

For Christ's sake. "Breaking in isn't easy," I say, but what do I
know. "I don't think my mother ever made it."

She rolls her eyes. "I know, *Mom*."

"Okay, but be smart about it. You know the cliché: Pretty young
girl takes the bus to Hollywood with ambitions of acting, ends up

on the street and posing nude for some creepy guy with a handlebar mustache who promised her a role in some movie."

She stubs her cigarette out on the gravel shoulder and laughs.
"Handlebar mustache! Ha! Listen. I'm not stupid. I know enough
to avoid the guy with the handlebar mustache."

I suspect she's poking a bit of fun at me, but I don't really care.
"I know, but even Marilyn Monroe once said, 'Hollywood is a place
where they'll pay you a thousand dollars for a kiss and fifty cents for
your soul.' "

Wow, I'm sounding more like James every day. But I'm actually
quoting my mother quoting Marilyn. It's amazing what happens
when you feel responsible for someone a little more helpless than
yourself. Just then an image of Denise swiping someone's wallet at
Frontier Days, and one of her appropriating my purse, flashes before my eyes. Maybe she isn't so helpless.

I glance up to see Jillian strolling back to the gasless car, shaking her head and shrugging. "No signal," she shouts. I do a mini
breathing exercise. For Christ's sake. What's the point of having a
cell phone if it won't work when you need it?

Denise sighs and looks at me. "Now what?"

Jillian plops into the driver's seat, sweating. "I need water." I
hand her a lukewarm bottle of water and scan the horizon for a
cloud of dust that would herald an approaching vehicle. Nothing
but heat haze.

"Well," I say, considering our options, "we can take a gamble
that there's a gas station in Hanksville and walk there together
through six miles of scorched desert. If we do that, we shouldn't do
it until dark, when it's cooler and we have less chance of melting
into the asphalt. It's almost five right now. It would probably take us
over an hour. Maybe even two."

Jillian runs a hand through her windblown hair. "What do you
think we should do?"

"Let's ask Larry!" Denise offers.

I shake my head. "Larry needs a nap. Jillian? Want to try your
pendant?"

"Ha-ha." She takes a long drink of water and adds, "I don't think we should walk anywhere. I'd probably just get us lost again." We crank our seats back to ponder our next course of action. "I'm sorry, guys," Jillian says quietly.

"Well, looks like we all might die before we're thirty," I drawl. Jillian rolls her eyes and gives me The Pinky, which is her sanitized version of The Finger. "Man," I add, "if everything happens for a reason like you say, there better be a good one around the bend."

"Maybe we missed a fifty-car pileup by leaving the interstate," Denise volunteers.

"Maybe we'll be rescued by a carload of really hot Mormons," Jillian says, grinning.

I cackle wildly. My head and stomach ache like I have heatstroke. "With our luck, it would be some bald guy with chronic halitosis who would force us all to marry him and make us give up coffee and wear our hair in long braids."

Jillian rolls her eyes. "No, it'll be some crazy fundamentalist Mormon whaddayacallem, *fanatics,* who murder us when they see that book you're reading on the backseat."

"It's a good book!" Jon Krakauer's indictment of Mormonism as told through the prism of a particularly grisly murder, *Under the Banner of Heaven.* I read it last year, but I thought rereading it in southern Utah might be interesting. Scene of the crime, and all.

"It might be the last book you ever read," Jillian adds morbidly.

Denise jumps in with "Wanna play twenty questions?"

"No," I say.

"I spy?" She starts playing invisible piano again on her lap, glancing nervously toward the horizon.

"I spy imminent death," I say.

"No, try again." Once again, I climb out of the car, which has become oven-stifling, even with the doors open.

Jillian smirks. "Then how about giving us a conversation topic worthy of the great and esteemed Leigh Fielding?" She and Denise also get out of the car and lean against the trunk next to me.

"Okay, who would we eat first if we ran out of food?"

Jillian and I just grin at each other like sharks. Denise fidgets, wiping sweat from her face with a palm.

"I think that vulture circling above us has dibs on you, Jillian," I say.

She whips her head back, scanning the sky. "Shut up!"

I ignore her. "How about this. There are two main things we're supposed to be figuring out at this age: relationships—or a satisfying career. And in my case, how to live past thirty. Pick a topic, and let's discuss."

Jillian makes like she's going to strangle me. "Leigh, if you say that again, you won't make it to next week because I'm personally going to strangle you. And why can't we talk about other things, like spirituality?"

"Because we're not fifty yet." And because if I have to hear about vortexes of energy one more time, I fear I may stab pencils in my ears. I stand tall and shade my eyes, searching for a vehicle on the horizon. "Jesus, doesn't anyone come down this road?"

Denise suddenly blurts, "I have to tell you something."

Jillian and I glance at her, nonplussed. "If it doesn't involve a can of gas in your backpack, I'm not interested," I say.

"Listen, that black car that's been, um, following us? I think it's Rick."

I can only stare while she continues. "See, Rick is kinda crazy. Well, not kinda, he is crazy. He was really abusive, actually. I . . . I think he might want to hurt me."

I find my voice. "You *think* or you *know* it's Rick?"

"Know. I know it's Rick," she admits quietly.

"But I thought he left you at the rest stop! I thought he abandoned you!"

Denise fidgets. "Well, not really. I escaped him, is more like it."

I find more of my voice—the part a teacher would wash out with soap. "For fuck's sake. Escaped him? What is he, the Hillside Strangler? Why didn't you just tell me the truth?"

"Oh yeah, right, like you'd give me a ride then. 'Hi, stranger, how about giving me a ride? I'm only being pursued by an abusive, lunatic ex-boyfriend who wants to kill me and has a police record.'"

Oh Jesus. What have I gotten myself into? Or what has Larry gotten me into? Thanks a lot, Lare. Real reliable. Real safe.

Jillian's jaw is resting on her upper chest. "We are going to call the police."

Denise looks alarmed. "Please don't! We'll be alright. I promise. I can handle him." She gives me a knowing glance, which I interpret as *I have a gun, remember*?

"I can't believe this," Jillian adds. "We could all be killed!"

Denise tries again. "Look, we're almost to L.A. And that's only two states away. And then I'm out of your life for good. Please don't leave me. Nothing will happen, I promise." Her lower lip starts to quiver. "I guess nobody wants to deal with me. But whatever, right? What else is new?" With that she starts to cry.

I feel it would be in my best interest to mollify her. We're talking about a girl who felt no qualms about holding my purse hostage in return for a ride; a level of irrationality even Whitney "Crack Is Whack!" Houston would frown at. What's Denise going to do if she feels backed into a corner now? Dump my medication down a toilet? "Denise, don't cry. We're not going to leave you. And I'm sorry to hear about what you must have been through, believe me. But Christ, what are we going to do about this guy?" What, indeed? Nobody has any suggestions. Six hundred miles to go and I've got two human barnacles on my ass. "This is insane," I mumble, cupping my face in my hands and sighing deeply.

We're quiet for the next few minutes, watching the sun slide down the late-afternoon sky, setting the distant buttes on fire. A small feeling of dread settles in my stomach. When I imagined my Unfinished Business Tour, I didn't envision it culminating with death by dehydration and/or at the hands of a murderous stalker in the Utah desert. "Okay," I say, getting rational. "He's obviously nowhere near us right now, in this godforsaken hellhole in the middle of nowhere, so maybe we've lost him." I glance at my bright cherry-red car, now screaming at me like a billboard: *Here we are!* it shouts. *Here we are!*

Jillian follows my gaze. "And I'm sure we'll blend right in with your fire truck of a car."

"Well, what do you want me to do?" I snip. "Get a beige paint job at the next gas station? Oh wait, we're probably going to die before we see the next gas station!"

"Excuse me for trying to be nice. *My* car still has a quarter tank of gas when the needle's on *E*."

I want to scream and drop-kick her little crystal pyramid into the desert. Instead of saying what I really want to say, which is childish and unconstructive, I say, "Oh, well. We won't be able to fill up at the pump, anyway, because we'll have bloody stumps for arms after Rick gets ahold of us." Which isn't much better than telling her we should have taken her highness's wonder car with the bottomless gas tank. We're silent and sulky for a few more minutes.

"Okay, let's refocus," I say, rubbing my face. "We've got to get out of here." Just as I'm about to suggest we try walking to Hanksville, Rick-be-damned, we spy an approaching vehicle in the distance, kicking up a cloud of dust in its wake. "Oh, please tell me it's not a black car," Jillian says. My heart vaults up to my throat, and I feel like I'm about to give a major speech before a surly crowd: Sounds are muffled, cold sweat dribbles down my sides, and I hear a clicking when I swallow. But . . . But then I relax a bit. By the size of the dust plume, it couldn't possibly be a car. We start waving and jumping. I'm nervous about flailing about so, advertising our weakness, because this is exactly the way most teen horror flicks begin. Hello, *Wolf Creek*? *The Hills Have Eyes*? But hey, like Jillian always tells me, if you put negativity out to the universe, it will only return to you tenfold. So I send hopeful vibes to the universe that it's a bus full of cheerful seniors en route to Vegas. We could compare medical war stories on our way to the blackjack tables at the Tropicana.

Our mystery vehicle turns out to be a colossal Winnebago. Relieved that it's not the black Acura or a pickup with a gun rack, we watch it park, craning our necks for a glimpse of who's inside. The driver, a chunky man in a plaid shirt and straw cowboy hat, exits first. He looks as if he's swallowed a medicine ball. A woman in a red sun visor, sunglasses, and high-waisted shorts gets out after him. She's wearing a thin American flag T-shirt through which I can clearly see her red bra. The medicine-ball swallower says, "You gals run into some car trouble?"

"We ran out of gas," Jillian volunteers, sweating.

The driver is stuffing handful after handful of dry-roasted peanuts into his mouth, talking around them. He tips the open jar in our general direction. I shake my head and smile.

"Helluva place to run outta petrol," he adds, chuckling and sweating. He tosses another handful of peanuts into his mouth.

"A helluva place, alright," I say. And even though I can see the front license plate is from North Dakota, I ask, "Where are you guys from?"

"Bismarck, North Dakota," the driver announces. A small bit of peanut falls from his mouth and lands on his chest.

I really don't know that much about North Dakota, and for once, I don't pretend that I do. I've got this terrible habit of acting like an expert on topics I have a nodding acquaintance with. Instead, I say, "I'm Leigh. And this is Jillian, and Denise."

"Bob and Peggy Lansky. We're hitting as many national parks as we can on our way to a swing convention in Reno."

The collective sound of our jaws hitting our chests is deafening. I absolutely love this. Who the hell just blurts that to total strangers? Bob and Peggy Lansky, that's who! Bob and Peggy are covered in vanilla, but they have spicy jalapeño centers.

"So what have you seen so far?" I ask, shading my eyes against the glare of Bob's belt buckle and trying not to projectile giggle. I place a mental bet with myself as to whether or not they'll mention the words *swinger, swap,* and *open marriage.*

"Oh, we seen Teddy Roosevelt, Yellowstone, Grand Teton, Arches, Canyonlands, Dinosaur, Flaming Gorge . . . Honey, did I miss any?" Bob asks, spewing peanut chunks.

"You forgot Ouray wildlife refuge."

"Well, that don't count as a national park."

Peggy flaps a hand at her husband and says to me, "He's just cranky that he lost at Scrabble last night." I grin madly.

"We'd be glad to help you gals out, with the gas and all," Bob says. "Got an empty gas can? We could pick some up for you."

I snap out of my hysteria and think for a minute. "I have one in my trunk."

I pop the trunk and we excavate it, heaving luggage helter-skelter. I find the empty red two-gallon gas can tucked neatly behind my wheel well. "Eureka!" I say, getting into the swing of things. (Pun sadly intended.) I hand Bob and Peggy ten dollars and the gas can. "I think there's a gas station in Hanksville, which should be just down the road."

Jillian pipes up. "Thank you so much for helping us!" She's still wearing an insane grin.

Denise and I come to our senses and echo her. "Yes, thank you so much!"

"Oh, shure, no problemo," Bob says. "Ain't no trouble at all." And they climb into the swing mobile to set out on their errand.

"We'll be back before you know it," Peggy shouts, waving.

Still smiling, Denise waves back, and I hear her say under her breath, "Thanks for swinging to town for us."

Jillian nudges me as they chug away from the shoulder, waving. "See? You just have to trust that the universe is looking out for you. And good things come your way."

I can't help but say in a newsroom voice, *"In today's news, three young women were brutally stabbed to death after their car ran out of gas in Bumfuck, Utah. Vacationers Bob and Peggy Lansky discovered the bodies, which had to be identified by dental records. Details at six."*

Jillian scowls at me. "Leigh!"

Denise chimes in with *"And now a special report on swinging! It's back. But is everybody doing it? Find out more when we return!"*

Jillian rolls her eyes. *"Wisconsin native Leigh Fielding was finally granted status as an adult today, after sixty cynical years on the planet. More after the break."*

"Hey, you are optimistic! Sixty years old. Whew!"

When she smacks me it smarts a little but feels good just the same.

CHAPTER NINE

This is what happens when your mother leaves and your older brother raises you.

Once, during my sophomore year in college, Jillian came to visit and we locked ourselves in Steve McCarty's dorm room to smoke pot. Seth, Wes, and my friend Amanda Sizemore were there, too, Amanda in her perennial *Buffy the Vampire Slayer* T-shirt. Amanda's the epileptic friend I've had since grade school. She was obsessed with Buffy and Angel, and I feared she'd set herself adrift on an ice floe after Buffy's final episode. Amanda was attending UW–LaCrosse, studying to be a social worker, which we all agreed should work out fine because she already liked ramen noodles and thrift-store clothing. Her boyfriend was in the physical education program, hoping to one day lead a gymnasium full of ten-year-olds in group push-ups and unsynchronized arm circles. In sixth grade, the kids cruelly called her Amanda Seizure. I told her it could have been worse. Her last name could have been "Fondle."

Anyway, we stuffed a towel in the crack under the door and passed Steve's pipe around, giggling and paranoid, grooving to *Morrison Hotel*. It was the first time Jillian or I had ever smoked pot, and it felt almost as risqué as the day we each bought a box of Summer's Eve in ninth grade to see how douche really worked. Sure, we'd gotten drunk a few times in high school, but the only kid who *didn't* drink in our graduating class was Ronald Kempf, because he was allergic to most fermented alcoholic beverages. At least that's what he told anyone who asked.

My first impression of pot was that it made my alveoli burst into flames. I coughed so hard tears poured down my cheeks. I can't even remember if we had a buzz or not, but stumbling from the dark black-lit dorm room into the bright hallway and the shins of the floor resident adviser had a sobering effect. Steve's RA was adorable, and every girl on my floor almost went into orgasmic convulsions every time they saw him eating a bowl of Rice Krispies in Blackhawk Commons. His name was Andrew, and I'm not sure if he smelled any wacky smoke, but I do remember him stumbling back at our exodus, startled but smiling at Jillian. "Hi," he said.

"I am not!" she sputtered, and we careened down the stairs laughing and terrified, locking ourselves in my room and drowning our eyes with Visine.

These are the tales I like to retell in Jillian's presence when we haven't yet had our daily laugh. While we wait for Bob and Peggy to return, giddy from the heat and slaphappy at the prospect of returning to the interstate sans Rick, I tell the story again. Jillian just smiles and shakes her head, amazed at having finally gotten away with something. (She spent most of high school grounded from the phone or car, and sometimes both.)

"Yeah, but remember when I made you eat your own pube?" she responds.

I roll my eyes. "Hey, do you want me to bring up the fling you had with Chad Macy?" Chad Macy was a man-boy partial to white sweatshirts. And while she was dating him, Jillian's menstrual cycle was not partial to a regular schedule. So, needless to say, his going down on her during this era was a recipe for disaster. And Mr. Macy's reaction to his soiled garments was even worse. Think Woody Allen meets the Ebola virus.

"Ugh! Please don't say that name." Jillian shudders. "I could die. I must have been brain-damaged."

"Still are," I chirp, and she gives me The Pinky again.

"So how is Ms. Seizure these days?" Jillian asks, smirking. Despite her dalliances with tarot cards, homemade granola, and hugging saints, Jillian has a delicious little wicked side that I adore. It makes it all the more palatable when she says things like "My third chakra feels a bit uncentered today." Secretly, I do kind of believe that it is possible for her to absorb her clients' negative energy like she says she does, but to admit that would upset the delicate balance of our friendship. I was the smartass skeptic (until Larry), and she was—and still is—the ethereal barefoot post–Haight Ashbury goddess with canary feathers on her lips.

"Jillian, you're terrible! And she's great."

I should confess I'm only bringing up these stories because I'm being a tad manipulative. I want to remind Jillian that we've been through a lot—moments both heartbreaking and hilarious—and our friendship will weather any catastrophe life hurls at it: distance, arguments, sickness, juvenile delinquents, liver-lipped men who provoke us to become people we're not. *Especially* liver-lipped men. Denise is listening quietly, smiling at the right parts. I suddenly wonder if she has any close friends. Were we hurting her feelings? "Denise," I say, "do you miss your friends?"

She shrugs. "Sure," she says, twiddling with a silver ring on her thumb. Then she adds, "But they've kind of been assholes this summer. You know how it is." I do? We all lean against the car, passing a bag of chips between us and watching the sun set.

"So do you really feel Larry's energy?" Denise suddenly asks. "Like, his persona?"

I nod, and she giggles.

"What's so funny?"

"Are you starting to like girls? Will you be a lesbian now?"

I roll my eyes and say, "Yeah, so look out. Tonight you'll wake up and hear me whispering sweet nothings in your ear like Stoner Ski Bum."

Jillian lowers her voice and says in a manly tone, "Hey, baby, what's your sign?"

" 'This way to Wall Drug,' " I blurt, and we laugh at Denise's expense. Everything's funny when you have heatstroke. Then I add, "But I don't think Larry would sound like that. He'd be more like a trippy stoner."

"Like, no way, dude," Jillian adds in a spacey voice. "My kidney is, like, totally inside your universe."

"Move over, liver. Now there's something meatier!" I say. Jillian laughs, but it goes over Denise's head. Then I remember that commercial probably aired before she was even born.

I breathe in the cooling evening air and watch a bluebird flit onto a piñon tree across the road. The buttes and cliffs in the distance glow orange with waning light. The car casts a long purple shadow. "This was actually worth running out of gas," I say. Of course, I can say this now, with a can of fuel and getting the hell away from here suddenly on the itinerary for the evening. An evening that will hopefully be devoid of any black vehicles transporting lunatics. But how could I have wasted the last six years just watching reruns of *Three's Company, Little House on the Prairie,* and *Facts of Life* while stuffing Newman's Own microwave popcorn in my mouth? I missed so much! Seth had once asked me, "If you knew the world would end tomorrow, what would you spend the rest of today doing?" (I think there's actually a law that everyone has to ask their boyfriend or girlfriend that question at least once.) Of course, I'd said something lame like "I'd spend the rest of today in your arms, listening to your heartbeat." Sick. Just sick. But strangely, I feel as if I'm living a new and improved answer to that question. I highly recommend experiencing this feeling, but try to do it without getting sick and having an organ transplant.

We feel a moment of panic twenty minutes later when Bob and Peggy haven't yet returned. "Do you think they forgot?" Jillian asks.

"Maybe they had to stop and have sex with a random couple," Denise says.

"You know, I had no idea there were swingers in Utah," I say, mystified. "Polygamy, sure. But swingers?"

"Physical love often challenges the restraints society puts upon it," Jillian observes. "People are complex creatures with emotional, spiritual, and physical urges that can be stifled by traditional monogamy."

"Whatever," I say. "People are monkeys that like to hump." Just like Geoffrey with a G.

Sometimes I imagine Jillian as Yoda, dispensing sage, solid advice instead of obtuse New Age riddles. I would sit cross-legged on a pillow before her and ask, *Why doesn't anyone seem happy with who they are?* And Yoda Jillian would turn to me on creaky joints and smile. *Yes, Leigh. Happy everyone is not with who they are. Yourself ask that question, hmmm?*

Jillian rolls her eyes at me. Denise contributes, "I once saw a show about a bunch of monkeys that had sex every time they fought! It was hilarious."

"Hey," I say ominously, "I think we're kind of close to where that hiker hacked his arm off to get out of the canyon."

"Leigh, would you quit it?" Jillian shudders, but her bright eyes are asking for the gory details.

Just then, we spy the Winnebago lumbering down the road. Bob and Peggy have brought enough gas to get us to Hanksville for more. We thank them effusively. Christ, what a relief. Before they leave, Bob thrusts a brochure into my hands. "Oh!" I say. My eyes dart around—at the brochure, at Jillian's feet, at Peggy's waist— confused about what they're supposed to be looking at, but they do ricochet off the flashy "Learn to Swing!" on the brochure's front page. Hoo boy. Jillian and Denise float next to me, watching anxiously. Jillian clears her throat and scuffs at the dirt with a toe.

Bob grins, oblivious to our discomfort. "If you have a chance, you should check it out. It's not all that complicated. Heck, if two old fogies like us can learn, you young gals should have no problem!"

Peggy nods enthusiastically and adds, "You should see how good we've gotten! We used to be more competitive—Bob was so jealous of the other couples! But now we're just in it for the fun. And it's fantastic exercise."

I force myself to chuckle, cutting her off before my brain is permanently damaged by the images copulating in my frontal lobe. You hear about these kinds of things happening from time to time. In chat rooms named Married, No Strings Attached. "Actually," I say, "I'm not really—" And that's when I look at the brochure again, *really* look at it, and notice that the brochure features a photo (sound of a needle ripping across the grooved surface of a record) of a spiffy young man in a zoot suit lifting a girl in a poodle skirt high into the air. Her legs kick out behind her: two shiny sticks plugged into saddle shoes. They are both laughing, having a terrific time with their wholesome pink cheeks and their swing dancing. *Dancing.* Swing *dancing.*

I can almost hear crickets chirping in Missouri.

"Well, gotta run. Don't want to miss the convention. Good luck, girls!" And with that, Bob and Peggy Lansky, swing dancers extraordinaire, board their Winnebago and lurch off into the sunset. Wearing crooked smiles, we watch them drive away.

After we top off the tank in Hanksville, use the restrooms, load up on more bottled water and snacks, and ascertain that we have indeed lost Rick (for the time being, at least), we debate where to stay for the night. Jillian argues on the merits of a shower, complimentary soaps, and a mint resting on a clean, fluffy pillow, and Denise rebuffs with images of harmonious camping and stargazing in Capitol Reef National Park. She even says something about a harmonica. I just want to sleep, and soon. We drive to the park and learn that all seventy campsites at the first campground we stop at were filled by three-thirty this afternoon. All of the sites at Cathedral Valley and Cedar Mesa, both half an hour away, are also full. The middle-aged bespectacled ranger suggests a campground in nearby Dixie National Forest. (Who knew southern Utah had national forests?) We're growing agitated. The sun has long slipped beyond the horizon, and we're washed in cool shadows. We climb back into the car. Jillian pops in a Jack Johnson CD and begins to sing along. I turn the volume way up to drown her out. I hate to say it, but listening to a turkey being shaved would probably do less damage to my eardrums than ten minutes of Jillian's singing. "What's wrong, don't like my singing?"

"Come on, Marianne Faithfull," I reply. "I adore your singing."

"Who's Marianne Faithfull?"

"Never mind."

The Dixie campground is also full. Twenty minutes later, after a wide-eyed and hyper-vigilant drive through a deer-infested stretch of semi-forested, curvy highway and one of those useless, juvenile two-part arguments over directions ("No it isn't," "Yes it is," "No it isn't," "Yes it is," rinse, lather, repeat), we lurch into the parking lot of Austin's Chuckwagon Motel in nearby Torrey. The night manager tells us there are two rooms left. "Your lucky night!" He grins at us and passes us our room key, and I notice he's missing his middle finger. Is that the penalty for an offensive gesture in Utah? The land where indulging in caffeine and too many earrings could land you some lake-of-fire-front property in hell, right next door to Dr. Mengele? I notice Denise signing the logbook again as "Amy Jasper," and this time I ask why. To deter Rick, perhaps?

"It's so wholesome!" is all she answers in return, flashing a brilliant white smile. I watch her return to the car with Jillian to fetch our luggage. I put the room on my American Express card. I don't mind. Jillian has announced that she will pay for half when we hit the next ATM, and as for Denise, she's lucky to afford a bag of Cheetos in the Snax machine near the motel parking lot. Unless she lifted someone else's purse at the last gas station. And if she did, I really don't want to know about it.

Our room is a generic composite of every motel room designed since 1990: the uncooperative window Climatron, the quilted nylon bedspreads in a muted pattern, the matching landscape prints above the faux headboards bolted to the wall, the coffeemaker and mini hair dryer near the sink, the raggedy local phone book, the drapes on a stick, the Gideon Bible in a drawer, the plastic-wrapped plastic cups flanking a plastic ice bucket on a plastic tray. Jillian wilts with relief that we have a clean shower and complimentary soaps. Cut-rate, to be sure, but still—they are individually wrapped. Denise and I fling ourselves on our beds while Jillian goes into the bathroom to take a shower. "Oh my God, there are little black flecks in the bottom of the toilet bowl," she says from behind the bathroom door, her voice heavy with disgust.

"And pubes everywhere! All over your pillow!" I shout. Jillian just gives a muffled, monotonous "Ha-ha." Denise and I snicker, and then the only sound from the bathroom is the hiss of the shower. "Jillian wouldn't lie on the top of the bedspread like this," I whisper.

"Why not?"

"Because they never wash them."

"Gross." Despite this acknowledgment, we don't get up. "Are you nervous about tomorrow?" she asks me.

I nod. Tomorrow we're going to Cedar City, where I will work up the nerve to visit Betty Resnick. Larry's mother, grandmother, aunt, cousin, or sister. (Or wife, even, though I'm not feeling that kind of vibe.) Well, this was one of the main reasons behind my trip, wasn't it?

"You'll be great," Denise says, followed by "And I'll be right back. I'm so hungry my stomach is eating itself." Then she promptly marches off to investigate the cellophane-wrapped sandwiches and mealy Red Delicious apples at Austin's Chuckwagon General Store. Jillian's cell phone, left on the end table between the motel beds, rings to the tune of "Annie's Song." I look at the caller ID. Geoffrey with a G. Ugh. It stops ringing before Jillian steps out of the shower.

Five minutes later Jillian walks out of the bathroom in shorts and a T-shirt, toweling her hair. "Did my phone just ring?"

"Um, yeah. It was Boy Wonder." She freezes, her hair dripping on the carpet. Just as she dives for her phone I grab it. "Jillian, re-member what we talked about. Be strong!"

She wrestles the phone away from my hand and listens to his message with her back to me. She hangs up and sits on the edge of the bed, staring at the blue drapes. When I can't stand it any longer, I blurt, "So what did he say?"

"Nothing, really. He just wanted to see how I was doing." She nibbles on a hangnail and adds, softly, "He doesn't want to get back together."

My heart rolls its eyes. "He actually said that in a message? After asking how you were doing? What a jerk."

She turns to me, crying. "I miss him so much."

I miss him like a plantar wart. And I hate seeing my friend turned inside out over this guy. What is the attraction? If my best friend could fall in love with such a putz, what did that say about her choice of me as a best friend? I sigh. "Sweetie, I know. But don't you think you could use some time alone to get some perspective?" She says nothing, just wipes away her silent tears. I try another approach. "What do you miss about him?"

"I miss his smell. The way he laughs. The way we could talk all night."

"The way he lied to you," I say. I pass her a box of tissues. Personally, I didn't think he had that great a smell. He smelled rather like sweat, dirty tube socks, and discount men's cologne. I found his laugh jarring and effeminate. And as for talking all night, I'd put my money on him talking and her listening.

"I know," she weeps, blowing her nose. "But I wasn't exactly the best girlfriend."

"Jillian, don't rationalize this. You deserve so much better!"

"But we knew one another in a past life. We have issues that carried over, that we have to resolve in this one. I'm sure of it."

Maybe they were Henry VIII and Anne Boleyn. "Well, it's your decision. Only you know what'll make you happy. But be true to yourself." In a last-ditch effort I add, in as serious a voice as I can muster, "And maybe you've already resolved your issues and learned your life lesson by standing up to him and leaving. Maybe you've set your karma straight." I wonder briefly if I've missed my calling as a semi-pretentious cut-rate motivational speaker.

She honks into a tissue, ignoring me. "We were going to spend the rest of our lives together. How could I be so wrong about some*one*—and some*thing*—so important? Our souls were . . . were . . ." Unable to name what exactly their souls were, her voice fizzles out and she just stares at me helplessly. Sometimes I want to shake Jillian and say, *Wake up! Guys don't want to talk about chakras and how parabens in cosmetics will kill you. Guys want to eat fifteen-pound hamburgers and reminisce about high school sports!* Well, unless you're trying to attract the Geoffreys of the world. But to say as much would be intentionally cruel. So I keep my mouth shut. I smile and nod at all the right parts. I try to be a friend, because I know she smiles and nods at half the stupid shit I say. And if you have the sensitive kinds of friends I do, and you're into conflict avoidance the way I am, this is how your world works. You just smile and nod and hope for a hurricane to blow in and change the barometer.

"God, I'm so stupid. How could I be so blind?" Jillian asks weakly.

I clasp Jillian's hands and try to think of something inspirational to say. "A million divorced people ask themselves the same question every day. Hon, do you think you'd really be happy with Geoffrey? Sharing custody of his kids with two ex-wives? Training for a million more triathlons and races that *he* wants to do? Watching him set off for work and wondering every day if you can trust him around hundreds of lonely women on treadmills? If you decide that's what will make you happy, then I'll stand by your choice. But Jillian, remember what you said about listening to yourself and trusting the universe. Take your own advice. You might find you're just having a moment of weakness. And if you try to go back to him, I'll haunt you after I die at thirty."

She groans and throws a pillow at me. Best of all, she doesn't return his call.

Jillian's phone call reminds me that I haven't checked my own voice mail in awhile. I have two messages: one from James ("Leigh, where are you? Why is your phone off? Call me the second you get this") and another from Wes. He doesn't leave the usual messages, like "I was just thinking of you and thought I'd see how you were doing. Call me when you get a chance." Oh, no. His messages are always something like "I was just thinking of the time your pants split down the ass when we went out in Chicago and you didn't realize it until we got home. God, that was hilarious." Sometimes he doesn't say anything when he calls and gets my voice mail—he just holds the phone out the window as the ice cream truck trundles past blaring "Turkey in the Straw" from loudspeakers. This time his message is such: "Hey, stinkfinger, just wondering if you've got any more interesting stories from the road. Lesbian stories, that kind of thing. Toodles!"

By now you've probably realized I'm not a typical girl. I don't yearn for a huge diamond engagement rock that's left a swath of dead or one-armed Africans behind it. I don't lie awake at night feverishly planning my future wedding or decorating schemes for my ideal home. And yes, my friends and I sometimes greet each other with distasteful pet names that would make Ron Jeremy blush. This is what happens when your mother leaves and your older brother raises you.

First I call Wes. He picks up after two rings. "Hello, fabulous baby!"

Now, you might think that Wes sounds like fairly solid, if a bit eccentric, boyfriend material. Oh, how wrong you'd be. While Wes has the Jack Tripper looks, they are more than offset by the Larry Dallas attitude toward women. I can't remember any of his relationships ever lasting beyond one month, a fact I attribute to his insufferable tendency to break up with someone—even a woman exactly matching his ideal—once the new-car smell has worn off. And it is always with a completely insane, Seinfeldesque excuse: Her laugh was too grating (read: her jokes drew more laughs than his); she didn't know what a two-point conversion was (read: she was too literate); she had too many shoes (read: she was perfectly normal, but he needed an excuse). This I attribute to two things: one, revenge for having his heart sent through the meat grinder by his high school sweetheart, Jenny Gillespie; and two, well, he's just got too much testosterone and his brain isn't yet fully developed. I don't mean that in a bad way. It's just a fact about human development that I've gleaned from reading far too many medical journals. (That's another side effect of being diagnosed with a life-threatening illness—you read way too much about human physiology and traditional and alternative medicine, thinking if you could just outsmart the dirty tricks your genes were playing on you, you'd somehow win.) In a generous mood, I'll also blame our generation in general, because we're always on the lookout for the next big new thing. Why buy this year's model when next year's will be so much better?

But Wes is sweet. Before and after my transplant he logged endless hours visiting me in the hospital, always bringing something unexpected: a bouquet of frog balloons, a giant beach ball, five episodes of *Mystery Science Theater 3000* on DVD, a jar of kidney stew. Give him ten years, and I think he'll make a great husband for someone. A very patient someone with an excellent sense of humor. Because we grew up together and watched each other go Quasimodo as we lurched through puberty, Wes and I never really considered dating each other when we reached high school. And by then, I was enthralled with Kevin Murphy's sexy teen angst/pathological lying and Wes was almost surgically attached to Jenny Gillespie's left hip until the fateful day he realized Mark Randall was attached to her right. I think he sees me as a kid sister (especially since he calls me kid or kiddo on occasion), though I'm several months older than him. Which gives me exactly what I need: another protective brother.

I tell him about running out of gas and Denise being chased by her crazy ex-boyfriend. Wes is alarmed, of course, as we all are. "Jesus," he says. "What are you going to do?"

Well, she is packing heat, I almost say. Instead I say, "I don't know. What can I do? I can't just abandon her."

"Sure you could."

"Whatever. Wes, you've got a bigger bleeding heart than I do. Why give advice even you wouldn't take?"

"You don't know that."

"Yes, I do."

"Well, I think you should call the cops. Fuck that noise. It could be dangerous."

"There's safety in numbers. We stick together and we'll be okay." Even I don't believe myself.

Wes ignores me and continues rambling on. "And I can't believe you didn't get Triple-A before a road trip." I can almost hear him shaking his head at my sub-par planning.

"It would be quite the investment, given the four miles I put on my car annually. And did I mention our cell phones were useless? Oh, I think I did. About eight times."

"Well, thanks for getting me all worried about you."

"Don't mention it."

"Hey, am I in your will?"

"Yeah, you're getting a bunch of Lance Bass posters."

"Aw, you know I love you, kid. Call me if you need me."

We hang up, and I feel better. Next I dial James. "Now where are you?" he demands immediately.

"Um, Torrey. Torrey, Utah."

"Where's that?"

"Between Moab and Cedar City."

"So are you still hell-bent on seeing Kate?"

I stick my tongue out at the phone. "Yes." Sometimes in the movies, you see people make crackling, staticky noises to prematurely end an unpleasant phone conversation. This would never work in real life, unless you were talking on a Hasbro walkie-talkie to someone with moderate to severe hearing loss. But since my reception is growing worse by the second, this may be a nonissue anyway.

"When are you coming home?"

"After I see Kate."

Despite a sudden crackle of static, I can hear him sigh and Marissa murmuring something in the background.

"Jillian's with me," I announce brightly.

"Is she mapping your course with a divining rod?" James snorts.

No, we're using Larry, I almost say.

"How are you feeling?" he asks. "Are you taking your meds?"

"Fine. And yes. How's work?"

We chat for a bit about nothing important. I've heard there are brothers and sisters that tell each other almost everything, laughing together over nutty relatives and coworker antics. They live on the planet Fiction. A few years before I got sick I tried truly getting to know my brother, if that's what you could call it. His first reaction was, I suppose, that of a teacher discovering that her smelliest, most illiterate student became a mini Degas when he picked up a paintbrush or chunk of sidewalk chalk. Like "Goodness, look what you've created! Oops, no, we don't *eat* the chalk." We attempted a few *meaningful* conversations about *things that matter*, but whenever I asserted something like "Don't you think Gram's garden was a fabulous metaphor for human existence?" James simply countered with a blank stare. We eventually tired of the whole thing and returned to leaving each other lists of toiletries that needed replenishing and phone calls that needed returning.

My reception suddenly dies and we're cut off. I'd say "literally and figuratively," but that would be stating the obvious, wouldn't it?

The next morning, something feels weird. I've been dreaming I'm on a sailboat with Wes, Jillian, and Denise. I'm in a wedding dress, and I think I'm getting married to Larry on the boat. But my groom is nowhere to be found. I run from stern to bow in a panic. When I tell Denise who I'm looking for, she merely says, "Oh, him? We threw him overboard."

After I haul myself out of the dream my hands move to my scar. It's still there, and Larry beneath. I'm nervous. What will I say to Larry's family?

"Denise, are you awake?" I whisper.

She mumbles something unintelligible and rolls over. Jillian's snoring softly next to me, hogging the bedspread. I get up, throw on shorts and a tank top, and go for a walk.

Today's the day. Do I still want to do this?

As I watch the rising sun inject the red hills with life, I'm convinced. Absolutely. I'm living every day like it could be my last. And my new schedule for that final day has nothing to do with impressing someone else.

I lift up a corner of my shirt, push down my shorts just an inch, and show my scar the sun. I trace a finger along it. How did you die, Larry? Was it a car accident while you were racing home to tell your family you just proposed to Hopi? Was it an embolism suffered during a flag football game with your nieces and nephews after Thanksgiving dinner?

I guess it probably wasn't cancer, because chemotherapy doesn't seem like a real kidney-friendly treatment. It's also unlikely he died from any other kind of terminal illness, which usually leaves your organs more trashed than a motel room in Cancún after spring break.

You know, when you consider the various exits from the planet we might one day take, terminal illness doesn't rank up there on most people's lists of Most Merciful or Best Ways to Die. But at least then you get the luxury of being prepared, of making some kind of peace with your life. With an accident, your last words to your mother could actually be "I wish I'd never been born!" as you storm out of the house, slamming the door hard enough to shake the pictures on the walls.

Was it a suicide, like my father? Did you give up on the world because you felt it had given up on you?

I know the feeling.

I can't believe I'm going to find out how he died, and how he lived. It's amazing, this gift he's given me. I wish I knew him.

In Jerzy Kosinski's *The Painted Bird,* a young Polish peasant falls hopelessly in love with a Jewish man she's never met based only on his photograph. The picture, along with dozens of other similarly doomed photos, fluttered across the countryside from a cattle car full of human cargo as it chugged across Poland to the gas chambers of Auschwitz. Maybe someone scattered the pictures through a tiny slot in a boxcar, the way a castaway on a desert isle would dispatch a desperate letter in a bottle to the wide blue sea. This bit isn't the entire plot of the story, mind you, but the image of a girl refusing to eat or sleep, refusing even to speak to her fiancé, over one photo of a handsome dead stranger with haunting eyes has burned itself into my mind.

That Jerzy dispatched himself years later by overdosing himself on barbiturates and putting a plastic bag over his head in the bath-tub didn't help matters much.

But this is the only analogy I can offer for what I feel about Larry and his kidney. I don't "love" him like a Polish peasant (that would be jumping over a psychological cliff of some sort), but the idea of him has embedded itself in my heart and won't shake free. The fact that his death has prolonged my own life only tightens the grip he has on my psyche. I know, he could have been some weird fifty-year-old who collected Barbie dolls and only spoke in mono-syllables, but . . . when I close my eyes and try to feel his energy, that's not the image I get.

Jeez, would you listen to me? I never thought I'd utter the phrase "feel his energy" without trying to poke fun at Jillian. But there's something to be said, New Agers be damned, about listen-ing to yourself. I'm beginning to believe that if we listen hard enough, we'll really hear the answers to our needling questions.

Take my friend Amanda. For two years she dated a lawyer with a symbiotic attachment to single malt Scotch and ethnic porn sites. I spied her crying over him at a wedding last winter and asked her in my best Oprah voice, "Well, what does your heart tell you?" To which she could only state the obvious. Her heart said to ditch the guy like a bridesmaid dress from 1988. Love, like fashion, must constantly evolve if it isn't to end up in a crumpled ball in the back of your closet. (A conclusion drawn from my stunning lack of expe-rience with the emotion as couched in romantic terms.) But the true moral here is that we usually know how to make things turn out okay. It's only a matter of acknowledging those steps and acting accordingly. I know, easier said than done. My omniscient mortal-ity does this to me.

I still think Larry was a peaceful, amazing guy. The kind of guy I'd stare at all night while working the courage up to approach. Don't ask me how I know. I just do.

We stop for lunch at a little bistro near the college. Afterward, we pop into a health food/hippie store so Jillian can stock up on gra-

nola, crystals, and patchouli. I kid. We're all stocking up on things
for the ride. Inspiration strikes as I slide my pears, snack-sized ap-
plesauce cups, low-sodium/low-potassium/low-taste cereal bars,
and cranberry juice across the counter, and I say to the clerk, "Listen. You wouldn't happen to know any Resnicks, would you?"

The clerk, a kind-faced man with wire-rimmed glasses, stares
blankly at me. Then he says, "The Resnicks? Sure! They're in my
ward."

His ward? Is that Utahspeak for neighborhood? I glance at Jillian, who's giving me a strange look I can't interpret. I lick my lips.
"Do you know a Betty Resnick?"

He grins. "Sure! Nice lady. Keeps to herself. Do you know
Betty?"

"Oh, I don't really." I feel my cheeks burn. "Okay, here's the
deal." I tell him the deal, beginning with me getting sick, having the
transplant, waking up in an altered state (mentally and physically),
and deciding to personally thank Larry's family for my new lease
on life. Denise ambles to the back to find the restroom. I flick an
eye up to the convex security mirrors and watch a bulbous, shiny
Denise investigate the cooler of drinks. She opens the cooler, withdraws two different bottles of juice, and compares their labels.
Denise, please don't steal anything.

"Wow," the clerk says. "That's some story."

"I know."

"Does Betty know you're coming?"

My cheeks are aflame, and now my forehead, too. "No. I've
been trying to work up the courage."

"She's really quite nice. I'm sure she'd be happy to meet you."

I take a deep breath and plunge into my next question. "Do you
know how Larry died?"

The clerk clears his throat. "It was a car accident."

I could collapse onto my pears in relief. It wasn't autoerotic
asphyxiation, or a murder-suicide, or some idiotic accident that
would have won him a Darwin Award. "Oh" is all I can manage.

"So you have his kidney?"

I nod.

"That's wonderful. I'm glad to hear he finally did some good!"

Whoa. Whoa there, clerkie. Somewhere inside of me, a balloon of ice water bursts. "What do you mean?"

The clerk glances at Jillian for some kind of clarification and, getting none, turns back to me. "You don't know anything about him?"

"No, not really." Every hair on my arms is standing at attention.

At this point four elderly women enter the store and the bell over the door gives a cheerful jingle. They push to the counter, and one of them asks, "Do you have wild yam cream?"

Jillian and I fade back, and the clerk gives me one last concerned look. "Stop by again, okay? Let me know how it goes with Mrs. Resnick."

We trip out of the store and Jillian clutches my arm. "Are you sure you want to do this?"

"Now more than ever." I unlock my car door and add, indignant, "You can't just do that! Just say something like that and leave me hanging! 'I'm glad to hear he finally did some good.' What's that mean?" I shove my bag into the cooler in the backseat, slam the cover, and turn back to Jillian. "It's criminal to leave someone hanging like that." A sudden thought galvanizes me and I turn back to Jillian. "Oh God, what if Larry was a criminal?"

"Maybe that guy just didn't like Larry," Jillian offers. "Great people are seldom appreciated in their own time. Look at Galileo. Heck, look at Jesus!"

Denise skips out of the store, sweatshirt bulging. The door jingles behind her. "What'd I miss?"

Fifteen minutes later we pull into the gravel driveway of a pocket-sized home straight out of 1954. It's perfectly square, white, and dwarfed by the split-level ranch homes flanking it. I've seen Barbie Dream Homes larger than this. I park and shut off the engine. We listen to it tick in the silent heat of late afternoon. My sweat glands have formed a union and are in the process of bargaining for better overtime pay. I am a human sweat faucet.

"Nervous?" Denise asks, swigging from her stolen juice.

I raise an eyebrow at her. "You have an amazing gift for stating the obvious."

"Leigh," Jillian says, "I'm sure you have nothing to worry about. Think of how long you've wanted to do this!"

Not that long, I almost say. I drum my fingers on the steering wheel. I close my eyes, focusing on Larry's kidney. I open my eyes. "Okay. Let's hit it." We step out of the car in unison, like the criminals in *Reservoir Dogs,* minus the gratuitous violence and criminal part.

Before I press the doorbell I say a small prayer to Larry or whoever is manning the controls up there: *Dear Lare, please give me the strength to meet your family. It's been a long road, and we're finally here. Oh God. I should just back out of this now. What was I thinking? I have trouble working up the nerve to order a pizza! Like I'm going to just ring this lady's bell and say, "Hi, guess who's filtering my urine these days?" Wait. I'm supposed to be praying. Right. Okay, um, whoever's listening, please help me get through this. For thine is the kingdom, and the power, and the glory. Forever and ever, amen. Thank you.*

I ring the bell. "Don't be nervous," Denise says, which only increases my anxiety.

"Maybe no one's home," I say hopefully. The possibility kicks a ray of sunshine through my field of vision, and I can almost hear a chorus of angels somewhere over Denise's shoulder.

Jillian rings the bell again, and this time we hear the unmistakable sound of an old woman shuffling to the door. "Maybe we could pretend we're Girl Scouts selling cookies!" I whisper irrationally. "Or we're Jehovah's Witnesses!"

"Knock it off," Jillian says through gritted teeth. The door swings open and her expression lights up. "Hello!"

"Can I help you?"

Mrs. Betty Resnick is wearing blue stretch pants with a sequined T-shirt tucked into her elasticized waistband. She's wearing navy slip-on canvas shoes. She looks like anyone's grandma, really. A working-class grandma who plasters her refrigerator with flag decals and drives a Buick with bad shocks. I'd bet my next paycheck there's a paper poppy stuck behind the driver's-side sun visor.

"Um, are you Betty Resnick?" I venture.

She nods. "Yes, and you are?"

I take a deep breath. "I'm really sorry for bothering you, but I'm Leigh Fielding. You might remember me? I wrote to you about . . . about my kidney transplant?" I am terrified and vulnerable. And apparently I may also be high. What was I thinking? This suddenly seems like the worst idea ever, like throwing a surprise party for a person recovering from triple bypass surgery.

Betty also sucks in a breath. We're both pulling so much oxygen from the porch, I wonder if Denise and Jillian may faint. Just as I'm about to apologize profusely and run back to the car in shame, she says, "Oh, yes! You received Larry's kidney!" She furrows her brow, as if we're here to demand a kidney from her as well. "What on earth are you doing here?"

"I wanted to thank you in person. I could have died without Larry's kidney, and I'm so grateful to him, and to his family, for giving me another chance at a normal life." Why, I don't sound nutty at all! My explanation sounds perfectly reasonable. Although it's not a sentence you'll probably utter during the course of an average day. Or ever. Denise and Jillian are just smiling benevolently behind me, like nuns in training. I remember to make introductions. "These are my friends Denise and Jillian." Everyone nods awkwardly.

"Oh my," Betty says. She seems confused, and adds, "Would you like to come in?"

As we enter Betty's living room, we're slapped by the smell of musty drapes and decaying carpeting. It's the smell of old rectories, of unwashed pillows. "You're from Iowa?"

"Wisconsin."

"Oh dear, that is a long way to come. You should have called ahead; I'd have made a nice ham dinner for all of us." She gestures to the sofa. "Please sit!" Denise and Jillian sit.

I want to hug her. She reminds me a little of Gram, had Gram subscribed to *Guideposts,* watched QVC, and worn clothing with elastic waistbands. "I'm so sorry to drop by unannounced, but I didn't have your number." (Well, I could have looked it up, right?) "We were kind of in the neighborhood, so . . . I just wanted to personally thank you and—" *Say it. Say it!* "Learn more about Larry." I look to Jillian and Denise for support. They beam at me from the plaid sofa, road-weary Miss America contestants. "Um, are you his grandmother?" I ask.

Betty nods and settles into a worn chair near the couch. I'm the last one standing (how often can I say that?), so I join Jillian and Denise on the couch. "Yes, I am. Larry's mother lives in Salt Lake City with her new husband. But we don't really talk anymore." She gives me a look that seems both regretful and self-righteous, and I wonder what kind of falling-out led to the emotional standoff. "His father, my son, passed on in '99. Lung cancer, bless his soul. Larry lived with me on and off, moved to Minnesota two years ago. He found a job with the railroad out there, thank the Lord. Wasn't making too much of himself here. The kid had the worst of luck."

I let this fact sink in. No nonprofit in Utah. Strike one. I'm also amazed at Betty's frankness, at her willingness to share intimate details of her life with a total stranger. Is it loneliness that cultivates such desperate disclosure in some people? "Was he married?" I ask.

"No," Betty says, looking perplexed. "He never seemed to meet any nice girls."

No girlfriend named Hopi. Strike two. "Did he have any brothers or sisters?"

Betty nods. "Just one. A younger brother doing his missionary work in Australia."

"Missionary work?"

"We're Mormon. Well, I was Mormon. Left the church a few years back." She sighs, but I detect a whiff of independence and good humor. "They don't quite like that much."

Mormons! *Ball!* One ball, two strikes. Runners on first and third. But we can recover from this. This is minor. I give myself a mini pep talk and mentally karate-chop the disappointment that's trying to sneak past the bouncer into the party.

Suddenly Betty cocks her head, like she's tuning in to a frequency only dogs and leprechauns can hear. "Would you like to see his old room?" She gestures to a door in the back of the house, past the tiny harvest-yellow kitchen.

I try not to leap up and salivate. "Absolutely!" I can actually feel the molecules in my body straining and pulling toward Larry's room, really throwing themselves into the campaign.

Betty pushes herself out of her easy chair. "My, you girls have come a long way. All this way to learn about Larry?"

"Pretty much," I admit. It did make one hell of a good excuse for a road trip.

"So what do you do back in Wisconsin?"

Ugh. I hate this part. "I work with dogs. Training, that sort of thing."

"I'm a student," Denise volunteers.

We all look at Jillian. "I'm a massage therapist." She blushes.

Jillian and I shouldn't care if anyone thinks our jobs are frivolous or that we're merely maids of a different stripe. But we do care. Because we like what we do (for the most part), and it's tedious to think of yet another way to defend the honor of your profession. Whenever Jillian tells guys about her job, they invariably turn their backs to her and hunch their shoulders like they have such aching neck muscles. This usually happens in a bar. And whenever I tell guys about my job, they laugh and walk away to order another beer.

Betty smiles and nods. "Oh, how nice."

Well, we're not molecular biologists, but hey, we contribute to Social Security and pay our bills on time. Mostly. We follow her through the kitchen to Larry's bedroom. My body hums with anxiety. She opens the door, and a stale smell puffs out. She flips on a light. "This is it."

I step in, my eyes adjusting to the light.

Have you ever had one of those moments where you discover a shocking habit concealed by a loved one? Say, Grandma's "massager" in a nightstand drawer, or a photo of Uncle Fred in Aunt Helen's girdle, or sixty-three progressively intimate e-mails in your boyfriend's in-box from a certain "kewlgurl84"? And space and time seem to have agreed that prolonging this *moment d'horreur* (if only illusory) would make for a great laugh? And how foolish and hot and ashamed you felt afterward, even though nothing had truly changed but your perception of reality?

That's how I feel right now.

An enormous Confederate flag is draped along the wall opposite us. Beady glass eyes stare at us from the heads of a bevy of taxidermied animals: Here's a stuffed fox poised on a log, defying the laws of gravity and decomposition. . . . Here's a raccoon glancing vacantly at us as if we'd interrupted her washing an apple. . . . There's a duck midflight . . . and nailed to a wooden plaque, a trout midswim. One entire wall has been littered with the heads of mounted bucks. Leather necklaces, belts, baseball caps, and handkerchiefs drip from their antlers. But wait, there's more: The pièce de résistance, the grand marshal of this parade of horrors, is the real bearskin rug splayed out on the floor, its eyes coolly regarding us. Bad enough to have your eyes replaced with marbles and your mouth propped open for all eternity, catching flies. Worse to spend the afterlife absorbing people's toe jam.

I look at Betty for an explanation, for a correction. I wait for her to say, "Hold on, sorry. This is Larry's crazy redneck brother Bubba's room. Larry's room is upstairs." Instead she says, "I kept it just how he left it."

Jillian looks at me nervously. I can taste something terrible back near my tonsils, a cross between bile and burned rubber. "Oh my God," I whisper.

"Wow," Denise says. "He was really into hunting, huh!"

"Yes," Betty says. "Yes, he was." The phone rings and she excuses herself before padding off in her Sensi shoes to answer. I can hear her careful, wary voice down the hall: "Hello? This is Betty." I can't hear the rest.

I tiptoe over to the dresser, which is littered with belt buckles, coins, and dusty sticks of deodorant. I open a drawer and carefully lift a sheaf of old birthday cards.

"Should you be doing this?" Jillian whispers. She peers down the hall toward Betty, who is still on the phone, nodding at whatever the person on the other end is saying.

I don't say anything, but continue gently rummaging through the contents of Larry's dresser drawer for more clues: an old watch, baseball cards, a Matchbox truck, movie ticket stubs, a small photo album. I'm tempted to shout "Eureka!" as I rapidly flip through the book, first craning my neck to see what Betty's up to. She's still on the phone, and I can hear her saying, "No, I really can't right now." Have to make this fast. The album's clear plastic sleeves contain various shots of people drinking, arms slung over one another's shoulders, more people posing in sunglasses at what appears to be a car race, shots of various cars at said race, a few pictures of girls in tiny shorts, and of course, pictures of orange-clad hunters posing in fields, proudly holding up the heads of their dead quarry for a final grisly portrait.

"Which one's Larry?" Denise whispers in my ear. I shrug, frustrated. There's no telling if he's even in any of these pictures, let alone which hillbilly he might be. As I flip to the end of the book, a yellowed newspaper clipping falls out. I read it silently. Jillian and Denise read it over my shoulder. I barely notice Denise moving her lips while she reads.

As I read the article, it dawns on me why it's so difficult to arrange visits between organ donor families and transplant recipients. Because someone winds up on a robust menu of antidepressants, or maybe their head explodes. In this case, I fear it may be me.

Larry didn't die alone. Drunk, he blasted through an intersection at about seventy miles per hour and rammed into a minivan driven by a deaf woman. She was killed instantly, along with her service dog. Her passenger was badly injured in the crash but survived.

My blood is being filtered by a kidney whose former owner killed a deaf woman and a service dog for the hearing impaired. Oh, and he severely injured a woman who, according to the article, volunteered extensively for a local literacy foundation. Can't forget that.

I start to have that feeling. That slimy, sick feeling you get where you want to slip out of your skin and run screaming down the hall to wash your hands for three days. I open my mouth, but the only noise that comes out is this high, almost inaudible whine. I clear my throat. Suddenly, I have trouble swallowing. And I'm itchy all over.

Jillian drops her jaw and stares at me. I can see her uvula. She also has an unattractive line of spittle connecting one of her bottom teeth to the roof of her mouth. Incredibly, it makes me want to giggle.

I touch my cheeks. They're hot, downy. Am I still real? I hear myself say, "I need to get out of here." I slip the clipping back into the album, then stuff the album back into the drawer.

We file out into the hallway, following Betty's voice. From what we can hear, it seems she's struggling to rebuff the advances of a telemarketer. She sees us and says with some resolve, "I have to go. I have company." She carefully places the phone back in its cradle on the wall. "Would you girls like something to drink? I have orange juice, milk, water . . . or I could make some tea." Betty looks at us hopefully. A bead of sweat snakes its way down my side, pooling at my waistband. Its coldness makes my skin pimple into goose bumps.

"I'm so sorry, but we really have to run."

"But you just got here!"

I knit my eyebrows together. I honestly can't tell if I'm disappointed or confused. It's exactly like the time Tommy Feducci pretended to like me for one day in sixth grade, and the entire class had a good laugh at my expense during lunch hour when he confessed the whole thing had been a joke. I can still remember the acidic film of tomato soup at the back of my throat. I can still remember staring at the orange ring in the bowl resting patiently on my tray. To this day I can't eat tomato soup.

I open my mouth to reply, but nothing comes out. Jillian glances nervously in my direction and steps in. "I know, and thank you so much for your hospitality. It must have been a real surprise to have visitors like us today!"

Betty smiles wistfully. "Oh, it was a wonderful surprise. It's just so nice to have visitors. And such special visitors!" She clasps my right forearm with a cool, bony hand—a lonely old woman desperate for her guests to stay. "Come back any time. I'm just so happy you stopped by. It was so nice to meet you." I smile, torn by guilt and disappointment. I squeeze her hand and manage a dazed "Nice to meet you, too."

"Keep in touch?" she asks, her eyes searching mine.

I nod and say, "Of course." Anyone would be lucky to have her as a grandmother.

I ask Jillian to drive. We're all silent for the first ten minutes. I'm turning my newfound knowledge over and over in my head, weighing it, considering the meaning of it all.

He has a Confederate flag on his wall. He killed a deaf woman and a service dog. His kidney is cleaning my blood. I finally break the silence. "Oh God, he stands for everything I detest. Oh, I could rip it out of me! I feel sick." I open my window and take a gulp of air. All of a sudden I'm reminded of a party a few years ago at which Wes bet some guy twenty dollars he wouldn't drink a bowl of flat beer, hot sauce, tobacco juice, and spit. The guy did, and promptly threw up in the bowl. He won another fifty bucks drinking his own puke.

Jillian glances at me. "Come on, Leigh, it's just an organ. It's keeping you alive."

"It's not 'just an organ.' It's a symbol for—for—" For what, I'm not really sure. For my recovery? For the "new me"? For gullibility? I don't know, so I change the subject. "You're the one who told me I was *channeling* him! *God*, I'm such a fool."

"Well, maybe you were channeling the good stuff."

"I think I'm going to throw up." I think of the guy at the party drinking his own puke and dry-heave theatrically. My eyes water in protest. "Oh my God. Oh my God! I can't live with that inside of me." It's an insidious joke. It's more than shameful and disgusting.

New taste in music? Gazpacho and falafel? New hobbies like metal detecting and kayaking? I invented it all! Could it be that I simply designed my perfect man like Build-A-Bear? Oh, and how I pranced around believing it, bragging about it, a grown woman professing a renewed belief in the Easter bunny and the tooth fairy. Like James said, it's called reality. And I need to pull up a chair and dish myself a whopping serving of it.

"Leigh, be rational," Jillian says. "That kidney is just a piece, *one piece* of a troubled person. It's still a gift!"

"I can't believe I thought I was assuming the characteristics of some dead creep. I can't believe myself." I bury my face in my hands. For a few months, I was reborn: I kayaked, bought new CDs, got a funky haircut. I could make challenging decisions, explore uncharted territory, speak up when my soup was cold and the Coke flat. I was the kind of person who believed she could do whatever she set her mind to, as long as she took her prednisone and Imuran on a daily basis and stayed kind to animals and other human beings.

I was a fool. Like Jillian, I rearranged myself to suit some guy. Unlike Jillian, my guy wasn't even alive! Or connected to reality in any way! I completely invented him!

"Wow. You just don't hear about dogs being killed in car accidents that often," Denise muses from the backseat. I can only glare at her. *What would Larry do?* my ass. "I mean, people, sure. But pets? I don't think I've ever heard of a dog dying in a car accident!"

"Denise," Jillian says sharply.

"I pinned all of my . . . *strength* on this guy. We asked him for fucking directions!" I lower my voice and tip my head. "Hello, Mr. Made-up Man. Where are you taking us today?" I answer myself in a higher voice. "To the land of make-believe! Where the streets are paved with sparkly self-delusions and the rivers flow with chocolate syrup! Wouldn't that be grand? Now turn left here, first you're going to romp around like an asshole at Zion National Park!"

I know I'm being difficult. But my pride has really taken a beating. Some people become withdrawn in the face of their own foolishness; I, apparently, become childish and prone to crude imagery. I sigh. "Maybe I need to just accept my fate. Learn to love pork rinds and Jeff Foxworthy."

Jillian shakes her head, smiling gently. "Oh, Leigh, you've always known what to do. You have a strong inner compass."

Jillian doesn't know me at all. Who is she talking about? Clearly, I'm clueless. I'm as lost as the rest of the twentysomething floatabouts that majored in philosophy and now work in banks, except I'm a terminally ill orphan who can't even get drunk when I have a bad day.

CHAPTER TEN

Nevada: Wide Open

M ost people don't become dependent on someone else, even a family member, overnight. Usually, it's a gradual process: an elderly aunt falling in the shower, breaking a hip, first needing help buying groceries and eventually requiring round-the-clock supervision . . . a grandfather unable to keep up with his house over time . . . a mother slowly succumbing to multiple sclerosis.

But some do become dependent on others overnight: a kid in a car sideswiped by a drunk driver . . . a father who has a heart attack in the middle of a business meeting . . . and me. After I got sick, there was really no way I could stay in school and afford my apartment, which had finally begun to reflect my personality. I was always tired, I was always in the hospital (or so it seemed), and I was always broke. So I said good-bye to my professors, to the people who would have rounded out my circle of friends, and to my roommate, a cloyingly nice girl in braces whose favorite outfit was a blue nylon tracksuit. James and Marissa helped me pack, helped me move all of my boxes and my bed and my dresser back home, drove me to dialysis appointments, shuttled me to and from doctor visits and tests. For their support, I will always be grateful. But it was as if I'd tasted *real* life on my own—danced on the sparkling stage of it—and someone in the wings had yanked me off with a huge cane. Late at night, thinking of the parties I was missing, the dates my friends were on, the careers they were preparing for, I curled into a little knot of resentment and sadness.

Then the medical bills started piling up, eating raggedy holes through the money Gram left us. I applied for Social Security disability benefits and Medicare, but as a transplant recipient under age sixty-five, my coverage expires in three years—isn't that a nifty little clause? I also applied for assistance under the state's Chronic Renal Disease Program, and let me tell you, nothing will make you feel like a senior citizen who lives in a refrigerator box like submitting the application forms for all of these programs. After a late night around a kitchen table smothered in bills and paperwork so confusing it could have been a home PC-assembly tutorial written in Bengali, James and Marissa decided the best thing would be for me to "limit my income" in order to qualify for maximum coverage with Wisconsin Medicaid. (Mindy, my boss at Fuzzy Navels, loved the whole "limiting my income" angle.) In the end, I was scraping by with a patchwork of cobbled-together funding streams that served to keep me walking and talking. It's a huge pain in the ass just to keep up with the paperwork, but you'd be surprised at what you'll do for just a few more sunsets, a few more episodes of *The Golden Girls,* a few more root beer floats.

And I was trapped. Every job for which I was qualified paid little and failed to offer decent health benefits. Let me rephrase that: Every job for which I was qualified and *interested in.* Even big-box stores offer health insurance to employees (with a hefty deductible and a waiting period of up to two years, of course), but what could be more soul-deadening than asking hundreds of people daily if they'd like a cart as they contribute to the trade imbalance with China? No, thanks. I'd rather die of kidney failure. You have to draw the line somewhere.

A few years back, James and Marissa even discussed adopting me so I could access James's health insurance, but that conversation fizzled when we learned his policy's cutoff age for dependents was twenty-five, and that it only applied to full-time students.

James holds the purse strings. Any presidential candidate who dares mention the words *single-payer system* is dismissed as a commie-pinko with probable ties to Havana. The price of medication continues to climb, and I'm off the Medicare tit in twenty-four months. Canada is looking mighty shiny right now. Maybe I could settle down with a good-hearted Canuck and raise orphaned reindeer. We could kayak the Ogoki River and I could learn to garden. I could go back to school, become a veterinarian!

But how to make my escape, that's the million-dollar question. I'm very open to suggestion.

We're hurtling down I-15 toward Las Vegas with Fleetwood Mac sanding the rough edges from our moods. Every revolution of my tires puts more distance between me and Larry Resnick's room-o'-revulsion, and it can't happen fast enough.

Lost his virginity listening to Jeff Buckley . . . ha! Probably lost it to a woman named Tiara Rose while listening to Toby Keith in the stained backseat of a rusty Chevy Caprice after the monster truck rally. Probably had to peel off a pair of tight acid-washed jeans and leopard-print bikini underwear to perform the act of debauchery. I shudder just thinking about it.

"Leigh, stop thinking about Larry," Jillian suddenly says, breaking the silence. She eases off cruise control when we get tangled in a sudden clog of cars. I shrink into my seat and focus on the semitrailer ahead of us. It's got one of those "How's my driving?" 800-numbers posted on the back doors, and I want to dial it to find out if anyone ever calls to commend the driver: "Hey, Truck Wranglers. Just wanted to let you know that Jim Bob is doing a bang-up job!"

"I'm not thinking about Larry."

"Leigh, I know you. You've got to stop beating yourself up over this."

I mock pummel myself. "I've only begun to beat myself up over this." I glance in her general direction while she rolls the window down. A candy wrapper swirls up from the floor and pelts my forearm. Above the din of highway noise and the ethereal harmonizing on "Rhiannon," I can hear her sucking air through her two front teeth: a reedy, almost inaudible whistle that makes the hair on my arms stand up, salute, and volunteer for active duty in wartime. Jillian does this without even realizing it, turning it into an off-key, nonsensical song. I can feel my blood pressure tiptoe up the scale. No black car behind us, but that's small consolation to me right now.

She stops tooth-whistling for a moment to ask, "Can I tell you something?"

"As long as it doesn't involve past lives, Native American mysticism, chakras, or cellular memory."

Jillian just gives me a pitiful look as she reaches for the volume and dials Stevie down to an indoor voice. I hate when people turn down the volume when I'm into a song! My minor irritation almost whirls into irrational, pent-up-in-a-crowded-car rage. I do a mini breathing exercise. *In for three—hold for four—out for seven.* "I have to come clean about something."

I glance at her. She's staring straight ahead, tooth-whistling again to gather her thoughts, I presume. "It wasn't Geoffrey's fault that we broke up."

Hearing his name again feels like being trapped in a bad dream. "What do you mean?" I'm half paying attention the way you sometimes do when a girlfriend wants to reanalyze her defunct relationship for the 8,395th time and you just want to eat a donut and take a nap.

"I . . . I met someone else, and . . ." she whispers so quietly I almost confuse it with one of her tooth-whistles.

"Huh?" I squint at her. She's mincing around what she means, but I'm fresh out of patience. I decide to get blunt. "You cheated on him?" The word sounds like a slap. Jillian's never cheated on anyone or anything, not even a spelling test in eighth grade. Not even when Paul Esben plugged the answers for Mr. Belling's final Advanced Chemistry exam into everyone's calculators. Jillian got the only B, and the only honest grade. (Sadly, yours truly fully admits to cheating. But I fudged three answers so it wouldn't look like I did.)

Red splotches bloom on her cheeks. "I wasn't happy for so long, and I sort of got close to someone at work, and it was a huge mistake and . . ." Her voice trails off, hoping I make the connection she intends. But my synapses are on a coffee break.

"What are you talking about?"

She fidgets and flips the cruise control on again as we exit the car clog. "Joaquin is another therapist at the day spa, and we sort of . . . The thing is . . ."

I try to digest this juicy tidbit, but all I can think is *From Geoffrey to Joaquin. Where have all the Steves and Brads gone? The Toms and Bills?* I take a deep breath as my synapses return from their coffee break and get down to business. "Wait a minute. I thought you and Geoffrey were engaged and happy and then all of a sudden he reveals this big crazy infidelity to you."

She avoids eye contact and jiggles her left knee. I can actually hear Denise straining to listen from the backseat. "Yes, we were engaged, but . . . I was so lonely. All he did was run the gym and train for the next big event. I got so tired of eating alone all the time, pretending to play along."

"I thought you loved that shi—stuff!"

Jillian shrinks a little. "I do, I mean, I did. I love hiking and biking and running on my own . . . but he got so competitive. That's just not me."

"I'll say," I add. Jillian barely lasted two weeks on the JV girls' basketball team and finished last at every track meet in eighth grade. And as sophomores we entered Fond du Lac's two-mile Walleye Run and came in second-to-last, gasping and wheezing. I can still see the trio of octogenarians that passed us in the home stretch. I can still hear our rallying cry as we summoned our last reserves of strength to cross the finish line: "Thunder thighs! Activate!"

"I ended it with Joaquin almost as soon as it began," Jillian continues. Her voice is rising, wobbling, quietly defensive. "The guilt was killing me, and I really love Geoffrey. I don't know, maybe it was my way to get his attention. To get back at him for ignoring me, I guess. I don't know. It's awful, I know." Her grip tightens on the steering wheel. Her cheeks are so red I can almost see them throbbing.

"That's one way of doing it!" Innocent little Jillian. I can't believe it. *I can't believe it!* But I'm relieved that the Jillian I knew and loved is still there beneath the weird robo-athlete she's become since Geoffrey stepped in as activities director in her life. This would certainly explain why she's been so snippy and withdrawn lately. Her heart wasn't broken four nights ago; it disintegrated weeks ago! Maybe even months. And she's been keeping it a secret for as long. I feel like a terrible friend for not figuring the whole thing out. How self-absorbed can I get? I sit almost slack-jawed, still trying to absorb this revelation. My virtuous, principled, trustworthy (if a bit flaky) best friend actually cheated—a *most* uncharacteristic behavior on her part—on the worst boyfriend she ever had. Well, garbage in, garbage out. Is that a sign or what?

Jillian glances at me, near tears. "I know. I'm an awful person."

"No, you're not," I say. (Like I'm going to say *I completely agree, you smarmy tramp* and do a tuck-and-roll from the speeding car.) "So did Geoffrey . . . ?" I ask gently. I almost say *return the favor?* but thankfully I don't.

Jillian gives a shaky sigh. "I don't know if he's cheating or not. He's been punishing me by spending all this time with this girl from Crunchtime, and whenever I ask what's going on, he just changes the subject. I think he's seeing her. I don't know. Probably." Her eyes well up with tears and she stops to take a deep breath. "I deserve it. I really do. It was the worst thing I could have done. We've been talking this to death for weeks. I thought we were patching things up, but . . . I was just so ashamed to tell you, and . . ." Her voice hitches and trails off again. I wonder if this is the best time for such a teary-eyed confession—barreling down a highway in a metal death trap surrounded by hundreds of distracted motorists driving giant bullets on wheels and all—but when the urge to purge strikes, I guess you have to obey.

"Does Meg know about this?" I'm embarrassed to acknowledge that I care which friend Jillian came clean to first.

Jillian shakes her head. "You're the first person I've told. I was going crazy trying to keep this a secret, but Geoffrey wanted to keep it between us. In case we worked things out."

"Never trust a guy who tells you to keep secrets from your friends," Denise blurts from the backseat. I shoot her a look, and Jillian visibly tenses. Denise shrugs at me, eyes large.

Suddenly I'm very sad for Jillian. Crushingly sad. I remember how things seemed in high school—the whole world was ours to discover, and there were a million paths we could take. We could meet anyone—we could move to Hollywood and become best friends with Drew Barrymore if we wanted. Why not? We were from the Midwest, and it had been drilled into our brains since kindergarten that if we worked hard, if we got up at sunrise and saved our allowance instead of pissing it away on Guess? jeans, there was no reason we couldn't be an Oscar-winning director, hanging out with Matt Dillon and Lauren Bacall in the Hamptons on the weekends and volunteering at an inner-city literacy center during the week. Or we could work at Kmart, if that was what made us happy. And then, as time went on, the naïveté began to stiffen and crack under the weight of reality. Hearts break. Jobs disappoint. Friends drift apart. Kidneys fail. It's all enough to make you start going to church again. Or drinking heavily. Or both.

I flip my visor down to block the glare from the setting sun and turn back to Jillian. "Sweetie, you could have told me the truth."

She sighs heavily, and her cheeks flush again. "I was ashamed." She glances at me, hopeful. "I'm so sorry. I just . . . didn't want you to think I was a bad person. God, I mean, I hate deception . . . and here I am, living a complete lie."

I contemplate this for a moment before saying, "Well, your spirit guide would have told me eventually."

She offers a watery smile. "Shut up."

So while chasing the sun at seventy-four miles per hour, we have the conversation about trust, honesty, being true to oneself, and third-person perception versus first-person reality. I tell her my qualms about her engagement to someone she's known for only a few short months, and a bunch of other things you tell your best friend when she makes a dumb but pivotal choice. I suggest that maybe this was the universe's way of extracting Jillian from a "wrong" relationship and steering her toward one that's right for her. She seems to like this explanation. Strangely, we also get onto the topic of anime and manga. (There's something about those voluminous eyes and unthreatening button noses. Even in kindergarten, I had a disturbing Voltron fetish.) Regardless, I'm thrilled to discover I haven't thought about my kooky kidney and degenerate donor for at least an hour.

Until now.

Dammit.

After stopping for a bite at a Burger King (where I order a veggie burger and receive, instead, a bun splattered only with ketchup, lettuce, pickles, and mayo), we're back on the road. We all applaud when we pass a sign reading LAS VEGAS . . . 29 MILES. Denise cheerfully announces that we are now twenty-nine miles to smiles. We listen to Willie Nelson and try to harmonize with the lyrics we know. As the sun sets before us, painting the sky wild purples and reds that ricochet around the car, we wind up in the "slow" lane behind a sputtering Datsun dragging a sparking muffler and belching clouds of bluish smoke up through our dash vents.

"Holy shit, that guy's car is gonna start on fire!" Denise announces, reaching for her backpack. She yanks out her sign-making materials and swings into action, feverishly penning a sign with her pungent black marker: "Dude, your muffler's on fire!" My eyes water from the noxious exhaust fumes filling the car.

At that moment a particularly brilliant spark leaps from his muffler. "Wow, she's right," Jillian says, whistling through her front teeth.

"Pull up next to him," Denise instructs. At this moment, we collectively discover that the driver of this highly flammable car is attractive in a way that many young men today are: His smile makes your thighs loosen and your mouth water, yet you can tell his hair probably smells like wet mittens. (Although my judgment shouldn't be trusted anymore; it's been so long since I've gotten laid that I'd probably relish an enthusiastic romp with Mr. Bean.) After some confusion on his part and lots of pointing and waving on our part, we both pull over on the shoulder of the road.

The driver of the flammable car steps out. I can hear Denise's and Jillian's backs crackle softly as they correct their posture. Smiles spread dreamily across their faces like dryer-warm quilts being smoothed over feather beds. They look like hypnosis on Valium in a vat of whipped cream. Rick and Geoffrey *who*?

"My car's on fire?" Mittenhead asks, a puzzled look on his face.

"Yeah, the sparks were fucking amazing!" Denise answers.

He crouches down to peer under his car and we all size him up. He has a lithe swimmer's body and loose, faded jeans that hang impotently over what could be either a very flat or very tiny rear end. He looks like the kind of guy that buys fireworks in bulk and drinks Budweiser from the bottle. I think he'd have quite a bit in common with James's friend Mark, who deep-fried a turkey and brought Thanksgiving dinner to the Hooters girls in Appleton last year. He packed everything—the squash, the stuffing, the green bean casserole—in insulated color-coordinated Pyrex Portables, which were pretty much the only things he got out of his divorce.

"And there was this huge cloud of blue smoke coming from your tailpipe!" Denise adds. A truck emblazoned with orange lights streaks past, sending a hot cloud of dust onto our cheeks.

Mittenhead sighs. "I didn't think it would get me to Vegas. It's been dying the last few miles." He shakes his head and grins. "It's a good thing you were behind me!" Jillian shivers, perhaps at her proximity to mitteny-fresh meat. "I'm Dave."

We introduce ourselves while the red sun is halved by the horizon. "Do you need a ride?" Jillian asks. I'm too stunned to say anything. By the time we get to Vegas I'll have a clown car spilling dozens of stranded motorists onto the strip, one after another. This thought triggers a personal cranial rendition of "Send in the Clowns," and I struggle to replace it with a more palatable earworm. Unfortunately, the only other song available in my brain at the moment is "Joy to the World" by Three Dog Night. I go with it.

I blink heavily, and maybe Dave can sense my irritation, because he says, "Don't worry, I only need a ride to Las Vegas. I'm hooking up with some friends there."

The next thing I know we're jamming his backpack into my trunk. I knock one of my rear speakers askew in the process. Dave lugs a guitar case from his backseat and tells us he's in a band that's just lined up a regular gig at the Whisky in Los Angeles. While we rearrange luggage, he pontificates on the music scene today. "What's your band's name?" Denise asks, and if there ever was a moment designed for the application of the adjective *starstruck,* this is it.

"Sardonic Coma," Dave says.

"I love it," Jillian and Denise say in unison.

"Right now we're exploring glam rock. A few T. Rex, Bowie, and Queen covers. We've got our own stuff, too. Sort of a fresh spin on the Killers and Interpol."

"So do you wear makeup and neon-pink spandex?" I say. Lately I've felt more free to be rude to men because, let's face it, I may not be the most desirable of mates. It's something of a defense mechanism. I mean, having a wife with the life span of a fruit fly might appeal to some guys, but when most men give up and settle in for the long haul, they want someone with a little more staying power. But you know what? I shouldn't even think like this. I could outlive everyone. They could invent a bionic kidney next year and test it on me, and I'll be the one shouting "Soylent Green is . . . *people!*" in a hundred years while a bunch of futuristic guys carry me from the room on a stretcher.

His sarcasm radar must be broken, because he smiles and says, "Spandex is a fad that died for a reason." Then he opens his guitar case and gingerly withdraws his guitar. "Ladies, this here's a Les Paul. My ticket to the big time."

And incredibly, he launches into Mott the Hoople's "All the Young Dudes," right there on the side of the highway. He stops playing and tries to act modest. Denise and Jillian swoon. "You just paid for your ride," Jillian announces heartily, grinning like she's just had a Mott the Hoople–induced orgasm. I love Jillian, but she has this tendency to become a bit obsessed with men who are so, so wrong for her. As evidenced by Geoffrey with a *G*, exhibit A. Also, see exhibit B, Joel Avery, Jillian's high school Svengali. Joel Avery actually tried to burn his house down when Jillian broke up with him—because every girl loves a pyromaniac with an eating disorder, right?

"Excellent," Mittenhead says.

"What about your car?" I ask, scratching an itch on the back of my elbow.

He waves a dismissive hand at it. "That shitheap can sit there and rot for all I care. It's a miracle it's gotten me this far."

"You're just going to leave it here?" I ask.

"Sure, why not?" Dave replies somewhat flippantly.

People who do such irrational things used to make me really nervous. And while I have recently embraced my inner irrationality, there's still a small part of me that will probably always wear sensible shoes and bring a sweater for later. That part of me is frowning right now.

Jillian tucks her chin and refastens her ponytail, corralling great chunks of her hair with an elastic band. "Where were you coming from?"

"Salt Lake City. Just visiting the 'rents." He runs a hand through his mitteny hair and beams.

I hate when people call their parents " 'rents." People who do that are real 'holes.

The rest of the cramped ride to Las Vegas goes something like this:

Dave: "So there's an A&R guy coming to our next show. I'm really hoping this time pans out. The music industry can be so damn cutthroat and disappointing."

Jillian and Denise, dripping with sympathy: "Yeah, I can see that. Truly."

Dave: "We cut an album last spring and we've been shopping it around. It's just hard to find people who appreciate real talent. It's all about publicity stunts and who you know. Or who you're screwing."

Jillian and Denise, stretching so Dave has a better view of their thighs: "Totally! So do you live in L.A.? And you're from Utah?"

Dave: "Yeah, I live in L.A. now. Grew up in Salt Lake City, though. Not the best environment for a glam band." (*Boyish grin.*)

Jillian and Denise, with heaving bosoms and damp lips (*giggle*): "Oh, I can imagine! How long have you lived there? How long have you been playing guitar?"

Dave, thinking hard: "Let's see. I moved out there in . . . Three years. I've been there three years. Been playing guitar since second grade, roughly."

Jillian and Denise, unbuttoning their top buttons: "Aw! So do you write music, too?"

Dave: "Absolutely! It's a little challenging, getting four heads all on the same page, but once in awhile there's this magic . . . I don't know; I can't explain it. It's like we're tapping into the collective subconscious. I really believe artists can dip into this psychic reservoir and discover thoughts and emotions they haven't even yet experienced. And when all four of us do this at once, it's just . . . it's just amazing." (*Meaningful pause and distant gaze.*)

Jillian and Denise, entirely naked and clamoring to sit on Dave's lap: "Oh, Dave, please father our children!"

Okay, this didn't really happen. But they certainly seemed to be auditioning for parts in his harem, the way they fawned over him.

I blink hard and the road doubles. I blink again. The sun has fully set now, leaving only a hazy band of orange clinging to the horizon. A few purple clouds linger in the sky. I notice cars turning on their headlights, so I turn mine on, too. Denise is painting her toenails black in the seat next to me, yammering about ol' Rick's band Kat Traxxx. "What a putz. I mean, Kat Traxxx? With three *x*'s? And you could train a seal to play guitar better than him." The smell of nail polish stabs my nostrils and makes my eyes water. I guess she can safely bitch about him now, with a new man in the car. Testosterone has that effect on some people.

CHAPTER ELEVEN

What Happens in Vegas . . .

Las Vegas city limits. When we hit the neon lights and saw the tourists milling around in shorts, it was like finally touching sand after treading jellyfish-infested water for days. Here we were in the magical land of Oz! There was Paris! The famous fountains at the Bellagio! The Flamingo! Palm trees and the MGM Grand, the Monte Carlo, the Tropicana, and Mandalay Bay! Caesars Palace! Bally's! Insane traffic! Shallow people! Hookers!

We drove around marveling at our sensory overload, discussing where to have dinner and stay for the night. There were simply too many choices. I tend to become paralyzed by indecision when confronted with such an array of options. I'm terrified of making a bad choice and missing out on something: a bowl of ginger carrot soup that I'll remember for the rest of my life, the most comfortable pair of shoes for a wedding, a considerate boyfriend whose long-range career plans involved more than memorizing lines from Bruce Campbell flicks, you name it. This is why I can't do online auctions.

Yesterday, I wouldn't have had this problem at all. I'd have sat very still and concentrated, then told you that Larry felt I should eat mushroom risotto at Postrio, sleep at the Bellagio resort, and feed no more than fifty bucks into the slot machines at the MGM Grand. But not anymore. Now I'm going to have to learn how to just pick a damn brand of toothpaste on my own and deal with the fallout afterward.

In the end, I left it all up to Denise, Dave, and Jillian. We checked into one of the 4,408 rooms at the Luxor pyramid (with the understanding that Dave would not be staying in our room with us), then spent about thirty minutes debating whether we wanted to gamble or eat first. In the end, hunger trumped greed. So that's how we ended up at Jimmy T's Hitching Post, where the Unfinished Business Tour has caught up with me. In fact, it is in the process of beating my enthusiasm right the hell out of me as I stand in a long line to enter the glass-hooded nirvana that is Jimmy T's All-U-Can-Eat Buffet. We shift our weight from foot to foot while we shuffle along at an amoebic pace with other slack-jawed tourists in pastel shirts. Jillian, Denise, and Mittenhead make up band names while we wait.

"How about this one? Dubious Bulge!" Denise offers. Jillian snickers.

"No, I've got it. Armed and Hammered!" Dave replies. He tries to top that with "Flesh Pendulum." Denise really likes that one.

They toss around a few more fake band names, trying to outdo one another while the line inches forward to intestinal duress. Ahead, I can see people jockeying for position at the carving stations. It's like an African watering hole, with the lions shoving the hyenas to the rear and the buzzards circling overhead.

"This is the Wilson Phillips of conversations," I say, yawning. "It jumped the shark a long time ago."

"Oh," Jillian says. "Jump the Shark! I like that one for a band."

My cell phone rings. It's James, and I'm not in the mood to field his latest inquisition, so I let it go to voice mail. Someday, I tell myself, James and I will be friends. Starting after the trip, after I find an affordable apartment of my own. This thought makes me smile a little. An affordable apartment is a primo oxymoron, just like *jumbo shrimp* or *tight slacks*.

Just like when Wes tells me that dying is a part of life.

A foreign couple is standing in line behind us. I eavesdrop on their conversation, of which I understand nothing, since I don't speak whatever it is that's coming from their mouths. Swedish, perhaps? Norwegian? But it involves considerable laughter, which I want to be a part of. So I introduce myself. They tell me their names are Hanna and Oscar. "Like Oscar the Grouch," Oscar gushes. They are both at least two inches shorter than me, and trim. They wear sensible walking shoes and breathable, hip clothing. They *are* from Sweden! Props to the Travel Channel for introducing me to Scandinavian accents.

Oscar and Hanna have rented a car and are traveling across the United States. So far they've stayed in a haunted mansion outside Baton Rouge and seen the Alamo and SeaWorld San Antonio, and here they are in line for Jimmy T's world-famous bread pudding and projectile diarrhea, by the looks of it. They went to the Liberace Museum earlier in the day and show me the Liberace magnets they've purchased there. We make a few jokes about Las Vegas buffets and I slowly say, "Well, at least they've got sneeze guards!" I stretch my face into a mask of exaggerated worry. "Stay away from the food if it's got a skin on it!" I'm shouting for some reason, thinking that volume might help with the translation. They nod and laugh, which kind of makes me feel like dancing. I always get a little crazy with a captive audience that laughs at all of my jokes.

Hanna leans toward me and whispers, "Oscar had, what do you say, the trots! After dinner at the Round Table Buffet yesterday!" She giggles.

The trots! Of all the American colloquialisms for diarrhea. Oscar smiles sheepishly.

They're so wholesome! Talking to them really cheers me up. They hail from Sweden! The country that gave us ABBA! And smorgasbords! And Volvos! I love them and want to leave with them. But then a surly hostess rips me from my new adopted fam-

ily, takes my money, and seats me with my original party in the refrigerated section of the restaurant. I sigh as we slide into our
booth, suddenly noticing the effect the air conditioning is having
on my entourage. "Jillian, your high beams are on," I tell her.

She blushes and crosses her arms over her chest, but not before
Mittenhead gets a good look. Our waitress arrives and takes our
drink order. "Bone apple teet!" she says before she leaves.

We traipse to the buffet and select our plates. I gaze down the
boulevard of kale-embedded salads and sauces and pooches of
mashed potatoes. The watery coleslaw appears to be a life-threatening bacterial infection waiting to happen. I return to the table
with an innocuous pita sandwich, a piece of blueberry torte, and
some kind of corn-and-pea salad that hopefully won't beat the shit
out of my kidney. Or colon, no pun intended. Dave returns to the
table with a mound of peeled shrimp and deep-fried items. Jillian
and Denise return with plates that look more like artists' palettes,
with evenly spaced colorful blobs of food. I miss the days when I
didn't have to calculate the effect my next meal would have on my
physical well-being. I miss being able to eat so many delicious,
squeaky cheese curds my chest would hurt the next day.

The busboy refills our water glasses every time we take a sip.
He has beautiful black eyes and a large, shy smile. He has chubby
cheeks like your favorite nephew at his first Communion. His hair
is well combed.

As soon as we're all seated we start to pick at our food and make
fun of it.

Denise takes a bite of pasta salad, frowns, and announces,
"This food has been prepared for people who are allergic to delicious."

"For people on taste-free diets," Jillian adds, giggling.

"The potato salad is as nuanced as Richard Gere's acting," I say
halfheartedly, even though I haven't had the potato salad. I'm trying
to have fun, too, but something about Dave bothers me. Maybe I'm
just being strange again. This is the kind of fun I'd rather be having
with Jillian and her family, or Marissa's crazy extended family, or a
family of my own. These are jokes to have with a sweet, absent-

minded mother and some snarky siblings that know everything about you, that tease you and yank open the bathroom door while you're on the toilet, shouting, "Now presenting!" just for laughs. I suddenly feel out of place, like I'm eating with strangers. I hardly even recognize Jillian. Who are these people? The jokes are flat. I've become a tourist in my own life. A clinical observer watching myself through a two-way mirror, charting my respiration and pulse in response to a foreign environment. Do they know I'm faking it? I want to go sit with my Swedish people.

Dave arranges his shrimp shells into a pile on his napkin and says, "I know! Here's the slogan: 'Got Bland?' "

"Feed your screaming brood!" Denise shouts.

"Did you know that one in seven Americans can't locate their own country on a map?" I ask, trying to change the subject and direct the spotlight my way. Everyone ignores me.

Dave holds up a petrified chicken wing and leers at us. "Welcome, ladies and germs, to 'Is It Edible?' The game you never want to play with a suppressed immune system!"

I guess I'll be sitting this round out. Every three minutes the busboy refills our water glasses. We all smile crookedly and thank him. After awhile we stop thanking him because his attentiveness has become cartoonish and discomforting. We stifle panicky laughs, the kind you get in church, while we watch him pour.

When we finish we wildly leave him a forty-dollar tip, because we're in Vegas and money is like confetti here.

"Hey, want to go play some blackjack?" Dave asks as we leave.

"Oh, I want to gamble!" Denise agrees.

"You can't gamble. You're not twenty-one," I say, but Denise ignores this. I turn to Dave. "When are you meeting your friends?"

Dave checks his watch. "They'll be here tomorrow."

His watch not only tells time, it sees into the future.

Jillian senses my hesitation. I can tell because she's giving me this look that says *I really want to do this thing you don't want to, but I don't want you to sulk over it.* "Want to go lose some money?" she asks me, slinging an arm over my shoulder. "What do you say?"

I just want to go back to the hotel to watch some bad *Love Boat* reruns by myself. I want to go mourn my loss of the good Larry privately, away from my cavalcade of capers. "I'm not feeling all that gambly," I say. "I'm going back to the hotel to take a shower. But you guys go have fun!" I'm being a disobedient little tourist. It's simply not the American way to watch reruns in your hotel room in Vegas. It's Vegas! I'm supposed to be blowing on dice and flinging them down the craps table, rubbing my hands together and shouting, "Come on, lucky number seven! Baby needs a new pair of shoes!" I'm supposed to be drunk at an all-night dance club, sipping a neon-blue drink and shouting a conversation with guys from Kentucky. I'm not supposed to be nostalgic or sick or lonely in the midst of friends. And relatively new acquaintances.

"Oh, come on, it'll be fun!" Denise interjects.

I make a reluctant face. "Nah, I'm just in the mood to hang out. I'll meet up with you later."

"Are you sure?" Jillian asks.

"You don't know what you're missing!" Dave adds.

I have a feeling that I do. I mine my purse for a ten-dollar bill and hand it to Jillian, feigning good cheer. "Play some slots for me."

Jillian plants a huge kiss on my cheek (*mwah!*) and says, "I'll miss you, because this will be *slots* of fun." She winks at me. Jillian never met a bad joke she didn't enjoy squiring about town.

Back at the hotel room, I rinse off in the shower and flop onto the bed, flipping through channels. But I'm restless. I decide to go for a walk on Las Vegas's legendary strip. On the elevator I try to recall scenes from *Swingers* to get me in the Vegas mood, but all I can think of is Jon Favreau's character just wanting to go home. A couple in matching cowboy hats and purple silk shirts get on the elevator with me, but they don't speak to me.

I fall onto a park bench near the strip and listen to the noise of sin. A herd of drunk girls stumble past me. It's a bachelorette party, covered in pink plastic penises and screamy laughter. Across the street, a trio of Elvis impersonators serenades a cotton-topped couple wearing matching Hawaiian shirts. At the end of the song the man gives the woman a chaste kiss. The Elvis impersonators shake their hips and curl their lips before moving on.

Las Vegas is an alien landscape, concrete, metal, and glass. It sounds like winning, but it smells like losing. Mostly it's just alive. People window-shopping, accepting flyers hawking "limited engagement" shows or time-share vacation properties, staring at the lights while they eat hot dogs and drink margaritas on their way to the next spending spree. I wonder if anyone else on the street has kidney disease. How many are widows? In remission? How many haven't been home for Christmas since college? I want to do a survey. I wish I had a microphone and a cameraman in a ponytail to follow me around while I interviewed people, recording human interest stories that tugged at the heart.

I wonder if anyone else in this sensory wonderland is as obsessed with death as I am. "You, sir, do you have a keen sense of your own mortality? Do you sit down to your eggs, toast, and coffee, shake open the paper, and flip right to the obits? Do you eat a bowlful of vitamins and medication daily? What? Where's the Flamingo? Turn left in Albuquerque."

Also, I wonder what my last words will be, when I'm on my deathbed. James's last words will be "I told you so," choked out in a raspy wheeze while Marissa weeps silently near his side. She's always clutching a purse and wearing a pillbox hat in this vision.

My last words will probably be "And he killed the service dog, too!" You have to picture me whispering this to one of the neighborhood kids, who for some reason have converged around my sickbed like I'm sprawled across the hood of an ice cream truck. In my old-age fantasies, I'm always surrounded by pleasant little children who sing songs and work on craft projects with me.

Sometimes I think it shouldn't really be that scary to die. I mean, I'd be in great company. Ella Fitzgerald. Thomas Jefferson. Gandhi. Malcolm X. John Lennon. And Gram and Dad, of course. In theory, it would be a fucking amazing reunion. I mean, even *The Simpsons* featured a vignette with Jimi Hendrix and Benjamin Franklin playing air hockey in heaven. Larry would be there, and I could return his kidney to him, handing it over like a box packed with an ex's belongings. *Thanks, Lare, it's been real, but you can have this back now.* Then again, he did kill a deaf woman and her service dog. Maybe he's roasting weenies in hell with Goebbels, Pol Pot, and Falco, who ended up there for unleashing "Rock Me Amadeus" on an unsuspecting public.

Jeez, would you listen to me? I'm playing Marco Polo with normalcy. Every time I get close it skitters away. Maybe I need to go into therapy. I *am* trying to balance work, friends, family, personal fulfillment, and a life-threatening illness, after all. It isn't easy, you know. You can't have it all like the women's magazines say. I remember how shocked I was to learn that of my five closest friends, Wes was the only one not on some kind of mood-regulating drug and seeing a therapist. I remember thinking at the time that he was the only one that probably *should* be on something, with his manic personality retreating into a dark, unshakable funk twice a year. He attributed it to the changing seasons, or stress at work, but I wasn't so sure.

I'm watching from the sidelines again during the couples-only skate, except this time the couples are my friends and their therapists. Is everyone truly depressed? When did our navels get so interesting? Or do we all just need someone like Gram's second husband, a former drill sergeant, to follow us around and bark in our faces when we get simpery? *Snap out of it, kid! There are starving people in China! We had to walk uphill both ways to our crappy jobs! On one leg!*

Please forgive me. Even when I filled out my power-of-attorney forms, giving James the right to pull any plugs should my body shut down, I was snarky. I read the optional questions aloud as we sat around the table, up to our chins in paperwork. "Let's see," I said. "If I am nearing my death, I want the following items . . ." I thought for a minute and then added, "A bag of sand from Lake Michigan, a signed copy of *The Odyssey,* and an original Picasso. Think you can do that for me, James?" Of course, if I were truly nearing my death, what I'd want most by my side would be my friends, family, and complete certitude that my life had not been in vain and that, yes, Virginia, there is an afterlife. I was similarly cheeky with the next question: "If I am nearing my death and cannot speak, I want my friends and family to know that . . . I never collected bumblebee-themed stuff, and I don't know who got that wacky idea in the first place." But what I'd really want them to know is that I love them, that I thank them for everything they've done for me, and that if their hall lights tap out a Morse code some Tuesday evening, there is an afterlife and I'm playing Jenga with Gram. Oh, and Elvis says hi.

I decide to call James. Marissa answers and I say, "May I please speak to the man of the house?" in a British accent.

He's silent for a minute when he finally comes to the phone. "Leigh?"

"Hey, James," I say. "I was just thinking about you."

"Oh." He sounds surprised. "Really?"

"Sure! What's new?"

"Not much. Just working. How's the trip? Where are you now?" When I tell him, he sounds wistful. "Las Vegas, huh?"

James had his bachelor party in Las Vegas. I try to imagine James having fun with the guys in Vegas, but the only picture I get is James pouting in the den at Marissa's parents' house last Christmas. The rest of us were playing Outburst in the living room, screaming the names of body parts that come in pairs and songs by Duran Duran as if our very lives depended on them. We were frantically shouting movies starring Robert De Niro when James left for a walk because he said he had a headache. He wore his anger like a wide-brimmed novelty hat. You could see it coming a mile away.

"Hey, James," I say, "remember how you used to call funerals Die Weddings when you were little?"

James chuckles. "What made you think of that?"

"I don't know." Just my morbid preoccupation with death, I guess.

"How are you feeling?" James asks, serious again.

"I'm fine," I say. "Great."

I consider telling James about what I can now refer to as the Larry Debacle, but I'm not sure we're quite ready for that yet. *Maybe when I get home,* I tell myself.

After I hang up the phone I watch the tourists trying to get the

most of their vacation experiences. I can hardly picture James swigging a margarita or compulsively ordering a blackjack dealer to hit
him. The bench suddenly buckles next to me. Why, hello, new
friend. Here is my new friend: white spiked hair . . . wallet chain
you could jump rope with . . . weaselly brown mustache. His jeans
begin an inch above his knees and he smells like stale cinnamon
gum and gasoline. He has a black eye. When he smiles I realize his
left front tooth is missing. It's like a little window to his uvula. He
leans in to read my T-shirt.

"'Vote for Juan.' What's that s'posed to mean?"

He leers in at my breasts as if willing them to grow. I can feel
them shrinking into my bra, trying to find a safe hiding place.

"It's kind of a joke. A play on a line from a movie. It's supposed
to be . . ." What? I guess it was supposed to be sassy and postmod-
ern on its cute fitted tee, but now it just seems kind of lame.

"Oh, is it that movie about that migrant-farmworker organizer
dude? You know, the guy who organized all them fruit pickers?"

It must be my pheromones. Or maybe I emit a low-frequency
siren heard only by parolees, porn aficionados, and guys who steal
your camera to take a picture down their pants.

"No," I simply say, inching away from his breath, which seems
almost drawn on, it's so intense.

"I'd vote for you," my new friend says.

"I'm not running for anything." I'd like to run *away* from something. Namely, him.

"You could. You could run for like, Secretary of Hotness." He
laughs at his own joke. "Are you alone?" He puts a sweaty hand on
my knee.

"You know, I don't think my fiancé would like that." I stand up
and wave at a random guy in glasses who appears to be about my
age, standing and waiting for something under the flashing lights of
the casino across the street. A ride maybe? His date? The Second
Coming of Christ? He turns around to see if I'm waving at someone behind him.

"Oh, you're engaged, huh?" He looks skeptical. I'd be skeptical,
too. I look and feel like a Nick Nolte mug shot. My hair is so frizzy

it seems to be running away from my head. Boy, do I feel sorry for my fiancé!

"Bye," I add, and trot through traffic to reach my fiancé across the street.

He is what Gram would have called big-boned (but what I would call deliciously squishy and huggable) and he has the smile of someone who volunteers at hospitals, reading books to children with leukemia, but who also really knows his way around a vagina. He's wearing glasses with quirky frames and a T-shirt that has an iron-on appliqué of an old R. Crumb comic. His hair is brownish, messy, and delightful—a little fiesta above his slightly sunburned face.

"I like your T-shirt," I say, smiling.

He smiles back. "Were you waving at me?"

"Yeah. I told that guy you were my fiancé."

He laughs. "And we're getting married down the street at the drive-through chapel?" We wave together at El Creepo across the street. He shakes his head and ambles off to pester a cluster of girls with shiny tan legs.

We introduce ourselves. His name is Chris and he's in Vegas for a comic book convention. A comic book convention! "Graphic novels," I marvel quietly.

He smiles wider. "In some circles. What do you read?"

"I loved *Persepolis* and *Maus,* of course. Also *Blankets* and *Palestine* . . ." I think for a minute of a title that might impress Chris. "*V for Vendetta,*" I finally blurt. *V for Vendetta* is about fascism and police states and anarchy and the real meaning of freedom. Things you tend not to think about while shopping for sweaters.

"Ah, yes, *V for Vendetta,*" Chris says approvingly.

H for Horny, I think. Thank goodness for the whole organ transplant and self-delusion thing! How else would I have ever started reading comic books? I'm so glad I'm wearing a skirt and not the flood-heralding pants I always seem to have on when I run into comely men back home. "Did you see the movie?" I ask.

"I did." He shrugs, as if to say, *Hollywood; what are ya gonna do?* Or maybe, *Meh.*

I suddenly remember that he appeared to have been waiting for something. "Sorry if I interrupted you. Were you waiting for someone?"

He shrugs. "My dad, but he's probably drunk at a blackjack table somewhere, throwing away my inheritance."

I squint up at the flashing neon lights. "My dad threw away my inheritance, too," I say. "So you're here with your dad?"

"It's this annual trip we take. Father-son bonding and all that. Who are you here with?"

"Some friends. They're gambling God knows where. I wasn't in the mood to join them, I guess."

"I hear that." Chris crosses his arms and gives me a considering gaze. "Hey, this is a little impulsive, but I found this crazy dive bar yesterday . . . lots of nutty people. If you're up for it, could be fun. There's a cocktail waitress there that's a real hoot." He smiles and shrugs. "Just a thought." He suddenly tips his glasses down the bridge of his nose to study me, still smiling. "You are twenty-one, right?"

"Ha!" It comes out much more like a bark than I would have preferred. I feel myself blush. "I'll take that as a compliment." This is something I've found myself saying way too much lately. Thankfully, he doesn't ask how old I am. Not because I would have minded telling him, but because it would have been a predictable follow-up question.

I consider my options. (A) Return to the Luxor and watch cable TV. Slip back into mediocrity. Live a life of quiet desperation and regret, wondering what could have been, like a miserable, dried-up neighborhood hermit on some shitty *Highway to Heaven* rerun. Or (B) continue having adventures—this time, without my kidney donor as a crutch. Make new friends, make wacky memories, make the most of my damn life. I shift my weight from foot to foot. He *does* have the kind of cute freckles that I like: a soft smattering across the bridge of his nose. I sigh and feel my lips form a smile. Okay, it's B.

A minute later we're in a cab on the way to Angelo's, a combination piano bar/casino/karaoke lounge. You can't ask for better than that. In the cab we joke with the driver, a rheumy-eyed man named Mick. Mick's scalp shines pink and vulnerable through his thin gray crew cut. We ask if we're on candid camera for *Taxicab Confessions: Las Vegas*. Mick says no, but feel free to take your top off anyway.

At Angelo's we're hustled off to a dark corner table by a cocktail waitress with a stiff bouffant like a dollop of meringue on her head. Her name tag reads "Flo." She winks at me and takes our drink orders (a water and a Coke for me and a Heineken for Chris) before zipping off again. The woman seated at the piano before us begins to play "Can't Take My Eyes Off You" by Frankie Valli. She's wrapped in black feathers, and her top is cut dangerously low. She may have been born before the discovery of Pluto. Just then someone hands the microphone to a gray-haired gentleman in tinted glasses and a beret. He's wearing at least fifteen pounds of gold jewelry. It sparkles over his polyester suit. His voice is fat and sassy, so rich it sounds greasy, and his lips graze the microphone during each chorus, sparking painful feedback.

Angelo's has the friendly, inclusive ambience of an R-rated *Sesame Street*, with the pierced and tattooed set, dowdy tourists, and bemused-looking locals yukking it up together at the smoky bar. The décor is "Christmas in a wood-paneled basement with mirrors." I notice a plastic air freshener plugged into a wall outlet near my legs. Chris smiles at me. "The guys working the front desk at my hotel told me they come here after their shifts. So I knew it had to be good."

"Yeah, screw fake Venice and fake Paris and fake New York. I don't like my gambling, prostitution, and binge-drinking tarted-up for families."

Chris laughs and I feel the familiar heady rush of a junkie, already scheming the next line that could make him laugh.

Flo returns with our drinks. She holds a palm out to us, making us guess our charge. Chris hands her a twenty and she marches off. "You think I'll be seeing any change from that?" he asks conspiratorially.

"Don't *bet* on it," I stage-whisper, a small paean to Jillian's humor. We listen to the geriatric singers for awhile, dutifully applauding at the end of every song.

"This is much better than staying in my hotel room watching *Mary Tyler Moore* reruns!" I shout over the clapping.

Chris applauds and grins. "If you could live in any TV show, what would it be?"

Now, this is my kind of conversation. I want to say *Real Sex* but blurt the second thing that comes to mind: "*60 Minutes!*" I chuckle lamely. "Not really. *Fantasy Island* maybe? My life lately feels a bit like *The Twilight Zone*."

"What's your favorite *Twilight Zone* episode?"

TV junkie that I am, I don't hesitate. "The one where the dying man makes the masks for his family that permanently change their faces to reflect their horrible personalities."

I try to imagine what I'd look like if my exterior mirrored my interior. I might be covered in cysts. I might just be one big cyst. Polycystic kidney disease . . . *poly* meaning "many," but in this case, those cysts aren't confined to just the kidneys. It's an equal-opportunity cysting disease. How long before my cysts spread to my liver? I hear Jillian's voice suddenly echo through my head: *Do not think like that, or you'll manifest it.*

Chris interrupts my thoughts with "I think you'd be just as pretty if your outside reflected your insides."

He turns red and I feel myself blush again. It was a pretty cheeseball comment, but I'd have felt mildly snubbed had he not said it. Flo comes around again. "How you kids doin'?" We tell her we're fine for now. She fishes an ice cube from my water and tosses it at a man jabbering on his cell phone at the next table. "Keep it down, motormouth!" The man ignores her. Chris and I start laughing. Flo collapses into a chair at our table. She nods briefly at the singer, who is robo–belting out Sinatra's "My Way" through the prosthetic voice box in his throat. "That's Denny," Flo says. "He's been dying of throat cancer for years. He sings this song almost every night."

"I can totally relate," I say. Once it's out of my mouth I realize

how insane I sound. Like I know what dying of throat cancer is like.
All of a sudden I've got the empathy belly for terminal illnesses?

"He don't care if he sounds funny," Flo continues. "Part of his
charm, I guess." She slides out of the chair. "You kids holler if you
need me."

After Flo zips off to deliver a tray of drinks to a table of men in
sport coats, I turn back to Chris. "I'm sorry, but did you tell me
where you're from?"

"Chicago."

"Oh, okay." Wow! Chicago. "I'm from Wisconsin," I volunteer.

"Hey! Where in Wisconsin?"

"A smallish city." My hand makes an absent brushing gesture. I
don't even think about it. My body has been doing lots of things
without permission lately. "Fond du Lac. You probably never heard
of it." *Fond du Lac* is French for "foot of the lake." Some people call
it Fondle Sack or Fun to Lick, but I don't mention this.

"Home of the Miracle Mile," Chris says.

"I can't believe you know that." I suddenly sneeze three times,
my nose irritated by the heavy rafter of smoke.

"Me, either," he laughs. "And gesundheit."

"You *are* from the Midwest."

Chris tips his head back and laughs with a capital *L*. I'm really
liking this guy's style already. I could curl up in his laugh and live
happily ever after. Denny finishes his song, croaking the final note
for an eternity. Afterward, he bows deeply and we all clap. I don't
know if we're proud of him or relieved he's finished.

Chris and I talk about random things for awhile: our mutual affection for dogs, irritating personalities on the Food Network
(Giada De Laurentiis . . . you know who you are), our families, our
jobs. Turns out Chris is a website developer. "Usually it's really dry,
for companies that make lawn tractors, or for insurance groups.
But once I did a site for a horror film a guy I know produced." I tell
him about how my friend Amanda once broke up with a new
boyfriend because he sang karaoke in a Michael McDonald voice,
and Chris clears his throat and shows me his Aaron Neville vibrato,

which is brave and pretty spot-on and makes me laugh. I suddenly hear myself blurt, "So I have a crazy story for you." See, I would never sing an Aaron Neville vibrato for a stranger. Instead, I will reveal intimate details of my life. I proceed to tell him the details of my kidney transplant, beginning with my keeling over at Fuzzy Navels and culminating with the highlights of the Unfinished Business Tour.

"Jesus! And here I thought my knee surgery was a big deal."

"You had knee surgery?"

"It's nothing. Old baseball injury." He shakes his head dismissively. "So you really gave a ride to a girl who stole your purse?"

I buff my nails on my shirt. "I believe in living dangerously." Lately, anyway.

"And your kidney donor—Larry—really had an accident that killed a deaf woman and a dog? That's really how he died?"

I nod earnestly.

"Wow. It's like a *Choose Your Own Adventure* gone wild!"

"Tell me about it," I say.

"Wow," he says again. "An organ transplant. I guess that's why you ordered soda." His eyes flicker. "Not that a person has to drink alcohol. I mean, anyone can have a Coke at a bar if they want."

I smile. He's adorable flustered. "Yeah, the whole kidney-failure thing really threw a wrench in my drinking schedule."

Chris turns serious as a senior citizen in a shiny purple suit grabs the mike and begins to belt out "Strokin'" by Clarence Carter. "I can't even imagine what that must have been like," Chris shouts. The singer behind him croons about strokin' it to the east and strokin' it to the west, thrusting his hips toward Chris's head. The piano player bops along while she plays.

I shrug. "It's not so bad. I know people who've had it worse." This is true, but I'm still proud of myself for acting so sanguine. Chris doesn't need to know about the time I cried myself to sleep in James's bathtub, fully clothed. Or that my first few post-transplant periods briefly sparked irrational fears that my body was rejecting my kidney. Or about my prepaid burial plot, right next to James's at Riverside Memorial Park. It is kind of a downer. I suddenly feel a fist of panic punch me hard in the chest, and I do a subtle breathing exercise. I visualize myself at seventy, tending a flower garden behind a seaside house in Maine. But my face is fuzzy, like I'm not really there. Like I don't exist. *Breathe, Leigh. Breathe.* I stare intently at the pianist and focus on the music. *Breathe.* The panic slowly subsides and I can breathe again.

"Still, you've been through more than most people our age." This is the part where some people stop seeing me as a complex individual who still enjoys sex and sarcasm. This is the part where I'm supposed to act stoic and humble, the Model Medical Citizen. I hate this part. "Well," Chris adds, correcting himself, "unless they live in a third-world war-torn country, I suppose."

I perk up. I like that he actually thought about this. "Very true."

"Did you read Dave Eggers's book *What Is the What*?"

"No, but it's on my list," I say. "My friend Amanda met him at a book-signing once. He signed her copy with a bunch of little moons and planets."

I'm suddenly struck by the arbitrary strangeness of my being in this very place, at this very minute. It's like that old Talking Heads lyric: "Well, how did I get here?" And I wish I could tell you. I watch a drop of condensation slither down my glass. I suddenly realize I'm homesick for a life I never really had. I'm homesick for Jillian's life, full of older sisters who tell me sordid stories about their pregnancies, and exasperated parents, and brothers that do handstands in the living room. The life she couldn't wait to shed. But I don't want to leave this place. I want this moment to become cosmic Silly Putty, stretched out and slow.

Chris seems to sense this and after finishing his beer, says, "Hey, want to sing something?"

I feel my mouth form a smile. "Uh—"

"Come on. Please? You only live once."

"This isn't really karaoke. It's a piano bar." I look around at the non-karaoke-style surroundings. Has it gotten more crowded in here?

He shrugs, smiling broadly. "So?"

I protest a bit more, and we go back and forth. I throw out all of my standard excuses (I can't sing, I'm not dressed appropriately, I can hardly give public speeches, I can't sing), but toward the end I'm only talking to myself because Chris is speaking with the ancient piano player, flipping through a songbook and putting in a request.

For the second time during the trip, I wish I could get stinking, piss-the-bed, eat-five-Whoppers-at-four-A.M., wake-up-on-a-strange-elderly-woman's-porch drunk.

He returns to our table and grins. "You can do this. You believe in living dangerously, remember?"

Right. I sigh heavily. "Okay, but I'm not to blame for causing tinnitus or permanent deafness in anyone within a three-block radius. Can I get people to sign a waiver?"

"Aw, you'll be great."

"What are we singing?"

"Kenny Loggins. 'Whenever I Call You Friend.' "

I want to hide in the nearest potted palm. Nonetheless, I step up to the mike near the piano. My heartbeat seems to fill the room. The intro starts, with the weird octave-jumping harmonizing that always reminded me of the Manhattan Transfer. Chris catches my eye and winks. It calms me somewhat, and I think: *Fuck it. Nobody here knows me. They'll have no way of contacting me when they wish to sue for auditory-nerve damage.* I study the lyrics and manage to channel a mildly tone-deaf Stevie Nicks. Chris has a plaintive voice that squeaks at the high notes. We share the lyric book and perform goofy eighties dance moves during the instrumental interlude (the Shopping Cart, the Axl Rose, the Cabbage Patch), much to the delight of the crowd. I can't tell if they're laughing at or with us, so I really ham it up. It's scary, this putting yourself out there . . . sober. But liberating. Chris is over the top the entire time, singing with gusto and making me laugh hysterically between verses. My laugh-singing comes out breathy and, I think, a bit self-conscious. We finish with a flourish and bow deeply. The crowd hoots and whistles.

"Not bad," Chris says, tipping the piano player ten dollars. She presses her palms together like she's praying and bows slightly in his direction. I notice that he's sweating generously on his forehead and nose. He wipes his face with the back of his hand.

"So why'd you pick that particular song?" I ask.

"First, it was a duet. Second, it was in the songbook. Third, who doesn't love Kenny Loggins?"

"His great radio rivals, the Captain and Tennille?" I'm happy when Chris laughs.

On our way out he asks, "Hey, want to try our luck at the slot machines?" We pick a machine that Chris deems "loose" after sizing it up. I wildly consider betting all of my money, but wisely, I opt instead for a single five-dollar bill, which I feed into the machine. The machine burps a stream of jangling noise, then clams up. Nothing.

Chris plugs in a dollar and wins the same dollar back. He considers what it means. "You know, this could be a metaphor for my entire life."

I laugh. "Well, you didn't win big, but you didn't lose big, either. Sometimes, life is nice without drama."

"I sure hope the Las Vegas Tourist Bureau doesn't adopt that as their new slogan."

"Well, it beats 'Vegas. Come for the buffets, stay for the craps.'"

He laughs. "Cute."

On the way out of the casino we spot a grubby male patron seated in the corner, repeatedly banging his head on the table. A wisp of hair from his comb-over flaps sadly with every blow. Chris whispers, "Must have lost big at the tables."

"Are you okay?" I ask the head banger. But he's oblivious to me. Then an idea hits me. This is going to sound terrible, maybe even mean-spirited, but I don't intend it that way at all. I grab a stack of napkins from the end of the bar. I time it just right and slide them under his forehead to absorb the blows. He keeps on banging, only now it mustn't hurt so much. It's muffled. Chris laughs, but it was the decent thing to do.

Later we buy lemon sorbet in Styrofoam cups. While we eat, we invent lives for all of the tourists milling about: a fragile, birdlike girl becomes the estranged daughter of a cult leader named Skippy Barnes. A rotund man with a receding hairline and pink loafers becomes an escaped convict who had been sentenced to life for chopping his mother up and storing her limbs in the freezer. An attractive blond couple is arguing over the discovery of birth control pills in the woman's purse despite the man's vasectomy. (This we actually heard.) Maybe it's the events of the past few days, maybe it's because this evening's encounter was so spontaneous and unexpected, maybe it's just Vegas . . . but my inhibitions seem to have taken the last train to Clarksville. We talk, and discover many more things in common than I have with even Jillian.

"You like Wilco, too?" I ask. Despite a no-show at the slot machine, my luck is certainly in tonight, taking calls and receiving visitors. Luck is a fickle friend, but I'm fortunate that she shows up when I need her most.

"Not only that, but I used to see every Uncle Tupelo show I could make." Wilco is sort of the reincarnation of Uncle Tupelo, an alt-country band that Denise would poke fun at me for liking.

"Wow. That was a long time ago! You must have been in junior high."

"I was."

I know better than anyone that long-term commitment to a musical fan base is no indicator of ability to commit to a relationship, but I still take this as a good sign.

Our conversation finally dries up around two A.M. "I'm glad that creepy guy hit on you," Chris says.

"Me, too. You can never have enough creepy guys in your life."

He laughs. "No, because you wouldn't have waved at me if he hadn't. And I'd be listening to my dad snore right about now."

It is one of the nicest things anyone has ever said to me. Despite wanting to stay right here all night, I sigh and tell him I should probably get back to the hotel.

He scribbles his phone number on a cardboard coaster stolen from Angelo's. "If you ever need someone to sing bad karaoke with, give me a call."

Chris steps to the curb to hail a cab for me. When it pulls up he offers a handshake, and despite my strong desire to turn it into a hug, I accept. I put my British accent back on and say, "It's been a perfectly lovely evening, Christopher."

He says, "Don't take any wooden nickels, see?" like a gangster from the thirties. I'm glad when he doesn't form a phone near his ear with an extended thumb and index finger, mouthing "Call me!" That was exactly what Seth had done after we'd met. Instead, we wave good-bye and smile at each other crookedly.

In the backseat of the cab, I slide the coaster into the back pocket of my skirt. It feels like a secret there.

"Having a good night?" the cabdriver asks in a husky voice, smiling at me in the rearview mirror. She looks like a retired show-girl in recovery.

I smile and say, "You bet."

CHAPTER TWELVE

I've had lots of practice inventing lives for people.

'm dragged from my light sleep by this sound: *Gong! Gong! GONG!* When I open my eyes I see Denise's face hovering inches from my own. She's grinning and smells of whiskey. My nostrils retreat from her breath, offended. "Wake up, sleepyhead! *Gong!*"

"What are you doing?" I mumble in the semi-dark, pulling the covers up to my neck. Light spills into the room from the hallway, and I can hear Jillian cackling wickedly from the suburbs of my consciousness.

"Guess what. You'll never guess."

I rake a hand through my snarled hair. Is this a bad dream? I'm tired and cranky.

"Jillian won five grand at craps!" Denise shrieks. She skips around the room turning on lights. I sit up, rubbing my eyes and blinking.

"What?"

Denise repeats herself: "Jillian. Won. Five. Thousand. *Dollars!* At craps!" Then she says, "Woo-hoo!" and skips around the room some more. Like a caricature, she's lugging around a half-empty bottle of cheap wine, which she takes a slug from.

Jillian and Dave stumble into the room next, equally drunk. "Hey, *chica!*" Jillian gushes. She crawls into bed next to me. She reeks of spiced rum, cigarette smoke, and taco seasoning. "We're totally going to Europe," she whispers urgently. Her eyes are large and blurry.

"You won money gambling?" I ask, annoyed, drawing the sheets up to my neck.

Jillian and Denise conga around the room doing the *Wayne's World* chant Jillian and I used to do in grade school, substituting the amount of Jillian's winnings for the original script: "We got five thousand *dollars*. We got five thousand *dollars*."

Dave throws himself onto the bed. "Man, you totally should have come with us."

I scratch my side and frown at Jillian. "You don't even know how to play craps."

She barely blinks. "Dave taught me. It's so easy! You'd love it!"

This irritates me. What's next—Jillian learns guitar and joins Dave's band? "You did not win five thousand dollars," I say firmly.

"Yes she did," Denise brays, cheering and dancing around. Even in my sleepy spaciness, I'm slightly jealous. The only thing I ever won was third place in a youth talent contest at the Fond du Lac County Fair for my impression of Donald Duck. And only three kids had entered the contest.

They yammer on, recapping the highlights of the evening among themselves. I feel even more left out, but I suppose it's my own fault. Whatever. Good for Jillian. Now she can travel in style. I plod through their celebration to the bathroom, shaking the pins and needles from my left leg. Inside, the bathroom lights are sterile and uncompromising. I study my face in the mirror. When did I get so many wrinkles! I look like my age in dog years: 196. I look exactly like a girl who had a kidney transplant a year ago and hasn't gotten laid since a past life.

I splash cold water on my face and read the back of one of the travel soaps the Luxor has conveniently displayed on the counter. I feel disoriented. I'm like that a lot lately. I blame the television commercials I've been catching at our motels. Commercials for local furniture stores, car dealerships, realtors. It's disconcerting. I don't trust these foreign jingles, these crazy accents, these wares hawked by colorful local sellebrities. Halladay Motors, Winks Fine Jewelry, Denny Ray's Floor Covering. Who are these interlopers? Where was my Rogers & Hollands Jewelry? My Les Stumpf Ford? My "Save Big Money at Menards"? I need to hear a familiar jingle, and I need to hear it soon.

I'm sure my disorientation has nothing at all to do with the fact that I've recently discovered that I'm harboring the kidney of a murdering alcoholic redneck. I sigh heavily and crank the faucets off, tightly. Now that I'm up, I could take a shower, but I don't have enough ambition. I sit on the toilet and discover that my visit to Jimmy T's trough has finally announced its ugly side effects. What was I thinking? I just need to vacuum-seal myself. I need to carry around a little radiation lamp to kill whatever bugs may be colonizing my lunch. Maybe I could borrow Denise's burgled forehead reading light and zap every spoonful before it hits my lips.

I languish on the toilet until my thighs grow numb. I listen to Jillian's giggles through the wall. Then Dave's voice: "Because he's a big liar!" It must have been the punch line to a joke because Denise and Jillian spew laughter. A few more years in James and Marissa's house, and this is what my life could become. Me sitting on the toilet listening to other people laughing through the wall.

Note to self: *Get a life if it kills you.* I close my eyes and smile a little. Am I ready for the rest of my life? What kind of life will it be? Two roads diverged in a wood and all that jazz. I'm back to a blank slate, so to speak. The Unfinished Business Tour is my kickoff to a changed life, despite the little setback with Larry. So far I've accomplished 75 percent of my goals. Not bad, but the biggest task remains. Am I ready to see Kate?

When I was five I lost my mom at the mall. As I wandered from store to store, peering helplessly down aisle after aisle of merchandise for a glimpse of her suede jacket or blond hair, I became sure that I would never see her again. And the fate that would befall me was the fate of little Adam Walsh, who was kidnapped and later discovered floating headless in a shopping mall fountain (so rumor had it among the macabre elementary set).

So I took action to avert that fate. I marched up to the help desk and informed the kind-eyed clerk in a wavering voice that I was lost. Could she please help me find my mom?

My mother didn't seem all that relieved to find me, I remember. More spacily amused at the concept of my daydreaming and wandering off than anything. Silly wabbit! But I recall the huge sense of relief my five-year-old self had at that moment. Mother and Child Reunion! A safe car ride back home to my Barbies and Cabbage Patch Kids! Chicken McNuggets for dinner!

Years later I would think that I should have asked for an exchange while I was up at the help desk. This mother is defective; she stares into her tea for forty-five minutes at a time and sings the same song lyrics over and over in the shower in different voices. She seems to be the reason my father's smile has been canceled for the season. So could I have a new mother? One who always remembers to pick me up from kindergarten? One who makes sure I'm wearing my helmet before I climb on my bike? One who packs my lunch every school night: peanut butter and strawberry jam on squishy white bread, an apple to keep the doctor away, a fun-sized Kit Kat, and a cool-crushing handwritten note on a napkin I could roll my eyes at in front of my friends but secretly cherish: *Love you, kid! Have a great lunch! Orange you glad I didn't pack a banana?*

But there are no refunds on family. Jillian likes to say that before we're born, our baby-spirit selves choose our parents while we're floating somewhere in the void. I guess we pick them based on some lesson our souls need to learn in the next life.

So apparently, in the great celestial waiting room between this life and the last, I discovered some coma-inducing hydroponic bud, because I must have been cosmically baked to have picked my parents.

I guess I shouldn't be so hard on myself for the whole Larry thing. I've had lots of practice inventing lives for people. Especially my mother.

I'm not sure I'm finished bearing the brunt of Jimmy T's revenge, but the fluorescent bathroom lights are doing something to my brain so I need to get out of here. I wash my hands and brush my teeth, at which point I discover the disturbing bulleted pitch on my tube of toothpaste: "Tastes great without the salty aftertaste!" What is this, a tube of toothpaste or a blow job? Since when do we live in a world where toothpaste has a salty aftertaste? Baffled, I rejoin the rest of the crew in the hotel room.

Jillian and Denise are in various states of undress at the table. They're playing strip poker with Dave. "Don't be such a cliché." I yawn and crawl back into bed.

"I thought you died in there!" Jillian says.

"In due time," I mumble, smothering my head with a pillow. "How long are you going to stay up?"

"Long enough for me to win all of Jillian's money," Dave slurs.

"Sorry, not gonna happen," Jillian retorts.

I must have dozed off, because I'm jolted awake by Denise's shrill "What the fuck do you think you're doing?"

A bucket of adrenaline pours into my arteries—like when you're about to nod off and the fire alarm explodes. While I wait for my heartbeat to subside I scowl and lift the pillow from my face. I have to rub my eyes because I'm not sure I'm seeing what I think I'm seeing. Dave is casually pointing Denise's gun at Jillian and Denise. He's tipped back in his chair, feet up on the small table in the corner of the hotel room. Jillian and Denise are just staring at him from across the table. Jillian's only wearing her bra and skirt. Denise is wearing a garbage bag for some reason.

"Just give me half of the cash," Dave slurs. He waves the gun around, aiming it at things in the room: the television, the lamp between the double beds, the window, my head . . . *my head*.

I leap out of bed too quickly and see spots.

"Jesus Christ," Denise whispers, rubbing her forehead. Her eyes are large and bloodshot. "Could you, like, not wave that thing around?"

Dave cocks the hammer and the gun makes a clicking sound. This infuriates me. "You fucker!" I say. I want to throw things at him like a major-league pitcher. I scan the room and grab an empty wine bottle by the neck. It's the deadliest object in the vicinity. A small stream of warm wine trickles onto my wrist. "Put the gun down," I say with as much authority as I can muster.

"Or what?" Dave asks, smiling. This pisses me off even more. People who don't take me seriously have consistently made my list of Top Ten People I'd Like to Push Down an Escalator. Along with people who aren't grateful for a ride when the muffler's falling off their car. So I smash the bottom of the bottle against the dresser and brandish the jagged glass neck at him. At least I try to.

Thunk! The green bottle vibrates in my hand, intact. "What are you doing?" he asks, laughing. Jillian and Denise just stare at me as if they've actually witnessed my mind leaving my head. I can hear the thumping bass line from a television down the hall, and laughter. *I'll tell them I was sleepwalking,* I wildly think. *Or I was possessed by the ghost of a jilted showgirl.*

I smash again and achieve victory in an understated tinkle of glass. Granted, I'm waving about four inches of harmless bottleneck at him, but why stop now? I've summoned my inner superhero; her fists are planted firmly on her hips. Her cape is flapping behind her. She stands for truth, justice, and anyone who has ever been given a painful wedgie. I poke my weapon at him, summon my most menacing expression, and say, "Go ahead, fucker. Make your day."

We lock eyes for three full seconds, although it feels longer than full Mass with Stations of the Cross. Then Dave cracks up.

Oh Jesus. Make *your* day? *Make your day?* I wait a lifetime to partially quote Eastwood in a real-life semi-dangerous showdown, and I screw it up? This is junior high English all over again, when my teacher almost laughed himself into a seizure at my dubbing a wee lad "toe-headed" in an essay.

"What?" Dave wheezes, laughing harder, and then I realize he knew there weren't any bullets in the gun. "Are you kidding me? 'Make *your* day'?" He has to bend at the knees, he's laughing so hard. He's still kind of drunk, I guess.

"The gun isn't even loaded, you dick," I answer, but it's too late.

My self-respect has left the building. In fact, my self-respect has entered the Dead on a Toilet phase.

"I know, Clint," he says. "But it was worth a try." He tucks the gun into his waistband, collects his bags, and saunters out of the room, still chuckling. "See you clowns on the flip side."

I look around for a hole in the floor I could maybe fall into.

"What the fuck?" Denise says. She looks like someone slapped her. "He just stole my gun!"

"Leigh, he had a gun!" Jillian shouts.

"Didn't you hear me? There weren't any bullets." I fall back on the bed. "No beanbag bullets, rubber bullets, or metal bullets," I mumble. "No rubber baby buggy bullets. Say that ten times fast."

"There really weren't any bullets?" Jillian is still staring at me, incredulous.

"No. I took them out in Cheyenne."

Okay, confession time again. Shortly after the gun was introduced to me, I did indeed get up in the middle of the night to furtively remove the bullets and toss them into a field near our motel parking lot. I may be paranoid, but not enough to believe we would run into bandits or an escaped and dangerous mental patient (this was pre-Rick, of course), necessitating an armed showdown starring me and everyone's favorite teenage runaway. More likely, one or both of us would have wound up shot in the spleen, robbed of money, hope, and dignity, and left to bleed to death in a sleazy bathtub in such a scenario. Probably, it would have been me. So it was "Adios, bullets."

"I can't believe that just happened," Denise mutters. "He totally stole my gun!" Then she explodes in gales of laughter. " 'Make your day.' You rock! 'Make your day.' "

I can't believe what just happened, either. Jillian, still staring at me in a slightly deranged way, cracks a small smile. Denise collapses next to me, laughing hard enough to warrant a lifetime prescription for nongeneric seizure medication. I close my eyes and say, "Well, it's official. I need to make new friends."

Denise looks up, grinning. "Why?"

"Because now you both know what a supreme fucking dork I am," I groan. "My secret's out."

Jillian snorts. "Your secret was out in the sixth grade."

"I really liked the part where you smashed the wine bottle like some kind of prison bitch," Denise adds. "Oh, and P.S., I knew you took the bullets out."

"You did?"

"Yeah. I figured you'd get all Mister Rogers and 'Safety First!' on me and shit, but whatever." She shrugs. "It beat you being all freaked out all the time."

Well.

Denise and Jillian fall asleep to an infomercial on some kind of exercise gadget designed to bilk a week's pay from desperate fat people. I stare at the ceiling for half an hour, feeling generally icky. I feel ashamed—sinful even, like the time the host missed my mouth during Communion and the priest had to bend down and pick it up from the carpet and refeed it to me. The Jesus crackers can*not* hit the floor where people's muddy boots have trampled, or it's like a venial sin. Maybe even a mortal sin. The priest just gave me a look that said *Worst. Sinner. Ever.*

I'm startled from my mooning by a raspy, irritated voice near my left ear. Jillian. "Stop tossing and turning. You need to get laid." A second later she's snoring again in that soft, funny way of hers. Then she mumbles, "I did not," and laughs lazily in her sleep.

I dream I am three years old. I am at a boxing match, perched on a metal folding chair in a shadowy crowd, bookended by my parents. My mother at my right, my father at my left. The room—a warehouse, a gym—presses hot air into our faces. Two men punch each other in the ring, grunting and jabbing, dancing and staggering. The crowd sighs. My father jumps up, yelling something that might be "Aw, come on!" My mother sits quietly, sipping a Pepsi through a clear straw, darting her eyes. Action in the ring. I stare at the man's overalls in front of me. People are faceless giants, jumping up, sitting down, rocking back in their chairs. Dust floats beneath the harsh white lights. A fighter's bloody mouth guard sails over our heads, trailing a comet tail of pink saliva. The crowd roars and rises in unison. The referee hammers the bell. My father picks me up and hoists me onto his shoulders. I ride above the crowd as we file out into the warm night. "Now, that was a fight," he says. We are all alive, birthdays are marked on the calendar, and we are going out for ice cream. My parents hold hands in the car.

This really happened. I'm sure of it. It might even be my earliest memory.

There's a song for every occasion, even the most esoteric of occasions. Take what we're doing right now. Leaving Las Vegas. Well, there's a song called "Leaving Las Vegas." Bland as canned mashed potatoes, but if I only hear it once a year, I don't mind it. However, there are some songs that should never be heard during a road trip. Not a snippet from the instrumental bridge, not a whisper of the chorus, not even just an opening note. Because these are songs that would incite violence among Quakers.

As we pull out of the parking ramp Jillian spins the dial and lands us squarely on some smooth songs popular long before personal computing. "Oh, I love this song!" She turns the volume up and begins to sing along to "Africa" by TOTO. I'm pretty sure she's mangling the words, but who am I to judge? I used to think that the Who's "Eminence Front" was "Livin' in Funk." I also used to think the chorus intro to Steve Miller's "Jetliner" was "Big ol' Chad at a lineup." Not "Big ol' jet had a light out," like everybody else who screwed up the lyrics. Nope. Not me. I was singing about a burly criminal named Chad. When everyone else misses the boat, I miss the ocean.

Denise joins in. And before I know it, we're all singing TOTO. Stool-softening music, true, but it makes me want to climb Kilimanjaro and run around with zebras. "Dust in the Wind" by Kansas and Band Aid's "Do They Know It's Christmas?" also give me goose bumps, a lump in my throat, and delusions of grandeur. I really belt them out when I'm alone in the car, screwing up the lyrics and trying out my vibrato.

"So what would our road trip anthem be?" Denise asks, flipping a wad of pink gum around her mouth with her tongue.

" 'Peace Train,' " Jillian suggests. A massage therapist, she's optimistic by nature. "Are we stopping for breakfast?"

"How about 'Highway to Hell'?" I say.

Denise ignores me and starts singing the "Wheels on the Bus" song.

This is one of those songs that incite violence. As she enters the third chorus of "round and round," I shout, "Denise, if you don't stop I'm going to drop you off in the desert to wander around and die of thirst. But first I'll bludgeon you with some luggage."

"Go ahead . . ." She starts to laugh. "Make your day."

Fifty miles out of town we spot one of those roadside museums/souvenir tchotchke stands/cafés, and I impulsively steer us into the gravel parking lot. A hand-lettered sign near the entrance explains it all: NED AND CASSIE'S MUSEUM OF VISIONS AND DESERT SOUVENIR STAND. SANDWICHES AND COLD DRINKS INSIDE. The yard is stuffed with rusty garden art, whirligigs, wind chimes, plastic flamingos, and industrial-looking metal sculptures.

"Are we really stopping here?" Denise asks.

"No, we're going to sell Avon door-to-door," I reply. We park and step out of the car to stretch, though we've only been driving for forty minutes. By now the gesture has become a habit. No deep vein thrombosis for us!

"Fascinating," Jillian muses, examining a fifteen-foot-tall dragon made from what appears to be old car parts welded together. The building that serves as the multipurpose roadside attraction is also a work of art, its walls painted with bright sunflowers, Kokopelli, constellations, rainbows, giant mushrooms, butterflies, blue skies, and dragonflies smoking hookahs. Obelisks, ship anchors, cacti, and an army of gnomes line the curving path to the front door. An old-fashioned bell jangles above our heads when we enter the musty shop. The proprietors, Ned and Cassie, greet us from behind a glass-topped counter: "Welcome!" Their sudden greeting startles Jillian, who jumps. It makes me laugh.

You know how people always seem to see the Virgin Mary in a burrito, or in a stain on a highway underpass? Well, nobody you've ever actually met . . . but you know what I mean? Well, apparently Ned and Cassie have collected numerous objects that have (A) been spiritually imprinted with a visage from beyond, (B) fallen into a puddle, or (C) been crushed by a portly ass at some point in history. These curiosities, shelved helter-skelter in the tiny shop, include items like a bath mat with a "Joan of Arc"–shaped stain and a piece of driftwood allegedly in the shape of Ganesha (if you held it at arm's length and squinted while running at high speed). Once our eyes get used to the interior gloom, Denise and I spend a few minutes admiring the artifacts and the stretch of imagination required to see whatever Ned and Cassie saw through a nag champa and pot-clouded haze.

"That shirt holds an image of Saint Michael the Archangel if you pull the left and right corners taut," Ned announces, startling me. Ned looks like a young Richard Dreyfuss, circa *Close Encounters of the Third Kind*.

I glance up and grin. "Oh?"

Denise snorts.

Ned stretches the shirt, which is just a plain blue T-shirt, and I see some kind of shape materialize in the fabric as he does so. It looks like a ketchup stain. I don't want to hurt Ned's feelings, so I nod enthusiastically. "Oh, sure. There he is."

"I don't see shit," Denise says. "Looks like a dirty T-shirt to me."

Cassie, ignoring Denise, proffers a little wooden statuette. "We found this in Bali, before Ned got sick. It's a hand-carved Buddha, but we think it looks more like Dom DeLuise." From the neck up, Cassie looks nothing like a hippie. She could be playing Harrison Ford's wife in a Cold War thriller. From the neck down, she's kicking the Hacky Sack around at a Dave Matthews concert.

Denise, sensing an opportunity to announce my ailments to the world, pipes up, "Leigh here had a kidney transplant."

"Oh man, that's some serious action," Ned offers softly. "That's nothing to shake a stick at. Well, you look great now."

"Thanks. It was about a year ago." I smile, not quite sure how to proceed. I'm curious about what happened to him. As people who have both been defined as "sick" at one point or another, we're members of a common tribe. So I ask, "What happened to you?"

"I was studded with tumors," Ned announces brightly. "I was a tumor sandwich."

Cassie clarifies things for us. "No he wasn't." She shakes her head at Ned. "No you weren't. You had one tumor."

"I meditated; I prayed. My friend Silvia did energy healing on me. And one day, my tumors were miraculously gone."

Cassie interrupts again, shaking her head. "He had chemo. But I'll tell you what. There's something to be said for emotional baggage from past lives carrying over. I had a regression and learned that in a past life I'd been shot in the heart on the battlefield. And I'll tell you what else, the cross that I bear in this life is heart disease." Her eyes widen and she nods earnestly at me.

Ned shakes his head. Now it's his turn to clarify. "Well, it was that or Jim." His tone grows conspiratorial. "She had a very painful divorce." He turns to Cassie. "Remember how you said your heart hurt? Like constant heartburn?"

She nods. "Oh, absolutely. It went on forever. My ex-husband really struggled with his path. He had extreme narcissistic behaviors that were not compatible at all with my self-actualization."

"In other words, he was a class-A creepo," Ned interprets for me.

I have to say, this concept appeals to me on so many levels. I had a false start with the whole kidney-donor thing (which, to tell the truth, I'm beginning to find mildly amusing), but this is different. Maybe in a past life, I was stabbed in the kidney by a jilted lover! And maybe there's something to be said for carrying emotional scars from pain inflicted in *this* lifetime. But PKD is genetic. So am I paying dues for my parents' debts?

Cassie snaps her fingers. "Did you see the bath mat with Eleanor Roosevelt on it?"

I smile and nod as she shows me, even though if you ask me, the image looks more like a wad of gum. But maybe we all just see what we want to see. Is there mystery in anything, or is what we see what we get? I look around at Jillian studying a display of crystals. I see a good friend with a huge, bottomless heart, someone who offered to give me a kidney when I got sick. I see a person who knows that I'm more like my brother than I'll ever admit. I see a person who believes 100 percent in angels and our souls going to heaven and feels true compassion and pity for anyone who doesn't. I see someone who consults a swinging pendant when faced with difficult choices and doesn't even mind when I laugh at her for doing so.

I look at Denise peering through a kaleidoscope, scratching a calf with the opposite foot. This one's tougher. A complete enigma now, and, something tells me, always. She's too cute, too easygoing and resilient for having come from a foster home. I mean, I can only relate in the context of my own orphaning, which wasn't *Sybil*-level traumatic. I grew up with adequate dental care, a set of encyclopedias, and piano lessons. I somehow doubt that Denise did, yet she's turned out to be more balanced than Jillian lately. (Although that's another unfair comparison, given recent events, so scratch that.) Maybe it's only having known her for a week. We all put on our best personalities when we're trying to impress people we just met. So who is she, really?

Honestly, I'm a little afraid of her. The gun? The psycho stalker ex? The stealing? It reeks of either deep-seated insecurity and maladjustment or a kind of thrill-seeking that you only see on television, because everyone else you know who's dabbled in it has gone to jail, died, or become the CEO of a multinational company. But what am I going to do? Leave her on the side of the road? I agreed to something, and now I'm following through. She is a person I will have known for exactly one week, and one week only. Strange to acknowledge this, but it's true. I don't have to be her friend or pseudo sibling and send her birthday cards. Do I? I suppose I shouldn't hash it over to death, and I should just let things ride. No pun intended.

I guess you could sum up my feelings for Denise in this phrase: "I like her, but . . ." And there'd be a long silence hanging after the *but,* because I can't even put my finger on why she makes me nervous. Well, okay, I can put all ten of my fingers on Denise's various behaviors and comments, but I haven't really felt compelled to delve any further. Hell, it's all I can do to chat about the weather with the teller at the bank most days. (Don't even get me started on the scripts I had to write before calling to order a pizza or make a hair appointment. Thankfully, that hurdle was cleared in high school around the time I got my first part-time job at Kohl's.)

I don't know. Maybe this is how all teenagers are. But it hasn't even been that long since I was a teenager. Have I forgotten already what it's like? All I remember about being seventeen is that I constantly tried to impress boys with limited vocabularies who drove too fast. Kind of like Bo and Luke Duke, come to think of it. God, I remember this one time in kindergarten (I'm going back a bit further here) I was so pissed because Angie Conrad got to be Daisy and I had to be Daisy Duke's homely cousin from out of town. But Angie Conrad had really fucked-up teeth with more ridges than a bag of Ruffles, bless her heart, so I can't begrudge her those few carefree days in the sun.

I do like Denise, from what little I know. She seems sweet yet crazy, generous yet self-absorbed. Unpredictable, yet even that has its own pattern.

She reminds me a little of my mother, come to think of it.

I'm barely surprised when she purchases an air freshener that looks like a slab of bacon, and a large inflatable vinyl Jesus from a rack of similar tasteless B-list, made-in-China novelties. (Fart spray and wacky Billy Bob teeth inserts, anyone?) On the box, Jesus' index and middle fingers are raised in a V: *Peace out, disciples.* We thank Ned and Cassie and say good-bye to their stand o' stains. But before we leave, I ask Denise to take our picture. Maybe when I download it later we'll look like a family instead of three strangers. Or maybe we'll just look like three lost-shaped people searching for answers.

CHAPTER THIRTEEN

Jesus is staying in tonight.

On I-15 to Los Angeles, with Denise's vanilla-scented bacon-shaped air freshener dangling on my rearview mirror next to Jillian's unscented New Age–shaped medicine wheel, we discuss the pros and cons of dating an agoraphobic. "Think about it!" I insist. "If you move in, he could never leave! Of course, you'd have to do all the shopping, even buy your own birthday and Christmas gifts. And you could never take a vacation. But that's a small price to pay for such romantic security."

"He could greet you at the door with a martini every day after work," Denise says, getting on board with the concept. She inflated her new Jesus minutes after his purchase. Now every time I look in the rearview mirror his flat benevolent face smiles at me from the backseat.

Jillian just rolls her eyes and laughs. "And when he cheats on you with a girl he met online, it's in your own bed."

I abruptly change the subject, my mind wandering already. "Jillian, I can't believe you won money gambling."

"I know! I never win anything."

I feel the urge to correct her. "No, *I* never win anything. *You* won every contest you ever entered since birth."

"Ha! Name one."

"Homecoming queen, junior year," I answer immediately.

She doesn't seem to hear me. "Can you believe Dave last night?"

"That's what we get for picking up strangers," I muse.

Denise smirks and asks, "So did you just watch TV all night? How exciting."

I've been waiting for this question. "Actually, I went out."

Jillian perks up and stops tooth-whistling. "Where?"

"I met a guy on the strip," I say casually, passing a Corvette from Kentucky. This is another line I've always wanted to use. Perhaps not those exact words, but close.

"What?"

"I met a guy on the strip," I repeat, smiling now.

"And you didn't tell us until now? Leigh!" Jillian smacks my arm. "So tell, tell."

I tell. There's not all that much to tell, but it feels good to have a secret to share.

"So. He's from Chicago?" Jillian asks, still grinning from ear to ear. Jillian is always trying to set me up with guys I would only find attractive or interesting had I eaten lawn fertilizer as a child. I elaborate a little, and you know how these things go. Don't want to get my hopes up, probably won't see him again, but if I do, it'll be just casual; if it's meant to be, it's meant to be; bladda-yadda-blah. You know, the mantras you say to hedge your bets and pad the fall in case he only wants to be friends. Jillian, predictably, tells me not to put that kind of energy out to the universe or I'll manifest it.

"So is he an agora-whatever?" Denise asks.

"Not likely, given that I didn't meet him in his own house."

"Well, I think you should definitely call him as soon as we get to California," Jillian announces. Right then, we hear an unfamiliar cell phone ring, to a hip-hop song that was popular in the mid-nineties, but I can't recall the name. "Whose phone is that?" Jillian asks, digging through her purse to make sure it isn't hers, and that she didn't accidentally change her ringtone from *Annie's Song* to what could very well be *Baby Got Back* by Sir Mix-a-Lot.

I also check my own phone, even though I know my ringtone is now only the best Beatles song ever. In the rearview mirror, I watch Denise's face redden. She quietly unzips her backpack, reaches inside, and the tinny beats cease.

Jillian stares at her. "You have a cell phone?"

Denise glances at Jillian, glances out the window, and then shrugs. "Um, yeah."

"Where did you get that?" I ask. "I thought you didn't have a cell."

"Sure I had a cell," Denise mumbles.

You will for sure someday, I think. *With a lidless toilet and your own little cot.* "You had that thing the whole time since I picked you up?"

"Yeah," she says, like, *Isn't it obvious, you moron?*

"Denise," Jillian says, "you could have helped us out when we ran out of gas!"

"I didn't have any reception there, either!"

"I'll fucking bet," I say. The dam has broken, and my anger is flooding the car. I'm riding it like a surfer. "Did you steal that, too, or is it yours?"

"It's mine!" Denise insists. "Jesus, everyone has a cell phone. Even drug dealers."

"Are you a drug dealer?" Jillian asks coldly.

"No! But everyone still has one."

Do I have the energy for this? I won't be chauffeuring Denise around after tomorrow. "You know what?" I ask. "I don't even care. Whatever. You have a cell phone. Congratulations." We drive in silence for a minute, and then Denise starts talking again.

"Well, we don't have the gun anymore now."

"That's probably a good thing," Jillian snips, emphasizing every other word. I feel an acute sense of ganging up on a girl eleven years our junior, ready to cast her from the tribe, primal and cruel. It's not a cozy feeling.

"So who called?" I ask, picking up the conversation I just couldn't let die.

Denise sighs. "A friend."

She doesn't seem to want to elaborate, and I decide to let it drop. One more day, I tell myself. *One more day.* And then what? Back to Fuzzy Navels and my regular television-viewing schedule, including nights watching the saga of the Latest Missing White Girl on 20/20 with James and Marissa? If I wasn't driving, I'd close my eyes and try to envision a parallel future for myself: my own apartment, decorated in funky, colorful furniture and vintage coasters. Witty refrigerator magnets holding a cache of fun photos recording my many escapades with friends. Potted plants and scented candles everywhere. A closet of silk kimonos I could greet my beaus in. Suddenly it hits me.

Why couldn't I have this? Like Jillian says, I create my own destiny. My future could be anything. I don't have to resign myself! I could let the Pottery Barn catalogue fall open to any page, drop my index finger down, and buy whatever it landed on! On credit, perhaps, but still! Yale? Why not! Midnight crocodile tagging in Costa Rica? Sign me up!

But what if you get sick again? a little voice asks.

Well, I think. *Well, then I get sick again.* Been there, done that, you know? How much worse can it get? I mean, really. Had I been born a Christian Scientist, I might be dead already.

Maybe what we all need is a good dose of perspective. I need to start reading biographies of people who have triumphed in the face of adversity. People like Franklin D. Roosevelt and Carrie Fisher. Or the next thing I know, I'm wearing my ratty gray bathrobe, eating turkey potpies, and watching reruns of *Gunsmoke,* only venturing out to get my mail.

We're deep in the Mojave Desert now. No towns to speak of, only flat, endless hardpan earth interrupted by jagged, rocky mountain ranges, open blue sky, scrubby vegetation, and searing sun. We're still thirty miles from Barstow on I-15, trapped in an Eagles song. It's hotter than a nuclear reaction, and my air-conditioning is wheezing like an asthmatic on Pikes Peak. I feel a little disconnected from the normal (ha-ha!) people in my life, so I mentally catalogue those I will be calling en route to the second-largest city in the nation. In no particular order, they are Meg, Wes, Amanda, James again, and, finally, my mother, parenting dynamo Katherine Fielding. Denise is sleeping in the backseat with her head resting on inflata-Jesus; Jillian is reading her book about the yogi; and, sick of music, I'm only listening to the rhythmic hum of tires on bumpy highway. We're all tired. Tired of driving, tired of talking to one another, tired of eating preservative-laden road food, tired of being crammed in the Saturn and smelling one another's feet. *Only four more hours,* I think. Unless we run out of gas or my wheel falls off again. Our patience with Riding in the Car Together has long since peaked and is now flirting with annoyance and, given the right conditions, temper tantrums all around. But it appears that we have indeed lost Rick and his black Acura, which is a small consolation.

I flip open the phone and dial Meg. While I wait for her to answer, I compose an impromptu list of things I would rather do than return to my old life:

10. Take seven SAT exams back-to-back.
9. Eat a bowl of paper clips.
8. Reroof my brother's house by myself.
7. Land a job as Dennis Franz's personal groomer.
6. Door-to-door fund-raising in Mississippi for the Atheist Alliance.
5. Hand out toothbrushes on Halloween in a rough neighborhood.
4. Get up at four A.M. to go Christmas shopping at Wal-Mart the day after Thanksgiving.
3. Try to grow a full beard.
2. Wear a suit of chum in shark-infested waters.
1. Enter a nationally televised dance competition.

Just as I finish my list I get Meg's voice mail, so I leave a message in an Australian accent. But I don't say, "G'day, mate!" Meg finds it funny when I do such things, which may be funny in and of itself. Or sad. I also get Amanda's and Wes's voice mail, so I leave messages for them, too. Without an accent. When I call James I get neither him nor his voice mail. It just rings and rings and rings, which is kind of weird.

I don't call my mother. I tell myself I'll do it when I get to L.A. (Not that I'll get anything other than her voice mail, but . . .) This hardly makes my nervousness subside. It's only like putting off that term paper until the morning it's due, which means that every smile between now and then will have a deadline hanging over it, muting it, and I know this. I am fully cognizant of this depressing fact.

In Barstow we stop for gas and snacks and I ask Jillian to drive. I pledge to be the best navigator ever. I will be the Nobel Prize nominee of navigators. I also bribe her with Gram's ultra-secret brownie recipe, protected by the family for seventy-six generations or something. I have no scruples whatsoever about spilling it in exchange for a passenger-seat view of road rage. I also tell her that since I don't do well in heavy traffic, we may die if I'm at the wheel. This seems to do the trick.

When we pass the exit to San Bernardino, Jillian gets drive-silly, and it's contagious. We do the Mr. Short-Term Memory routine Tom Hanks made famous on *SNL*, repeating, "Hey, I'm from San Bernardino!" over and over, laughing each time. Denise just smiles, a distant, puzzled look on her face. How sad to have missed *SNL* before it became a pasteurized wasteland! My very youth was established on a foundation of early-nineties *SNL* bits. My friends and I would have entire conversations in *SNL* skitspeak: "I'm Hans . . . (and I'm Franz) and we're here to pump . . . YOU UP!" and "Well, isn't that spay-shul!" and a few years later, "Makin' copies!" It's a wonder none of us were strangled during this phase, actually.

I have only experienced southern California vicariously through films and television shows, so my impression of what to expect involves pool parties attended by thin, tan cokeheads, movie wrap parties up in the Hills attended by thin, tan cokeheads, and impromptu parties in the parking lot near a popular neighborhood taco stand. These parties are attended by cops and gangbanger hooligans. So imagine my surprise to learn that just east of L.A.—adjacent to the metropolitan area, in fact—there is skiing! Wilderness hiking! And fishing! I tell you, I'm like a child on Christmas morning.

So the plan is to just kind of get there, get to downtown Los Angeles intact, and hang out for the rest of the day. Find a café, have a little dinner, see the sights. Then consult our various maps and (A) check in to the Chateau Marmont because I've only had my junior suite booked since childhood, (B) return Denise to her rightful owners, and (C) figure out how to find my mother. My stomach flip-flops at the thought.

Traffic. Brake lights and stoplights. I turn off the air-conditioning. We open our windows, let our hair flap in the wind. Palm trees and hot breeze. Billboards, phone lines, and smog. "Jillian, you're a fantastic driver," I say. Air redolent of orange blossoms, wildfires, and car exhaust. Los Angeles. She's here somewhere. She grocery shops here, banks here, and maybe even has another family here.

Another family. Do I have a half sister or brother? What would he or she be like? What is their daily routine? Does she make their sandwiches before school? Or does she moon about the house quoting Katharine Hepburn?

Maybe she's in an institution. I wouldn't be surprised. How would I react to that news? Maybe James has known all along. I become suddenly, inflexibly paranoid, like I've smoked three joints in a row. Not that I've ever done that. But I can imagine what that would be like. If she were institutionalized, would she recognize me? Or would she flash me a showy smile, throw her arms out, and greet me with "Bette, darling, I love what you've done to your hair!"

Would the staff try to guilt me into visiting all the time because see-ing a sane family member who cares makes them sleep a little bet-ter each night? (Well, sane in the loosest possible terms.)

Maybe she's dead. But surely I would have been notified. Doesn't someone call you when that happens? When your es-tranged mother keels over from a brain aneurysm at the local Safe-way? Or has whatever bond we once shared been so completely severed that her name has slowly faded from my birth certificate? Disappearing ink for my disappearing mother.

Jillian interrupts my paranoia with an urgent command. "Quick, tell me where to go." I notice that she's sweating from the strain of concentrating so intently.

"Take this exit," I impulsively answer. "Get off here." Who knows where that will take us! I flap my map around madly, trying in vain to pinpoint our location.

"Merge onto the I-10 West," Denise interjects confidently. "You don't want to take that exit, believe me."

Jillian merges. "Where do I go next?"

"Take the Sunset Boulevard exit. But you've got about twenty miles to go yet. We're going to the Marmont, right?" Denise seems to be in her element. But her face has a weary expression, like re-cess is over and it's time for long division again.

"How do you know where we're going?" Jillian asks, nervous.

"Just trust me. I looked at the map."

More traffic. L.A. is an endless traffic jam, with fake tits and palm trees and salsa on the radio. *Sunset Boulevard.* I can hardly stop myself from leaping out of the car to dance in the street. This street is *legendary.* How many other streets have movies, musicals, songs, *and* television shows about them?!?! The final scene in *Annie Hall* was filmed here! There's the Laugh Factory; the Virgin Megastore, former site of Schwab's Pharmacy, where F. Scott Fitzgerald had a heart attack in 1940. Farther down, we would find the Comedy Store, the Argyle, the Viper Room, the Whisky, the Roxy, and half a mile south of the Strip on Santa Monica Boulevard is the Troubadour, where a besotted John Lennon heckled the Smothers Brothers. "Jillian, you're really doing a fantastic job," I say. I try to sound reassuring and impressed. I don't want the ride to end.

Sullen, ratty-looking kids with purple and green hair smoke on the sidewalks. Tourists in lavender polos and khaki shorts take pictures of one another posing in front of the giant Bullwinkle statue at the Dudley Do-Right Emporium while sculpted couples on rollerblades weave through them. Across the street is Union, known for its competent Caribbean fare and the occasional celebrity guest. Two blond women in heels and sunglasses walk out, laughing and flipping their shiny, full-bodied hair. Guess which one uses Suave and which uses the more expensive salon product? I can't tell, either! It's so exciting. I could spend days here taking notes and making up complicated lives for everyone. If people watching were an Olympic sport, I would have a consistently decent final showing. I would make my country relatively proud.

My heart is ready to leap from my chest and I lock eyes with a homeless man who looks like my father if I squint. I've driven two thousand miles and traveled back in time twenty-two years. But then, maybe we never shed the ghosts from our pasts. It's what I'm here to find out. I'm here to find out if it's possible.

We note Bar Marmont on our way to the hotel of my dreams. Lord, I miss booze. I can say it like that because my becoming an alcoholic at this point is about as likely as Tom Cruise shooting an ad for Zoloft. *My kingdom for a pair of functional kidneys.* I have surpassed my peer group, skipping the marriage, mortgage, kids, and Roth IRA entirely. I am treading water in the sixty-plus demographic, but I'm not even thirty yet. It's amazing how you'll compromise when your life is at stake. No more martinis? But I can live another ten years at least? Excellent! I'm so there! No experimentation with drugs, smoking, late-night parties, or kinky sex? Point me in the right direction! No more processed meats? Meat schmeat! (Actually, that one wasn't all that difficult, given that I've been seeing a cute little puppy face with huge watery eyes in every hamburger for the last ten years or so. Not that burgers are made of

dog, but you know what I mean. So I'm kind of a vegan now. A
vegan who wears leather and eats honey, capsules encased in
gelatin, and the occasional cookie made with egg and butter. And a
tiny serving of plain skinless chicken if Marissa makes it the way I
like. Because I don't want to be rude. But that's it. So maybe I'm
not a vegan after all. But I really, really admire them. And if my kidney fails and I go back on dialysis, I can have bologna again. But no
bananas. Weird, huh?)

The Chateau Marmont looks like a castle on the side of a hill,
hidden in dense foliage. You just know there's at least one, maybe
two A-list stars lounging around the secluded pool on any given day.
Belushi overdosed on heroin in one of the bungalows in 1982. (A
moment of silence, please, for one of the original Blues Brothers
before the bastardization of the franchise.) Jim Morrison swung
from a drainpipe on the roof—a moment later reenacted by Val
Kilmer in Oliver Stone's slutty movie about the Doors. Jean Harlow
and Clark Gable were rumored to have trysted in one of the suites.
John and Yoko slept here, of course. And the eclectic, glamorously
grungy décor (vintage Art Deco meets Moroccan meets Gothic,
chic bohemia) suggests that the anecdotes are only getting started.
After we park the car in the cavelike hotel garage and stretch our
legs, we make our way through the dim retro foyer to check in. The
clerk has a laid-back sense of humor and a chic polish, with red
Bettie Page bangs and a fitted green velvet jacket. She makes a
small self-deprecating joke when she's looking up my room, and
you can tell she'd be fun to get high with. Jillian and I dump our
luggage in the room, which is an eccentric throwback to 1940s
Hollywood, with a black-and-white tiled floor, a chenille bedspread, and olive vinyl-backed diner chairs in the kitchenette. We
freshen up in the aqua-tiled bathroom: three faces jockeying for
mirror time. Denise wants to bring her inflatable Jesus down to the
pool, maybe to use as a float in the water. I let his air out and drape
him over the back of a chair. "Jesus is staying in tonight," I say. But
not me. I'm ready for tapas around the pool and some serious relaxation.

• • •

Hanging out at the Marmont proves to be an excellent antidote to Riding in the Car Together for too long. We order fruity drinks (nonalcoholic in my case, but do I even need to mention that anymore?), share a plate of hors d'oeuvres (which Denise keeps calling "whores duh-vores") at a patio table, and toast friendship, being young and single, and getting to California intact. As twilight falls, the hotel staff walk around lighting candles. Night-blooming jasmine opens and infuses the air with perfume, making Denise's continued and purposeful mispronunciation of various items on the menu more bearable. We can barely hear the traffic from the Strip through the tangled palm trees, ferns, and hedges. We are surrounded by attractive people in expensive sandals. They look like people pretending to hide from their own celebrity.

"Well, here we are," I say, tipping back in my metal patio chair. Candles throw strange shadows across our faces. The sound of the waterfall cascading into the pool calms me.

"Here we are," Denise echoes, smiling. She pulls the strings from the hood of her red sweatshirt back and forth.

"Ready to go to your aunt's place?"

Denise shrugs. "I guess so." She pops a bite of bruschetta into her mouth. I try to imagine what it could be like to adopt Denise, to give her a good life beyond a broken foster care system and the care of a reformed drug-addled aunt. I could be her James! I could send her to college! Oh, how proud I'd be on graduation day. . . . I picture Denise smiling at me in her cap and gown, clutching her diploma and waving at me from the stage. Then I think, *What am I, nuts? I can't even send myself to college!*

Jillian just watches us carefully. "Looks like we lost Rick after all," she finally says.

"You know what?" Denise announces. "I can just call a cab from here."

I'm taken aback by both the offer and the false confidence in her voice. "Denise, we took you this far. It's no big deal." It suddenly occurs to me that maybe Denise doesn't want us to see her aunt's home. Maybe she doesn't want us to meet her aunt. Maybe she's ashamed because calling someone a crack whore has become so commonplace that it's turned into a term of endearment in some circles—and her aunt *really is* a latter-day crack whore.

Denise fidgets, rubbing one frayed and dirty sweatshirt cuff between her left forefinger and thumb. "Seriously, guys. She doesn't live too far from here. I'll just call a cab. I mean, you've already done way too much for me."

Which is probably true, but something feels off-kilter here. Why would Denise insist on a 1,900-mile ride but abdicate the final few blocks? It occurs to me again that she could be lying. What if she's really homeless? With nowhere to go? What if she ends up hooking to pay for a new meth habit she contracted simply because I was too lazy to drive a few blocks farther, too careless to make sure she had a safe place to sleep for the night? Then a more sinister thought burbles to the surface and pops: What do I do if she *is* homeless? What if her aunt is actually a burly, gold-toothed pimp named Ice Dawg? I wish I got out more. And was more assertive.

"Denise," Jillian interjects, "we can give you a ride."

I jump in. "Yeah, we made it this far together. Besides, I'd kind of like to meet this aunt of yours. Make sure you get there safely."

She gnaws a hangnail, considering this. "Well," she says, "okay. But don't say I didn't warn you."

This peculiar instruction stops my tongue behind my teeth. I try to think of a reassuring quip, something to put us all at ease, but instead I'm simply relieved that she has something of a home base after all. And really. How bad could it be?

As Denise directs us farther down Sunset toward Beverly Hills, a curdled feeling expands in my stomach. The houses are getting bigger. The landscaping is growing more elaborate. Pretty soon the houses disappear completely, tucked away from prying eyes and cameras. "Are we going the right way?" I ask, uneasy.

Denise nods. "Turn left here."

I turn left. She directs us down a few more streets to Mulholland Drive, winding up and along the ridgeline of the Santa Monica Mountains. The city glows, hazy and sprawling, behind us. We pass several more streets named after canyons before Denise instructs us to pull up to a gated driveway flanked on each side by a massive wall of foliage. The letter *B* curls in wrought-iron elegance on each gate. "Your aunt lives here?" Denise doesn't answer.

Jillian frowns. "I was not expecting this."

"Neither was I," I say under my breath. *Maybe her aunt is house-sitting,* I try to reassure myself. But I'm not falling for it.

"Park for a second," Denise orders me. Again, I obey. She hops out of the car and skips around to a keypad/intercom-type box. She punches in some numbers, and the gates slowly ease open. I almost have to rub my eyes. This is not a house. This is a steel-and-glass fortress—an architectural triumph, really—buttressed by palm trees, illuminated Japanese gardens, and potted topiaries that have been manicured to within an inch of their lives. This is a dwelling that would make Jesus hang his head in shame. Or throw rocks. Jillian can only tooth-whistle in awe.

"Your aunt lives here?" I ask again.

"Park over there. By the golf carts." I park under a massive oak tree and stare at her, waiting for clarification. Denise seems oblivious to my mounting panic and confusion. She hops out of the car and heads for the house. Er, mansion. Jillian and I just gape at each other.

Suddenly Denise's blond head looms large in my field of vision. "Well? Are you coming or what?"

I exit the car, and for a horrible minute I'm sure Denise has dragged us here to rob the place. But how does she know the entry code? Maybe she stole it. Maybe she *is* part of an interstate identity-theft ring! My mind is spinning like an unbalanced washing machine.

We follow her down a winding path, past several flat, underlit pools, up a series of concrete staircases, and finally into a foyer so unique, so Art Deco on speed, it's almost hideous. *Denise has a key, ladies and gentlemen*. But I've got no time to consider this, because the ceiling is a mile over our heads, anchored by a modern iron-and-glass chandelier that has likely been specially commissioned for a fee surpassing my total lifetime income. It is larger than my childhood concept of planet Earth. To my left, the rock wall is weeping, and to my right, Jillian practically is.

Denise walks around, nonchalantly flipping on lights. "Thirsty?" she asks. We follow her, like dumbstruck puppies, into the kitchen. You know those home and garden shows called *I Want That!* or whatever? Well, if I were more into consumerism, I'd nod my head vigorously in agreement if someone were to say that right now. The walls are the color of butter, accented by real, honest-to-God paintings on stretched canvas. No churned-out Thomas Kinkade prints here, folks! The smooth cabinets are crafted from some kind of dark red tropical hardwood, the absence of which has probably led to the decline of at least seventeen species of insects in the Amazon rain forest. The appliances are nowhere to be seen (save for a flat-screen television tucked tastefully under a cabinet), but as an avid watcher of home improvement shows, I know that they are concealed by appliance garages. The refrigerator has the same facing as the cupboards, and one or more of the drawers will also be refrigerated. There are three sinks. With aerodynamic silver faucets. And two islands. Granite countertops and a heavy-duty commercial range that may never have been used. Real hardwood flooring and strategic recessed lighting. A bizarre metal sculpture to my left, like something out of *Beetlejuice*. A glass wall about a football field away that opens to a patio with an enviable view of the Hollywood Hills. Denise pulls open a cupboard door and is bathed in cool white light. "Water?" She offers a rectangular bottle of Fiji water.

I shake my head and slowly say, "Denise, does your aunt live here?" But the question is more a formality at this point. The jig is up. And I've been had.

Denise sighs and slides onto a polished metal stool. "I'm not a foster kid, okay? I live here with my parents. Well, with my mom and stepdad."

"Where are they?" Jillian asks warily.

Denise shrugs. "Europe, I think. It's hard to keep track."

All I can do is stare at her. She stares back. "Look. I'm really sorry I lied to you. It's such a long story, and . . . I don't know why I did it." Her voice trails off. She drops my gaze and takes a swig of water. "Are you sure you guys don't want anything? *Jugo de naranja?*"

I finally snap. "Who the hell are you? What else have you lied to me about, Denise? If that's your real name!"

"Why did you do it?" Jillian asks, going into concerned-social-worker mode. "Why did you lie?"

I prefer to use a more confrontational approach. "So how did you end up at a rest stop in Minnesota, Denise? Private jet crash in the woods?" My anger is actually making the room vibrate. Or maybe my eyeballs are shaking in their sockets.

"Look. There really was a Rick, and he lives in Minneapolis. I met him online. He really did turn out to be an asshole. So it wasn't a total lie, right? I could have just charged a plane ticket home, but . . . I just wanted to do something crazy. I was bored. I mean, I've done everything already. I was, like, in rehab at twelve. So what else am I going to do? My parents couldn't care less what I do." She seems lost in thought for a second, then finishes with "I don't know why I stole your purse."

"She stole your purse?" Jillian asks me.

"You played this whole charade because you were *bored?*" My voice echoes through the kitchen. A refrigerator kicks in, humming quietly. "Nice fucking excuse for an excuse."

"I just got carried away. It was totally impulsive. I thought you looked like a nice, normal person, and I sort of just decided to do it on the spot. It was totally spontaneous. It started with one little spontaneous lie and then it just kind of grew and grew from there. I was, like, *I can't believe I'm getting away with this,* and then it was too late. But we had fun, right?"

Yeah, I think, *if your definition of fun involves being a lying sociopath.* "You're a total sociopath!" I declare. "You made up a whole fucking persona, just for fun. That, to me, is the definition of a complete sociopath." Well, that and listing one of your hobbies as "genocide" on your eHarmony account. "You should be in prison," I add. "You can't . . . You just can't *do* that to people!" I flounder for words.

Denise frowns. "I'm not a sociopath. I'm just understimulated."

"How can you be understimulated? You live in a fortress on Mulholland Drive! You've got a digital camera so advanced it practically hasn't even been invented yet!" She was the kind of girl that could get involved in a major bank heist. Does she want to graduate to bit parts in John Waters films someday? Poor little understimulated rich girl . . . With no Symbionese Liberation Army to kidnap her, she invents her own madcap adventures.

"So where'd you get that gun?"

"Does it matter anymore? And yes, my name is Denise, by the way. I stole the gun from Rick, if you really care."

"If we can believe any of that," Jillian replies sarcastically.

I just shake my head and look around the kitchen. No sweet little boy named Jarrod. No abusive foster parents. The party in Aspen must have looked like a camping trip to her. I'm suddenly depressed. "Why?" I ask. It seems to be the only word my mouth will make. In a movie I might have slapped her, but I don't have the energy. And honestly, I'm a little afraid of her.

Denise just looks at me, confused. "I used to be an actor?"

"What?"

"I was. Ever see *The Year Santa Skipped Christmas*?"

I had, but I wasn't about to admit it. "No," I practically spit. What kind of explanation is this?

"I was in that. Also, I was in *Remember Georgia*. That one had a talking cat." She rolls her eyes as if to say, *Producers and their wacky talking cats. What can you do?* "I'm auditioning for a small role in a pilot for fall. Can you guess what the role is?" Denise manages to look both coy and lewd.

"I don't care," I say.

She doesn't seem to hear me and says, "A teenage runaway, of course!"

I can't even conceal my disgust. "Let's get out of here, Jillian."

At that point I happen to glance out the window . . . and see the black Acura pull up. I crouch behind the counter. "Jesus Christ, it's Rick! Oh my God. He found us. Well, Denise, are you happy now? We're all going to die!"

"Relax," Denise says. She almost yawns as the front door opens. A short, thin man in a navy polo and khaki slacks walks in, a helplessly furious look on his face. "This is Luis," Denise announces. "Luis works for my dad." She folds her arms across her chest and directs her next comment to Luis. "*Spies* for my dad is more like it!" Jillian and I can only stand there like slack-jawed mutes. For the second time in mere days, I have lost my power of speech. My mind is stumbling around in shock like an unattended accident victim. But I start to sense the line connecting the dots: the California plates . . . the expensive black car . . . Denise's relative nonchalance during most of the trip. Of course it wasn't some lunatic stalker. "I guess you could call him my . . . *manservant*," Denise adds, smirking. It was her fucking . . . *man*servant!

Luis fumes. "I told you not to call me that! Where is the respect!" He doesn't seem to know what to do with his body and ends up shaking a flustered finger at her. "You just wait until your mother and father return from Europe! Flying to Minnesota to meet some . . . *bribón*! And then hitching a ride with strangers! Shame on you!"

I begin to have this vague fear that I could be arrested for simply associating with Denise. What if she's really thirteen? And here I am contributing to the delinquency of a minor! Oh my God, I want to get the hell out of here.

"*Stepfather*, Luis! You call him and I'm going to call the INS."

"You wouldn't."

"Try me."

Luis looks at me, helpless. "You see what I have to live with?"

"You can always quit, Lu," Denise singsongs.

Luis throws his hands up. "She is impossible, this girl!"

I have never agreed more with a sentiment in my entire twenty-eight years on the planet. "Jillian," I say on our way out, "we have just crossed the country with the Antichrist."

* * *

In the car, we're silent for a long time. We drive down a dark street lined with palm trees. "I knew something wasn't right about her," Jillian says softly, breaking the silence.

I want to cry, but I can't. Instead I let out a bitter "Ha!"

I try to remember a time in my own life when I've pulled such a stunt. The only thing I can think of was when I told Sarah White in third grade that I was born with a Venetian caul and could therefore see ghosts. Oh, and another time I told a few of my second-grade peers that I was a secret descendant of one of the popes and a nun. But that ended in elementary school! Did I ever tell an exorbitant lie when I should have known much better? Did I ever pretend to be someone I wasn't? Maybe I exaggerated a little now and then when I met a guy I wanted to impress. Maybe we told the waiter at Olive Garden that it was one of our birthdays when it really wasn't, just for the free cake and amusing singing. Maybe we gave out fake names once in awhile to deflect obnoxious men, and I seem to vaguely recall my friend Amanda once convincing a would-be suitor that she had sung in a rock band that toured Japan. (This was a lie that had especially hilarious results.)

I also remember the time a boy drove 250 miles to see Jillian, and she taped a note to her apartment door explaining that her grandmother had just died so she had to leave town for the funeral. In reality, she and I were watching from the window, hiding and shushing each other, as the poor guy read the note and walked back to his car, dejected. She really beat herself up over that, especially since her grandmother was very much alive and would have smacked her upside the head for telling such a lie. (Oh, the reason for the lie was that he turned out to be an Amway evangelist.)

"I guess being a child star does that to you," Jillian suddenly says.

"So does being born without a soul," I say meanly. I wish I could try on a new personality, even a new life, if only for a weekend.

Then it occurs to me. I had.

Jillian continues. "You know, some people lead double lives and their own spouses don't even know."

"Maybe we're all actors in a play," I say grandly. Then I think, *Maybe it's intermission and all the lights are brightening and I'm just discovering now that what I've thought was real all along has only been a farce.* When we reach a straight ribbon of road, I turn and give Jillian a serious look. "Nobody will believe this, you do realize that."

Jillian smiles and says, "I especially liked the part where you said, *'If that's your* real *name!'* "

I laugh, although I don't want to, and Jillian grows thoughtful. "Remember when Helen told you that your guardian angel was named Denise?" she asks. "Maybe there's something significant about that. Maybe this Denise was supposed to change your perception about things."

"Mission accomplished." We're silent for a beat, and I ask, "Jillian, am I really that gullible?"

She gives me a pained look. She's totally onto me. "Does the pope shit in the woods?" This was something people said in high school.

I want to say, *Let's ask your pendant.*

"Well, everything happens for a reason."

"Does it?" I ask. I remember Denise's excitement about something as cluttery-kitschy as Wall Drug, her occasional goofiness. *I'll miss that,* I think. Was that the real Denise or simply an act? Will this just be an anecdote I relate over and over at parties? A riddle I'll never solve? Probably. I know myself. I obsess over things. I once spent three days trying to remember that it was Rosalind Russell whom my great-aunt had once served at a restaurant in Chicago. Maybe the whole thing will come to mean about as much to me as my former coworkers at Kohl's. I see their shapes in my mind, but no longer their names or faces. Their time in my life was fleeting and random, as I was to them. But if nothing is random—if, as Jillian says, there's a reason for everything—then there's a reason for Denise. It just might take me awhile to figure it out.

But then again, that might be a load of crap.

* * *

The next morning, after a deep sleep at the Marmont, a shower with the exquisite complimentary toiletries (Marmont exclusives, I'm told), and a sunrise walk down the Sunset, I feel better. Jillian and I share a poolside plate of sun-dried-tomato-and-basil quiche and fresh strawberries. In her so-cool-they're-*next*-season sunglasses, silk paisley halter smock, two-hundred-dollar jeans, and kitten heel thongs, Jillian is completely at home around the Marmont pool. In my scratched Target shades, black tank top, old-ass frayed jean skirt, and paint-dappled flip-flops, I am completely at home in a bowling alley.

"So I'm thinking of moving back home," Jillian suddenly announces.

I give a little squeal, and I'm not the squealing type. I also clap. "Yes, you should! We could get a place together in Madison!"

"I mean, Geoffrey and I are definitely over. And Colorado holds so many wonderful, but now so many sad, memories for me." She toys with a strawberry stem.

I try to compose myself. "Jillian, I think you could do well with massage in Madison. Or even Milwaukee."

She gets thoughtful. "I'd have to build up my clientele from scratch, but it's possible." She pops the last bite of quiche into her mouth and asks, "So what's the plan?"

"Well, we could start looking for apartments next week. . . . Are you thinking downtown, by the capitol maybe?"

Jillian smiles. "No, I mean for today. I know there's something you've been wanting to do." She makes a librarian-looking-over-her-bifocals face in an effort to remind me: chin tipped down, eyebrows arched, subtle grin.

"Oh." Freshly vulnerable from my last catastrophe, I'm not sure I'm ready for the *Tyrannosaurus rex* of tasks, but I haven't come all this way to just eat quiche around a pool (although now I'm wishing I had). "Well, it's time to see if Kate Fielding still exists," I say mysteriously.

"When did you last talk to her?"

"I don't know. A few years." I sip my iced tea. Seven, to be exact, but I don't tell Jillian this. She does know, however, that my mother has no idea that I have PKD and a new kidney. It occurs to me that this is quite a load to dump on an estranged parent. But being left by a parent is quite a load to dump on a child, too.

Jillian scrapes at a bit of cold cheese with her fork. "Do you have her address? Are you sure she's still at the same number?"

"Well, every time I call her I get this automated voice mail system. I do have an address. I guess all we can do is just, um, go there?" Wow, it sounds so sad when I actually say it out loud.

Jillian pushes her sunglasses up, perching them above her forehead. "Leigh, you came all this way and you don't even know if you can even find her?"

I laugh self-consciously. This is true. Maybe I really don't want to find her. Especially now that I'm here. My early naïve bravado has faded into a tepid, nervous search for the fire escape. If I'd *really* wanted to find her, I would have done my homework. There are twenty K. Fieldings in the Los Angeles phone book. I checked last night. I try to imagine how demoralizing calling all of those numbers would be. Anyway, she could have a new last name to go with her new life. She could be Kate O'Malley, or Katie Sullivan, or Katherine Kress.

How badly do I want to see her? Better yet, *why* do I want to see her? Am I really such a masochist? Maybe James was right. She'd written us off long ago. Her silence tells me that we mean nothing more to her than a pair of knee-high boots she'd worn in high school: fun—if a bit cramped—then, completely forgettable now.

Maybe I never had a mother at all. Maybe I imagined ever having a mother. I might have crash-landed in Gram's backyard in an egg-shaped pod, like Superman or Robin Williams as Mork, bumping my head hard enough to get amnesia about my home planet. And maybe I wandered around like P. D. Eastman's lost baby bird, asking every creature in my path, "Are you my mother? Are *you* my mother?"

I shrug and lamely say, "I guess I was just taking a chance. It was a long shot. I sort of said to myself, 'If you can find her, it's meant to be. If not, well, then, maybe everyone's better off.' " I kind of say this to appease Jillian, but a small, perverted part of me actually believes it.

Jillian continues. "Do you need to hire a private detective or something? How curious are you? Leigh, what if she's . . . not well? What if she's remarried and you have half siblings?" We've discussed the various twists and turns my mother's new life could have taken many times before. But repeating the conversation within perhaps twenty miles of Kate's new home seems to blow Jillian's mind a little, and she slumps back, staring at me. "I'd want to know, wouldn't you? Maybe they could give you a kidney if your new one fails! Maybe you have a half sister who's a perfect match!" Jillian gets excited when she thinks she's found the solutions to my problems, especially those medical in nature.

"And maybe neon bandannas tied around your thigh will come back in style."

Jillian ignores this. "Well?"

I stand up and shake my left leg, which has fallen asleep. If I don't do this now, I never will. I try to think of a witty comeback, but when I open my mouth, what decides to come out is "Well, what? Let's go before I change my mind."

We plot our course to my mother with phone directory maps cross-referenced against the laminated map of Los Angeles we picked up yesterday. It feels like deciphering a code, or maybe studying for an exam—*connect these dots and the desired result will be yours.* I wait for some kind of emotional reaction to materialize in my gut, or maybe my heart, but I realize I'm just clammy. Jillian offers to drive, because I seem a bit divorced from the ability to concentrate in heavy traffic. "Are you sure you want to do this?" she asks.

"No," I answer, almost before she's finished asking the question. But I've come this far, haven't I? I stare out the window at the palm trees and traffic. The sunlight melts into the smog, creating a hot, bright blanket. I feel suffocated. *James is right,* I think. *I should just leave her in the past.* But I'm not sure I share his innate ability to move forward without looking back over his shoulder at least once. I'm always looking backward for clues. I suppose it's why I needed to reconnect with Seth, and it's most definitely why I'm directing Jillian to turn left at the next block and right two streets later.

I try not to think about how successful my reunion with Seth was. Christ, life is sure difficult without a pendant or magic kidney to guide you.

"1764 Meredith Street," Jillian says, pulling up and parking before a small olive-green Craftsman bungalow on a quiet side street. She turns the car off and we sit silently, staring at the house. Tucked in by exotic vines and shrubs that would never make it through a Wisconsin winter, this is the house my mother calls home. Maybe, anyway. A network of overhead phone and power lines connect it to its neighbors, and a cinder-block wall lines the driveway that, I assume, ends in a garage in the backyard. The windows along one side are imprisoned by wrought-iron grates. They really add a safe, cheerful, family-friendly ambience.

"Hey," Jillian says brightly, perhaps to psyche me up for the task at hand, "I think I saw this place on *Flip This House.*" And she's right: It's exactly the kind of home that a developer would buy for half a million, install new appliances in the kitchen, and resell for three-quarters of a million.

"I think I saw the owner on *Flip This Family,*" I answer, still taking it all in. This feels so much different from meeting Larry's grandma. For one thing, this is my estranged mother—a woman who abandoned me, got herself lost, and probably doesn't want to be found. My face is suddenly warm, and I'm having trouble inhaling fully. I feel like someone's tightly rolled me up in a length of R-30 fiberglass insulation. Jillian pivots in her seat to face me but says nothing. She's waiting for me to make the next move.

Fuck it. *"Take big risks,"* I think, and open the door. I make my feet march up the sidewalk to the front door. My legs feel as if they have become lengths of garden hose. I am vaguely aware of Jillian slamming the car door and trotting across the lawn to catch up with me.

Before I can run back to the car, I force myself to ring the doorbell.

It is at this point that I realize I have no idea what I'm about to say.

I mentally sprint through several possibilities: *Hello, I'm Leigh. Remember me? . . . Mom, it's me. Your daughter. I'm sorry to drop by out of the blue, but since you never called or wrote . . . Mom, James called you an asshole. . . . "Here's Johnny!"*

The silence stretches on and on, like eastern Wyoming.

"Someone's coming!" Jillian says in a strange voice. She's standing at my side. I'm peripherally aware that the someone in question has lifted the curtains at the window to our right to check out our visual credentials and props (or lack thereof). Even I look down to see if I'm holding religious literature of some nature. I'm suddenly sure of nothing at all.

At that moment, a flood of eerie calm envelops me. I wonder if this is the sudden clarity some people exhibit before they die in a natural disaster of epic proportions. At least that's what it looks like in the movies. I turn to Jillian solemnly. "Thanks for doing this with me." Before I add, *I couldn't have done this without you,* a man in glasses opens the front door.

"Help you?" he asks. I suddenly forget who I am and why I'm here. All I want to know is whether or not this attractive older man is my stepfather. He's certainly dressed like *someone's* stepfather, with sensible leather sandals, khaki shorts, and the requisite middle-manager's white polo shirt with a blue stripe on the collar. His dark hair is graying at the temples. He has a mustache and goatee, also graying.

He's waiting for an answer. I blink and stammer, "Um, is this"— I rummage through my purse for the address even though I committed it to memory long before President George W. Bush fainted after choking on a pretzel—"1764 Meredith Street?"

He nods, and I can sense he's growing impatient.

"Does Kate Fielding live here?"

He stares at me for a second. *This is it,* I think. *My past, present, and future, about to collide like a hungover twentysomething and a Sunday* I Love the 90s *marathon on VH1.*

"She did," he answers.

I'd like to say I fainted, but unfortunately, reality is always much less attractive and cinematic than the late Aaron Spelling would have had you believe. When my possible stepfather said those two words—"She did"—I sat down hard on the porch, filmed in cold sweat. Well, more like my legs just collapsed and my ass plopped down where I stood. Possible Stepfather and Jillian helped me up and into the house in which my mother lived. Past tense.

"Would you like some water? I have iced tea in the fridge."

I manage to nod. "Water. Yes. Please. Thank you."

Jillian whispers, "Are you alright?"

I nod some more and take in my surroundings: dark built-in shelving, walls painted with colors that could have been named Colonial Brick and Harvest Moon, the perfect Mission-style décor, Pottery Barn living room showroom circa 2006. The couch upon which I sit is covered in stiff yet supple brown leather. It doesn't feel like anyone really lives here, let alone a man who once knew my mother intimately, quite likely.

When the man returns with an ice water (plus lemon slice!), he sits in a chair next to the sofa. "Feeling better?" I take a sip and nod even more, until it feels like I've turned into a bobble-head doll my-self. We make brief introductions, first names only. His name is Brad.

"Want to tell me what this is about?" he asks.

I decide simplicity is best. "Kate was my mother," I say. "Still is, I guess." This time I do sound like I could be in a Lifetime movie starring Jacqueline Bisset and Judith Light. I'd totally watch it if I wasn't in it right now.

"I knew Kate had children," Brad replies, his tone softening. He shakes his head. "God, I don't know what to say. What on earth are you doing here?"

"I haven't talked to her in seven years. I guess I just wanted to see her." Hearing myself say those words compresses my heart, as if someone's attached a vacuum to my dorsal artery. I will myself not to cry.

"I'm sorry," he says, his eyes soft. He shrugs, leans forward with his elbows on his knees, and clasps his hands together. "I suppose you'd like to know what happened."

"Yes," I say. The understatement of the century. Someone beeps a cheery greeting as they drive past on the street, reminding me that the world couldn't care less about the drama unfolding in this living room. It kind of pisses me off.

He rubs his forehead and says, "She left about three months ago. She didn't want to get married. We'd been together for about nine months prior to that. It took me a long time to start dating after my divorce, but when I met Kate everything just clicked. She moved in shortly after we met. Then, this April, she met someone else." He looks bewildered at this confession.

I've missed her by three goddamn months? I ask the first question on my lips. "Where'd she go?"

"London. He was British. Would you like some more water?"

My mother is a serial abandoner. "London?" I frown. "Um, no more water. I'm fine." I look at Jillian; she gives me an intense look in return. "I can't believe this," I continue. "I missed her by three months." I slump back on the sofa, my mind crammed with questions. I lean forward again. "Did she ever talk about me? I have an older brother, too. James. What was she like? Do you have pictures of her?" Slowly, I let my mind process the information rushing in: My mother is not dead. She's not in a facility for the mentally disturbed. She's not living in a dumpster in an alley, turning tricks for heroin. Nope. She's just a flighty, irresponsible, emotionally frigid slut with intimacy issues.

I immediately feel guilty for thinking of her as a slut. She is my mother, after all. Was.

"I'm not much of a photographer. But I do have a few pictures of us from trips we've taken." Brad reaches under the polished cherry end table to my right and pulls out a small photo album.

Déjà vu. Will a newspaper clipping fall from these pages to announce that my mother has been murdering homeless people and burying them in the backyard? "I'm sorry to say she didn't talk about you much. She just told me you and your brother were living with your father and that she hadn't seen you in years." He darts his eyes back and forth between Jillian and me before adding, "She said he wouldn't let her see you."

I take a deep breath and blurt what my deeply ingrained sense of fairness demands I blurt: "My father died twenty-two years ago. My grandmother raised us until she died, too. James and I have been on our own since then."

He makes a face like he's processing a difficult algebraic equation. "Jesus Christ."

In my head, the Zombies' "She's Not There" plays on a loop.

"I'm so sorry," he adds. "I had no idea." I pick up the photo album and begin to turn the pages. Jillian looks on next to me.

And there she is. It's like a kick to the heart via my eyes. Her hair is a laid-back honey color now, and her smile is similarly relaxed, California-style. She's wearing a white tunic, with a fuchsia flower tucked behind her ear. She's sitting at a seaside table somewhere. The sun is setting behind her. Her nose doesn't look like mine, and I wonder if she's gotten it fixed.

"That was taken in Maui last fall," Brad explains. He almost seems embarrassed.

From the picture, she could be anyone. She is a stranger.

The rest of the pictures are similarly impenetrable: shots of her posing at picnics, smiling on hiking trails, shading the sun from her brown eyes on a sailboat, feeding a carrot to a horse. She is laughing in the last one, and it almost seems obscene. I don't remember her laughing, ever, unless she was performing a scene from a movie.

I hand the photo album back to Brad. "Thank you," I say. He looks supremely uncomfortable.

Jillian suddenly asks, "Did she have any other children that you know of? I mean, other than Leigh and James?"

Brad shrugs. "Not that I know of."

"What has she been doing for the past seven years?" I ask. "Was she acting?"

Brad shakes his head. "She kind of bounced from one thing to the next. When I met her, she was dabbling in real estate. Flipping houses and talking about becoming a licensed real estate agent. Right before she left, she wanted to open a bistro."

"Did she even cook?" I don't remember her cooking. Just sewing those damn puppets and hanging scary masks on my bedroom walls.

"She was taking classes."

I look around the living room again for signs that she once inhabited it. "How long have you lived here?"

"Twelve years," he says. The fact seems to both satisfy and exhaust him.

I nod as if satisfied. But I'm far from it. We talk for a bit longer, bringing each other up to speed on the details. He's sorry to hear about my kidney transplant, and sorry that Kate was such a shitty mother.

So am I.

I'm okay, really. Nothing has really changed for me. It's just the things I'll never know about her that get me: her favorite color, if she had any allergies, if she was a generous tipper at restaurants. And it's the things my mother will never know about me. For instance, she'll never know I have PKD. She'll never know I had a kidney transplant, which isn't exactly the kind of thing you mention offhandedly in the annual Christmas newsletter. She'll never know her future grandchildren, in case she has any. And she'll never know me, and all the little things in my daily life that make me who I am. In the end, isn't it always the little things that get you?

Later that evening, after a philosophical patio dinner under tiki torches, stars, and rustling palms, Jillian and I decide to close the day with a drink at Bar Marmont. Sort of a farewell toast to Denise, my mother, and my perception of Larry. I lie on the bed in our room, waiting for her to finish getting ready. Lord, I'm tired. I feel like I could fall asleep right now, easily. I'm also uneasy because, despite my exhaustion, my pulse has been racing, which is a new development. I haven't had any symptoms like this since that night in Moab. But I have to face facts. My body, despite my medication, could be rejecting Larry. I realize I've already rejected him emotionally; I suppose the coup de grâce would be a final physical rejection. But I'm probably overreacting. I don't feel feverish. I don't ache. Still, I'll call my doctor next week, get in earlier for my next checkup. It couldn't hurt.

You might say it's been a draining week.

Jillian stands on tiptoes to survey her rear in the bathroom mirror. "Are you sure these pants don't make my butt look funny?"

"Your butt looks fucking hilarious in those pants." Jillian gives me a look. "I'm kidding!"

"This whole outfit cost less than thirty dollars," she adds.

I'm thrilled to report that bargains and frugal purchases are well respected—even envied—among my circle of friends.

Jillian curls her lips over her teeth to apply a final coat of lipstick. "So should we rent Denise's old movies tonight? What was the one, *Santa's Too Hungover for Christmas,* or something?" She's been making an effort to be especially cheery since our stop by my mother's last-known residence.

"You know, I do remember her from that. It was *The Year Santa Skipped Christmas,* by the way."

"I never saw it."

I yawn and watch the ceiling fan lazily slice the air. "She was cute. But her acting left much to be desired." I lift my head and add, "Hey, are you almost done in there? I need to pee before we leave."

"Yeah, yeah. Keep your pants on."

"I don't think that would be advisable." Jillian and I stick our tongues out at each other while she exits and I enter the bathroom. I check my teeth for dinner debris in the mirror before moving on to the task at hand. Why did I have to wear the most bathroom unfriendly outfit in the world? I wrestle with my drawstring linen pants and finally manage to untie my Gordian knot. I don't like talking to people while I'm peeing, so there's a moment of silence. Someone is playing a Rolling Stones disc down the hall: "Waiting on a Friend." It's muffled through the wall, but I can make out the lyrics. One of their most tolerable songs, in my opinion—right up there with "Gimme Shelter." People say you're either a Stones or a Beatles person, and you can't be both. But I disagree. The Beatles are my days, but once in awhile, when I'm being completely honest with myself, the Stones are my nights. I'm schizophrenic that way. I finish my business, wrestle back into my pants, turn to flush, and stop. A chill marches across my skin.

Coffee, I dimly think. But this is far from Starbucks. This is old blood. Just a few drops, blooming and diffusing until I almost could have imagined them.

But I know what I saw.

I do a frantic mental count to determine when my period is supposed to start. Not for two more weeks. I close my eyes and count to three. When I open them, the water in the bowl is unreadable. The proverbial tea leaves have disappeared. I gingerly touch my abdomen. And suddenly, there it is. The pain has been there all along. I can feel it humming like electricity along my scar—faint but present.

I must have been standing there for some time, because Jillian calls, "You fall in?" Her voice could be coming from across a canyon.

I snap out of it and flush the evidence. "Jillian?" I don't recognize my own voice.

"Yeah?" I step out of the bathroom, and her eyes register concern at my expression. "Leigh, what's wrong?"

My heartbeat fills my ears. Everything's wrong, all wrong. This can't be happening again. But it is. I open my mouth and make it real. "There was blood in the toilet."

Jillian snaps her purse shut and grabs my hand. "We're going to urgent care."

Something in me takes a step back. "It was just a little blood. A few drops."

"Still, don't you think you should get this checked out right away? It might be really serious!"

I take a deep breath. Do a breathing exercise. An emergency room in Los Angeles. It could get messy. It could be complicated. "Here in Los Angeles? Forget it." The prospect of fighting a mob of diseased and bleeding people for treatment in a massive foreign city is about as appealing to me as anchoring the *NBC Nightly News* in nothing but an adult diaper.

"Leigh, this is your health—your *life*—you're talking about. You need to see a doctor immediately."

I close my eyes to think for a second.

Jillian continues, determined. "If you saw blood in the toilet, I really think you should get that checked out."

I should have remembered Jillian's hypochondriac tendencies before opening my mouth. For Jillian, every new freckle is a malignant melanoma worthy of an immediate rush to the hospital. "Jillian, think about this for a minute. By the time I actually get through the line to see an unfamiliar stressed-out resident who hasn't slept in four days, I could be comfortably at home seeing my own familiar doctor, who knows me by name, and every type of medication I'm currently taking by heart."

"You aren't thinking, Leigh."

"Kidneys don't fail overnight. It can be a long process." I'm beginning to really dig my heels in.

"Leigh, you don't know that for sure."

"The paperwork alone will take a month to process. I'd probably be exposed to some kind of mutant skin-dissolving bacteria in triage. And then I'd really get sick."

"Leigh, you already are sick!" Her voice bounces off the walls. I raise my eyebrows at her, and she lowers her voice to repeat herself. "You already *are* sick."

Thanks for the news flash, I think. "Have you not seen the documentaries on emergency room care in major metropolitan areas in the United States? It's insane!" I hear a woman laughing brightly in the hallway as she walks past our room. Ah, to be part of that kind of world. "They'd just do a bunch of tests to make sure I could fly home and meet with my transplant team, when the *real* diagnosis and treatment will occur. Why not avoid all of the tests *here*, when I will be subject to them at home again *later*?" I try to keep my voice logical and clear. I refuse to set foot in any sort of medical madhouse.

I can't be sure, but I don't think Jillian has blinked once during this whole discussion. Her eyes are wild. Her hands are on her hips. She is not about to yield an inch in this argument. "You just basically said you don't know whether you're stabilized enough to fly home." She sighs. "How do you know you're even okay to fly?"

Fuck. "JILLIAN! I'm not going to an emergency room in Los Angeles!"

"Yes you are, and I'm driving."

Then I remember: My own doctor's numbers are programmed into my phone. "I'll call Dr. Jensen!" Why was this not the first thing to come to mind? Probably because my mind has been so completely messed-with this past week and a half that by now it has the synaptic activity of a bowl of cottage cheese.

Wisconsin is two hours behind us. It's not too late to call. Jillian plops down on the bed and sighs heavily while I dial.

"Hello?"

"Dr. Jensen? This is Leigh Fielding. One of your kidney patients?" I always say this, even though Dr. Jensen and I go way back. I think I've seen him more than some of my ex-boyfriends. "I, uh, is this a bad time?"

It sounds like he's on the tarmac at an airport. "No, not at all," he says, although his tone suggests otherwise. "What can I do for you? Any problems with your prednisone?"

"No, my medication is fine. It's just, well, I'm on vacation, and—"

"Oh, right! How's the trip going?"

"Fine. Um, but I just noticed a little blood in my urine."

"I see." I hear faint traffic sounds in the background. "How are you feeling?"

"Okay. I don't think I have a fever. But there is some pain in the area. I guess what I want to know is, should I go to the emergency room here? Or should I come home? Am I okay to come home?"

Jillian is watching me intently from the bed. I'm standing near a window for better reception.

"On a scale of one to ten, how's the pain? Is it sharp?"

"About a three. Wait, is ten the highest? If it is, then I'm a three."

"Have you noticed blood in the urine any other times? Pain in the kidney?"

"Um, no, not really." I absently run my hand along my scar. "Maybe just a little pain, a few days ago." *That Larry, always doing the sensible thing,* Denise says in my head.

"Okay. Well, you're going to need an ultrasound or an MRI to see what's up."

"Should I come home?"

"I can't be sure without seeing you, but it sounds like you'd be okay coming immediately home. But to be on the safe side, you could go to a local urgent care facility. Just to check things out. If things get worse, I suggest you do so right away." I can hear a blinker ticktocking faintly in the background. "Leigh, I have to run. If things don't get any worse, come home and we'll get you in for a look-see right away. Sound good?"

"Okay. Wait—"

"Yes, Leigh?" There is a whiff of distracted impatience in his voice.

"Does this mean my kidney is failing?"

"Let's not jump to conclusions. We'll run some tests and get to the bottom of things. 'Kay?"

I feel slightly deflated, but he did give the advice I was looking for. And what do I want, anyway? A shoulder to cry on? An arm-in-arm stroll through the park? He's my doctor, not my father. He has a flock of other patients to tend, many with more demanding issues than mine. I'm lucky to even have his private phone number.

I hang up. "Well?" Jillian demands.

"He said I should come home," I say.

"Are you lying?"

"Yeah." I shake my head. "No! I mean no. He said I should come home for some tests, but if the pain got worse, I should have it looked at right away."

Jillian nods. "Okay. Well, let's get you packed and on a plane." Despite her general mistrust of the Western medical establishment (and conventional agriculture and organized religion and a global-ized economy and the military-industrial complex, ad nauseam), Jillian has put a lot of stock in the physicians charged with my own care. If they give me a directive, she and James can be counted on to see that I'm following it.

I look around our charming little Art Deco room, with its original plumbing fixtures and slightly musty smell, sad to be leaving it pre-maturely. "So much for my relaxing vacation." *Chateau, I hardly knew ye.*

"I think the relaxing part of the vacation flew out the window when you picked up Denise," Jillian says, beginning to refold the maps and brochures we spread open on a bedside table. "Oh, and don't even think of stealing all the shampoo samples. We split them fifty-fifty."

CHAPTER FOURTEEN

Wisconsin: Life's So Good

I'm on a plane now, lucky enough to have found an immediate red-eye flight home (with only one layover—in Atlanta, of course) and even more lucky to have a friend willing to drive my car back to Wisconsin. I haven't been on a plane since junior high, when I flew with Jillian and her family to Massachusetts for her cousin's wedding. So I'm twitchy. My hangnails are a pulpy mess. I look up at the vents and little ceiling dashboard. Why do they still have the light-up NO SMOKING sign? Hasn't everyone gotten the memo by now? I can't stop jiggling my legs. And my ears are popping already. I contemplate paging through one of the magazines I picked up at LAX, but I'm too lazy to bend over and rummage through the carry-on bag I stuffed beneath the seat in front of me. A woman behind me is reading *Goodnight Moon* to her toddler daughter, who keeps insisting she reread each page. "Read it again, Mommy. Now again. Again now." It both annoys me and breaks my heart. James told me once that Kate threw my favorite book in the garbage when I was four because she was sick of reading it to me. That book was *Corduroy,* and, oh, did that small bear put a lump in my throat. If I could have leaped into the pages to rescue him from the empty store, to reassure him that it wasn't just Lisa who could love him without the button, I would have.

I have an aisle seat. The bedraggled woman sitting to my immediate right flips impatiently through the *SkyMall* catalogue. She's wearing red plastic clogs, and every so often, I catch a whiff of her feet. They smell like soggy corn chips. She informs me that she'll need to get up and climb over me to brush her teeth after the snack, and maybe again later on, because she has braces. So basically, forget about taking a nap. And forget about eating, because of the putrid smell of decaying feet. I'm too agitated to eat or sleep anyway.

I've had the last five hours to focus on what's potentially happening to my kidney, and to be honest, I'm sick of thinking about it. I've been worrying about and trying to make peace with my illness for years, and frankly, I just want a little vacation from my own head for awhile. Because clearly, a physical vacation didn't help much. Instead, I think about my last phone conversation with my brother, almost two hours ago.

He answered the phone with a confrontational "So? Still feeling alright? Where are you? Did you see Kate?"

Caller ID—a bittersweet service. "Hi, James," I said, already defeated. Might as well cut to the chase. "Um, I'm coming home."

An aggressive silence. "Did something happen? Something happened."

I reflexively held up a hand in protest. I noticed that I gestured much more when I spoke with James. "It's nothing to worry about; I spoke with my doctor—"

"You spoke with your doctor? About what? What's going on?" His voice was riding an escalator.

I made a concerted effort to remain calm, but when James grew agitated, he usually dragged bystanders with him. "Just a small bit of blood in my urine."

"Leigh! Jesus Christ." I could almost imagine him beginning to pace, his eyes wild. "I told you this trip was a bad idea."

"I probably would have shown symptoms at home, too," I argued in a small voice.

"Symptoms." There was another silence while I heard him processing this. "Of kidney failure?" Then, he roared: "Jesus Christ, Leigh!"

I held the phone away from my head, wincing. "Settle down. I booked the next flight home."

"Which airline? When will you get here? God, Leigh, I just knew—"

"I'm not going to talk to you when you're like this. I'll call you when I land."

I flipped my phone shut, my body exhausted, but also humming with the thrill of semi–civil disobedience. My phone rang again almost immediately—guess who? I turned it off.

Gram told me that when James was a little boy, he would lie on his back for hours playing with a stick, making spaceship sounds. He could invent an entire world with items found in her junk drawer: bits of string, Popsicle sticks, old batteries, multicolored rubber bands. He also kept a journal, with the kind of thoughtful observations a young, sensitive boy might make prior to puberty: secret aspirations to be the best basketball player in school, pitiful ruminations on the mystery of girls and whether they would ever like him, feverish plans to see a late-night showing of *The Empire Strikes Back* with friends. He'd written everything in a kind of comedic/journalistic style, as if he were reporting things years after they'd happened, and for the benefit of a semi-public audience. He was always remarkably insightful.

A flight attendant phones in the preflight safety show. I try to pay attention to be polite, but I don't think she notices. She's looking over all of our heads, weary of the inane chitchat and dazed expressions. The engines cycle up, making the soles of my feet vibrate.

And then Mom left. And Dad died. And James stopped journaling, preferring instead to turn things inward, compacting the pain and hurt deep inside until they turned to coal. When Gram—who was our last bridge to a relatively carefree life—died, James aged fifteen years overnight. It was as if he looked around, picked a wife with an attractive pedigree and traditional interests (i.e., Jell-O molds, baking, and gossip), accepted a job with excellent benefits and mediocre duties, purchased a life insurance policy, opened a Roth IRA, bought a sensibly priced home with good resale potential, and called it a day. The worst part is, sometimes I wonder if he gave up on himself because of me. I know, how self-absorbed to even think that. It's all me, me, me, right? But James is the most responsible person I know. He has never bounced a check, missed an oil change, or swum within an hour of eating. That I know of, anyway. He does the right thing. . . . Whether he wants to or has to is unclear. I'm leaning toward "has to."

But before Gram died, James's car was much more likely to smell of stale beer and French fries. He was more likely to come home at four in the morning with bloodshot eyes and a hankering for Doritos. He laughed more. Now he is stoic. He drinks black coffee and golfs. And I can't imagine how anyone would find that amusing.

What if we crash? What if I never get to see James again? I strain to recall our last conversation. Had we said anything momentous or meaningful? This is a dim prospect. The flight attendant finishes her monologue. She makes direct eye contact with me and smiles. *We won't crash*, her smile seems to say. I remember my friend Bridget telling us about her days as a flight attendant, and how one time a fur-draped woman in first class consistently ignored her, averting her eyes with every offer of food, water, or other amenity. The woman's husband eventually told Bridget, "Sorry. She doesn't speak to The Help." It almost seems made-up, doesn't it? This was a woman so surreally disconnected from reality and humanity that it frightened me badly for weeks afterward to know people like her existed. I smile back at the flight attendant.

It occurs to me that James's stodgy transformation was a lot like me with my weird new habits after Larry. But for James, the catalyst was Gram's death. Let's examine the evidence: Before Gram died, James listened to AC/DC and Quiet Riot. After Gram died, he listened to sports talk radio. Before, he drank Budweiser directly from the can and sometimes belched the alphabet. After, he drank St. Pauli Girl from a pilsner glass and burped discreetly into a cocktail napkin, if at all. Before, he dated girls who wore fringy pink boots and cracked huge wads of neon gum at the table. After, he married a woman who once had a pink canopy bed and considered sour cherry Altoids gum risqué because it made you salivate and say "Oh! Oh! Oh!" Before, he was a big brother. He could be goofy. He rented an apartment and had rowdy Super Bowl parties. After, he was basically a father to a moody adolescent girl. He could be baffled and overwhelmed. He made an offer on a house with low-maintenance siding and puttered in the garage while his wife hosted Pampered Chef parties. He purchased a vehicle that received the government's highest front- and side-impact crash-test ratings. He prepared the guest room not for his first child, but for his sick little sister. This last thought makes me want to do something heroic for him.

I listen to *Goodnight Moon* for the fourth time as the plane speeds down the runway. The little girl behind me sleepily echoes her patient mother. " 'Goodnight mittens. Goodnight kittens.' " As we lift into the sky, I can feel the wheels tuck into the silver belly of the plane with a thud. I close my eyes. *Goodnight brother. Goodnight mother.*

After landing at General Mitchell International Airport, I head to the baggage claim and ponder my next step: call a cab, I suppose. I'm exhausted, despite sleeping for at least an hour on the plane. I've used the bathroom twice since leaving Los Angeles, studying the bowl intently for further signs of distress until the auto-flush whisked any possible evidence away. Both times the same slight tinge of accusing dark blood stared back. What I find even more alarming is this: The pain in my kidney has begun to sharpen and amplify. What started as the low strumming of an acoustic guitar has morphed into a four-piece band specializing in Kiss covers. And my joints are starting to ache.

At the luggage-go-round I watch three battered suitcases pop through the curtain of clear plastic strips and ride the conveyor belt to their yawning owners. I fumble through my purse for my cell phone and flip it open. Almost five A.M. I lost two hours with the time zone change. The layover didn't help, either. James will be up making coffee in half an hour. I snap it shut. Here's my bag, handle tied with an old knot of red yarn. I retrieve it, extend the handle, and lug it behind me to the bank of sliding glass doors near the airport's main entrance. I step into the muggy summer morning to find three taxis idling near the curb, their drivers sitting in air-conditioned comfort. One of them steps out to help me with my bags. Moths beat their wings against the cab's orange running lights. "Want to take a road trip?" I ask him. He's tall—at least six feet tall—with friendly brown eyes.

He laughs and asks, "Where would you like to go?" His accent is East African, maybe. He has a reassuring smile.

"Do you know where Fond du Lac is?"

CHAPTER FIFTEEN

"I'm not offended. Are you offended?"

In urgent care intake there is a blond little boy with a nail that's been driven through the palm of his hand. His cheeks are shiny with tears and he wails while a triage nurse examines him. His mother repeats, "Shhhhhhh, shhhhhhh," like a mantra while she rubs his back.

"Am I going to die?" he asks, his voice hitching in his chest.

His mother smooths his fine blond hair. "No, sweetie, you're not going to die."

"We're going to make you good as new again," the nurse says. "You're being very brave."

He seems to consider this, sniffling. "Then will I get a toy?"

His mother kisses his forehead. "After we see the doctor, sweetie." Two nurses in baby blue scrubs roll the little boy back to an exam room on a gurney, and his mother follows.

I close my eyes in the waiting room and reflect on what's been a marathon of a morning. Upon returning to Fond du Lac, I directed my driver, Abdi, who was Somalian as it turned out, to drop me at James and Marissa's place. (It's funny; I've never quite been able to call it my own home.) I parked my luggage in my room (see, but I have no trouble calling their guest room my room) and freshened up. After countless hours of canned air and treated water in planes, airports, and motels, my hair and skin were barely on speaking terms with me. I looked like a grubby composite of every "before" picture ever taken.

I looked exactly like what I was. Sick.

James and Marissa were both at work, I was relieved to find. The house was a cool cave with all the shades drawn. I fixed myself a peanut butter and jelly sandwich, plopped in front of the TV, and absently flipped through a few morning show pep squad routines. I gave my mail a joyless perusal (bills, a Victoria's Secret catalogue, *Entertainment Weekly*), wondering how I would get to urgent care without my car. Now that I was home, my next order of business was to solve the mystery of what exactly was transpiring inside of me. I could call another cab, but my checking account was on the floor, wheezing and clutching its chest. So I decided to call Wes. He was, of course, shocked to hear from me. "You're where?!"

"Home. Here in Fond du Lac."

"I thought you weren't coming home until next week!"

"Me, too."

His voice begins to shift from surprise to apprehension. "What happened? Are you okay? You sound . . ." He didn't finish.

"I'm just exhausted." And disappointed. And terrified. And tired of being terrified.

When I told him what had happened and where I needed to go, he simply said, "I'll be there in fifteen minutes."

I've been triaged and registered for over an hour, and I thank God I always have my info at the ready: ID, medication list, contact info for my nephrologist and transplant team, and Medicaid card. Without these golden tickets, I could be waiting all day. Suddenly another nurse, with a honey-colored ponytail and also in blue scrubs, approaches me, smiling. She's so young I want to see her ID. "Leigh? You can come back now."

Wes closes the *Men's Health* magazine he's been flipping through and catches my gaze. "I'll be waiting right here."

I smile, again reflecting on how I won the friendship lottery. "Why are you so good to me?"

I catch Wes giving the nurse a furtive once-over before he smirks at me. "Just tell your brother to keep those checks coming." He winks, and the nurse laughs politely. I just roll my eyes.

I follow her back to the exam room in the observation unit. I know exactly what comes next: the tech has me pee in a little cup and takes my vitals: blood pressure, weight, temperature, respiration, pulse. The attending nurse pops in and asks me a million questions about my medical history (which I have committed to memory). They toss me into a sexy patient gown and I wait for the next panel of tests. The attending physician comes around with a stethoscope, asks me a million more questions, and makes a differential diagnosis. They draw some blood and check out my transplant scar and access. (I've got an arteriovenous fistula in my right forearm to allow access to my veins and arteries during dialysis. I was kind of hoping I'd never have to use it again.) Then a nephrologist, Dr. Gupta, stops by and chats with the attending physician. Dr. Gupta has a lyrical Indian accent and shiny black hair cut in a choppy bob. She also looks younger than me, and I suddenly realize why old people are usually wary around doctors. She submits me to yet another physical exam and reads my file like she's studying for a test. Which I appreciate, believe me. I check my watch: almost ten-thirty. God, I'm tired. I wonder if Wes is still waiting, and if anyone's told him what's going on. Dr. Gupta frowns over my lab results.

"Leigh," she says, "simply put, your kidney is failing. This seems to be a chronic rather than acute rejection, which is fairly common among cadaveric transplants. Right now your kidney is functioning at roughly 20 percent of capacity. It looks as if it's gradually shutting down. A healthy blood urea nitrogen value is between 10 and 20 milligrams per deciliter. Your BUN is 48, and your creatinine is 4.2. As I'm sure you know, this is also too high, although we're going to have to get a better reading later with a controlled 24-hour urine analysis. Let's see . . . blood pressure 150 over 95, too high. You are also slightly anemic." She consults her clipboard again. "And you reported having flulike symptoms recently?"

I nod helplessly. "Um, yeah?"

"Okay. Your blood work does show you having a very mild infection, but this is common among people who are taking immunosuppressants. Easy to treat. We have contacted your transplant team for the next course of action, but we do need to admit you for further observation and immediate treatment."

Christ, I'm the Beirut of health! But she's not finished with me yet. "We're going to have to perform a biopsy to see if we can learn what's causing the failure. Depending on the results, your transplant team will develop a treatment plan. This may be as simple as an adjustment in medication if the kidney still has potential. If not, there's a small chance that it would have to be removed to prevent continued infection. You'd be able to stop the antirejection medications, which is the good news. The bad news is that you'd also have to go on hemodialysis again until another suitable transplant can be found." She stops rattling off my roster of medical misfortunes to catch her breath. "In the meantime, we're going to tackle your anemia, your CMV, and try to get your BUN and creatinine numbers back to normal." Dr. Gupta pauses again and smiles at me. "I hope I haven't overwhelmed you. Do you have any questions?"

I feel like I've been smacked in the face with a tractor tire. "CMV?" is all I can manage.

"Cytomegalovirus. It's a member of the herpes family. Don't worry, we can take care of that pretty easily." Her smile seems to say: *Herpes are silly!*

Herpes has a family, and I'm host to the reunion. Well, isn't that cute. It's perfect, really. I clear my throat and say, "This is all happening a little fast!"

"Sometimes organs do fail rather quickly. But the sooner we treat your other symptoms, the sooner you'll be back on the road to good health."

Back on the road to good health. Should be a long, grueling trip, but I have no choice. So sign me up. I'm ready to get back on that bus. As long as nobody tries to steal my purse.

Dr. Gupta claps her hands together. "Okay. First, let's get you prepped for the biopsy."

I suppose it's time to call James again.

James and Marissa come to the hospital to see me later that afternoon. When he sees me in my hospital bed, flanked by machines, hooked into tubes and monitors, James greets me with "Well. This is a familiar sight." He sighs deeply.

I've been bracing myself for their visit since my last two phone conversations with James, both of which made me feel like I'd just completed a triathlon in a sumo wrestling suit. All I can offer is a weary apology.

"How long are they keeping you here?" Marissa asks gently, settling into a chair next to my bed. The strap of her purse falls from her shoulder and she centers the bag in the middle of her lap, where it rests like a fat bulldog. James paces to the window, peers out, and then leans against the sill to face us, arms crossed.

I shrug. "They'll probably release me after my final blood work is in, to make sure I'm stable. Maybe tomorrow? I don't know. We'll have to see what my doctor says."

Marissa nods her head with this glazed look on her face. Marissa gets more excited about televised Packer games than she does about most real human dramas. You know how I said Meg and I had a gulf between us? Well, Marissa and I aren't even in the same galaxy. In fact, I doubt we're the same species.

James pushes off the windowsill and drops into a nearby chair. He props an ankle on the opposite knee and starts to jiggle it violently. I can tell he's mentally composing a mini lecture. "Leigh, you can't overexert yourself," he finally says, uncrossing his leg and leaning forward, elbows on knees and hands clasped. "I worry about you so much."

This is kind of a breakthrough, the acknowledgment and public confession of a mildly feminine emotion. Despite my better instincts, I toss out a sarcastic response. "You? Worry? Never!"

Sensitive to James? Me? Never!

"Of course I fucking worry," he continues, anger beginning to color his voice. And his face.

"Shh, sweetheart," Marissa scolds. The penalty for swearing in front of Marissa is to be called a term of endearment. But it could be worse. She could make us suck on a Testamint, which I've actually seen in her purse.

"James, I appreciate the worry. But what am I going to do? Live in a bubble?!"

"I know! Does anyone want a beverage?" Marissa interrupts, eyes wide and eager to change the subject.

"No, thanks," I say, beginning to soften. I direct my next statement to James. "You never even asked if I had fun on my trip."

He leans back in the chair and crosses his arms. "Okay. How was your trip?" He pauses, and adds, "Did you meet Kate?" It's an almost accusatory question, but I can feel the hurt behind it.

I'm hesitant to tell him much with Marissa in earshot, because the presence of a spouse changes the whole sibling dynamic. "Can you get me a water?" I ask her. "I am kind of thirsty."

"Of course!" Her eyes dart between James and me, and I get the feeling she's relieved to be sent on an errand.

When she's gone, I say, "No, I didn't find Kate." We talk about her so rarely, it's almost as if the air grows thicker when we do. It becomes hard to make eye contact—like we're both embarrassed to be products of such a human being.

"She's in London now, with some guy." I tell him about Brad. Another man left behind, another Kate Fielding castaway. "He was a nice guy. Clueless but nice. He showed me pictures of her."

"What did she look like?" He's trying not to sound eager, and doing a poor job of it.

"Pretty. Like anybody's mom, really. Brad said she was into real estate." I try to read James's reaction, but his expression barely changes, except to say *I told you she didn't want to be found.*

"I guess the acting thing didn't work out so well," he snorts.

"And you know," I say, "that's fine. I, for one, am okay if I never see her again." Now that I've said it, I feel slightly better. Life can go on without her, it means. It also means I'm one step closer to actually believing and accepting this.

"So you couldn't find her," he says again, as if fact-checking the situation.

I shrug and fiddle with the call button on my bed. "We could if we really wanted to."

"I don't want to."

A nurse in comfy sneakers and a ponytail pops her head into my room to check my vitals. "Hi, Leigh. Dr. Jensen will be here in a bit to go over your lab work with you." This is Greta. Earlier today she told me, in a mildly mischievous tone, that Dr. Jensen's cell phone rang to the tune of "Proud to be an American." I liked her immediately. She sees James and asks brightly, "Who's this?"

"My brother, James."

James's face breaks into a winsome smile and he tips her a small salute.

"Nice to meet you, James!"

"Likewise."

They make small talk for a minute while Greta updates my chart, and she tells him I'm one of her favorite patients. So cooperative, so pleasant. I feel like I'm a fourth grader listening in on a friendly parent-teacher conference. But I'm glad for the interruption, because it's had the effect of shifting James's emotional gears. I'm always a little heartsick when I watch James interacting with virtual strangers, because he's so charming and open. He seems to reserve the resentment just for me. Is it because I remind him of our parents? Because I've become such a burden? When he turns to me after Greta continues making her rounds, his face is still cheerful. "So the rest of your trip. What else did you do?"

I push my introspection into the corner, collect myself, and begin to talk. Unexpectedly (to me anyway), James chuckles at all the right parts. At the last second I decide not to tell him about Denise, but I get into the nitty-gritty details concerning my self-delusions about Larry and meeting Betty Resnick. I tell him about running out of gas. "You ran out of gas in the middle of the desert?" Old control-freak James is trying to crash the party, so I jump in.

"Oh, that was no big deal. Jillian was driving and kind of spaced out."

"Big surprise there," James says, rolling his eyes.

I ignore him. "We were rescued by two swing-dancing retirees in an RV. They were from North Dakota, on a mission to see every national park in their path." I feel my cheeks grow warm as I recall our mistaken impression that they were swingers. I decide not to tell him about my car breaking down, because James would probably be a little less understanding about that one. He's big into preventive maintenance and regular tune-ups and would just lecture me about the perils of irresponsible auto ownership.

I even tell him about going to the karaoke bar with Chris in Las Vegas. I enjoy reliving my trip and become quite animated. He's silent for awhile, digesting everything. He shakes his head and slowly smiles at me like I'm finally an adult. "I get it now. The new hobbies. And you actually sang karaoke? Did anyone sustain lasting hearing loss?" I make a fist and shake it at him: *A wise guy, eh?*

James smiles. It went so much better than it could have! "I'm glad you had a good time," he says. "I really am." His smile fades. "I just wish . . . This is just so disappointing." He's clearly referring to the potential failure of my kidney transplant.

"Tell me about it." I take a deep breath before saying the rest. I've been turning it around in my head for the past few hours, and I just need to ask before I lose my nerve, while the climate is still fresh and open to possibilities. "James, do you ever wish you didn't have to take care of me?"

He stares at me, frowning a little, trying to process this. I rush on. "I mean, you've done so much for me, and I don't know how I'll ever repay you. Do you ever wish you didn't have to worry about me? I sometimes worry, I don't know, that we're stunting each other's growth. I just wish you could be . . . less stressed out. Free to do what you want." It all comes out in a rush.

He's silent for a beat, and I almost feel like I've hurt his feelings.

"Wow. Where to start?" He sighs, running a hand through his hair. "Leigh, I'll admit it wasn't easy. But I didn't mind. I don't mind. You're family. We take care of each other," he trails off, wistfully. I've rarely seen James like this. Suddenly he adds, "Do you remember how sick Dad was before he killed himself?"

I'm taken aback by his question. "Not really." The truth is, I thought we were all sick back then—sick from missing Mom. Sick from watching the stack of mail addressed to "Katherine Fielding" grow on the dining room hutch, patiently awaiting her return like an abandoned pet. Sick from seeing her dusty half-used bottles under the sink: nail polish remover, tanning lotion and hair gel with crusted caps, economy-sized vats of Redken conditioner for color-treated hair. They seemed to have joined Dad in his vigil for her return.

"Dad was really sick. He stayed in bed all the time."

Well, by that yardstick, half the people I know are terminally ill for at least a few weeks of the year. "I thought he just missed Mom."

"PKD is genetic, right?" It's a rhetorical question.

I nod. In the hallway, a Dr. Roth is being paged.

"And didn't Grandpa Dan die of kidney failure?"

"No, it was a car accident."

James is determined to find the elusive genetic connection. "Well, maybe Dad had PKD, too."

I have to admit, the thought has crossed my mind. Almost daily. But then I'd always conclude something else because the disease never claimed him as one of its own. There were no weekly rounds of dialysis, no amber bottles of medication lining a kitchen windowsill, no frantic trips to the hospital—at least, that I was aware of. I was six.

James sighs wearily. "I guess we'll never know." He scratches a mosquito bite on his calf and looks at me. "Maybe I'll get sick someday, too."

"Don't say that." I hate thinking of James getting sick.

I try to think of something funny to say. Something to lighten the mood. A man walks past my room carrying a bunch of GET WELL balloons. They seem to fill the hallway, bobbing and dancing. One of them features a monkey. So I say, "Hey, I know what could help make things easier for us. We could get a helper monkey. He could do our taxes and field visits from solicitors."

James scowls and says, "He'd shit all over the house." Like I'm serious, right? But that's the beauty of James.

"No he wouldn't! You could train him. And he would wear a diaper."

James starts to smile.

"How about a helper orphan from a country beset by natural disasters and insects the size of cats? We could call him Little Ming-Lai. He could sleep in my room and mow the lawn for you. Marissa's mom would say, 'Little Ming-Lai, you're an inspiration to us all.'" Marissa's mother was always finding inspiration in the wheelchair-bound or unfortunate. As long as they were children from other countries and spoke only when spoken to.

James chuckles a bit at this. He and Marissa's mom, Vicki, have what you would call a hate-hate relationship. But they still send each other cards and gifts on birthdays, like two diplomats aiming nuclear warheads at each other but shaking hands on TV. Whenever James gets the obligatory birthday card in the mail from Vicki, I announce, "You got some hate mail today."

If we were in a movie there'd be a montage of us watching the sunset through my hospital window, bonding while a Nick Drakeish song rambled on in the background, and then later James would crack open a photo album featuring the only pictures we have of our mother, and the camera would pan in to catch a single, secret tear trickling down his cheek. Instead, I make jokes about monkeys in diapers and James announces that, man, he's really got to drop the Browns off at the Super Bowl, just as Marissa comes back with three bottles of water, saying, "What did we ever do before bottled water?"

My biopsy results are officially in. The verdict? Larry is the AMC Pacer of kidneys. They've added a few new pills to my daily regimen because there are pharmaceutical giants to keep in business and it's great training for my next career as a Colombian heroin smuggler. (Actually, I'd probably eat cat vomit if it meant I could stick around to see poverty eradicated in Africa—or the United States, for that matter. But then I'd outlive all my friends and grandchildren, which would be the pits.) Next Wednesday I go in for more tests to see if we need to remove Larry from my life for good. I've grown used to him, and like a spouse, he's come to inspire, frustrate, cheer, and depress me over the past year. And now he's finally walked out on me, leaving me with a whole body and no kidney to support it. To be honest, I think I'm still in shock. As are James, Marissa, Wes, and Jillian. She called from the road this morning and I told her the news.

"Oh, hon, I'm so sorry," she said, crestfallen. "Are you okay?" She was in Minnesota, just a day away.

"No," I said honestly. "I'm really not."

She made a sympathetic, heartbroken noise, and we were silent together on the phone for a beat, letting the ramifications of the situation settle. I could hear the whistle of wind in her open car window, the distant jocularity of a DJ on a strange radio station, and something inside of me had to catch its breath.

I felt the self-pity percolating within me, so I changed the subject. "You didn't see Geoffrey, did you?"

"No," she said somewhat defensively.

"Good, because if you get back together with him—"

Jillian groaned. "You'll haunt me after you die at *ninety-seven*."

"Thirty," I said, laughing. Jillian just told me to shut up.

We were so optimistic a year ago, you know? It's like I spent a year crafting a bamboo raft to get off the island, with all of my friends and relatives as the cheering investors, and the damn thing sinks on its maiden voyage.

So? I'm back on the evening dialysis shift on Mondays, Wednesdays, and Fridays, for three hours a pop. I have my good days and my bad days. And I have a new and improved diet. (You thought post-op food restrictions were fun? Well, just try the fun-free dialysis diet, where chocolate, French fries, and cheese are strictly off-limits! You'll never enjoy the nutty deliciousness of bridge mix at another family function again!)

My regular nephrologist, Dr. Jensen, is an old fart on a conveyor belt, but once in awhile, he'll say something that cracks me up. Yesterday I overheard him saying to one of the other dialysis patients in the unit, "Keep your hopes up. A good transplant match will come up before you know it. And it is summer. More accidents." Then he winked gruesomely, checked his watch, and strolled out.

At the St. Luke's dialysis unit, ten of us are propped in reclining chairs all in a row, like we're getting a newfangled spa treatment. An infusion of baby blood à la Monty Burns, perhaps. We're the evening-shift club, and let me clue you in to the members. Bob Vollrath, a retired postal worker, sits to my right. Bob's a really great guy, if you don't mind unsolicited advice. I don't, because you can learn a lot about a person by the kind of advice they dispense. Let's take Bob. He always says things to me like "The secret to a happy marriage is separate checking accounts" and "Pain is nature's way of telling you that you're still alive." From this, I can deduce that Bob has had some financially related marital woes and may or may not be a masochist.

Mary, the gardening kind of grandmother you see on arthritis ads, sits to my left. Her grandkids sometimes visit when she's dialyzing, coloring in books on the floor and playing spaceship. We, the dialysis patients, with blood-filled tubes connecting us to whirring machines, get to be aliens in the ship's basement. (This actually speaks to the excellence of the St. Luke's dialysis unit. With nothing to hide, they allow visitors. Some centers don't.)

Shirley, to Mary's left, is a fortysomething English teacher with lupus who occasionally grades students' papers during her treatment. She's quiet and new to dialyzing. Her husband is currently testing to be her donor, and we're all rooting for her.

The last station on that side belongs to Hector Sibley, who uses his age and condition as an excuse for rude, curmudgeonly behavior. He's been on the evening dialysis shift for years. In fact, he remembered me from over a year ago and greeted me with "You again?" when I returned last week. I said I missed him too much to stay away for long.

I'm told that he recently got into trouble with Nurse Ratched (not really her name, but it gives you an insight into her personality), and now Mark is the only technician who will work with him. It started when Nurse Ratched asked, "Mr. Sibley, what are you doing?"

Everyone looked over to see Hector's right hand cupping one of her breasts while she strapped the blood pressure cuff on his arm. "I'm touching your boob," he answered in a reasonable, plaintive tone. Like, duh!

"That's not appropriate, Mr. Sibley," Nurse Ratched responded. "Remove your hand immediately. Mark, can you come here, please?"

Last year he was infamous for a stink he made about the reading materials he could bring to the center. "But why can't I have *Playboy*?" he asked. "I'm only dying here."

"It might offend the other patients."

"I'm not offended. Are you offended?" he asked Helen. She just shook her head and turned back to her Bible. She was reading it from start to finish. That's all I really know about Helen, who is still dialyzing, but now on the morning shift.

I don't know the other patients yet, but I will soon. It's a bittersweet friendship forged, because you always enter the unit with a twinge of trepidation in your stomach. Will the same cast of characters be in today, dialyzing through their catheters? Will Mary be knitting and listening to a book on tape? Will Bob still be sitting next to me, serving nuggets of advice and reminiscing about life in the 1950s? Or will I need to buy another black dress for a funeral? Will I find that someone has thrown up the white flag, cried uncle, and retreated to a quiet death at home facilitated by hospice?

Happily (or not, depending on how you see things), everyone is in this evening, joking with the techs, reading, or filling out bills. While I'm dialyzing I decide to watch season four of *Mr. Show with Bob and David* on the portable DVD player Wes and Jillian bought to cheer me up. To my right, Bob has tuned the television set to one of the twenty-four-hour news channels. And surprise, surprise, Michael Jackson is on. "Does it piss anyone off other than me that Michael Jackson owns the publishing rights to hundreds of Beatles songs?" I ask the room.

"Who cares?" Hector shouts from three chairs away. Fair enough, Hector. Fair enough.

Nurse Ratched comes by to check on me and rag me about my diet. "Evie says you had a bad report card," she says. Evie, the dietitian, likes to call our lab printouts our report cards, which everyone finds insulting.

I try to look earnest and innocent. "Well, I'm still readjusting to things on dialysis again. I'm just not used to it yet. My diet wasn't so strict with the transplant."

Nurse Ratched is having none of my earnestness and fixes me with an impassive stare. "Follow the meal plan Evie develops for you. Are you taking the Renagel with meals?"

"Yes." Christ. We only went over this a thousand times already. I catch Bob rolling his eyes as she strides down the line to hassle someone else. I imagine the ten of us chained to benches in the bowels of an old wooden ship, rowing and rowing in dreary unison to power our dialysis machines while Nurse Ratched paces near us, slapping her palm with a horsewhip.

While I listen to the droning of the dialyzers, I start to day-dream. I imagine the scenario I've imagined dozens of times, where my mother learns that I'm dying of kidney failure and decides to donate one of her own kidneys, which matches perfectly. "This is all I can give you," she would say. "This is it." She would slide her nail file into her purse and walk to the window, staring down over the parking lot below. Her face would be pale in the late-afternoon light.

I would feel an urge to smile and tease, "Giving me life twice? That's all?" but I'm too sad and relieved to say it. Because she could give me life and take it away in one breath.

I stare at the two 16-gauge needles taped onto my right forearm with pressure bandages. I feel my blood exit and reenter my body, cool, clean, and foreign. Distant, like a child who's vacationed with grandparents and returned home to Mom and Dad with a huge sense of entitlement. I am bionic. I am scared. Mostly I'm scared.

I stare at my ceiling for a minute, drained. It's only ten-thirty in the morning, and I'm ready for bed. And I'm hot. James and Marissa have central air, but they only turn it on when it cracks ninety. According to the thermometer hung helpfully above the back deck, it's eighty-eight degrees out. Close enough. In my third (well, maybe we're up to four or five . . . it depends what you count) act of insubordination in my relationship with James, I pad down the hallway and turn the thermostat down to a cool seventy-two degrees.

I decide to clean my room to try and wake myself up. As I toss dirty laundry into a pile, I feel something hard, flat, and round in the back pocket of a skirt. When I pull it out, I can't help but grin. It's the coaster from Angelo's, with Chris's phone number scrawled across the back in blue pen. Well, well. I catch myself in the mirror, still smiling like an idiot. It's so old-fashioned; like a real, honest-to-goodness paper chain letter! It's like a time capsule back to junior high, before e-mail and text messaging. For a minute I almost convince myself that it's a fake number.

He probably won't even remember me. And I'll have to say, *You know, the girl with the kidney? My donor killed the service dog, too? We sang a Kenny Loggins song?* I wonder what new websites Chris is designing. I wonder if he's got the new Wilco album. I glance at the stack of graphic novels next to my bed and grin. Chicago isn't that far away. I tell myself that if I'm going to do it, if I'm going to work up the courage to call him, I have to do it today or I'll have seven years of bad luck.

I can convince myself of almost anything.

The days crawl by. I'm sleeping too much, getting migraines, watching too many shows on The Learning Channel. The upside is that I'm learning a lot. I return to the hospital for more tests. I go to dialysis three evenings a week. I miss being on the road. I'm not Jack Kerouac or anything, but I miss it. The herds of growling motorcycles (or as they're known in emergency rooms around the country, "donorcycles"); the families in minivans bogged down with luggage and Auto Bingo tiles; wiping the layer of bugs from my hot windshield at a gas-station franchise that doesn't exist in Wisconsin. Hell, I even miss Denise and her signs. The thought sends a gurgle of regret and anger into my heart. But only a little.

The hospital calls. My kidney's inflammation has decided to stay; it's signed the lease and rearranged the furniture to its liking. They tell me that though they usually leave a failed allograft in place, there are certain atypical symptoms I'm exhibiting that don't look so good. Why do they say that? "It doesn't look so good." If you're going to introduce me to some bad news, you don't have to prime it with such a stinker segue. I wish I could say, *Just give it to me straight.* Like in medical shows from the seventies. But part of me doesn't really want to know.

They want me to see a counselor in case I'm feeling depressed. "Why would I be depressed?" I ask, too sharply.

I am driving in my car thinking of Gram. She died comfortably at home, surrounded by family and friends. She ordered us to celebrate her. "I want a celebration of my life, and that's a direct order." She did not want a typical funeral, with easels of family photographs leading to a casket in which she'd been painted and sprayed and molded into someone she would have poked fun at in life. Her friends sang songs and read poems by Rumi and Emily Dickinson. They put pink scarves on the lamp shades and burned incense and candles. I think Jillian would have really liked them.

Forty-five miles an hour. This is the roller-coaster road, the road Dad used to floor it on, to make us whoop in the backseat. The memory of him chuckling at our euphoric backseat fear exhilarates me, and I reach desperately to uncover more: *Think! Think! Surely there is more here!* But I come up empty-handed. I feel my car sink in the first valley, momentum carrying me to the crest of the up-coming hill.

After Gram got sick, she shrank. Withered. Like watching November creep into her body, eat the fat, suck the shine from her hair, make her eyes scary and huge. Still, she could smile, ask me about the boys I wouldn't be dating for another four years, tease James for having long, mullety hair and skinny girlfriends in tight jeans with zippers at the ankles. Hospice set up shop, gentle volunteers who softly transferred the excess lotion from their hands to mine and told me about their children away at college while we fluffed pillows for Gram and waited. They gave me a name for the new shape of things. Gram was *dying*.

Fifty-five miles an hour. I sail over the hill, floating in my seat for a split second. I think of Larry's withering kidney in me. Am I *dying*? I press the accelerator to the floor to gather speed for the next hill. Trees whip past, silvery green in late summer. I can outrun anything. The dry cornfields are spiked like a pineapple plantation. It hasn't rained in weeks. Through it all, the crickets hum in a blurry chorus.

Gram was awake, ghostly in her white sheets. She smiled, politely declined the ice cream sandwich my aunt Sally offered. Somebody played Enya on Gram's stereo, although I know she'd have tossed that CD like a Frisbee into the field if she could. I frantically tried to find her favorite Joan Baez album in the wooden bin near her fireplace. Gram fell asleep.

Sixty-five miles an hour. I fly over the hill. My tires might be airborne. My organs seem to float ponderously inside of me. My hair lifts from my forehead, and I smile reflexively. The trees are a blur against the gunmetal gray sky. I am flying, defying the law of gravity and the law of the land. My roller-coaster ride begins to feel dangerous. What if I crash into a tree? What if, indeed. Two crows flap angrily from the ditch, frightened by my recklessness.

I failed to find the CD, of course. And I missed Gram's last breath. She died asleep, pumped full of morphine. People wept and held her cool, dry hand. Her lips drew back, blue and waxy, framing her airless, cavernous mouth. It seemed impossible that she had ever kissed with those lips, and I remember thinking how cruel that was. The blood settled in her veins, purple.

Seventy miles an hour. I convince myself I might leap into the sky as I crest the next hill. Just launch right into space. What a relief that would be! The wind feels like pins on my arm, a rake in my hair. A strand whips my eye, stinging and sparking tears. What if I let go of the wheel? What if I stop pedaling? I lift my hands from the steering wheel and close my eyes. I commandeer the thin ribbon of road. The road is mine: this one thing, real and hard. And something small taps me on the shoulder: *Getting a little melodramatic, are we? Move over and slow the hell down.* It even sounds like Gram. At the last second, I open my eyes and drift to the right, because you never know. I don't want to kill anyone. And I meet a police cruiser at the top of the hill, driving at me. It's cosmic, really. I veer away, lay off the gas pedal, and watch the needle on my speedometer slip down to a reasonable speed. Well, I asked for it, didn't I? The cruiser whips around and lights flash large in my rearview mirror. I crunch onto the shoulder and park. My heartbeat fills my ears, crowding out the crickets.

The police officer, a wiry man with a mustache and dark sunglasses, greets me with "Too nice of a day to die, don't you think?" He's no Officer Hottie.

I want to tell him every day is too nice of a day to die. He tells me I scared the bejesus out of him, gives me a $224 speeding ticket and a seat belt fine. I let him pull away first, pretending to fuss with my seat belt, purse, radio. I drive cautiously like an old man, weeping all the way home. The grief has no outlet but my tears, so I open my mouth. I don't recognize the sounds coming out, but it feels good to release them. Eight miles later the gray clouds finally break, releasing fat raindrops that hail onto my car and smear the dead bugs caked on my windshield. The fields around me reach up, thirsty, to catch the rain.

· · · ·

The next morning I have one of my bad days. Jillian's doing energy work on me at her house, hovering her hands over my abdomen. I can feel their heat through my T-shirt. Jeff Tweedy drains from the stereo, aching and spare, and I can hear children shrieking as they run through a sprinkler on the neighbor's lawn. Suddenly I can't breathe; it's like someone's dropped an engine block on my chest. I struggle to sit up and take a deep breath.

Jillian steps back, her mouth an alarmed O. I press a palm to my chest, close my eyes, and try to inhale. It's funny how the simple desire to breathe will supersede any other desires you may have ever had in your life when your lungs decide to play hooky. Seth? Life without PKD? My parents alive, together, and hosting a Currier and Ives holiday gathering? Fuck all of that; I just want to feel fresh oxygen sliding down my trachea, right now.

"Oh my God, Leigh, are you okay?"

I shake my head. "I can't breathe."

"Deep breaths. Relax." She rubs my back and I manage to settle down a little.

Tears fill my eyes and the room doubles. I blink and release them. They spill down my cheeks. One lands on my lip, salty and warm. I cover my face with my hands and try to memorize the way they feel: dry and smooth, fleshy. They smell like the lavender soap in Jillian's parents' bathroom. "I don't want to die," I whisper.

"You're not going to die, sweetie."

The tears fall freely now, like a monsoon after dry season. I look up to find Jillian's clear, concerned eyes. "I'm so tired. I'm just so tired."

"I know. Just relax. Let it out."

Jillian holds me with her safe, familiar arms. My cheeks are slick with tears. I try not to get her sweater wet. I wish I were still a Catholic, or maybe a Pentecostal or a devout Baptist with a close personal relationship with Jesus. I envy people with such clear, unyielding faith. Oh, wouldn't it be lovely to imagine traveling down that tunnel, toward the proverbial light . . . certain that on the other side I would rejoin Dad, Gram, and an assortment of extended relatives who have preceded me? Just the thought that this is a possibility floods me with relief and loosens my chest enough for me to take a deep breath. How simple! How comforting! But then, as usual, the questions come creeping back, setting the deep taproots of stubborn weeds. In heaven, if there is such a place, will the Jews and Palestinians get along? Will God let them in, or will they be turned away by the bouncers at the gates for fighting in line? Will we all wear white billowy robes, or maybe the clothing we're buried in? I don't trust Marissa to dress me appropriately for the afterlife. Would we even need clothes, or will we be *so* over the whole nudity thing? How old will each of us look? If I die at thirty, could I look fourteen if I wanted? What language will everyone speak? Won't it be crowded? Will our pets be there? What about gorillas that know sign language? Will there be a waiting list for appointments with Jesus? What do we do every day in the afterlife? Are there organized activities, like shuffleboard? I think I'd really miss eating.

Or it could be the Buddhist afterlife, and I could just come back to rehash all of the old bullshit because I'm not ready to shed my identity, ego, or gender and become part of the great big sha-zaam in the sky. But just the thought of the kinds of lives I'd be stuck with next gives me a stomachache. If I had kidney disease in this one, what's next? I'd better kick out the good works if I don't want to end up an Ann Coulter clone in the next life. Good Lord, I'd need a heart transplant!

And soon enough, I can't shake the feeling that it's just that cold hole in the ground awaiting me, next to the future resting places of James and Marissa. This can't really be happening. Surely it's a trick. Because I'm not ready for this. I've never been so scared in my life.

The day of my surgery arrives. It's down to my last few hours with Larry. How should I say good-bye? I take an early-morning walk and listen to Lynyrd Skynyrd on my iPod. I watch an old *Dukes of Hazzard* episode on TV Land and then three laps of a NASCAR race, which is as much as I can stomach. I can't eat anything (doctor's orders), but if I could, I would toss a few pork rinds down like rice at a wedding. *Good-bye! Good luck! We'll miss you!*

Marissa and James drive me to the hospital. I'm doing my breathing exercises, trying to focus. I retell myself the only story that kick-starts my faith in death being not an ending but a transformation: A little boy is talking to his newborn sister in her nursery. His parents overhear him on the baby monitor. He says to the infant, "Tell me about God. I'm starting to forget." This really happened, as far as I know. It's much better than the stain of Mary on the underpass.

"We'll be praying for you," Marissa says, hugging me tightly.

"I need all the prayers I can get," I say, winking.

James hugs me next. "We'll be waiting just down the hall. Don't worry. It'll be fine. You've gone through worse. You're a fighter."

I like James calling me a fighter. I feel scrappy and tough. I curl my lip at him and grin. They wave good-bye, and then I'm alone, shivering.

Nurses wearing pale blue cotton pants, cheerful print tops, and institutional smiles breeze past. They carry clipboards, blood pressure cuffs, and medication. They look important and comfortable, saving lives and caring for the sick. I care for the spoiled dogs of well people. I want to save lives, too. Pet lives *and* people lives, although that level of responsibility scares the hell out of me. But I think I could do it.

I hate the smell of hospitals: plasticky and sterile, like a mountain of Band-Aids. But with undertones of antiseptic, secret death. I hate the sounds of hospitals: squeaky rubber shoes on tile, toneless announcements on the PA system, the soft droning of televisions in semi-private rooms . . . and the endless noises of machines. Beeping, whirring, sucking, hissing, humming. I guess I just hate hospitals. As the old saying goes, familiarity breeds contempt.

One of the physician assistants checks me in and the countdown to surgery begins: paperwork, signatures . . . final lab work and testing . . . a change into stylish hospital duds . . . vitals taken once again . . . prep work . . . Dr. Jensen breezes in wearing squeaky tennis shoes and pale green scrubs, outlining the procedure one last time. . . . His eyes swim behind his glasses. . . . "This will be easy-peasy," he says. . . . He smells of garlic and industrial-strength germicide. . . . I think of his cell phone ringing to "Proud to Be an American" and smile. Then, in whirls the ultimate tour guide: my anesthesiologist. "Ready, Leigh?" he asks, eyes twinkling between his surgical mask and hair cap. He's cute in a Pauly Shore kind of way, which does nothing to relax me. I lay on my back in the operating room, grinning and admiring the ceiling. The lights blind me while Pauly Shore injects me with a tranquilizer that could probably knock out the entire population of Lithuania should it enter the water supply. Why can't I listen to music during surgery? I want to hear "Hey Jude" one more time, in case I don't wake up. *Oh my God don't think that whatever you do just think positively yeah just be positive.* I guess Jillian's New Age Physics lesson stuck. "Are you alright?" Pauly asks, but my lips suddenly feel like inflatable rafts, incapable of forming a sentence. I manage a numb nod. The ceiling tiles have become woozy tectonic plates, shifting and forming new continents.

Well, Larry, I think as I go under, *it's been one hell of a ride.*

I dream I'm awake during surgery. My mother is wearing latex gloves and a surgical mask. I'm splayed open like a perch fillet. My eyes dart around the operating room. She's poking around in me, pulling out organs willy-nilly. "We don't need this," she exclaims, brandishing my shiny liver. "Or this." My blood trickles down her arms, scarlet. *I have nothing left,* I try to say. But I can't open my mouth. She yanks my heart out and frowns at it. "Dead weight, sweetie. Just dead weight." She tosses it into a corner. I can't defend myself. I'm five! What can I do?

I open my eyes. I'm in a hospital room. It's cool. Bandages and an IV needle are taped to my right hand. Hissing and beeping machines surround me. I feel disembodied. And dopey. I'm Dopey, Sleepy, and Grumpy rolled into one. Too bad there weren't any other dwarfs: Melancholy, Anxious, and Medicated. Twenty-first-century dwarfs. I could be them, too.

"She's awake," Marissa says. Her voice is sharp, alert. The voice of one who can be depended on. I like this voice.

The noise of a scooting chair. "Hey, kid," James soothes. His warm hand smoothing my hair. "Welcome back. You did great." My eyes swim over to his. I begin to cry.

I spend the next two days recovering and watching terrible daytime television. I plan my next road trip in my head, although transient-friendly dialysis centers are infamously dirty and dangerous, at least according to the St. Luke's evening dialysis shift. Seattle in August might be nice . . . or the Carolinas in springtime? I'll have to do some research. I'm lucky enough to have my own room, and I sprawl out. I take over the room like a virus, scratching and belching and farting as freely as I want. I can heal in peace, except for the seemingly endless stream of nurses and social workers and technicians and doctors who come to assess my vitals, levels of various substances in my blood and urine, my mental and emotional state, nutritional intake, medication levels, and general hygiene. I'm tethered to an IV drip. But don't get me wrong. I don't mind.

James and Marissa visit again the morning after my surgery, bringing my portable DVD player and the complete run of *Freaks and Geeks,* one of the best television shows ever, which is why there are only eighteen episodes. *Knight Rider*? Eighty-four episodes. "How are you feeling?" James asks.

"How are *you* feeling?" I ask in return. James sprained his ankle yesterday while mowing the lawn; he tripped on a mole hole. His ankle is wrapped in peach-colored gauze. He hobbles to a chair and falls into it.

He grins. "I know you are, but what am I?"

I laugh and say, "I actually feel okay. I've been through worse.

I've felt better. I'm used to it by now." I know my abdomen should feel like a burning building, but I'm on these fantastic drugs that have stamped the pain down into a cozy little campfire. "I feel kind of stoned," I confess.

"How do you know what it feels like to be stoned?" James asks, feigning shock.

I raise one eyebrow halfheartedly.

"So Dr. Jensen says you're healing really well," Marissa says, smiling like a cherub on an inspirational poster.

"Boy, do I feel sorry for you." I take a sip of water through a flexible straw. "In a few days you'll have two invalids in the house!"

"I resemble that remark!" James protests. Apparently, he has not only sprained his ankle; he has also been surgically implanted with the late Rodney Dangerfield's sense of humor. James clears his throat. "Dr. Jensen also said you can come home in three days."

"Unless my liver decides to bail on me, too."

His face darkens. "Leigh, don't joke around about that."

We're contemplative for a moment, and then my uncle Steve, his wife, Luann, and his three freckle-faced, gap-toothed daughters conveniently show up and present me with a gigantic Boyds teddy bear and *Chicken Soup for the Surviving Soul* (which is actually for cancer survivors, but whatever). The conversation turns to space exploration, which happens to be the distraction du jour on CNN.

My room starts to sprout bouquets of flowers: elegant potted orchids, dainty pink tea roses, grand gladiolas. Meg sends a cheerful vase of sunflowers and a long note that brings tears to my eyes. My two coworkers at Fuzzy Navels (minus boss Mindy, who still has a week left seducing every busboy in Europe) send me a small basket of scented soaps and lotions. My aunt Fran and her "roommate" bring me a cast-iron Japanese teapot and a bale of green tea. We watch *The View* together and bitch about gas prices. Marissa's mother brings me a classy soy candle that smells like tomato leaves. She also brings me a not-so-classy electronic *Wheel of Fortune* game that I've seen on her toilet tank. Do I have to tell you I will not be playing this one, not even if I had a fake arm and you paid me with money still warm from George Clooney's front pocket? Jil-

lian and Amanda, my first nonfamily visitors, come the next morning. They knock quietly and tiptoe in, grinning like idiots behind a
monstrous potted peace lily. "Hey, you!" they stage whisper, waving.

"You can talk louder. It's only me in here."

I'm fine alone with either Jillian or Amanda, but the three of us
together don't have the best track record. Jillian and I have been
best friends for so long that we fight like sisters over the most inane
things, even though we usually make up almost immediately. We
have, you might say, our own special way of relating. But when you
throw another friend into the mix, it gets complicated. (Witness
our troubles when Meg entered the picture.) At that point we tend
to undermine each other, puffing ourselves up by calling each other
out on our peacocking, letting no amount of bullshit pass. I still remember the infamous *Golden Girls* conversation, when I asked
Amanda and Jillian to name which Golden Girl they most identified with. Amanda immediately named Sophia, the sweet curmud-
geon. (Although I'd have pegged her for a hybrid between Sophia
and Blanche.) Jillian thought for a minute and nodded decisively. "I
also have to say Sophia."

"But you're totally a Rose!" I protested, trying to set the record
straight.

Jillian pouted. "I'm not an airhead!"

The challenge was too easy, too blatantly false, to ignore. "Do I
have to tell the story of the white sandals? The ones you thought
were perfect for a full day of walking at Summerfest and you got
blisters in ten minutes?" I chided. "Or the time you thought you
were following me in my car and you were actually following a couple in a minivan? Or the time you consulted your swinging pendant
in the vitamin store to see which brand of multivitamin the universe wanted you to buy? Admit it, you are Rose to the core."

Jillian retreated to nurse her wounds while Amanda looked on,
uncomfortable. We didn't speak for days afterward. I admit, sometimes I'm an asshole to Jillian. I don't know why I have to burst people's bubbles. It must be the James in me.

"So how did it go?" Amanda asks, hanging her purse on the back
of a chair. I haven't seen Amanda in weeks, and I have to say, she

looks amazing. Her brown hair has been highlighted with sassy copper and blond streaks, and she's wearing the black ballet top that I spent all spring trying to find. She's also unnaturally tan, but it's a small oversight.

I quote my doctor verbatim. "The good news, according to Dr. Jensen, is that I am physically ready to go back on the transplant waiting list, pending final approval by my transplant team. The bad news is that once again, it could be years before a suitable matching organ becomes available. But he's optimistic about finding one soon, so I guess that's good."

I catch Jillian looking warily at my drainage tubes and IV. "I'm totally tubular," I quip.

"Why can't we give you a kidney?"

I purse my lips, trying to think of an adequate response. Jillian and I have been through this before. "You probably don't even have my same blood type."

"What type are you?"

"I'm an O. Universal donor, not so universal a recipient. Do you even know what type you are?" I hear a haughty inflection in my voice that I don't care for. This is what the three-person-friendship dynamic does to me.

Amanda thinks for a minute. "I'm pretty sure I'm A positive. Or negative."

"I might be AB negative," Jillian announces.

"Jillian, less than, like, one in two hundred people or something are AB negative. Anyway, I don't want you to do this. I already told you last year."

They give each other a smug *the baby's just tired* look, which I am amazingly able (dare I say mature enough?) to ignore. I steer the conversation to Amanda's recent engagement, and then a food service worker busts the party by bringing me a bland, institutional lunch that includes a small bottle of soy-based Vanilla Supreme Ensure. "What am I, eighty?" I complain. "No wonder I have no sex life."

"With anyone other than yourself," Jillian brays, laughing much harder than necessary. I throw a piece of Jell-O at her and hit the box of tissues near my bed instead.

Wes visits later that afternoon, with his Little Brother, Keane, in tow. Wes is not only a teacher; he is also a Big Brother. Sometimes to his own students, which is the case with Keane. Lots of girls find this incredibly charming until he tries to give them a drunken back rub late at night, which is Wes's segue into I'll Just Put It in a Little to See How It Feels. (So I've heard.) But luckily, Wes has appropriate boundaries and is actually a good role model for anyone younger than eleven. Keane, sporting a graffiti-worn cast on his right arm, has a two-foot-tall paper Flat Stanley cutout in tow. Flat Stanley also has a cast decorated with graffiti.

"How's the patient today?" Wes leans down to kiss my forehead. He smells so good you just know somewhere a girl is pining for him.

"Other than feeling like a dissected frog and so tired I could sleep for an ice age, great!"

"Keane, you remember my friend Leigh, right?"

Keane nods vigorously, making his sandy brown hair flop up and down. "Will you sign my cast? And Flat Stanley's?"

Wes clarifies things. "Keane wanted to 'cheer up' the hospital patients and get autographs on his cast and on Flat Stanley."

I beam at Keane and say, "Absolutely!" I scrawl my name on both casts in a fragrant red marker.

He frowns at my signature. "You sure have messy handwriting." He swings his feet under his chair, staring at me. "What's wrong with you?"

"I've got an infection in my kidney," I answer. "It's really doing a number on my handwriting."

"Oh. I had an infection in my toenail last summer."

"That doesn't sound too fun!"

"It was pretty gross. Hey, what's this?" He points to one of the machines surrounding my bed.

"A time machine. Want to travel back to the Wild West?" An image of Denise begging me to stop at the 1880 town zips through my brain, triggering a pang of . . . regret? Do I actually miss that nut?

Keane shrugs, uninterested. Apparently he's one of those kids that could give a rat's ass about getting his sheriff's badge at the 1880 town. "Mr. Flynn is taking our class bowling next weekend. Are you going?"

I smile, as I always do when I hear Wes referred to as "Mr. Flynn," and say, "Probably not. But it sounds like fun!"

"So what's next?" Wes asks me, turning serious.

I sigh. "Back on the transplant waiting list, I guess."

Wes considers me thoughtfully until I start to squirm. "What?" I ask.

"Why can't I give you a kidney?"

I roll my eyes. What is this, a plot? "Thanks, but that's pretty serious, Wes."

"You dying is pretty serious, too," he replies. Keane is flipping through channels on the television, ignoring us.

"You're joking, right?"

"I'm not joking."

We just stare at each other, letting the power of this new suggestion hang in the air. Keane giggles at something on TV. "Wes, you're probably not even a match, but if you were, I'm not sure I'd let you do this. I'm not your . . . wife."

"No, you're my best friend."

I find this deeply touching but try not to let it show. "Until you get married. Wes, think about this."

"Who do I have to talk to about getting the tests to see if I'm a match?"

I grow tight-lipped. Don't get me wrong—I'd be the happiest, most grateful, most blessed (and I don't use that term lightly) person on the planet if one of my friends or family members gave me a kidney. But I'm also afraid of such generosity. Afraid that my body would reject it, and we'd both be out a kidney. Afraid of my donor getting sick. And the very weight of this debt—what would I owe my donor? The world would be a good start. In some cultures, I'd be my donor's manservant for life. Er, womanservant. Butler.

And maybe I'm afraid of getting my hopes up again. The disappointment when most of my relatives failed the compatibility testing during the first go-round nearly crushed me.

"We shall speak of this no more," I say cryptically, in a robotic voice.

Keane taps Wes on the arm, bored. "I'm going to get some more autographs."

"Okay, just hold on for a sec."

Keane jiggles my plastic IV tube, which startles me. Where do such bold, brave children come from? "Hope you get better." He skips out of the room waving Flat Stanley like a flag.

Wes kisses my forehead. "Bye, kiddo. I'll call you later."

"Don't call me kiddo."

"Okay, twiddletits," he whispers.

CHAPTER SIXTEEN

Heaven, hell, limbo, or what?

'm serious, Leigh," Jillian repeats.

We're sitting in James and Marissa's hosta-rimmed backyard under the cold shade of a purple sugar maple. I shoo a fly from my arm. "Jillian, we've been through this before. Now can we drop it?" I try to keep my voice pleasant, but I hear the faintest edge of irritation creeping in. Jillian and Wes have been hounding me since I left the hospital about undergoing the tests to determine whether or not they are potential donor matches for me. They think their persistence will eventually wear me down, and I'm hoping my naysaying will outlast their persistence.

"So what is it? You like being sick? I know you don't like being sick. But maybe you're used to it. Maybe you've been sick for so long that you're afraid, because you don't know who you might be if you weren't sick." Jillian leans back in her chair and crosses her arms like a cut-rate guidance counselor hoping her theory has struck a nerve with the juvenile delinquent pouting in her office.

"I tried that last year. I was a metal-detecting, comic-book-reading weirdo."

She feigns a patient smile. "I'm sure there are a thousand other people on the waiting list who wouldn't be so stubborn and ungrateful."

I sigh heavily. "Jillian, I'm grateful for the offer. Believe me. But I'm just scared that you would get sick. Even if you're a match, which is a long shot, what if there are complications during surgery? It's not like donating blood. You're not in there for an hour and then it's cookies and juice. This is major, invasive, removing-one-of-your-critical-organs surgery. Recuperation takes weeks. *Months* even."

Jillian locks eyes with me. "I know that." We listen to the late-summer crickets. Somewhere down the street a lawn mower growls to life. Maybe she has considered the risks and benefits. Maybe she's made a list of the pros and cons of giving me one of her kidneys on the back of an old grocery receipt: Leigh will live to be ninety and stop bitching about dying by thirty (pro). *This gift is priceless, nonrefundable, and Leigh is incapable of fully appreciating it (con).* It's the best karma money can't buy (pro). *Leigh's body could reject it despite every precaution, and we'd both be out a kidney (con).* Leigh could go off dialysis and become a happier, more spiritually evolved person. We could take trips together (pro). *Once again, we could both be out a kidney (con).*

Suddenly Jillian interrupts my daydreaming with "So I'm flying back to Colorado tomorrow to get the rest of my things, and then I'm driving back home. For good." At first I'm not sure how to react. We've had a few "moving back home again" episodes before, so I settle for cautious optimism.

"Wow, that's great! Where are you going to live?"

Jillian smiles. "Chicago. I found a place in Wicker Park that's pretty affordable—my friend Grace needs someone to take over her lease when she leaves for grad school in London. I'm looking for a roommate, if you're interested."

"Grace?"

"From the yoga retreat I went on last winter."

Right. I wonder which neighborhood Chris lives in. My whole face is smiling. Well, if I've been waiting for opportunity to knock,.

here it is, bashing a foot through my front door. But I need to consider a few things. First, how will I support myself? My gig at Fuzzy Navels is not exactly my long-term career plan, but it pays the bills for now until I make a few decisions about the future. And I'd miss my coworkers and clients, canine and human. Second, I'd need to find a new nephrologist and dialysis center. This is not as easy as it sounds. I *like* my routine. I *like* my doctors and nurses. My dialysis center is clean, well lit, and staffed by friendly, knowledgeable people. There are no bloodstains on the floor, no loose needles out of sterilized packages. No awful scenes with people passing out around me. Well, not many, anyway. Third, I need to talk to James and Marissa about things. We may have been reluctant housemates sometimes, but we've developed a kind of symbiotic familiarity over the years. James is right, we're family. He's all I have, and I depend on him much more than I'll admit.

Jillian must sense my unease, because she adds, "We can go job-hunting together. I'm sure you'll find something you like. It's Chicago!"

Funny how life works. I thought James was the one keeping me in Fond du Lac, and my PKD, and my dialysis routine. But all along it was just me.

Can you believe we live in an age when women still don't have the right to vote in at least eight nations? And America incarcerates more citizens than Russia? And polar bears could be extinct in our lifetimes? And more people know the names of judges on *American Idol* than on the Supreme Court? And grown (sort of) women believe they are assuming the personality of their kidney donor, use him as a crutch, really, to do things they should have done years ago?

I know. It's crazy.

I didn't need Larry to change my life. All I needed was myself.

Jillian leans forward, crossing her arms on the glass tabletop. "But first, you have to give me a *good* reason why I can't even test to be your donor. I haven't heard one yet."

· · ·

There are many cumbersome tests a potential organ donor has to undergo to determine compatibility: blood tests, urine tests, X-rays, colonoscopies, sonograms, CT scans, psychological evaluations. It's enough to challenge even the hardiest supporter's will. But my friends are tenacious, and now I come to learn, masochists. Generous, selfless masochists, one of whom I could be indebted to for life.

Jillian failed the first screening for blood type, as I knew she would. Both Wes and Amanda (a late but insistent entrant in the Potential Donor Parade) cleared that particular hurdle. Wes fell by the wayside during the human leukocyte and cross-matching antigen testing. And ultimately, Amanda was ruled out by her fiancé. I can't say I blame him for putting the kibosh on things. . . . If my future wife's kidney was on the block for a friend I have nothing in common with, I probably would have done the same. Meg even called to tell me that if not for her baby and precarious emotional state, she'd have been first in line to determine a match.

Well, it was a long shot anyway. But am I not the luckiest girl on earth to have friends willing to risk their own lives to save mine?

A few days later I'm cleaning my room, throwing old clothing onto a pile for Goodwill. I'm boxing other unwanted items— CDs, books, stuffed animals, candles, picture frames, and photo albums—for a yard sale the neighbor is having. I tell myself I'm cleaning up for the sake of cleaning up, but I know I'm slowly acclimating myself to the idea of moving. It feels healthy and necessary. I feel like I should be in an insurance commercial: *When things are changing in your life, one constant remains: State Farm is there.*

Marissa pads down the hall in her Tempur-Pedic slippers and knocks softly on the doorframe. "How are you feeling?" she asks. In our family, this question has long since replaced "Hi!" and "What's going on?" as the greeting of choice.

"Pretty good," I answer, wiping a hand across my sweaty forehead.

"Oh, you're giving this old coat away?" She sits on the bed next to me and picks up an outdated black leather coat lavishly given to me by my old boyfriend Kevin Murphy, who never met a poor financial decision he didn't like.

"Well, I don't want to look like a time traveler from 1995."

Marissa chuckles. She smells like the Burt's Bees almond-milk hand cream I gave her last Christmas. She plucks a CD from the box on my bed: Hootie and the Blowfish. It pains me deeply to admit I own this. "You're giving this away, too?"

I smile and try not to cringe. "It's yours if you want it."

"Thanks! I used to love these guys."

Of course you did, Marissa. That's why we love you.

Marissa grows quiet and taps the CD against her thigh. "Leigh, I've been wanting to tell you something."

Uh-oh. They're going to move to Eau Claire. She's fallen in love with her pastor and is divorcing James. I search her green eyes for a clue, but she has the world's best poker face. It could be serious. James has cancer. No, Marissa has cancer! A feeling of dread pools in my stomach.

She clasps both of my hands in her own, and a gigantic smile blooms on her face. "We're pregnant."

My mouth opens involuntarily. "What?"

"I'm due in February." She's beaming at me, searching for a response, and it suddenly hits me. I'm going to be an aunt! I snap out of my daze.

"Marissa, that's fantastic! Oh my God!" I launch myself into her arms. We embrace like real, live sisters. "Wow, when did you find out?"

"Well, I knew last month, but I wanted to be absolutely sure. I've had friends who had early miscarriages, so I didn't want to tell anyone until I was a bit further along. And then you got sick, and the timing was just all wrong. But I think it's right now. So here we are." She offers me a vulnerable smile.

I'm going to be an aunt! I sit back, amazed. *There's a tiny person in Marissa.* Well, this certainly expedites and validates my decision to move to Chicago. I'll make it work. I have to. And when I come to visit, I'll bring contraband books and CDs and candy and loud toys like drum sets and battery-operated space weapons. I'll be the funtastic aunt! We'll take trips to the Discovery Learning Center and Lincoln Park Zoo to feed the goats handfuls of pellets you can get for just a quarter. When my niece or nephew is a teenager, he or she can visit me in Chicago and return home with wild ideas and a smart mouth. I get to be the fun aunt! I'll make it all work. "Well, I'll be out of your hair in no more than a month or two, once I get my feet on the ground in Chicago. . . . I'm moving in with Jillian, as soon as I find a job and a new dialysis center." I'm jabbering and stop when I notice that Marissa looks confused . . . even crestfallen.

"Oh? You're moving?"

I rush in with "Well, nothing is set in stone. I haven't even talked to James about it yet."

Marissa continues as if she hadn't heard me. "This is going to be such a huge change. I'm a little nervous about everything. It would be nice if you could stay. I'm sure I could use the help!" Her forehead scrunches in worry, but then she shakes her head to clear things. "But you don't have to. I just thought it would be nice, you know?"

Maybe she suspects I'm scared to leave. Maybe this is Marissa putting training wheels on my life change: *You don't have to let go just yet. First learn how to balance, how to steer. "Just keep pedaling. . . . Keep your eyes focused straight ahead!"*

Maybe she just wants help changing diapers.

We've grown used to one another, to the little trips and sighs of our daily habits. We're a family. I shrug and grin, because I get to be the helper monkey. "Marissa, of course I can stay as long as you want me to. It'll all work out. I'd love to help you when the baby comes."

She smiles benevolently. She almost looks relieved. "Wonderful! Now do you want to see the ultrasound pictures?"

An hour later, after adjusting to the baby news, calling Jillian, and looking at pictures and a few old notes I find in my dresser drawer,

I once again discover . . . The Coaster. With Chris's number. Impulsively, before I can think it to death, I flip open my cell phone and dial. Carpe fucking diem. It rings. And rings. And then he picks up. "Hello?" His voice is deeper than I remember. For a minute I think I dialed a wrong number. My nervousness catches up with me and I forget my own name, whom I'm calling, and what day it is. I catch a glimpse of my messy blond head and gaping, anxious expression in the mirror and snap out of it.

"Chris? Hi. Um, you probably don't remember me, but we met in Vegas? Leigh Fielding? With the kidney transplant?" It all comes out in a rush. Well, at least I didn't add that part about Larry killing the dog, too.

Silence. Then: "Oh, wow! I totally gave up on you. How are you?"

"Great. Great!" I ramble on about coming across the coaster with his number and a few other mundane things and then I announce that I'm going to be an aunt. Luckily, it just so happens that he's an uncle, so we bond over our mutual aunt/uncle status for a few beats. I tell him about my kidney failing, and he's sorry. He asks all the right questions, which I answer succinctly but in an upbeat voice. He tells me about his new job doing a website for a reclusive lunatic Brazilian—a former soap star–turned–public relations magnate. He regales me with anecdotes that illustrate the Brazilian's insanity. We laugh together, and it's like crawling into a down comforter on a cold night.

"So when are you coming to Chicago?" he asks me. I almost have to look over my shoulder to make sure he's not talking to someone else in the room. It makes me want to dance, and I do the twist next to my bed, quietly.

"Actually," I say, grinning, "funny you should ask that."

One of the nurses at dialysis has been badgering me to do a PKD Walk for the Cure this fall, and I actually signed up last week for the one near Chicago. Jillian and I plan to visit the new apartment and scope out our future neighborhood afterward. And Chris? Is

meeting us at the walk. It's not a date-date, so I don't mind Jillian
being along. Besides, I want her objective opinion on him.

The day of the walk dawns crisp and sunny, perfect for planting
mums along a sidewalk, or stretching out on a chaise lounge to eat
a caramel apple while you watch someone else plant the mums for
you. Because registration begins at nine and the walk starts at ten,
I've been up since five. Well, technically, I was up almost all night
because I was so damn nervous about seeing Chris again. I listen to
Yankee Hotel Foxtrot and watch the sun rise during my drive, singing
along when I know the words. Jillian updates her to-do list and
chats on her cell phone with Meg for half the drive. It's the kind of
thing I'd find rude if we weren't practically family.

Over the past few weeks I've raised $9,325 for research from
my friends and family, with $1,750 from James's employer alone. I
confess that I got pretty misty-eyed when I saw the grand total. But
here's the weird thing: Someone in California logged on to the PKD
foundation website (www.pkdcure.org, everyone go there now!),
found my fund-raising page, and donated $5,000. Okay, it was
Denise. It had to be her because I know no one else in California
other than my mother's ex-boyfriend Brad, and at this point the late
Fatty Arbuckle was more likely to be my mystery sponsor than him.
What made me 99 percent sure it was Denise is that the sponsor (I
hesitate to use the word *donor*) called herself *Amy Jasper*. Right.
The fake name Denise signed at every sleazy motel we stayed in.

Last weekend I rented her old B movies. And honestly, she
really was a cute kid. Sort of a poor man's Jodie Sweetin from *Full
House.* After I was certain that I wouldn't type the words *lying
klepto* or *ethically bankrupt,* I answered her donation with a personal e-mail, which the Web donation system was set up to support.
Just something simple thanking her for such eye-popping generosity, wishing her well. She wrote back almost immediately: "Audition tomorrow. Fingers crossed! When's our next road trip?" I
replied: "The year 2050? ☺ Again, I'm humbled by your donation.
THANK YOU. Take care of yourself. P.S.: Good luck on the audition. Let me know what happens." There were so many more questions I wanted to ask, but I decided to save them. Denise is the

kind of person who will let you know exactly what she wants you to know. And that may or may not be anything resembling the truth. I'm not sure whether we'll stay in touch, or if we'll ever reconnect in person, but I'm glad to know that kind of spontaneity is just a phone call away. And I'm glad to know her. As much as anyone *can* know a crazy girl like that.

Before we get to the walk, I need to fill you in on everything else that's happened over the past few weeks. Okay, here's the quick wrap-up. Other than raising more money than I ever imagined I would for PKD research, I met with an adviser at UW Oshkosh to outline the remaining undergraduate classes I need toward my bachelor's degree. I started classes last week, and they're pretty pedestrian, but the profs seem alright. Then, next spring, after I've got more gen eds down and the new baby has joined the program currently in progress, I'm moving to Chicago to finish up. The University of Illinois, if they'll have me. Jillian and I will be roommates, which illustrates the human capacity to forget, forgive, and tune out. If I can deal with Jillian's sage-burning rituals and questions during movies, and she can overlook my cynical comments and freakishness about household chores, we should both be alive and chummy a year from now.

Oh! And here's the best part: After I finish my bachelor's degree? I'm applying to the College of Veterinary Medicine at the University of Illinois at Urbana. This is the deal, baby. If I crack the books and make like the high school brainiac I once was, I think I can pull it off without losing too much hair—perhaps even on a partial scholarship if I'm lucky. It's this or peddle hammers at the Home Depot (or write doggie report cards my whole life), so I need to make it happen. It may take awhile, since I'm not sure I can handle a full class load while on dialysis, but like Gram always used to say, particularly while awaiting phone calls from the various suitors jockeying to take her to the latest Paul Newman flick or out for a good Wisconsin fish fry the following Friday, "A handful of patience is worth more than a bushel of brains." Which always left me with disturbing mental images, but I think we all get the gist of her meaning.

Once I get to Chicago, I'll have to find a new nephrologist and dialysis center until another transplant becomes available, but this is what life is all about. It's about change. People quietly take such gigantic steps every day, no training wheels necessary.

In the meantime James and I go for walks and watch films by Christopher Guest (when it's my turn to pick) and Michael Mann (when it's James's turn). We talk about our childhoods, and about the new baby, and about Mom and Dad and the kinds of parents we want to be. We take care of each other, nagging about diet, exercise, and, in James's case, relaxation techniques. I taught him how to do my breathing exercise to help with his stress, mostly for a good laugh. The other day I spied him doing it while on the phone with a client.

I'm also back to work at Fuzzy Navels, which I was surprised to find I *missed*. My boss, Mindy, is talking about expanding operations and exploring various employee benefit packages. To include health insurance. I'm not holding my breath, but this is a good sign. Also, Jillian is making me a list of part-time job opportunities in Chicago that offer health insurance.

After work and dialysis I help Marissa paint the baby's room lavender. Shirley from dialysis has found a donor—her husband wasn't a match, but it turns out her sister is. We had a party for her last weekend, catered by our dietitian, Evie. Even Nurse Ratched came, bearing a croquet set that we set up and played right away.

The drive is much too short, and I ask Jillian to consult my MapQuest printout when I see the Golf Road exit. A few short turns later, and we enter the Busse Woods Forest Preserve, the kickoff spot. Hundreds of cars are parked in neat rows. They gleam hopefully in the early-morning sunlight. Children with balloons tied to their wrists and daisies and butterflies painted on their cheeks play tag between their parents, who gossip and clutch goody bags and pull official WALK FOR PDK T-shirts and caps over their heads. Other people register for raffle prizes, stuffing blue scraps of paper with their names and addresses into plastic buckets. Everybody looks wholesome and optimistic in their sunglasses and comfortable walking shoes. I should have no trouble spotting Chris.

There are so many people just like me! Wry, hopeful, disappointed, excited, scared, laughing, mixing-it-up-at-the-walk-in-T-shirts people. We're here to raise money to fund research that might cure the disease that marks maybe half the people here. For the disease that probably claimed one of my grandparents and possibly would have claimed my father. A sense of urgency underlies the picnic-in-the-park feel to the day, and I almost expect Michael Buffer to jog onto a stage to kick things off with perhaps the most famous behest in the English language: *"Lllllllet's Get Ready to Ruuuuummmble!!! In the far right corner, polycystic kidney disease, with its deadly reputation and frustratingly evasive maneuvers. In the far left, a crowd of the most determined people you don't want to fight over the last Tickle Me Elmo in the store. At stake? The lives of twelve and a half million people worldwide and a trip for two to Cancún for the best fund-raisers here today. And will the owner of the blue Honda Accord, license number NJE-266, please report to the registration tent? Your lights are on."*

The cool morning air on the golf course smells like dew and coffee, which must be coming from the Starbucks tent. It reels me in, and after my first delicious sip of Fair Trade Blend, I scan the booths for the registration table, where I'm meeting Chris.

"Are you nervous?" Jillian asks, her eyes gleaming. Clearly, she wants me to be, because this is the kind of obvious question that only serves to whet the appetite. It's like when your grandmother leans in with fresh-baked chocolate chip cookies on a platter, asking, "Hungry?" Of course you're hungry with hot, buttery deliciousness in your face, and of course I'm nervous right now with hot, buttery deliciousness about to *be* in my face.

"Do farts stink?" I ask, slightly annoyed.

"Actually, some don't. Like mine, for instance." She caws laughter at her own wit.

I decide to ignore her. A young L.L.Bean–type couple pulling twin girls in a red Radio Flyer wagon trundle past, chatting animatedly about a trip to an aquarium. And then I see him, talking to an elderly woman in a wheelchair near the registration table. He's younger than I remember, but his hair is still crazy in a comfortable, caffeine-addicted way. He's wearing sunglasses, so I can't tell if he's seen me. But he has, and waves. I break out in a smile and make a beeline for him. We hug, which I was nervous about. Would it be awkward? Should there even be a hug? If so, who should initiate it? But in the end, we both do, and it feels like we've done it a thousand times. He smells like the perfect seaside vacation you saved three years for—fresh, relaxing, memorable. The woman in the wheelchair politely excuses herself and rolls off into the crowd.

"Thanks for meeting me here," I say.

He pushes his sunglasses up and grins. "Thank you for suggesting it!" At this point he notices Jillian. We make introductions, and I try, subtly, to get a reading on her first impression. She seems pleased, but Jillian seems pleased 99 percent of the time, even in the face of a shortage of crystal pyramids. Even in the presence of a cynical smart-ass like me.

I step back to take him in. Yep, still eminently huggable. Freckles on the bridge of his slightly crooked nose? Check. Quirky mannerisms? Check. Two appealing distinct brows above trustworthy, intelligent hazel eyes? Check. Ability to make me do the two-step below the belt? Check. We've spoken on the phone at least five times in the past few weeks, so there's something of a long-distance comfort level there. But there's still that stomach-churning mystery, so I've made a list of things we could talk about on the walk to avoid any awkward silences:

10. Whatever happened to Danny Pintauro?
9. The most awful way to learn there isn't a Santa Claus.
8. Best and worst breakup, wedding, and funeral songs.
7. Celebrity we'd most like to see tossed into a pool full of water moccasins.
6. Best nonmainstream coming-of-age book and/or movie.
5. Sequels Hollywood will churn out next year, and why they will fail.

4. Greeting cards you'll never see (e.g., "Since your stroke, Grandma, you may not remember me . . . but I want to wish you a happy birthday anyway").

3. Best and worst smells in the world, excluding the obvious. And why.

2. Things we ate as children that we wouldn't ingest now for less than $7,638.

1. Heaven, hell, limbo, or what? Wacky religious stories from our youth.

Luckily, Chris is a talker. He tells me an amusing story about his childhood arch-nemesis, Henry Kaplan, while we check in and pick up the goody bags, which contain a key chain, trial-sized Aveda hand cream, a Clif Bar, two packets of Tazo herbal tea, a few coupons (buy one loaf of bread, get the second one free at Panera; five dollars off an oil change at Valvoline; ten dollars off an FTD floral arrangement), and a CD by the acoustic trio currently entertaining us with their musical stylings in Tent Four, Illusion Plus. Plus what, I don't know. Pretension?

I know whatever this is with Chris could crash and burn. Talk to me again next week and maybe I'll have found out he's married already. Or maybe we return to Vegas and get married ourselves, at a drive-through chapel, freaking everyone out. Maybe I find out he's gay. Hey, it could happen! But I'm a new me again. Older and wiser, but open. Accepting. I breathe life in, relish the weight of every laugh. I make direct eye contact and ask for what I want. And when what I want doesn't turn out to be what I need, I can reshelve it and try again.

We read some brochures on the latest research and clinical drug trials (which have been promising in halting cyst growth in mice), but this may have been a bad idea, since it's too late for me. My original kidneys are long gone. Chris seems to sense the subtle shift in my mood, so he tries to cheer me with a story about his friend Gene's glass eye and, of course, the glass-eye high jinks. It works, because I crack a big smile. Jillian takes this as her cue to tell an embarrassing story about me (the time my gynecologist mistook my botched eyebrow pencil job for a melanoma), which I put the kibosh on almost immediately. "I'll tell you later," she says, winking large. We all buy a PKD wristband for two dollars each and munch on free bagels at the refreshment tent.

"So where are we going next summer?" Jillian asks, rubbing her palms together briskly. "Thailand? Africa? Sweden?"

"Sweden!" I say, thinking of the couple in line for the buffet at Jimmy T's Hitching Post. Then I remember that as a result of that trip, I'm probably qualified for extra-strength Medicaid to the power of four. My checkbook is now more morose than Eeyore after losing his entire family to an ALPO roundup. "Actually," I say, bringing my enthusiasm back to earth, "how about something a little less pricey. Another road trip maybe?"

She laughs reluctantly. "I'm still not over the last one."

"This fall my brother and I are driving to Graceland," Chris offers. "Maybe you could do a theme road trip."

"What, like to all the Civil War battlefields?" I think of Bob and Peggy Lansky, visiting every national park they could cram into a two-week window.

Chris rolls his adorable eyes, but he's still smiling. "Not unless you're a retired postal worker who collects stuff from the Franklin Mint."

Ah! An opening for Jillian, and she takes it. "Has Leigh told you about her metal detector?"

"Shut up." I shove her semi-playfully, almost into a child's bouquet of blue and white balloons, while she snickers.

Luckily, Chris ignores this to continue his train of thought. "After *Sideways* came out a bunch of people took road trips to visit the wineries featured in the movie. You could do something like that, with a different movie. Or you could just go to Burning Man."

"I'm liking the themed road trip idea. We could do our own *Assassination Vacation!*" I wait for Chris to get my Sarah Vowell, darling of NPR, reference, and he does: He smiles and nods approvingly.

"Eww!" Jillian says. "How about Route 66? Where you can get your kicks!" She starts to sing in her turkey-being-shaved voice.

I loudly clear my throat. "Or we could go to Amish country. We could bring Denise so she could practice for a role in the remake of *Witness*," I say.

"Yeah," Jillian says, stooping to retie a shoelace. "That would be all we need."

"They're remaking *Witness*?" Chris asks, puzzled.

"No," I say. Then I remember a trip Seth used to want to take, before his tastes changed to all-inclusive Caribbean golf resorts. "How about Seattle? Bumbershoot?" I knew Jillian wouldn't pass up an opportunity to dance barefoot in a peasant skirt, smoking clove cigarettes, with her tribe.

She claps her hands and it sounds like a shotgun. People look over at us, startled. "That's it!" She links her arm through mine and begins to plan. "We'll go to Mount Rainier, and Pike Place Market, and, oh my God, Leigh, we have to. We could go whale watching! Let's go. Seriously. Can we?"

I laugh and shrug. "Sure! But maybe we should fly." So that's my next trip, I guess.

There's one last thing. Finding my mom? Well, that mystery has been on hiatus for over twenty years. I don't see why a few more would hurt. Given my dialysis schedule and Marissa's impending delivery, I truly don't care much to pursue Kate right now. Especially since it's obvious she doesn't want to be pursued. But every so often I fire up Google and research private investigators. Or PIs, as they say on the street. When the time is right, I might follow through. Or I might not. It's funny how sometimes when life reshuffles your priorities, the things you think you want so badly turn out to be things you don't really want after all.

My road trip is over, somewhat anticlimactically at that. In many ways (at least the obvious ones), I'm back to square one. But I'm no longer the same person. And I know this sounds totally cliché and hokey as hell, but I feel like my real journey is only beginning. *Gah*, I know. But cut me some slack. I have my own blood filtered and pumped back through my veins like some kind of freaky science experiment three days a week. You could say it's a draining experience, and I do apologize for the bad pun.

I need a new hobby, right? I wonder what I'll get with the next transplant! I hope it's Ping-Pong. I've always wanted to be really good at that.

I kid. I don't need some kind of crutch to become a Ping-Pong master. All I need is myself. And two paddles and a little white ball.

I shade my eyes as we make our way to the crowd gathered near the starting point. I am amazed at the hundreds of people gathered here today for one reason. Some people are wearing T-shirts reading IN MEMORY OF . . . with a photo of their deceased friend or family member. But the air is alive with hope and determination. I find myself a little choked up, so I visualize what I want to manifest: I am a veterinarian. . . . I am a second transplant recipient. . . . I am a wife on her honeymoon in New Zealand. . . . I am a mother reading *Corduroy* to her four-year-old adopted son. . . . I am eighty years old, packing for a photo safari in Kenya with Jillian.

The thought makes me shiver, and Chris gives me a look of concern. "Cold?" He smiles and wraps a shy arm around my shoulder. "Want to start a fire on the golf course? I'm sure we could find something flammable around here."

"That's okay," I say, smiling. "I'll be fine once we start walking."

About PKD

Polycystic kidney disease (PKD) affects more than 600,000 Americans and an estimated 12.5 million people worldwide. In fact, PKD impacts more people than cystic fibrosis, muscular dystrophy, hemophilia, Down syndrome, and sickle-cell anemia—*combined*. While there is no cure for the disease, the PKD Foundation is working tirelessly to fund scientific research and clinical trials that could lead to one. For more information, visit www.pkdcure.org.

Acknowledgments

There would be no *Driving Sideways* without the indefatigable support of my agent, Laura Blake Peterson. Thank you for believing in me, for holding my hand during the scary parts, and for giving Leigh a chance to share her story. Thanks are also due to Tracy Marchini for working behind the scenes to help make it all happen.

To Jill Schwartzman—could a first-time author be any luckier to have such an awesome editor in her corner? Thank you for your patience, commitment, and spot-on insights. Plus, you're just plain fun to work with.

I owe a heap of gratitude to Hope Benthien, Wendy Jensen, Leeann Busse, and Stephanie Huff for their friendship and encouragement over the years. Thanks for the memories, many of which found their way into Leigh's adventures.

I would also like to thank the following early readers: Esri Allbrittin, Connie Vera, and especially Cindy Mehus, the best friend a girl could have. Thank you for being such a good sport and a damn fine traveling partner. Horsehair medicine wheel notwithstanding.

For sharing the ride, for their understanding, and for putting up with me on a near-daily basis, I extend my thanks to Kevin De-Cramer; Pat McKeown; Teresa Thiel; Lori Uttech; Mike Derr; Jeff Hinds; Anita Konen; and especially Linda Phillips, whose thoughtful reading of the manuscript and helpful feedback—especially the reminder that not everyone enjoys bathroom humor—were invaluable.

Special thanks to Dr. Patrick McDonough and Dr. Eric Gibney for their medical input and to Rhonda McDonough for the assist.

For trusting me with their experiences with PKD, for their enthusiastic support, and for helping me "get it," I owe a great deal to Aimee Sutton and Valen Cover. I am honored by their friendship and humbled and inspired by their courage.

The list of things for which I'm grateful to my parents would require enough paper to wipe out the boreal forest, so I'll leave it at this: Mom? You set the bar sky-high with your gentle warmth, generosity, and talents—and you make it look so easy. Dad? Thank you for telling stories, for writing things down, for making all of us laugh, and for reminding me that some people *do* enjoy bathroom humor. For all this and for keeping our home well stocked with books, I love you both. And to my brother, Jake, and sister, Maddie, two adorable kids who grew up into amazing adults: Oh, the stories I could tell but won't because I love you both to bits. Thanks for your friendship and for sharing this journey with me.

Thanks also must go to my extended family for their unwavering enthusiasm; and more thanks go to Daisy the Amazing Barking Dog for her foot-warming company, chapter by chapter.

And to Jason, my husband and first reader: Thank you for giving my heart a home.

About the Author

J ESS R ILEY is a grant writer who lives in Oshkosh, Wisconsin, with her husband and their dog. *Driving Sideways* was a finalist in the 2005 James Jones First Novel Fellowship. Visit the author's website at www.jessriley.com.